Agent for Justice

Agent for Justice

Duke Southard

5/8/2004

To Clark —
With my appreciation
for your support —
all the best.
Duke Southard

HotHouse
PRESS

For information about permission to reproduce
or transmit selections from this book in any form
or by any means, write to
Permissions, Hot House Press
760 Cushing Highway
Cohasset, MA 02025

This book is a work of fiction. The characters are products of the author's imagination. Any resemblance to persons living or dead is purely coincidental. While some locations in the book actually exist, they are used only as points of reference and events that occur in them are purely fictitious.

Library of Congress Cataloging-in-Publication Data

Southard, Duke
Agent for Justice / by Duke Southard
   p. cm.
  ISBN 0-9700476-6-5 (hardcover)
1. Teachers—Fiction. 2. Connecticut—Fiction. 3. Mentally ill—Fiction.
4. Revenge—Fiction.
I . Title.
  PS3569.O759A73 2003
  813'.54—dc21
                   2003013373

Printed in the United States of America

Book design by Harold Coughlin

Hot House Press
760 Cushing Highway
Cohasset, MA 02025

DEDICATION

This book is dedicated
to those public school teachers who
perform their crucial work with an
unselfish and steadfast devotion
to their students.

Prologue

His previous scouting trips around the perimeter of the lake led him to this secluded spot on the shore where darkness would surely bring at least one boat within easy range. The unknown result of how his attempt to "make the bastards pay" compounded his excitement. The late afternoon eroded into a sensual summer evening and a disconcerting calm descended upon him as he made his final preparations. The expected moral dilemma over his plan didn't materialize. Any residual guilt clearly had been rationalized.

"So," he said aloud as though speaking to a comrade in arms, "just where the hell is the guilt?"

He pulled the night vision binoculars from his backpack and stepped into that nebulous world where fantasy and reality become one.

"Tonight," he whispered, "my liberation begins." His quiet chuckling assumed a quality of madness as it bounced off the trees surrounding the small clearing. With great care, he unpacked his scuba gear, each piece of equipment reminding him of how chagrined his diving instructors would be if they had any idea of his plans for using their expert training.

* * *

Nancy Yates slipped the provocative note into her husband's briefcase, sure that he would discover it soon after settling in behind his huge mahogany desk at Lakeside Realty. She calculated that the phone would ring within ten minutes, confident that the answer to her suggestion would be a resounding yes.

With their two children married and settled into the ever-repeating human cycle of birth, school, love, marriage, career and children, Bill and Nancy Yates loved spending any free time in each other's company. While other married couples seemed to search for reasons to be apart, they looked for excuses to be together. Their unique relationship was the envy of most of their friends.

The slumping real estate business around the big lake forced Bill to log long hours at the agency, and Nancy had decided that it was time for one of their "trysts," a euphemism they jokingly assigned to any planned romantic encounter. The power of their love for each other coupled with an ever-present sexual attraction made these rendezvous feel almost illicit. Nancy and Bill usually behaved like two quivering, nervous adolescents when they had one planned.

As Nancy sat sipping her morning coffee on the veranda overlooking the lake, quite predictably, the portable phone rang.

"Bill's opened his briefcase," she said as she lifted the phone to her ear.

"I accept your invitation and will be at the town dock at the appointed hour." Nancy chuckled at Bill's mock formality, picturing him sitting with his feet thrown casually on his desk, an impish grin spread across his face.

"What sort of treat might you have in mind for our boat ride, Nancy?"

In spite of her age and experience, Nancy felt her face reddening as memories of past "trysts" flitted through her mind. "I promise it'll be worth your while. Just think about me today, and I'll have the boat all ready to go and a nice picnic dinner, too. See you at five!"

Bill smiled and hung up. He turned and looked out at the lake through the large picture window behind his desk. The picturesque setting was his livelihood. He and his staff were working overtime to convince their wealthy clientele that they needed to upgrade their social status by moving into more elegant properties. Lakeside Realty, under Bill's able leadership, performed this task quite well, even in the slow times, and the Yates's lifestyle certainly had not suffered during the recent downturns.

Nancy had just a brief wait before Bill arrived. Their boat, an eye catching *Chaparall SSi 285*, always attracted attention at the town docks, especially when Nancy was at the helm.

"Classy lady, classy boat," Bill said in a whisper as he walked briskly across the parking lot separating the town docks from the row of buildings lining Main Street. Nancy waved as soon as she saw him, her wide smile making the distance between them irrelevant. He decided that his good friend Ray, owner of a sprawling RV and boat complex, had been absolutely right. A woman like Nancy should be in a boat like this. The sleek vessel, its twenty-eight feet length dwarfing most of the other boats around it, was a perfect match for her.

* * *

"Tonight'll be a pretty good test," he said quietly to himself. "The worst that can happen is they'll find my body floating in the lake and that might not be all together bad." His wonderfully restorative black periods convinced him that constant conversations with one's self was more a curative than a sign of dementia. He remained on the positive side of that well known but ill-defined edge between genius and lunacy. At least two hours of daylight remained before he could attempt his first mission.

He settled into a collapsible canvas hunter's chair, holding his compact but powerful spear gun across his lap. Just once, during a scuba exercise, had the gun been used for its designed purpose. Then he had adapted it for a use he would be trying tonight for the first time on a real target.

The large triangular shaped rock, a full eight inches across the bottom, took hours of grinding before he was satisfied that it would serve his purpose. The stone weighed in at just over thirty pounds before he began the tedious job of hollowing it out with the grinding attachment on his portable electric drill. He formed the rock into what looked like a huge replica of an ancient arrowhead, an efficient killing instrument used by so many Indian tribes during their hunts. It had been a relatively easy task to mount the rock, now weighing less than seven pounds, on the end of the spear.

The practice sessions in the privacy of his yard, surrounded by thick woods and undergrowth, proved that his weapon was well suited to his purpose. His personal arrow effectively penetrated any of the targets

3

he constructed out of the variety of materials used in boat building. Whether it was wood or vinyl or fiberglass, the powerful spring loaded gun would deliver its seven-pound load, creating a gaping hole, surely enough to send any boat to the bottom of the lake. The exterior of the arrowhead stone duplicated many of the submerged rocks in the big lake. Any investigation into the accident he was preparing to cause would quickly conclude that the boat had gone down due to contact with an unseen boulder lurking just beneath the surface of the lake.

*   *   *

The large blacktop parking lot still held the warmth of the day. The shimmering echoes of heat rising underfoot did not distract Bill's attention to his wife, looking absolutely gorgeous as she stood at the controls of their favorite toy.

A warm, gentle breeze blew her beach cover open and revealed her voluptuous figure, only slightly covered by his favorite outfit, a brilliant yellow bikini. His expectations for another wonderful evening with Nancy increased with each step toward the boat. Just before boarding, he turned back toward the docks, sure that everyone would be staring at his beautiful wife.

"How did I ever get so lucky," he called to her, bringing a slight blush to her cheeks. He jumped onto the deck and gave his wife of twenty-four years, a genuine, full body hug with a gentle but insistent pressure in the pelvic area.

"You are incorrigible, Bill Yates!" she teased, fully aware of the effect that her bikini usually had on him.

After the normal "how was your day and what's new" greetings, they set about checking the boat one last time before leaving the dock. Bill untied the bow line of the glistening craft and the boat slowly glided backward away from the dock. A semi-interested older couple sat on the bench nearest the dock observing the scene.

"What an attractive young couple . . . those were the days, huh, Emma?" The words of the gray haired gentleman drifted to him over the blatting of the powerful engines, causing him to smile. Bill, with his own half-century mark rapidly approaching, wasn't feeling much positive excitement about his life changing from the "These are the days" mode to the nostalgic "Those were the days."

"Everything's relative, I suppose," he mused, joining Nancy at the helm as she turned the boat toward the open water and opened the throttle. After a few seconds, the powerful craft settled into a comfortable planing mode, the town docks and their quaint New England village backdrop quickly receding behind them.

Bill and Nancy Yates knew the big lake well. Eye contact and a nod of the head this way or that by either one of them easily communicated what the other was thinking. There was no need for shouting over the rhythmic pounding of the water beneath them or the moderately noisy blatting of the huge engine. A married couple in tune with each other, they could finish the other's sentence without arousing resentment or animosity. On this perfect summer evening, with a minimum of expression or body language, they agreed to shut the engine down when they reached the "broads," a unique New Hampshire name for the widest and deepest part of the big lake. For the next two hours the boat drifted slowly with the current as they enjoyed the picnic supper. When the sun finally completed its fiery plunge into the western edge of the lake, Bill moved to the front of the boat and started the engine. A nervous excitement swept through both of them as they set a course for their favorite cove, an isolated spot on the northern side of the lake. The timing of their arrival would be exactly right. They had spent enough evenings in the cove that they knew if they arrived just as the deepening dusk turned to darkness, the loons would provide a welcoming chorus of unique calls and the closest human being would be at least a mile away.

After a fifteen-minute cruise across the huge lake, the *BiNaY II* gradually slowed. A lengthy discussion led to the naming of their first boat, finally compromising on the

"*BiNaY*," for <u>Bi</u>ll and <u>Na</u>ncy <u>Y</u>ates. The result didn't exactly indicate a depth of creative genius but they were relatively satisfied. When they graduated to the larger vessel, they simply attached the "II." They agreed with a sometimes rollicking good humor, that naming the boat had been more trouble than naming their children.

As expected, the quieting of the engine allowed the call of the loon to be heard. In the gathering darkness, the startling diverse calls came from several different directions.

They assumed an eerie quality, unsettling to city vacationers used to nothing but road rage horns and sirens but an absolute joy to nature lovers.

Bill warily guided the *BiNaY II* slowly into the cove, aware of the number of slightly submerged rocks in the area. As they reached their favorite place, he cut the engine and gently lowered the anchor. When it struck the bottom, he turned to look back at Nancy.

"We're at about thirty feet, I'd guess," he said. She was lolling on the rear seat against a backdrop of the towering pines lining the shore, their silhouettes quickly being gobbled up by the darkness. She had discarded her beach cover-up and her short blonde hair shimmered in the reflection from the running light at the stern of the boat.

She matched his good-natured leer with her most flirtatious smile. The discordant yet haunting calls of the loons echoed across the cove, increasingly insistent in the enveloping darkness.

*   *   *

With just a faint light remaining in the sky, he used his night binoculars to follow the boat as it slowly made its way into the cove. He loved the cacophony of the loons but his small twinge of regret at the intrusion on the natural sounds of the lake was quickly dispelled. The excitement of finally addressing his desperate need for justice assumed control.

As the obscure plans for revenge began to form in his mind, his physical condition assumed even more importance. Whatever final plan emerged from the turmoil in his mind, he was sure that he would need to be in shape to execute it.

He chanted his often repeated mantra as the boat inched

its way into the cove.

"I am, as they say, of sound mind and body." He heard the engine stop and, through the Bushnell binoculars he saw that it was better than he had hoped. For his first time, he wanted justice served on at least a moderately wealthy specimen, and he was confident that the occupants of this fancy Chaparral would fit into that category. After clicking through the numbers and arriving at the red "10," the strongest light gathering mode, he scanned the situation. The man obviously was dropping anchor, and his female companion seemed to be draped across the rear seat. The old adage about sound carrying better across water allowed him to almost distinguish the words in their conversation from over a half-mile away.

"Don't want any damn human individuality interfering here," he said aloud. The people in the boat had to be like the civilians bombed into oblivion during a war. The psychological problem of pilots who dwelled on thoughts about those poor souls are well documented and he wanted no part of it. The results of this first excursion were not decided yet, and he didn't want the compassionate feelings of his teaching days getting in his way. The boat rotated on its anchor line, drifting until the stern faced him.

"What could *BiNaY II* mean?" The question shot through his mind but was dismissed, likely some family significance that he did not want to know about. He snapped on the lens covers and slid the binoculars back into their leather case.

He peered at the boat through the gathering darkness. The loons quieted and the lake assumed its usual nighttime calm, as though exhausted from the business of the day. Well before dark, he had arranged everything that he would need for his swim in exact order on a large blanket.

After proceeding through his mental checklist of equipment and finding everything in good order, he prepared for his mission. He slipped the breathing apparatus over his shoulder and scooped up his mask, fins, the weight belts, tanks, and hoses necessary for spending a couple of hours in the water. The last item he grabbed was his personal pride and joy, the spear gun he had purchased ostensibly for fishing.

He walked slowly to the edge of the lake and set the spear gun and its lethal ammunition aside, quickly going through the pre-dive preparation rituals. The adrenaline rush began, accompanied by the thumping in his chest. Satisfied that he and his gear were ready, he picked up his gun and the spear and slipped his feet into his flippers, reaching down with his free hand to pull the straps over his heels. He walked awkwardly into the lake; the darkness of the water, the sky and the surrounding forest blending together into a surreal environment. When the water reached his waist, he turned and lay gently on his back. The umbrella of stars overhead created a sharp polarity with the feel of the weapon he held in his hands. Just before he submerged, he looked out toward the boat and noticed that the running light had been turned off.

"That will make this even easier," he said before slipping beneath the surface. He swam toward his appointment with the *BiNaY II*.

* * *

Bill Yates had flicked the switch for the running light, leaving the boat in total darkness. The night sky had never been more beautiful. At that moment, with the startling quiet descending upon them, they might have been the only two people on earth. He slowly made his way to the stern where his precious wife was waiting. The familiarity of their years together had not diminished their playful passion for each other. Bill sat down next to Nancy and slid his arm around her. She nestled her head against his shoulder and they both looked up. On other nights such as this one, they would launch into long philosophical discussions about the universe and how humble and insignificant they felt in the face of God's creation. Tonight, after a few wordless minutes admiring the haze of stars in the Milky Way, they turned to each other. For the next hour, the boat served as a floating platform for their lovemaking, the delicious sensuousness enhanced by the quiet environment of the warm evening.

* * *

He surfaced several times on his swim out to the *BiNaY II*, certain that the two people on the boat were not expecting any visitors. Even if they had been watching, it was highly unlikely that they would be able to see him. Each time he came to the surface, the erotic sounds of the couple carried across the water to him. He allowed memories of a passionate encounter with his own wife on the deck of their cabin careen through his head. He swallowed the bitterness welling up in his throat, and his mission assumed even more importance. If they had only let him do his job, they could have been out here making love instead of these people. Each time he surfaced, his agitation increased. He was practically hyperventilating, not good at any time, and especially problematic in his present circumstances.

He listened for what seemed an eternity but actually had been only a half-hour, waiting for the couple on board to finish and get underway. The buoyancy of the water combined with the air tanks strapped to his back allowed him to float effortlessly, even with the extra weight of the gun and the spear. As expected, his eyes became accustomed to the dark, and he caught an occasional glimpse of the people in the boat. He fought the vague feeling of jealousy in order to stay focused on his mission for the evening.

The star filled sky and the warm lake water had a mesmerizing effect, but the dream-like state exploded into reality as the man on board stood and walked to the cockpit. The running light came to life and provided a marvelous backlighting for the woman's figure as she stood, naked from the waist up, and pulled a sweatshirt over her head. He grudgingly slipped beneath the surface as the man pulled the anchor onto the boat. The charts he had committed to memory showed the water in this section of the cove to be about thirty-five feet deep. He needed to be just under the boat when it began to move so that he'd be able to see well enough to direct the spear to its target. For all of his planning of this first serious act of revenge, he still had no idea how it would end. Sinking an expensive boat was a minor part of his fantasies of vengeance entertained during his black periods but causing a few wealthy people some pain in their pocketbook would indeed be a start.

Drifting just a few feet under the bow of the boat, he waited for the engine to start. If the driver took off at full throttle like one of the obnoxious summer show-offs at the town docks, there wouldn't be time to fire his gun.

The rumble and vibrations of the engine coming to life reached him at the same time. He swam to a spot about twenty feet in front of the bow, anticipating that as the boat started out, it would head directly toward him. His eyes thoroughly accustomed to the blackness just beneath the surface, he waited until he saw the shining white hull directly over him. He raised his gun and fired. The hollow rock penetrated the fiberglass, creating a large hole and sending splintering cracks in every direction.

The hours of backyard practice and preparation paid the anticipated dividends. All of his rehearsals had been on stationary targets, and he jerked the rope attached to the spear, not sure what would happen. With a giddy sense of relief, he felt the rock slide back through the hole in the side of the boat. The spear tumbled toward the bottom of the lake. He followed the line to retrieve it, still not aware whether the damage he had inflicted was sufficient to call this first mission a success.

Using his most powerful swimming strokes, he quickly distanced himself, moving in a direction opposite of where the boat had been heading. When he felt safe, he slowly made his way to the surface. The second his head cleared the water, he slipped his goggles off and glanced around. The dark cove was as quiet as ever. He listened, straining to hear any sound at all but there was nothing. No more than five minutes had passed between the time he fired his weapon and his resurfacing. The boat should still be in the cove after sustaining the damage he was certain that it had. Like a water ballet dancer, Brad spun slowly in a three hundred and sixty-degree pirorette. The silence on the lake was profound. He started back toward the shore, convinced that the first mission of his "liberation" had failed.

*　*　*

Nancy and Bill Yates were enjoying the afterglow of a passionate and erotic lovemaking session. After Bill raised the anchor, he glanced back at Nancy, smiling as she stretched, teasing him with her bare breasts before slipping her sweatshirt over her head.

"I'm the lucky one," he called to her, a reference to a running good-natured argument over who was more fortunate to have the other. He started the engine and pushed the throttle forward. The boat started to glide through the smooth liquid mirror the cove had become.

The solid thump on the bottom of the boat was muffled by the increasingly loud engine noise as Bill struggled without success to bring the craft to planing speed. Nancy's presence behind him was palpable, and he glanced over his shoulder. The ambient light of the stars and the boat's running lights reflected the worry in her eyes. As always, her husband provided the reassurance as he just shrugged his shoulders and smiled. He had collided with many rocks in his years on the lake, and this sound just wasn't the same. The boat hadn't even trembled when they heard the noise. The lake was full of logs, lost oars, and other accidental jetsam, none of which causes anything but nuisance damage.

A minute later, when the performance of the powerful boat degenerated into a sluggish plodding, Bill knew that something was very wrong.

"Would you just take a quick look below, Nance?"

Nancy anticipated the request and was standing at the top of the stairway leading down to the cabin. Bill slipped the throttle into neutral just as Nancy's quavering voice drifted up from the cabin below. "Oh, my God!"

Without the forward momentum supplied by the engine, the severe listing toward the starboard side was obvious.

"What's wro. . . ?" Bill's question faded into nothingness as he peered down into the darkened cabin.

Nancy had turned to climb back on deck, and he could see the swirling water follow her with each step. The instinctive reactions of the well-seasoned lake boater took over, even as he reached to help Nancy clamber onto the deck, her face contorted with disbelief. The enervating adrenaline rush had the unique effect of calming him. He leaned against the railing as though still enjoying the magnificent star splattered sky.

The two-minute battle to get to full speed had carried the *BiNaY II* into the center of the broads, the deepest part of the lake. Bill calculated that the nearest land would be Rattlesnake Island, at least a mile away. The black night enveloped them. Only a sprinkling of distant village lights

11

providing any sort of reality to what had so quickly become a surreal situation. The boat was taking on water at a rate that overwhelmed the bilge pump and would send it to the bottom of the lake in minutes. Any hope of help arriving before the *BiNaY II* slipped beneath the surface was useless. Bill turned all of his attention to Nancy.

"Get the life jackets. We've got to get off this boat now!"

Nancy, trying desperately to control her ascending panic, pulled the cushion from the long sideboard seat. She grabbed two of the never-used life jackets and threw one to Bill. He shut down the engine. His vision of the *BiNay II* settling in the sand two hundred feet below the surface was anathema to him. He yanked the key with its flotation key chain from the ignition and jammed it into the small pocket of his swimsuit as though certain he would be using it again.

After an awkward moment of sorting out top from bottom, they managed to help each other into the life jackets. Bill took Nancy's hand and led her to the stern of the boat, now lifting out of the water. He helped her down the ladder as he untied the ring buoy and handed it to her.

"You use this. You know I've always been a better swimmer anyway." She smiled in spite of the circumstances. The same life ring had always served as just a nice decorative touch on the boat.

When Bill descended the ladder and settled into the water, he reached for Nancy's hand.

"We'll stay together and go toward Rattlesnake, OK? Shouldn't be a problem; it really isn't that far."

"Thanks for such an exciting evening!" she said. They shared a brief chuckle as he worked his way closer. "I love you."

"Love you, too. Now let's get going." He kissed her lightly on the cheek and they started toward the shore of Rattlesnake Island.

The soft glow from the millions of stars dotting the sky lent enough light so that the couple could barely discern the silhouette of Rattlesnake Island. Bill's estimate of a mile to the island from where the boat went down was accurate. The brilliant orange life jackets provided more than enough buoyancy, and little effort was necessary to stay afloat.

Their major concern remained fatigue. The sinking of the *BiNaY II* was traumatic and emotionally draining. They held each other tightly as they watched from a short distance away as the boat slid beneath the surface, its stern standing straight up in the air for a few seconds before its dive to the bottom. After a full minute of floating without moving, staring at the still rippling water as though expecting the boat to resurface, they set out again for land. Making forward progress was not difficult, and they covered the first half-mile in less than an hour.

Nancy, using the life ring as one might use a surfboard, propelled herself forward faster than Bill, but safety seemed better served if they stayed together. The island loomed closer in the blackness, and their confidence rose with each passing minute.

"What'll we do if we land on a deserted part of the island?" Nancy called into the darkness.

"I could give you one of my usual wise remarks, but I don't think you'd appreciate it." His laugh rippled to her but was interrupted by a single deep breath, a wordless gasp for air.

Nancy stopped her forward progress. She turned to look at Bill, expecting one of his familiar leers. Instead, she realized that he had stopped kicking and was floating on his back. A searing panic set in and she paddled toward him. His eyes were open, staring into the night sky as if searching for an answer to a profound but unanswerable question. She grabbed his arm, frantically searching for a pulse. There was none. The sparkling canopy of stars overhead, so beautiful minutes before, suddenly became a crushing presence around them. In sheer desperation, she placed her mouth on his and tried to blow air into his lungs. Fighting the numbing sensation tingling throughout her body, she whispered his name into his ear, over and over. The whisper became louder with each syllable until she was shouting. The shattering reality that Bill was gone threatened to immobilize her completely. Finally, a despairing calm settled over her, and she began to make her way to shore, one hand on the life preserver, the other firmly grasping her husband's life jacket. After what she was sure must have been hours, they arrived on the shore of Rattlesnake

Island. Drawing strength from the pure desperation of her predicament, she pulled Bill's limp body through the soft sand until it was completely out of the water. She knelt beside him, the incongruity of the awesome beauty of the clear night clashing with the desolation of death. She looked down at him and the clutching fingernail grip she held on her emotions left her. She put both hands to her face and rocked back and forth, sobbing.

*   *   *

A noise outside startled him out of a fitful, restless sleep. A large red 6:58 stared back at him from the nightstand. He rubbed the fuzziness from his eyes and clicked on the television, using the remote to surf through the channels until habit brought him to WMUR, the only station that called New Hampshire its home.

The two announcers were preparing for the cutaway to commercials with phony bantering. He caught the superimposed graphic scrolling across the bottom of the screen even before the deep, bass voice of John Tancredi intoned the upcoming news story.

"WINNIPESAUKEE BOAT ACCIDENT CLAIMS ONE LIFE" made the circuit from ear to brain to final comprehension. The female version of Tancredi reiterated that there had indeed been a tragedy on the big lake overnight, and the breaking story would lead the morning news show after the commercial break.

"Oh, shit!" The loud exclamation echoed around his room. It was one of those rare moments when subtle intuition becomes screaming truth, when gut level feelings turn to sickening reality.

He puffed up his pillow and, with grim fascination, waited for the talking heads to reappear and begin to fill in the details of what happened on the lake. The glorious aroma of the fresh-brewed coffee wafted up the stairs, but he resisted the temptation to race down to the kitchen. Instead, he stayed rooted to the spot, refusing to miss any part of the story.

He smiled in amazement. Even last night, he had observed the nightly ritual of grinding coffee beans and setting the automatic timer on the coffee maker after returning from what he already was calling his "mission." He couldn't remember a night when he hadn't prepared the coffee; it was one of the few habits left over from his life with his wife and the inconsequential connection was more compulsion than ritual. The link between the coffee and his wife reminded him of the purpose of his mission, of his need for liberation, of his festering anger and bitterness. The touch of remorse that crept in when he first heard of the fatality was pushed aside by a deeper feeling of justice being served. There were bound to be unforeseen events as he carried out his missions and if someone had the misfortune of being in the wrong place at the wrong time, then it must be destiny.

Fifteen minutes later, he sat on the modest deck overlooking the dense woods surrounding his house, sipping the strong home brewed coffee. A sense of detachment washed over him. His first mission had been an unqualified success, and he had no control over extraneous, unplanned circumstances that arose while he carried out his objectives.

"The bastards have begun to pay," he muttered as he immersed himself in reconstructing the events of the night before.

Bradford Wallace,
Educator-1964

"I touch the future – I teach"
Christa MacCauliffe

After graduating from the University of Connecticut, Bradford A. Wallace stood ready to begin a career of influencing the lives of untold numbers of children. Brad, like generations of neophyte teachers before him, possessed the naive idealism, yet unbridled enthusiasm unmatched by beginners in any other profession.

The process had not been an easy one for him. His father, John Wallace, as patriarchal and authoritarian as he could be, delivered a seemingly endless series of long-winded lectures about schoolteachers. "Those who can, do, Bradford," John would bristle. "Those who can't, teach!"

His father's many vicious diatribes against schoolteachers, the "feeders at the public trough, those leeches of society," achieved the opposite effect from what the senior Wallace had hoped. Brad became even more determined to pursue a career in education. Mr. Lehner, his sophomore English teacher had redirected his life, and he was sure he could do the same for any number of young people. "The noblest of professions" was his constant rebuttal to any argument his father put forth.

Sandra Wallace teased her son unmercifully about his "five year plan" as he changed majors three times. Ultimately, she convinced John that they needed to support Brad for the fifth year, "even if he is only going to be a schoolteacher."

When the principal of Hampton Village High School called to offer Brad his first teaching position, he was happy that his mother was the only one at home. Sandra Wallace, the life-long buffer between his father's harshness and his own ebullience, would join him in his enthusiasm.

Hampton Village High School, a small school in western Connecticut, provided a perfect beginning for Brad's career. With just over six hundred students, the environment was more like that of an exclusive private school. Hampton Village, a wealthy bedroom community northwest of the Hartford-Springfield area, attracted a wide variety of professionals with its picturesque Berkshires setting and visionary zoning ordinances. The two-acre minimum lot size eliminated any chance of lower income housing, and the majority of the residents lived in spacious mini-estates and gentlemen's farms. The tax base allowed ample funding for outstanding community services and schools; the residents assumed the responsibilities of citizenship with avid involvement in every phase of operating the town.

Only a few of the more experienced members of the staff could afford to live in "The Village." Brad found an apartment in a predominantly middle class town twelve miles from the school. The commute, at first dreaded but soon welcomed, became an opportunity to prepare mentally for the day and reflect in the afternoon. As engrossing as the preparation for his new life was, nothing could compare to the thought of the first official day of school: a new staff orientation day. Whenever those thoughts surfaced, his stomach fluttered with a positive nervousness.

Bradford Wallace would soon be Mr. Wallace, social studies teacher. He could not wait. He joined six other new staff members for the first day of new teacher orientation.

None of them had teaching experience. The obligatory university student teaching programs were helpful but an unrealistic taste of a full time teaching position. From their first introductions, a unique camaraderie developed, a common bond of uneasiness and anxiety coupled with the excitement and challenge of their new careers.

Two women and five men comprised "the magnificent seven," as they were calling themselves by their first lunch together. The men, none of whom had military experience, shared a mutual concern about the possibility of being drafted as President Lyndon Johnson's promise of a "Great Society" juxtaposed with a rapidly escalating war in Vietnam. All five had benefited from student deferments during their college days but those had lapsed with graduation. Their new profession was considered a critical skill, and all five had filed the request for a change in draft status from 3S to 2A. The presidential election of 1964, just under two months away, could change everything, and many of their hurried lunch discussions revolved around what might happen to them if Barry Goldwater became the President of the United States.

The two young women of the magnificent seven, Josie Campbell and Harriet Long, relished their position as the single and available females of the group. At the close of the exhausting first official day of school with the students, the new male staff members planned to celebrate by hoisting a few beers at Pete's Pub just over the town line. Brad flattered the two women with an invitation to join them. All agreed to meet at Pete's at 4:30 that afternoon. By 5:00, the first beer had loosened any lingering inhibitions, and the opening day of school anecdotes began.

As the humorous stories about the first day faltered, they were replaced by more serious and more tiring philosophical discussions. When Harriet informed the others that she was heading home for a quick supper and early bedtime, all but Josie and Brad agreed that it was time to go home. After a quick calculation of who owed what on the check, five of the seven said their good-byes with the promise to make the "meetings" at Pete's a regular occasion. Brad's quiet invitation to Josie to stay around for just one more drink was readily accepted, and their evening lasted through a pepperoni and mushroom pizza and several hours of comfortable conversation.

"Stay tuned for the ten o'clock news." The voice from the television behind the bar intruded.

Brad and Josie looked at each other in surprise. "How on earth did it get to be ten o'clock?" Brad was the first to ask.

After paying their bill and combining their loose change for a tip, they walked toward the door in silence. Only a few cars were left in the darkened parking lot but theirs were at exactly opposite ends.

"I really enjoyed this evening, Brad," Josie said as she started to her car. Brad turned and walked along side her. Unlike the hours of animated conversation in Pete's, no words were spoken during the leisurely walk across the lot. They walked close together but without touching until they arrived at her green 1962 Chevrolet Corvair convertible.

"Well, Josie, Ralph Nader wouldn't be very happy with you. You'd better be careful driving this car," Brad joked.

"My Dad gave it to me for graduation and I'm sure that he wouldn't give me a dangerous automobile." She smiled at his discomfort.

"Sorry, Josie! I'm sure he wouldn't. . . . I was only teasing," Brad stammered, regretting the mild faux pas. "Nader is such a complete jerk anyway; nothing but a stupid communist."

Josie responded to the sharp edge that had come into his voice. "It's OK, Brad. I know you were only kidding. Relax!"

His awkwardness vanished when he looked at Josie and saw her smile.

"I feel like I'm fourteen and on my first date," he confessed.

"This isn't a date," Josie corrected, "but I know what you mean. Thanks again for a wonderful evening. See you tomorrow."

Brad closed the door for her and watched her drive away. The next day at school couldn't come soon enough.

*   *   *

The first four months of the magnificent seven's tenure at Hampton Village High School passed in what seemed like a few days. The debriefing meetings at Pete's occurred spontaneously, usually spawned by one person's suggestion. The sessions evolved into such powerful therapeutic tools that only rarely would someone miss one of them. Usually, the one who suggested they meet would have a particular problem that needed to be explored and, by the informal and unwritten rules of the seven, that issue would be the first one discussed. The commonality of classroom experiences was a revelation every time they met. The spirited camaraderie carried each of them through the difficult times, whether those times were caused by a problem student, an unreasonable parent, or an unfair evaluation by a supervisor. The magnificent seven acted as buffers for each other against the inevitable discouragement that follows the blind idealism of most beginning teachers.

The approaching Christmas vacation brought the usual mixture of excitement and chaos to the school, and the young teachers met on a regular basis to help each other deal with the common problems of the season. Josie and Brad's friendship deepened on a daily basis and naturally became a major item of discussion among the gossipy adolescents who happened to be in both Miss Campbell's English class and Mr. Wallace's American Government class.

Brad had all of the qualities necessary for attracting women. His light brown, wavy hair, longer than was fashionable until the Beatles made it so, contrasted with his dark brown eyes. Just over six feet tall, he had a slim, athletic build and a wide, impish grin that spread across his face with just the slightest provocation. Josie and Harriet shared the opinion that he could make a woman feel as if she were the only person in the universe, even in the most distracting of environments. His penetrating eyes had a sparkle and vitality that Josie found slightly disconcerting at times. As the months passed and the self-protective layers of his personality and character were gradually peeled away, Josie spent much of her time thinking of Brad. With just the right combination of good humor and seriousness, he could put her completely at ease. She felt a depth of comfort that she had not experienced with any other man.

The one concern she had, one that was easily dismissed, was Brad's intensity when discussing injustices of any kind. His eyes would lose their sparkle, darkening into a grim, brooding glaze that she found transiently frightening. During one of the late afternoon sessions at Pete's, a political discussion evolved into a heated but friendly argument. Rich Lane, the most articulate and intellectual of the seven and a colleague in Josie's English department, enjoyed playing the devil's advocate. He counted upon Brad to be the first to rise to his bait. The discussion began with Johnson's presidential campaign's use of a frightening political television ad depicting a beautiful young girl picking flowers just as the brilliant white light of an atomic bomb explosion obliterated the screen. The message was clear: Barry Goldwater was dangerous.

"You know," Rich said, "Maybe Goldwater has something; maybe he's not such a loose cannon after all."

"Oh, yeah, and maybe we should send all the Negroes back to Africa!" Brad's words came out in a low hiss, his passion impossible to ignore.

"Got you again, Brad. We're really on the same side, you know!" Rich's voice and friendly demeanor diffused the heat of the moment, and the friends shared a mild, mutual chuckle. With the discussion directed toward the racial issue, Harriet Long mentioned the horrible murders of several Civil Rights activists in Alabama but quickly wished that she hadn't.

"Those murdering bastards should pay!" Brad shouted, his hand slapping the table in front of him. His six friends looked at him in unison, shocked at the intensity of his response. Josie caught the foreboding gaze in his eyes just before it vanished.

Josie and Brad-1966

"The greatest of these is love."
I Corinthians

Josie Campbell and Brad Wallace shared many of the rare qualities that make just a few teachers special and memorable. Both received the highest accolades from supervisors, peers, and, most importantly, from their students during their first two years at Hampton Village. Their commitment to the profession provided substantial benefit to their lives. Chaperoning dances, taking field trips, advising student clubs, and tutoring academically challenged students allowed Josie and Brad to spend most of their waking hours together. They chose to announce their wedding plans at the annual staff Christmas party, which would lead to a barrage of amiable jokes about using Josie as a draft deferment. The escalating war in Vietnam threatened to remove most of the critical skill draft exemptions from the teaching profession, but married men benefited from John F. Kennedy's removal of them from the pool several years before.

Prior to their wedding announcement, Tyler Spence, one of the magnificent seven, would be drafted. Tyler's unexpected call had come in October, and Superintendent Dr. Chris Howard's plea could not change the collective mind of Tyler's draft board. A melancholy, tearful farewell session of the seven colleagues came to an abrupt conclusion when Brad launched into a vehement and impassioned denunciation of the inequity of the draft process. His embarrassed apologies afterward eased everyone's mind as they said goodbye to Tyler, but Josie once again noticed the frightening glaze come into Brad's eyes as he concluded his tirade.

"Those bastards on the draft board should go over there themselves," he snarled.

*   *   *

Josie Campbell, determined to establish her own identity, prevailed over her parents' objections and in June of 1966, the Hampton Village Community Church became the setting for her wedding. The Campbells, a prominent Hartford family with connections at the highest political levels, wanted Josie to follow tradition and be married in her home church, but Josie quickly pointed out that the Hampton Village Community Church was her "home" church. The loyalty she felt toward her students played an important part in her decision. As soon as the word spread about the impending marriage of two of the most popular teachers in their school, the students began making plans for their own celebration and Josie would not be the one to disappoint them. Brad agreed that Hampton Village had become their home and the wedding would not be complete without their students taking part.

"How do you figure I got so lucky?" Brad whispered to Rich Lane, his best man, as they stood at the altar watching Josie and her father make their way through the throngs of students standing at the rear of the church.

Josie, with bridal radiance casting an aura around her, looked more beautiful than ever. In her self-deprecating manner, she often referred to herself as "chunky" and struggled without success to lose several pounds before the wedding. To Brad, and other admiring males in the congregation, the extra pounds, if indeed there were any, were certainly spread over the right places. The tightly cinched wedding gown displayed her voluptuous figure to good advantage. Brad's eyes remained riveted on her as she walked down the center aisle of the small church on her father's arm. As they drew closer, the gleam in her hazel eyes shone through her veil.

Robert Campbell gently unhooked his arm from his daughter's and mumbled "I do" in answer to the traditional "Who gives this woman?" question. Robert flashed the common look a father tends to give his future son-in-law as he passes his daughter over, a glance that quietly shouts, "You had better be good to her!" Then he moved to his seat in the front row next to his wife. Brad's parents looked on with warm approval.

Brad, using both hands, gently folded Josie's veil back, then took her hands in his and looked at her. Her eyes now glistened with dampness, the residual effect of the organ's rousing "Here Comes the Bride" still touching her.

"Are you happy?" Brad whispered. She answered with a demure smile and slight nod. They turned to the minister and the service began.

The Great Society
and Tyler Spence

"The Great Society rests on abundance and liberty for all. It demands an end to poverty and racial injustice."
Lyndon B. Johnson, 36th President of the United States

Slightly built and smaller in physical stature than many of his young male students, Tyler Spence caused the school administration legitimate concern about his ability to handle discipline but he was a magical presence in a classroom. Soft spoken by nature, he had the uncanny ability to address a class with just enough volume to force his students to listen. Two administrative observations eliminated all concern about his talent. He was living proof that great teachers are born and have instincts and timing that cannot be taught. He was, by anyone's standards, a "natural."

As the newest member of the Mathematics Department, he was assigned the least desirable schedule. To assuage some degree of his guilt, his department head added an *Advanced Algebra I* class to his four sections of *Basic Mathematics*. Each of his classes contained the maximum twenty-five students, including many of the most challenging in the ninth grade. The daunting assignment would have tested even the most experienced instructor. With five sections of freshmen and a large auditorium study hall assignment, Tyler had drawn the most difficult teaching load of any of the magnificent seven. The unfairness of his assignment often occupied a portion of the therapy sessions at Pete's but Tyler himself never complained. He loved teaching, smiling as he let his friends grumble about his situation. When he volunteered to be the class advisor for the Class of 1968, the largest freshman class in the history of Hampton Village High School, no one was surprised.

With the abolition of student draft deferments and college campus demonstrations increasing in number and intensity, Tyler worried about the prospects that his younger brother, Bobby, a freshman at Brown University might be drafted. Two weeks into his second year at Hampton Village, Tyler's own draft notice arrived. His weekly call to Bobby began in typical fashion, checking on his brother's health and well being. As if an afterthought, he mentioned his notice at the end of the conversation. "Don't worry about me, will you? Everything'll be fine. OK?"

He returned to reviewing his lesson plans for the next day, plans that now included a short announcement to his classes that he would be leaving them soon, but "only for a short while."

*   *   *

The summer of 1966 tumbled by, the Wallaces spent much of their time in a newlywed glow of happiness as they prepared for the coming school year. Their rural life was a safe and idyllic cocoon, far removed from the harsh reality of racial violence and political protest intensifying in cities across the country.

Late in August, the exciting anticipation of another school year was reaching a peak.

After a morning of grocery shopping, Josie stopped at the post office to pick up their mail while Brad visited the hardware store for a few home improvement odds and ends. When Brad arrived back at the car, Josie sat reading the annual letter from Chris Howard, welcoming the staff back for another school year and laying out the schedule for the first two days of staff meetings. An animated conversation about the upcoming year, their tenure year, they kept reminding each other, lasted the entire trip back to their apartment.

The phone was ringing as Brad unlocked the newly repainted door to the apartment. Leaving the overflowing bags of groceries at the door, he raced to answer it. *"What is it about a ringing telephone that makes people practically kill themselves trying to answer it?"* he wondered as he slammed his knee against the kitchen table.

"Hello," Brad said, just slightly out of breath.

"Chris Howard here, Brad. How's your summer been?" Brad stuttered a bit before answering. A call from the Superintendent is rare.

"Really good, Dr. Howard. We just got your letter today. We're both anxious to get back," Brad answered, his response sounding like a feeble attempt at ingratiating himself with his boss. An inordinate period of silence preceded Chris Howard's reply, making Brad even more nervous.

"Bad news, Brad," Chris said, emotion choking his voice. "It's Tyler Spence. He's been killed in Vietnam. I need to ask for your help in spreading the word with his closest friends. The principal will be in touch with everyone about the arrangements and all the details but I wanted you to know first. I'm really sorry, Brad. I know how close that group of yours is. I'll talk to you again soon. Truly sorry. . . ." His voice dropped to a whisper as he hung up.

Josie, carrying two of the bags Brad had left at the door, came into the kitchen and found Brad leaning against the door jamb, his eyes watering but simmering with a cold, angry stare. An inexplicable shiver raced down Josie's spine.

"It's Tyler, Josie. Those bastards got him." Then he went to her and wrapped his arms around her in a desperate embrace.

*   *   *

Unsettling nighttime sweats awakened Brad at regular monthly intervals. Two weeks after the crushing memorial service for Tyler, Brad awoke at two in the morning, his pajamas soaked. Not wanting to alarm Josie, he slipped quietly out of bed and fumbled his way to the bathroom. He turned on the cold water faucet, cupped his hands under the still lukewarm water and waited for it to turn cool. A few splashes on his face calmed him and he sat down on the toilet, reconstructing the moment when he awoke.

"Just a stupid dream," he said softly, as though saying the words could convince him that it was just that. Tyler's face, covered with blood, floated before his eyes. He remembered that same image just before waking. What began as a vague memory crystallized and Brad could hear his friend's voice.

"It's not fair, Brad," the voice had said. "You've got to do something!"

Brad stood up, went to the sink and splashed more water on his face. He took one final glance in the mirror, expecting to see Tyler's face looking over his shoulder, then tiptoed back to the bedroom, relieved to find Josie still sleeping soundly. He slid into bed, the bottom sheet cool and damp from his sweat, and stared up at the ceiling. For the rest of the night, he fought an urge to awaken Josie and tell her about it but knew that she likely wouldn't understand.

"You're right, Tyler. It isn't fair. I've really got to do something." He muffled the words into his pillow. Josie stirred but did not awaken. After the fitful night's sleep, Brad did not hear the alarm and his wife jabbed him with a pointed elbow in the ribs to get him moving.

He stood in the shower and let the hot water massage the tense muscles in his neck and back. Tyler Spence's visit in his dreams opened a pathway to feelings locked away in a dark corner of Brad's mind. An intrusive notion that he must correct such injustices began to bring him to the edge of despair.

He turned and let the hot water cascade over his face. With his eyes tightly closed, Tyler's ethereal image appeared again. The utter futility of it all washed over him like the water beating on his face. The chaos of the times mirrored his own feelings. John F. Kennedy's "New Frontier" had fired his imagination six years before, but the promise disintegrated under Lyndon Johnson. The festering anger and bitterness blended into a sad frustration. When he would listen to his students present their oral current events assignments, Brad would assume a modern Don Quixote stance as he listened to the endless reports of world problems. In a Walter Mitty fashion, he walked along side of Martin Luther King in a nonviolent protest march, faced down Governor George Wallace on the steps of a school in Alabama, or locked arms with a group of anti-war demonstrators.

His anger festered. "You're never going to do anything but protect your own ass," he said through the penetrating stream of hot water. As he turned off the water, he allowed his promise to Tyler to find a place in the corner of his mind reserved for inequities that he would address later.

The Hartford Move

"To the rest of the world, The United States must look like a giant insane asylum where the inmates have taken over."
Art Buchwald (1968)

Until June of 1968, Hampton Village High School appeared immune from the insanity that engulfed the rest of the country. The tragic assassination of Martin Luther King in April intensified the explosive social and political unrest. Escalation became a catchword for explaining everything. The Vietnam War escalated; anti-war protests escalated; anti-protest protests escalated; draft evasion escalated; inner city violence and rioting escalated. With just a few Black families in town, Hampton Village residents easily adopted a superficial racial tolerance and an empathetic attitude toward the nearby communities struggling to control dangerous tensions in racially mixed neighborhoods.

During their four years at the school, Josie and Brad Wallace's popularity and effectiveness escalated as well. As their methodology professors had promised, each year in a teaching assignment became easier. With less time required for basic preparation, more time became available for innovative projects. The Wallace husband and wife team developed a reputation for creativity that earned them the respect of their administrators. The same imagination and artistry also gained the grudging admiration of their peers; a respect always tempered by professional jealousy.

Rich Lane, the advisor for the school yearbook and one of the magnificent seven, couldn't contain the secret any longer. When he told Josie that the seniors had dedicated the school yearbook to Brad, she beamed with pride. The final class day, Wednesday, June 5 would be the perfect time to inform her husband that her suspicions had been confirmed by a visit to her doctor.

31

Using the final class day as an excuse, she invited Brad out for dinner to their favorite Hartford restaurant, ostensibly to celebrate the end of the semester. The day already had been a special one, a career highlight for Brad, but as they were ushered to a quiet corner table in the small, dimly lit cubicle just off the main dining room, Brad sensed that there was more to come. His wife glowed and he waited for her to share the excitement.

"What's going on, Josie?"

Josie smiled, her cheeks coloring slightly, and said, "Why don't you try to guess?"

Brad reached across the table, signaling for her to put her hands in his. "Are you sure?"

"Yep, confirmed by Dr. Capaldi yesterday. Do you have any idea how hard it was to wait to tell you? I guess the hopeless romantic in me just wanted a special setting."

They looked at each other, their glistening eyes reflecting the candle wavering between them.

"When?" Brad asked.

"The doctor says it could be a Christmas baby. Wouldn't that be something?"

"Oh, wow, what a day this has been," Brad stammered as the waitress approached.

The dinner at the elegant Hostelry Restaurant was exquisite, and the euphoric Wallaces cut into their monthly entertainment budget by adding a large shrimp cocktail, dessert and a bottle of their favorite red wine to the occasion. Between giggling and "I can't believe this" looks, Josie and Brad spent their celebration dinner in lively conversation about their careers, children, and their wonderful students.

"We've really got to go, Brad. The waitress gave us the check a half hour ago." Josie looked over at Brad and once again felt a pleasant tightness in her throat. In that moment, the overwhelming problems of the world could not have been further removed from their minds. What truly mattered existed right there at the small table in the Hostelry.

"I love you, Josie," Brad said. "I think you're probably the only thing that keeps me sane sometimes." Reluctantly, they stood to leave. Brad pulled the cash from his wallet and added a generous tip, due more to the occasion than the service.

"I keep you sane? What in the world does that mean?" Josie's question, more rhetorical and joking than serious, was left hanging as they left the restaurant and walked to the car.

The trip home began with a solemn pronouncement from Josie. "Seat belts are now mandatory in the Wallace automobile. We have a child to think about." Brad just smiled as they both buckled up. Before they were halfway home, Josie unhooked her belt and moved provocatively closer to her husband. The rest of the ride seemed like seconds as they teased each other with caresses and sideways hugs and kisses.

The front door of their apartment had barely closed behind them when the passions aroused in the car enveloped them. Josie dismissed his timid "Is this OK?" by guiding him against the hallway wall and pushing her body against his. Sensing that his concern was real, she whispered in his ear.

"Doctor said no restrictions for now, Brad." Their perfect evening ended with a long and languorous lovemaking session. The elation with the direction their lives were taking served to increase the passion level several notches. Just before her exhausted husband fell into a deep sleep, Josie heard him whisper, "My God, I'm going to be a father."

Her senses still tingled in the glowing contentment of their love-making when she turned toward him. "What did you mean I keep you sane?" she said to Brad's back. Then her thoughts shifted to the child in her womb and she was smiling as she fell into a sound sleep.

*   *   *

The clock radio on the overflowing nightstand next to Josie's side of the bed awakened Brad as Josie struggled to switch off the music blaring from their favorite radio station. Brad was the first to shake loose the wine-induced cobwebs from his head. The initial words out of his mouth were, "I'm going to be a father!" This startled Josie into action and she fumbled her way to the switch, he realized that the noise emanating from the radio was not the usual lively music.

"Wait just a second, Josie." She pulled her hand back and the deep voice of the announcer buffeted them with the shocking news. In mid-sentence, his voice faltered, leaving Josie and Brad to fill in the missing segments.

". . . critical condition in a Los Angeles hospital. His wife Ethel is with him and a medical bulletin will be issued later this morning. More details will be upcoming on the regular news broadcast at 6:30."

"What the hell has happened now?" Brad pulled Josie closer to him, his stomach beginning to churn as he made the connections. Robert Kennedy was campaigning in Los Angeles and his wife's name was Ethel.

"Damn it, Josie, something's happened to Bobby Kennedy." Then he was out of bed and running into the living room to turn on the television. He had most of the details even before Josie joined him on the sofa. The kinescope replay of the chaotic scene following Kennedy's victory statement in the California primary was repeated twice as Josie and Brad sat in stunned silence, holding hands as they stared at the murky black and white images on the screen.

"We'd better get to school, Brad. You know what it will be like." Josie's voice intruded on the surreal state of Brad's mind. He agreed with a perfunctory "yeah" then squeezed her hand. The serenity and content-ment of the night had been rudely displaced.

As the steam from the shower filled the small bathroom, Brad stood motionless, ignoring the sharp needles of hot water. It was indeed, "déjà vu all over again," as Casey Stengel or Yogi Berra once said. He couldn't remember which. The face of Tyler Spence formed in the mist. Had it really been two years since he was killed? The same desolation and helplessness he felt when he heard about Tyler settled over him. With a substantial degree of desperation, he tried to convince himself that he could not be the only one with a sense of hopelessness. The poignant cry of Tyler to "do something" reverberated in his head.

"One of these days," he said, speaking toward the showerhead as if it were a microphone. "One of these days I'll make a difference, God damn it!" Brad dried himself, watching the bathroom mirror clear as the steaming mist gradually dissipated. He drew some measure of strength from the eye contact with the resolute image reflecting back at him. Some day, he would do something; he was certain of it. He stared at his image for a few more seconds, then hurried into the bedroom, the happiness of the night before retreating into the crushing reality of whatever this day might bring.

*   *   *

The political and social turmoil of the summer of 1968 framed the turbulence in the personal lives of the Wallaces. The assassination of Robert Kennedy became the catalyst for Brad to look beyond the serenity of Hampton Village and its sheltered life style.

He and Josie arrived at school expecting to handle a universal emotional crisis among their students. They instead found a discomfiting lack of interest in the fact that Bobby Kennedy would likely die during the day. Even given the overwhelming Republican nature of the town, the general lack of compassion toward the Kennedy family was surprising and disappointing to the Wallaces. Brad offered a ten-minute reprieve from beginning the final exam in his first period class to talk about the situation, but without exception the students wanted to begin the exam immediately. The complacent attitude prevailed on the second day as well, even though Kennedy had died during the night from the gunshot wound. Josie and Brad found these times to be "going through the motions of life" days while most of the student body appeared blissfully disconnected, more interested in completing finals and beginning the upcoming summer vacation. A change from the contented and self-absorbed student body of Hampton Village High School had to be made if he had any chance of fulfilling his personal promise to make a difference.

*   *   *

Without informing Josie of his intent, Brad placed a telephone call to Jim

McBride, a former classmate serving as Director of Curriculum and Instruction in the Hartford School District. Two weeks later, Hampton Village High School lost its graduation speaker, yearbook dedicatee, stellar teacher, and coach to Hartford West High School, a racially blended school on the west side of the city. Brad thought, perhaps in Hartford, he could do something to make a difference and return the gaze into the mirror with conviction. Just maybe Tyler Spence would look on approvingly.

His explanation to Josie for the rather sudden decision to move did not include any reference to Tyler, but focused on the increase in salary, the generous benefit package, and the need to provide for the well being of the new baby. She accepted his belief that the change would be for the best. Their rural environment with its bucolic calm would not change. Brad would simply become another of the thousands of commuters who ventured daily into the city to make a living, then returned at night to the safety of the suburbs.

In her heart, Josie knew that her husband could not be a time clock teacher. The same dedication and effort he demonstrated at Hampton Village surely would apply at Hartford West. On two separate occasions, she shared her concern about his tendency to become immersed in the life of his students and what that dedication might mean to them if he were teaching in Hartford. Both times, he made her feel foolish and she gave up. Finally, with less than her usual enthusiasm, she supported his decision.

Josie Campbell Wallace

"There are two kinds of weakness:
that which breaks and that which bends."
James Russell Lowell

Josie entered the second trimester of her pregnancy in late July, just as the Connecticut Berkshires were suffering through an extended heat wave. The temperature soared above ninety degrees for twelve straight days, and the natural discomfort associated with bearing a child increased in direct proportion to the oppressive heat. The annoying ritual of morning nausea had subsided, replaced with the increasing aggravation of weight gain and emotional instability. Brad often teased her about her tendency toward being "pleasantly plump," and she accepted the joking with a good-natured confidence. Despite Brad's constant reassurance that she was as attractive as ever, Josie looked in the mirror, searching for proof of his claim that all pregnant women had a radiance, a glow that set them apart.

"Sounds like a great pick up line, Brad," she said on more than one occasion.

One sweltering morning, after Brad had left for his *Management Techniques for School Administrators* class in Hartford, Josie walked the half-mile to the Hampton Village Public Library as briskly as she could. The combination of the prolonged heat and humidity mixing with the musty pungency of the old building accentuated the old book library smell. She found her way to the Psychology/Philosophy section, hoping that this stultifying environment didn't trigger a relapse of her morning sickness episodes. After just a few minutes of browsing, she had four volumes cradled in her arms. She walked toward the check out desk with her head down, absorbed in the reviewers' blurbs on the back of the book that topped off her pile.

"Well, good morning, Mrs. Wallace." The cheerful greeting startled her and she looked up. The voice was that of Gladys Markham, the legendary librarian who had to be at least three times her age. Josie wondered absently if Miss Markham ever addressed any patrons by their first names. Opening each book to the inside front cover with deliberation, the librarian handed her the small card from the inside pocket and waited for her to sign her name. During the date stamping process, she became aware of Miss Markham's eyes flitting between the titles and her somewhat rounded stomach. Miss Markham peered at her over the bifocals pinching the end of her nose. After the last book was stamped and handed across the desk to Josie, she looked directly at her with a mixture of curiosity, interest, and concern.

"Is everything all right, Mrs. Wallace?" Her question seemed harmless and innocent enough but Josie found it intrusive.

"Why do you ask?" The harshness was evident in Josie's voice and the librarian reflexively cleared her throat and leaned back, a few loose gray hairs escaping from the tightly wound bun sitting like a halo on the top of her head.

"I mean, this selection of books isn't your usual, you know. I just thought that you might be having a problem. . . ." Gladys Markham's voice trailed off into the oblivion of embarrassment.

"Sorry, Mrs. Wallace, I didn't mean to be nosy," she said, stammering while recovering her librarian's demeanor.

Josie just mumbled a hurried "That's OK" and hugged all four of the books to her chest as she turned and left without looking back.

The added burden of four heavy volumes of psychology textbooks made the return walk to her house even more difficult and, as the screen door closed behind her, Josie regretted not waiting until Brad returned home with the car later in the day. She shed her blouse and bra before she arrived at her bedroom door and within minutes, stood under a cooling shower. The resentment of Gladys Markham and her intrusive old-biddy behavior swirled down the drain with the soothing water of the shower. Resignation replaced indignation. What mattered was the comfort she hoped to draw from her books, especially *The Psychology of Anger*. The morning incident with Brad, just one of a continuing series over the last few months had been the catalyst for the library trip.

"Bitches!" she had heard him shout from the living room, startling her and sending the cup she was drying crashing to the floor. She scurried in to find him standing by his chair, the newspaper flung in sections across the floor.

"Daley might as well set up a fucking police state in Chicago; we are supposed to be a damned free country," he said as though addressing a group of friends in a locker room. He seemed unaware that she had entered the room. When his eyes finally focused on her, he flushed with embarrassment. He mumbled an apology and went about picking up the *Hartford Courant* scattered around the room.

She adjusted the shower toward the warmer side and turned to allow the water to massage her neck and back as she soaped the front of her body. Showers of more than five minutes were a luxury in the Wallace household and hers already was pushing ten. Two extra minutes eased a bit more of the tension from her neck. She turned, enjoying the sensuousness of the water cascading over her breasts and protruding stomach. As she pulled aside the shower curtain, her partially obscured reflection in the fogged, full-length mirror across from the tub looked back at her.

"This is radiant?" she said out loud. "This is glowing? Brad, you must be crazy." She toweled herself down as the droplets of fog slowly disappeared from the mirror. When she finished, the mirror had completely cleared and she stood in front of it, turning so that her profile was reflected. She imagined Brad's basking in the intellectual stimulation inherent in his postgraduate course, his outburst of the morning likely forgotten. As troubling as his powerful irrational lapses were, she turned her attention to a more immediate concern, maintaining her own stability throughout the rest of the pregnancy.

Still naked, she went to the bedroom and propped up the pillows against the headboard of the bed. The stack of four books from the library had fallen over at the foot of the bed and one, *Nine Months-An Anatomy of a Pregnancy,* lay on the floor face up. She stooped to pick it up, feeling awkward and ungainly as she bent over. She stacked the books together again, put them next to the pillows and climbed into the bed. The windows on either side of the room provided strong cross ventilation and for the next two hours, as the hot summer breeze blew across her body, she read about what she could expect in the next four months. The book at the bottom of the pile, *The Psychology of Anger,* could wait until another time.

The Christmas Baby

*"God never promised us a quiet journey,
only a safe arrival."*
Author unknown

The rejuvenation Brad expected with the move to Hartford West High School was quickly realized. Hampton Village became a receding memory as he faced the challenge and excitement of being a social studies teacher in a large ethnically and racially mixed school. Josie was correct; he could never be a time clock teacher. Within a week, the "Sorry, dear, I'll be home late for dinner" phone calls were coming on a regular basis. Josie spent the latter part of the month of September preparing her classes for her replacement, and the Wallaces' dinner table conversation remained relatively balanced the first month of school. Each had much to say in answer to the ritualistic "So what's new and how was your day?" questions. The evolution from sharing experiences to one-sided monologue occurred gradually.

"Chris Howard visited my creative writing class today," Josie mentioned one evening, pleased that the busy Superintendent would take the time. Before she could expand upon her story, Brad interrupted with a lengthy description of a demonstration lesson he had given that day to his entire department.

"So, what were you saying about Chris Howard?" he asked when he finished. The condescension in his voice infuriated Josie.

"It wasn't important; certainly not as important as what's happening in Hartford."

Missing his cue, Brad moved right into a narrative about his deft handling of a potentially explosive discipline problem in the cafeteria. "Not much like Hampton Village," he concluded.

41

When the end of September came, the subtle disinterest he showed in Hampton Village no longer was a factor in their conversations. He was free to share the infinite variety of experiences at Hartford West while her day consisted of being the stay-at-home housewife waiting for their baby.

Within the first few weeks, Brad faced more challenges in his enervating new environment than he had seen in four years at Hampton Village. Most of his morning commute was occupied with thinking about his lesson plan for Current Events class, his first of the day. The class of seniors encompassed a full spectrum of academic levels and racial mixtures, and he had to draw upon all of his creativity and innovative teaching methods to keep the class on track. His other classes in American Government and American History required planning, but the familiarity of the subject matter eased the demands considerably. The human chemistry of those college preparatory classes reminded him of Hampton Village and presented no challenge to a quality teacher. The Events class represented a major reason for coming to Hartford West. He happily accepted the responsibility for dealing with the diversity and enjoyed the chance to soothe the simmering tension among the various elements in the group.

By early October, Brad's department head and principal already were suggesting to the rest of the faculty that they might want to observe the new teacher. The subtle, intangible genius of a gifted teacher was obvious and the transformation of the Current Events class into a cohesive and cooperative group solidified Brad's reputation.

*   *   *

Brad left for school a full half-hour earlier than usual on the brilliant, crisp mid-October day. Although there was no magnificent seven at Hartford West, several of the younger faculty members formed an unofficial breakfast club. On alternate Fridays, they would meet in the teachers' lounge for some camaraderie and sharing before school began. For their first meeting, he agreed to be the bearer of the donuts, and he knew what

MacDougal's Bakery was like at that hour of the morning. The extra half-hour would allow enough time to pick up a nice selection of the "best donuts in Hartford" and to deal with the early morning glare as he drove due east directly into the sun.

Since she had stopped teaching, Josie was adamant about having breakfast with him before he left for school and agreed the night before that this morning they would just have coffee.

"I certainly wouldn't want to ruin your appetite for those donuts," she had said. During the night, she was quite restless and Brad had set his internal alarm clock. He awoke minutes ahead of the alarm and slipped quietly out of bed. Josie stirred and he sat next to her, bent over and kissed her on the cheek.

"Just stay in bed this morning, Jos. You didn't seem to sleep very well. Are you ok?" he had asked.

"I think so but I'll take you up on your offer. Don't stuff yourself with too many of those low calorie puffed pastries. Love you." Then she turned on her side and fell asleep.

*　　*　　*

Josie was startled awake by a sharp cramp in her stomach, and she felt the dampness soaking her wool nightgown. The fuzzy morning cobwebs disappeared with the next sharp pain and she was instantly alert. She threw off the heavy quilt and looked down to find the bed saturated. The realization that her water had broken coincided with the undeniable knowledge that something was terribly wrong. She drew in several deep breaths and sat up, dangling her feet over the side of the bed. A momentary relief was replaced by another cramp, so painful that she instinctively lay back on the bed.

"I've got to do something," she said aloud, as if needing to talk herself through whatever was happening. She sat up again but this time a wave of dizziness and nausea forced her to drop her head to her chest and close her eyes. After the queasiness passed, she struggled to her feet, using the bed to push herself into an upright position. For a few seconds, she stood still, gathering her courage to set out for the kitchen and the only phone they had in the apartment. Her initial panic eased, replaced by a less dramatic sense of apprehension. The need to stop at the bathroom on the way to the phone was overwhelming. Taking a few steps toward the bedroom door, she steadied herself against the doorjamb.

A number of large picture frames holding various diplomas, awards, and certificates lined the walls of the short hallway to the bathroom. Josie sent several of them crashing to the floor as she held out both arms, struggling to keep her balance. She fought the return of the nausea as she finally made her way to the toilet, the simple process of urinating providing a strange feeling of well being. Still unsure of whom she should call when she finally arrived at the phone, she stood uneasily, her legs wobbling as if she had just climbed several flights of stairs. All positive feelings disappeared as she flushed the toilet. The paper she had used swirled around the bowl, a bright red streak obvious even as it disintegrated in the water. She steadied herself against the wall, peering into the bowl like a gypsy fortuneteller peering into a crystal ball.

"What the hell is happening?" she hissed through gritted teeth. She had to get to the phone quickly. The room began to go out of focus again when she felt a warm gush of dampness between her legs. The panic she had felt earlier returned, more powerful than ever. Without checking to see what the fluid might be, she lurched down the hall to the kitchen.

"Stupid extra charge for an extension. . ." The exclamation was interrupted by yet another powerful stomach cramp, strong enough to stop her progress toward the kitchen phone. The world was spinning and she leaned against the wall to try to regain some of her composure. Another sharp pain sent her sliding down the wall. On her hands and knees, she covered the last few feet to the kitchen in a desperate crawl, ignoring the sticky wetness between her thighs. Head down, she finally arrived at the long cord hanging almost to the floor and looked up, unsure if she would be able to stand to dial the phone.

"Oh, God, I'm going to die right here, on the kitchen floor." The words came out in a shout and echoed through the room. She summoned a last surge of extra strength. Clinging to the wall like a rock climber, she pulled herself into a kneeling position, following the cord to the receiver. Steadying herself against the wall with one hand, she reached for the receiver. The dial tone buzzed loud enough for her to hear, and she cradled the phone against her ear with her shoulder as she leaned back against the wall. Her hand again fumbled up the wall until she found the circular dial. Pushing the dial around one full time drained most of her remaining strength. She listened as the number rang twice before the operator answered with the typical nasal twang that seems a prerequisite for the job.

"Operator. How may I help you?"

The effort required to answer pushed her toward a frightening edge.

"I need an ambulance. Please hurry. 21 Sycamore Drive. . . ." Then the darkness descended.

*   *   *

About halfway through the first period, Brad's class was in the midst of a heated but controlled discussion of the pending teachers' strike in New York City. As had become the norm, the students prepared themselves for the friendly debate on a subject close to his heart. He leaned back in his chair, comfortable but resisting the temptation to prop his feet on his desk. While most teachers kept the classroom doors closed as if they wanted no intruders on their domain, Brad's doors were always open. Just as one of his more adept students invoked the name of Albert Shanker, the Teachers' Union president, Brad noticed Mike Costello, his principal, hesitantly raising his hand to knock on the window of the open door.

Mike, already one of his favorite administrators, made a point of being visible around the building. Dropping in and out of classes was not unusual for him. When a classroom door was open, he would slip in, capture the atmosphere of the class then just as quietly slip out. When Mike signaled for him to come to the door, Brad hesitated. A quick glance around the room told him that his students were so involved that they wouldn't miss him. The tight, pained expression on the principal's face showed from across the room. When he reached the door Mike took Brad's arm and guided him into the hall.

"I'll take over here, Brad. Josie's been taken to the hospital and you'd better go home now. She's OK but you really need to be there." Mike's expression contradicted his words.

When Brad walked back into the classroom, his students searched his face for reassurance that he was all right. He scanned the room again, sensing the bond that had formed between him and this class in just two months.

"Just a little problem at home, folks, not to worry. Your favorite principal will take over and you can just continue what you're doing. I'll see you tomorrow."

Mike remained at the doorway, waiting to be invited in. Brad's slight nod indicated that it was now all right for the principal to enter his personal empire. As they passed, Mike suggested that perhaps a quick phone call to the Emergency Room at Covington County Hospital would be a good idea.

"Use the office phone," he said. " Just tell Joan I said it was OK." Brad mumbled an appreciative thanks, well aware that school policy required teachers to use the pay phones for personal calls.

"And, Mr. Wallace," Mike called after him, "drive carefully and don't race!" The gentle giggles of his students faded behind him but not before bringing a tight smile in response to the admonition.

"Sounds just like my mother," he said softly. Many of the students in the room were thinking the same thing.

Joan Potter had been alerted to the situation and ushered Brad into the office with a flourish, dialing the hospital's number as she handed the receiver to him. The Emergency Room nurse recognized his name and was well trained in handling these situations.

"She is stabilized, Mr. Wallace, but Doctor Capaldi would like you to come in as soon as possible," she said, her voice a clipped, professional monotone.

"It will take me about an hour to get there; I'm leaving right now." Brad answered, handing the phone back to Joan. She looked at him as though expecting an answer to an unasked question. He waited, sure that she would eventually come out with it. He wasn't disappointed.

"What about the baby, Mr. Wallace?" she finally asked. He left the office without a response, amazed and bewildered that he didn't know the answer.

*   *   *

The trip to Covington County Hospital normally takes about an hour from Hartford, but Brad arrived at the Emergency Room entrance in less than forty-five minutes. No spaces were available in the small parking lot nearest the entryway. A previous experience with a "CARS WILL BE TOWED AT OWNER EXPENSE" sign forced him to careen through the large upper level parking area, finally finding an empty space at the far end of the lot. His hand shook as he reached for the keys in the ignition. The trembling spread through his entire body by the time he locked the car.

The sprint from his car to the large sliding glass door left him winded and gasping as he waited for the automatic to creep open. As soon as there was enough room, he squeezed through. Approaching the nurses' station, he felt as vulnerable and helpless as he ever had in his life.

The partition wall at the station, filled with the usual dire "DO NOT" signs, came to his shoulders. Any visitor approaching the desk had to peer over the top to see the nurses sitting behind it.

"May I help you?" drifted up to him, emanating from the white cap sitting on top of a curly black bed of hair below. Engrossed in the paper work in front of her, the nurse appeared to want to conduct her business without ever looking up.

What if I had a real emergency here? he thought without forming the words. "I'm Brad Wallace; my wife was brought in a while ago." The announcement came out in a strange high-pitched voice that he barely recognized as his own. His tone, not at all subtle, brought the white cap on fuzzy black hair out of her chair. She turned her back to him, proceeded directly to the swinging door separating the station from the outer room, unlatching and opening it in a single motion.

"Follow me, Mr. Wallace," she said. "She's in Cubicle Four." His mind functioned in an adrenaline induced high-speed mode. He was not happy with this entire situation, from the coldness of the bitchy nurse to his apparently very ill wife being placed in a cubicle.

"I'll find Doctor Capaldi and send him in. He'll explain everything," she said, her aggravating calmness coming through as pure apathy.

The nurse opened the door to Cubicle Four but did not enter. Brad pressed by her. When he was fully in the room, she turned and let the door close behind her. He glanced around, already formulating a letter of complaint in his mind about the nurse and the cubicle. A cubicle surely was a misnomer for the room in which he stood. He moved toward the single hospital bed in the center of the room, guarded by a floor to ceiling privacy curtain. The complete array of medical equipment lining the walls penetrated his perplexed mental state, impressing him in spite of the situation.

"Josie?" Brad whispered through the filmy but opaque curtain. When no answer came back, he found the opening in the curtain and pulled it aside. He had prepared himself for seeing Josie by picturing her as he had said goodbye that morning, adding a more disheveled look. She was sleeping but somehow the harshness of whatever she had been through showed clearly on her face.

"How can someone who is asleep look so tired?" he whispered as he reached beneath the blanket and found Josie's hand. He squeezed gently, not intending to awaken her but needing the reassurance that a soft human touch always supplies. She stirred ever so slightly and opened her eyes. It seemed to take an enormous effort to turn her head towards him. When she saw him, she returned the pressure on her hand.

"I'm really sorry, Brad. I just couldn't help it." He just looked at her, puzzled but forcing a comforting smile.

"It's OK, hon. Now, if you're up to it, tell me exactly what happened." Josie saw the brief questioning glance, sighed and closed her eyes. Brad didn't know anything. She started to tell him what she remembered about the morning. They both clung to that invisible edge separating composure from emotional chaos.

"Oh, Jesus, I should've never left you." Brad sat next to her on the bed. In a few disjointed sentences, her narrative reached the call to the operator, the last thing she remembered before fainting.

"It was a boy, Brad, a boy, just what we wanted. . . ." Her voice faded to a whisper. As she hesitated, unsure how to proceed with the next part of the story, the door to the cubicle opened and Dr. Steven Capaldi knocked, simultaneously announcing his entrance.

Brad stood as the doctor pulled back the curtain. In spite of the anxiety of the situation, he couldn't help but notice how much younger the doctor appeared to be since Brad last saw him. After a quick handshake and mumbled reintroductions, Capaldi directed Brad to sit in a small folding chair against the wall while he checked on his patient. He pulled the privacy curtain closed, leaving Brad to stare across the room, studying a large poster illustrating the skeletal system of the human body. His annoyance with being separated from Josie increased as each minute passed. When the doctor finally appeared again through the split in the curtain, Brad pushed it fully open and brushed by him, moving directly to Josie's side.

"So, what's going on?" Brad asked. He sat on the edge of the bed and reached for Josie's hand.

"First of all, Mr. Wallace, you certainly can't blame yourself," Capaldi began.

"What the hell does *that* mean?" Brad asked. Josie's insistent squeezing caused him to pause.

"There's no need to get angry. I'm sure you know that I'm doing everything that I can in your wife's interest. All I meant is that Josie's problem might not have been so dramatic if we'd gotten her to the hospital sooner. There was nothing you could have done to prevent the premature birth, even had you been home at the time." The doctor paused again.

"By we, I assume you mean me, right? And might it be possible for you to stop talking in riddles? What do you mean, dramatic? What are WE talking about here?" Brad's agitation caused the doctor to change his approach.

"Why don't we step outside in the hall for a moment?" He turned to Josie, smiled, and led Brad into a protective alcove in the hallway. Josie simply smiled back, her trust in her obstetrician blind and unequivocal.

Any pretense of civility disappeared when the two men left Josie's presence.

"Are you going to explain what happened to me, or what?" Brad tried to stay composed, but could feel contempt growing for his wife's doctor.

"When the ambulance had arrived to your house, your wife was on the kitchen floor having lost a lot of blood. She had been going through premature labor. When the paramedics brought her back to consciousness, they delivered the infant en route to the hospital. The infant was still born. It's difficult to say whether the infant had vital signs when she first went into labor. Let's remember that the important thing is Josie's just fine. All the bleeding is stopped and there's nothing to worry about. Your job is to help your wife through this," Capaldi said, using a clipped, professional tone that the average person often finds so condescending.

"What exactly do you want me to help her through, Doctor? You just told me she was fine."

"We'll have to do some repair work, Mr. Wallace."

Brad fought the impulse to scream at the good doctor. "What in the hell are you talking about with this repair work shit? What is she, a construction site?" Brad's anger level turned up yet another notch but Capaldi wasn't biting.

"The obvious damage to Josie's uterus from the hemorrhaging might have been prevented with quicker treatment, Mr. Wallace. Of course, we can't be one hundred percent sure of that." He stopped again.

"And. . . ?" Brad insisted.

"And, sir, it's very likely that your wife will not be having any children of her own. I think this sort of news should come from you, don't you agree? She'll otherwise recover from the incident completely, of course."

Brad's seething indignation erupted into a bitter fury directed at the composed and confident doctor facing him.

"I thought doctors gave this sort of news in person; you know, the couple sitting there holding hands, supporting each other, all that sort of stuff." His encounter with Dr. Steven Capaldi crystallized his long held conviction that doctors and teachers differed most in the major area of human compassion.

"She's lost a lot of blood so you can expect her to be tired for a few days. Call the office and we'll schedule an appointment." Capaldi ended his part of the conversation and offered his hand.

"You've been a great help, Doctor. Thanks a lot!" He turned away from the offered handshake and walked toward his wife's cubicle, leaving Steven Capaldi to absorb the icy sarcasm in his voice.

A short time later, Josie was settled in her own room. She drifted in and out of a medicated sleep, in her waking moments encouraging Brad to go home. Several hours later he relented after her parents arrived. He promised to return later that evening, kissed his wife gently on the cheek, and left the hospital. The ride home passed in a blur as he focused his attention on what might have been different if he had stayed home that morning.

The scene greeting Brad when he walked into the kitchen brought on a wave of nausea. The small maple table was tight against the wall; a small gash marred the paint where Josie had pushed it as she staggered toward the phone. The not-quite-matching chairs were scattered and askew next to it. The furniture clearly had been pushed aside as the ambulance crew hurried to tend to Josie, who probably lay crumpled under the wall phone across the room. His eyes followed two faint black lines, smudges from the wheels of the rolling stretcher, across the white vinyl floor to a large blotch of smeared red. Moving as if being pushed from behind by some invisible force, he crossed the kitchen and stood looking down to where Josie likely passed out. The dried red stain spread out in a pattern that showed clear evidence of a hasty attempt by someone to wipe it up. The seed of guilt that the doctor had sown came into full flower as Brad let the replay fade away with the image of Josie lying there in a pool of blood. He steadied himself against the wall, his mind reeling from the real possibility that he could have lost her.

He noticed the red light indicating that the automatic coffeemaker was still on, just as he had left it earlier that morning. He reached for a large mug, one of many lining the open shelf next to the telephone.

"Never even got her morning coffee," he said as he filled his mug almost to overflowing in his preoccupation with the scene around him. The coffee had continued to strengthen as it sat in the pot. The aroma had an undeniably burnt tinge as it rose from the mug. Brad made his way to the living room, burning his upper lip on the scalding hot liquid as he tried to sip it while walking to his favorite chair.

"Dammit," he muttered as he set the cup on the rounded arm of the chair, carefully balancing it as he had so many times before. The ringing of the phone from the kitchen startled him and he returned to answer it.

"Hey, what's going on?" The welcome voice of Rich Lane echoed in his ear. Brad launched into a detailed description of the events of the day, a narrative that included an unflattering portrait of Dr. Steven Capaldi. Rich listened without interruption, just an occasional gasp emanating from his end of the line.

"I'll stop by and see her tomorrow if you think she'll be up to it," Rich said after Brad's story concluded.

"I'm sure she'd like that and thanks for the call. It was good to talk to you." As he placed the receiver back in its cradle, a picture of the handsome young doctor flashed through his mind. He remembered fighting the irrational jealousy that began every morning when Josie had her monthly appointment. The strong smell of the coffee drifted in from the living room and he was drawn toward the scent. His rage at the doctor diminished but only slightly as he reached the chair where the cup remained balanced. Steadying it with his hand, he collapsed into his chair, with a heavy sigh.

During the next fifteen minutes Brad entered his first black period. At first, he thought he certainly must be going insane; later, as disturbing as they sometimes were, he would welcome the respite the periods provided. It was as if he squeezed his eyelids together, shutting out the physical world around him, except that his eyes were wide open as the nightmare played out.

Frantic images clawed their way to the surface of his mind, each one saying the same thing.

"You've got to do something, Brad." Tyler Spence was first, followed in quick succession by famous people like John F. Kennedy, Martin Luther King, Jr., and Bobby Kennedy. The news photograph of the three dead Civil Rights workers in Alabama appeared. With each image, his world grew darker. Dr. Capaldi emerged, holding a six-month old infant in his hands, his dead son. A final blackness came as he laid his head back and imagined Josie, lying on the kitchen floor, needing help but without him there to give it. Finally, he drifted into a fitful, troubled sleep, whispering over and over again.

"God, help me. . . ."

Black Periods

"One cannot tell what passes through the heart
of man by the look on his face."
Japanese Proverb

The Monday after the long Thanksgiving weekend, Josie Wallace returned to teaching. Dr. Capaldi's required one-month convalescence period was painfully slow and she was more than ready to resume her duties. Josie's students wanted her back and the long-term substitute allowed the contract issue to drop with only a subtle hint to the principal that she expected to be working on a daily basis for the remainder of the year.

For Josie, returning to a demanding academic environment was exactly what she needed. She loved the surroundings, even with its occasionally phony extended family atmosphere. The emotional entrance into her homeroom served as a catalyst for the natural vitality and energetic dedication with which she was blessed. Like a fine Broadway actress who leaves all personal emotions behind as the opening curtain ascends, Josie entered her world and felt its support enfold her in a protective haven from the consuming grief she left behind.

Despite Brad's insistence that the doctors were correct in calling what happened a premature still birth, she refused to place the loss of her infant son in that category. For the long month of recuperation, she spent much of her time each day staring out the side of their bedroom window in the direction of the cemetery in the distance. It was as though the outcome of that awful day could be changed by reflecting on what Bradford Jr. might have become.

Now, the genuine empathy of her homeroom students rattled her composure. Her ingrained professional demeanor was disintegrating.

"Will you please stand for the Pledge of Allegiance?" The intercom intruded on the moment and Josie was thankful. The nervous young man, a new recruit likely forced into the stable of reluctant announcement readers by his English teacher, barely whispered into the microphone. His announcement allowed her to turn away from the room full of students and toward the faded American flag sagging under the weight of accumulated chalk dust in the corner. With her back to the students now mumbling their way through the Pledge, Josie had enough time for the dampness in her eyes to dry. When she turned back, she was ready to begin the job at hand, once again leading these docile but malleable students to an understanding of what civilized behavior was all about.

"Listen to these announcements, people. You never know when one of them might apply to you." Her presence in the classroom demanded attention and the murmur of the students faded quickly to silence as they plunked themselves down into their seats. The daily announcements droned from the speaker behind her head while Josie glanced around the room, realizing how absolutely unattractive it was. Her substitute obviously wasn't strong in classroom décor. She began to construct bulletin boards and poster decorations in her mind.

"Enjoy your day at Hampton Falls." The whispering voice became a bit louder and more enthusiastic as the relieved young man ended his first day of announcements with the traditional closing phrase.

"I am back in business," Josie said happily, absorbing a touch of the collective vitality of the group of young adults as the dismissal bell sent them spilling into the hall.

* * *

Brad's commute to Hartford took him past the Mountain View Cemetery every day. He passed the gaudy entryway less than a mile from his house before his first sip of coffee from the travel mug balanced on the dashboard. Each morning, he would catch a glimpse of the rows of headstones as the fall sun ricocheted off the surrounding trees and shed some light on the graveyard. With a barely perceptible nod, he acknowledged his son's burial site on a daily basis. His ritual would have surprised Josie. Not many days went by without one of their philosophical discussions, arguments really, about whether the six months Brad Jr. had spent in her womb qualified him as a human being. Playing the role of devil's advocate, he honestly believed that Josie's devastation could be reduced to manageable grief if he could convince her that their son had never been a sentient being.

"He should be buried," Josie argued. "We owe him at least that."

"That's really not logical, Josie, and you know it." Brad finally agreed, won over by his awareness of the closure effect of a graveside service. The only other contentious issue in the discussion about the service concerned the wording on the inlaid stone grave marker but in the interest of domestic tranquility, Brad acceded to his wife's wishes.

The driveway entrance to the cemetery was guarded on both sides by large marble statues of the archangel Michael, brilliant white wings fully extended as if standing at the gates of Heaven itself, ready to do battle with any evil attempting to enter. The ornate wrought iron sign announcing the name of the cemetery arched over the narrow entryway, each end entwined in Michael's hands. Brad drove through the gate in the gathering dusk, calculating that about ten minutes of daylight remained for his visit. He parked the car in the usual place, a small cul-de-sac at the end of the main road through the center of the graveyard. He walked briskly toward Brad Jr.'s marker. The inscription stared up at him.

BRADFORD J. WALLACE, JR.

INFANT

The letters glowed in the grayness of the late November afternoon. They provided all the inspiration he needed.

"You weren't six months, son. You didn't have a chance to be anything." The emotional darkness enveloped him from every side. The catalog of jarring wrongs that accompanied the blackness came to him, the final image of Josie lying on the kitchen floor in a pool of blood.

"That bastard Capaldi," Brad hissed, his breath forming a misty

cloud in the air. "He should have known." Without dwelling on the possibilities, he turned to walk back to the car, the light from the real world
creeping in.

"Goodnight, Brad, Jr.," he called back as he opened the car door.
The short ride to the house provided ample time for Brad to realize how
refreshed, almost renewed, he felt after a visit to the blackness.

"Like living two lives," he said aloud. "Time outs from life that just
might keep me sane. . . ."

*   *   *

For the first time since what she now referred to as the "incident," Josie
entered the kitchen without hesitation. Her first day back at Hampton Falls
far exceeded her expectations. The conscious effort to resurrect the unbridled zeal for her career in education reached a new level; its fire fueled by
the reality that the other career, motherhood, was never going to be a part
of her life. For educators like Josie, the excitement and demands of good
teaching required an energy unlike any other profession. The first day revi-
talized her and she couldn't wait to share all of the details with Brad. She
planned to come home immediately after school to prepare a special meal
in celebration of her return to the classroom but couldn't resist when the
remaining members of the magnificent seven suggested that they have a
quick beer after school to celebrate her return. Brad usually arrived home
by five or five-thirty, and she was so touched by their concern that she was
sure there was plenty of time to spend a half-hour or so with the old gang.
As had happened so often in the beginning of their tenure at Hampton
Village, the session stretched out a bit longer than expected and the late
afternoon sky was a murky gray when they left Pete's Pub. Rich Lane, as
always the consummate gentleman, walked Josie to her car. The two English
teachers, now in their fifth year together in the same department, shared a
professional respect that had developed into a deep friendship. She wasn't
surprised when he asked the question.

"So, Josie, how are you really?" The same question asked by an
acquaintance is easily diverted or ignored but she was flattered at his sin-

58

cerity and nonplussed by her response.

"I'm doing all right, especially now that I'm back here." He continued to look at her with questioning eyes. A faint blush came into her cheeks. "No, really, Rich. Honest, I'm fine."

"I'm just so sorry, Jos . . . I know how much this baby meant to you. It's got to be really hard." The emotion on his face was impossible to ignore and Josie again flushed. For a few seconds, they looked away, each searching for composure.

"I just wanted to tell you that, that's all, Josie. I am truly sorry." Josie opened the car door and sat down heavily.

"Yeah, I'm sorry too, Rich." She reached out and took his arm, squeezing it gently. "You're very sweet and I'm lucky to have such a good friend." She squeezed his arm once more, this time with a bit of extra pressure then let go and pulled the door closed. Looking straight ahead so he wouldn't see her eyes filling, she started the car and drove out. A glance in the rear view mirror revealed Rich standing in place, Pete's red neon sign reflecting from his face as he watched her leave.

* * *

The dinner that Josie put together was not at all what she had planned. She arrived home just minutes before Brad and was defrosting some frozen spaghetti sauce when he walked in the door. It would not be a wonderful celebration dinner but the occasion was happy enough for a dinner of leftovers.

"Welcome home!" she called over her shoulder as she flipped the icy block of sauce over in the pan. Brad crossed the room and wrapped his arms around her waist, lightly kissing her on the neck. The pleasant domestic scene dispersed the blackness from the cemetery and he slipped into the role of attentive husband.

Josie blended the usual preliminaries into a single run-on sentence, giving him only a few seconds to respond before moving on.

"I had the greatest day, Brad!"

The one-sided dinner conversation that evening covered every minute of Josie's day at school. Brad couldn't remember a time when she had been so animated and excited. It was as if she had begun a new life. Her infectious enthusiasm increased a notch when she described the gathering at Pete's after school.

"Did everyone make it?" Brad asked, wanting to at least assume a vicarious part in the afternoon. He missed the collegial companionship of the magnificent seven despite the fulfilling challenge of Hartford West.

"Every one who is left was there; it was so great of them to arrange it just for me," Josie said, her fervor causing a ripple of jealousy to flutter through Brad.

After dinner, he insisted that Josie relax in the living room while he cleaned up the kitchen. For the first time since moving his career east to the big city, he realized how much of what they shared as a couple came from the commonality of experiences in Hampton Village.

"Did you miss me today?" Brad hollered into the living room over the voice of the local weatherman on Channel Five. Her answer only temporarily covered the disquieting concern roiling in Brad.

"Of course, honey. What a silly question!" The response he really wanted was for her to put her school work aside, come into the kitchen and physically brush the worry away with at least a connective hug. When that did not happen, he took three steps to the doorway, peering around the corner like a child playing hide and seek. Josie's attention was riveted on the materials spread out on the coffee table before her, intent on tomorrow's school day and ignoring the bleating television. Brad retreated back to the kitchen and finished his cleanup chores. He watched the soapy water creating a whirlpool effect as it drained from the sink, taking the last remnants of the spaghetti sauce with it.

That night, they made love with more passion and urgency then they had since Josie became pregnant. Brad's earlier concern vanished in the depths of Josie's sensuousness. Lying in the dark, he listened to her measured breathing as she slept. Surely all would be well, even without a Brad, Jr.

He followed Josie into a satisfied sleep.

Harriet

"In the soul of human beings at their best,
there is an unconquerable spirit."
Paul S. McElroy

Harriet Long enjoyed the rural environment and bucolic farm country surrounding Hampton Village. The rolling hills and crisply edged fields overflowed with pleasant reminders of her childhood on the family farm in southern Vermont. Her background provided fertile ground for Rich Lane's merciless teasing.

"You can take a girl out of the country but you can't take the country out of the girl," he often said. Harriet accepted the good-natured laughs at her expense, actually enjoying the attention. "What's that perfume you're wearing, Harriet, Estee Lauder Essence of Barnyard?" Rich varied the question but the theme remained the same. She admitted her disappointment to Josie when a day went by without Rich's kidding.

As Harriet's fifth year wore on, the magnificent seven (who were now the magnificent five) noticed a change in her. The five years at Hampton Village High served only to convince her that she had much more to offer the educational community at large. The signs of her "professional itch," and her need for self-improvement became more obvious than ever at the second monthly faculty meeting in October. After that, none of the staff doubted that Harriet would soon be leaving the small school behind.

Harriet had returned from an exciting National Defense and Education Act Science Seminar in Chicago, an event that consumed most of the summer, and she wanted to share her experience with the faculty. She presented her seminar report on a brilliant fall day, the type of day when the faculty's collective body language would have forced the principal to call an early end to the meeting. Instead, Harriet led the staff through one of the most inspirational faculty meetings in memory. For an hour and a half, her humor, knowledge base, and teaching expertise mesmerized the group. Any doubts about Harriet's future being somewhere beyond Hampton Village were summarily erased that day.

As pleasant as her teaching assignment was, much of Harriet's energies for the remainder of that school year were directed toward exploring the many options available in the field of science education. The amiable harassment of the magnificent five continued unabated throughout the year, interrupted briefly by the dispiriting tragedy of Josie and Brad Wallace. One Friday afternoon in May at Pete's, she announced that she had accepted an offer of a teaching fellowship at the University of Chicago.

Harriet graciously received the standing ovation of the staff as she accepted the compulsory going away plant at the final faculty meeting of the year. The meeting lasted less than an hour and a short time later, the Magnificents retired to Pete's.

When Josie stood to offer a toast, the group was unusually quiet, almost introspective. English teachers rarely have difficulty finding words for any occasion and until she had their attention, Josie was confident that her training would not fail her. All eyes were raised to meet hers. She faltered, wishing that Brad, who accepted the invitation to join them, had not been late.

"Here's to Harriet," she began, then her voice left her. Faced with the loss of another important person in her life, she crumbled before the emotion of the moment. Rich Lane, seated to Josie's immediate right, stood and put his arm around her.

"Come on, Jos, this isn't her eulogy, you know," he said, failing to lighten the mood. Leaning closer to her, he tightened his grasp just a bit and dropped his voice to a whisper. "We can do this," he said, announcing to the rest of the group that the toast would be delayed while he made a few remarks about their departing colleague. As he started, Josie sat down, and his arm fell to his side. She reached for his hand and gave it a hard squeeze.

"Thanks a lot," she said, looking up at him, but Rich was already enjoying his final chance to use Harriet as his personal foil. He never glanced down.

The toast became a hilarious ten-minute Harriet roast worthy of the best of Don Rickles. By the time he finished, any tension had been diffused and Josie stood once more, offering a well controlled but tender toast. The five then turned all of their attention to the refilled beer glasses in front of them. Several beers and two hours later, Brad finally joined the group, apologizing for being late for the reunion but clearly excited about something. Grabbing a chair from the next table, he wedged his way between Rich and Josie. He rapped a spoon between two of the many empty bottles scattered around the table. The clinking, a move someone might make at a wedding reception, gathered everyone's attention. He cleared his throat and delivered his startling announcement.

"They're going to make me an assistant department head. Can you believe that?"

Harriet was the first respond. "That figures; I'm having my going away party and I get upstaged again. I don't believe you, Brad!" Her scolding only made them all laugh; the humor of her complaint exaggerated by the fuzzy thinking that comes of consuming too many beers in too short a time.

The others joined the fray in quick succession, only Josie holding back. In his pragmatic, physical education teacher style, Jack Hopkins chimed in with a question they all had.

"What the hell, Brad. You've only been there a year. There's gotta be other guys in the department with more seniority."

"And more talent and ability." Loud guffaws followed Harriet's smirking thrust.

The noise from the increasing number of patrons threatened to drown out much of their conversation. The jovial mood of the group turned more melancholy. The alcohol intake slowed but not before affecting the usual transformation of the six close friends. Somberness and philosophy replaced the earlier rowdiness and joking. Finally, it was truly time to wish Harriet the traditional Godspeed and farewell. Each in turn made the expected promises, with absolute sincerity and honesty. In their hearts they knew how life has a way of interfering, of refusing to let people keep their promises, no matter how noble or well-intended, but they made them anyway.

"We'll be sure to keep in touch. Don't forget to send your new address when you get something permanent," Josie said.

"Yeah, then we'll all have a free place to stay out there. And, hey, I've only been joking all these years about your name. It is possible for someone named Harriet to be attractive." No one acted surprised when Rich followed the serious request with an entertaining diversion but the reality of the situation kept intruding. By now, they were all standing and Harriet was on second and even third hugs with some of them. Brad, the last in line as Harriet made her way toward the door, provided a final pep talk.

"You're a great teacher, Harriet. Just keep your integrity and you'll go places," he said. He gave her the last hug and goodbye of the night.

Harriet turned and hurried out the door, plainly worried about where her own emotional state might take her. The remaining five were left in her wake, speechless until Rich tried to put everything into perspective.

"Well, at least we can go visit if we want. Better than going to the cemetery to visit Tyler. Only four of us left now, Josie." He moved toward Jess Grogan and Jack Hopkins, who stood there as though waiting for someone to tell them that it was all right to go. All three men extended their hands at the same time and finally managed to connect with each other after several tries. Brad clutched Josie's hand and started toward the door but Rich caught them before they had gone very far. He gave Brad a warm and firm handshake then turned to Josie.

"It's been some year, hasn't it, Jos?" He moved closer and gave her a lingering hug.

"Thanks a lot, Rich. You saved the day with that roast. Be in touch over the summer, OK?"

"Yeah, sure," he said as he watched the Wallaces disappear through the door.

The short ride home from Pete's gave Brad enough time to describe the events of the day to Josie, with the offer of the new position being by far the most important. As they turned into the driveway, the subject changed to Harriet.

"I wonder if we'll ever see her again," he said, not really expecting any answer.

*   *   *

Later that evening, Harriet stood in the hot shower reliving the gathering at Pete's. The stark reality of change washed over her. For five years, Harriet's simple life consisted of this small one bedroom apartment, Hampton Village High School, and the occasional social outings with her teacher friends. Now that she was about to escape from this quite comfortable rut, a depressing sense of loss settled over her. The final hugs and good-byes reminded her how likely it was that contact with her Hampton Village friends would gradually diminish, dwindling down to a Christmas card exchange, if that. She felt much older than her twenty-seven years. She turned her back to the showerhead; some of the tension drained away and with it, some of the sadness.

As Harriet toweled off, she forced herself to concentrate on the elation she felt when she first received the news about the offer in Chicago. She was thrilled with the prospect of living in the city. The desperately trite remark she made in her farewell speech at Pete's that afternoon rang in her head.

"I'm going to make my mark on a larger stage," she said, and instantly regretted it, embarrassed even in front of her good friends. The larger stage, she hoped, might include more dating prospects as well. Hampton Village fell well short in the available male category. The medicine chest mirror cleared of the moisture from the shower and she looked at her reflection. There was no reason for the young woman she saw peering back at her to become the old maid her mother feared.

Harriet's dark brown hair, damp and matted from the shower, hung in curled ringlets down to her shoulders. Her hazel eyes seemed flecked with green, a highlight of an attractive face. Her rosy, apple cheeks set off a smooth complexion that showed not a single sign of blemish. As she looked down at her breasts, she smiled, thinking of the dire predictions that the braless craze would lead to a generation of sagging women.

"Hasn't happened yet," she announced to her reflection, her smile widening. The mirror cast back a vivacious, attractive and shapely young woman.

"What is it that you are missing?" she asked her reflection, a clearly rhetorical question because she already knew the answer. "All work and no play makes Jill a dull girl," she said, as if the question needed to be answered aloud. "God, I'm talking to myself," she said with a giggle.

She brushed her teeth, went to the darkened bedroom, and stretched languorously across the queen size bed that occupied most of the room. The night still clung to much of the heat of the day and just a light summer breeze wafted over her as she lay flat on her back. She had compounded the luxury of the huge bed by investing in shocking pink silk sheets. With only a few dating disasters to her credit, she was certain that her male friends thought of her as their asexual buddy and pal.

Wouldn't they be shocked? she thought as the warm air flowing across her naked body contrasted with cool silkiness of the sheets under her and she allowed her almost nightly excursion into erotic fantasy to take over.

"Look out Chicago, here I come," she said much later as she fell into a contented sleep.

Another Bad Dream

"Never ignore evil."
#967- Life's Little Instruction Book, Volume II

Josie had gotten up with him as usual and soon the unique aroma of sizzling bacon seeped through the opening at the bottom of the bathroom door. Continuing to shave with one hand, he reached for a towel rack on the back of the door with the other hand and pulled it open.

"Hey, Jos, what's the special occasion?" Bacon and egg breakfasts were usually reserved for weekend mornings. When no answer came back, he finished his shaving routine and found Josie in the kitchen. She was facing the stove, turning the splattering strips.

Without turning around, she addressed the wooden spice rack above the stove.

"You really don't know, do you?" The question was asked in a tone reserved for forgotten birthdays and anniversaries. "It was just a year ago, Brad. Only a year but it seems like yesterday. . . ." In a single motion, she turned and was clinging to him.

Brad wished that he had initiated the revisiting of their grief but it was too late. "I'm sorry, hon. I just wasn't thinking. I'm really sorry." The need for emotional support and comfort replaced Josie's brief flash of anger and they stood entwined in silence, the only sounds in the room coming from the crackling pan of bacon and Josie's light sniffling.

"This is probably a silly question but why the special breakfast? It's not like a day to celebrate." Brad's soft voice clashed with what he had said.

"Commemorating isn't the same as celebrating," Josie said flatly.

The delicious breakfast was eaten in a quiet, subdued atmosphere. This was not the time or place to resume their ongoing discussion of Brad, Jr.'s degree of "humanness" when he died. Brad waited for Josie to initiate any conversation. She remained somewhat distracted, even aloof,

67

until he left for school and he made a mental note to call and check on her during her planning period at school. This was also a day to make a special effort to visit his son's gravesite on the way home.

*   *   *

One image dissolved into another. In his waking moments, when Brad tried to resurrect the dream, he thought of the mesmerizing effect of watching a series of the same still pictures over and over again. The scenes in his dream film loop were upsetting and he awoke to find his pajamas soaked with sweat. The tone for the whole day had been established that morning and the sad anniversary precipitated the dream.

As he lay there, drenched in his own sweat, he let the film loop spin through his mind, the catalog of images becoming more disconcerting with each play. No one new appeared in this dream, but this time the picture of each person was different than they had ever been. As the repetitive loop spun through his mind, he saw each person in the moment when they crossed the fine line between life and death.

First, there was the ever-present Tyler Spence, a regular in Brad's night reveries since his death in Vietnam. Tyler was lying on his back, mouth gaping open, a slight froth of spittle mixed with blood trickling from each corner and slowly making a path down his cheeks toward his ears. Tyler dissolved from view, replaced by Martin Luther King sprawled out on a motel balcony, a pool of blood gathering under his neck and shoulders, his eyes staring toward the sky as if in his most fervent evangelistic prayer.

The clarity of his memory of the images fascinated him. He experimented with slowing them down a bit, absorbing every detail. King's picture faded into what looked like a single frame of the famous Abraham Zapruder film. John F. Kennedy lay slumped against Jacqueline, a large part of his head missing; all recognition of the world around him splattered throughout the limousine. Then the face of Robert Kennedy superimposed itself over the frame, this moment of passage captured and frozen forever by a photographer who happened to be in the right place at the right time. Whether JFK or RFK had actually crossed over in these images wasn't important. He was confident that they knew where they were headed at the time. The loop focused on the most gruesome picture of all, the bodies of three black men hanging from a branch of an enormous oak tree. The sixth and final episode on the loop, sandwiched between the return of Tyler Spence and the horrifying scene of the lynching, depicted a well-formed but obviously premature child, bathed in blood and mucous, its tiny eyelids closed tightly in death. Brad closed his eyes, stopped the spinning loop and concentrated on the image of his infant son.

"I can do something about Capaldi," he said, a clear picture of the doctor forming in his head.

The Physical-Weirdness

> "All men, when backed into final corners,
> will develop teeth and claws."
> The Red Badge of Courage by Stephen Crane

The Hartford City School District required that any teacher under contract must have a complete physical examination every two years. Early in Brad's second year in the district, he received a terse note from the central administrative office stating that he must submit a physical form by December 1, 1969, or risk being terminated. After sharing the letter in the faculty room and having many laughs about the use of the word "terminated," as if those who did not have physicals would be executed, he decided he had no choice.

Dr. John Simms, the Wallaces' family doctor on paper but a man who would not recognize either of them on the street, performed the routine exam and administered the required blood and tuberculosis tests. As the exam progressed, Brad found an unexpected compatibility with Dr. Simms and when he was escorted into the doctor's office for the final consultation, he was prepared to share some of the weird thoughts that occupied his mind on occasion.

Simms provided the perfect opening immediately.

"So, Brad, other than the standard things that we've already discussed, are there any other health issues you think I should know about?" The doctor, with two children at Hampton Village High School, was well acquainted with Brad's former reputation at the school.

Brad looked at the doctor, weighed his inclination to trust him and floated a small trial balloon. He watched Dr. Simms' reaction closely then decided to proceed.

"I think I'm pretty good physically, Doc, but sometimes I wonder about mentally."

71

"Really?" Simms asked, his eyebrows arched a notch. "Now, whatever would that mean?"

"I'm really not sure. It's just that I have some pretty strange nightmares and sometimes get really angry when I see things that are so unfair." Dr. Simms' obvious interest showed and Brad began to hesitate. "You know, just some strange feelings once in a while. Stuff like that. . . ." He deliberately faded out, giving the doctor his chance to respond. The revelation of his black periods could wait.

"I guess I'd say that you're representative of probably ninety percent of the population, Brad. The major difference is that you're able to express your worries in this sort of a forum. You wouldn't believe some of the thoughts I've heard from patients.

"Haven't you ever heard one of your students verbalize a frightening thought, like wishing he could harm or kill someone? Most human beings, thankfully, have an ability to stop short of allowing rage to overcome them, even in the direst of circumstances. Just because we hear about the jealous husband killing his wife's lover doesn't mean that every cuckolded husband does it. Get my point, Brad?"

Brad saw where the conversation was going and withdrew.

"Yeah, Doc, I get it. So, you're pronouncing me fit enough physically and mentally to teach those hormone-crazed adolescents?"

"Without a doubt, Brad. I'm just sorry that my kids missed out on the chance to have you as a teacher. I wish my reputation, as a doctor equaled yours as a teacher. You've got nothing to worry about. I signed your form and left it with the nurse. You can pick it up on the way out. By the way, I'm really sorry about the loss of your child last year. Real tough situation." Brad extended his hand and they shared a firm handshake.

"Thanks. Especially hard for Josie but, you know, everything happens for a reason. God's will and all that. See you in a couple of years. Thanks a lot!" Then he was out the door.

"What a fine young man," Doctor Simms said to the closing door.

Brad hurried to the car, glancing over his shoulder as though Dr. Simms would be running after him at any moment, suggesting an emergency trip to a psychiatrist. He was breathless from the brisk walk across the long parking lot and sat for several minutes before thinking about starting the car. The comment that the doctor made about most people being able to hold rage in check resonated with him. This physical had been a good idea after all. He could be whatever he needed to be. His black periods would serve as release valves for his anger and frustrations. The rest of the time, he would fit comfortably into the expected mold for the rest of the world. It all was so easy.

"Thank you, THANK YOU, THANK YOU! Dr. Simms," he murmured as he turned the key in the ignition. Dr. Steven Capaldi's face once again floated before his eyes.

* * *

Brad's physical with Dr. Simms lasted only an hour. There was plenty of time to make the long trek into Hartford. He'd arranged for a substitute for the whole day, and an appearance at school would only upset the system. With good substitutes practically impossible to find, sending one home with only a half-day's pay was not an option.

In a rare display of spontaneity, he turned his old Ford Fairlane toward Hampton Village High School. Josie's lunch period came during the fourth time block of the day, and the timing might be just right to surprise her and join her for lunch.

Force of habit turned the car into the teachers' parking lot, but he caught his mistake and circled around, finally parking in a visitor's space in the front of the school. "You can never go back," he whispered, remembering his first and last visit to his former high school when just a freshman in college. He glanced at the small groups of students scattered around the grounds on what had become a beautiful fall day. The sun still held enough power to supply abundant warmth for them to enjoy their lunch outside. A few called to him as he walked toward the entrance, enough of a greeting to be sincere but not quite enthusiastic enough to be an invitation to join them. Though not a true veteran teacher, he knew enough about the fickleness of high school students to understand that most of them saw his leaving them as somewhere between treason and abandonment.

He entered the school, ignoring the ALL VISITORS MUST REGISTER AT THE MAIN OFFICE sign and proceeded directly to Josie's classroom. His route took him by the cafeteria where the fourth block students stood patiently in line, the freshmen, as usual, stuck at the rear. *No doubt hoping they might have at least ten minutes to eat,* he thought, smiling. The walls of the corridor that housed the English department classrooms were lined with the usual pep banners and home made signs begging the football team to PLUCK THE EAGLES! Or BEAT WESTMINSTER! The door to Room 102 stood wide open and Brad walked right in, resisting the impulse to shout "Surprise!" For just the smallest fraction of a second, Rich Lane, Jess Grogan, and Josie looked at him as if he was an intruder but their reaction quickly turned warm. Josie reacted first.

"Brad, what a great surprise!" a genuine pleasure obvious in her voice. The three friends had arranged four of the one-piece student desks into a square, and it took a moment for Josie to extricate herself from the maze of stainless steel legs and folding arms. Their partially consumed lunches were spread out in front of them. Josie met Brad halfway across the room and put her arms around him. He returned her warm embrace and kissed her lightly on the cheek.

"Watch out for those PDA's, Jos. You now how our administration feels about that," Rich called across the room. Brad laughed out loud. Hartford West had either moved beyond the rule concerning Public Displays of Affection or given up trying to enforce it.

"Why don't you join us?" Jess asked. "I'll run down to the café and get you something, whatever you'd like." Brad appreciated the sincerity of the offer. Good friends are indeed hard to find.

"How'd the physical go?" Josie asked, expecting the simple pat answer. Brad did not disappoint her.

"Disgustingly healthy, no problems," he answered. Jess had climbed out of his seat by now and insisted on knowing what Brad would like from the cafeteria.

"Thanks, but I think I'll pass. I just wanted to stop and say hello to Josie. I've got the rest of the day off, not to rub it in or anything. It's such a gorgeous day maybe I'll hit the links. Why don't you walk me out to the car, Josie? I really just stopped by to say hi."

"Are you sure we can't convince you to stay?" she asked. As an answer, he took her hand and guided her toward the door. As they walked down the hall, the few students they met greeted Josie with exuberance and enthusiasm, dampened only by Brad's presence at her side.

"God, I've only been away a year," he said with more disappointment than he wanted to show.

"They're kids, Brad, you know that. Don't let it bother you. Thanks a lot for coming by. I do appreciate that."

After walking the remaining distance to the car in silence, Josie rephrased her original question.

"So the doctor said you were fine?" she asked. They squinted at each other through the brilliant glare of the sun glancing off the car. There was expectancy in her voice, as if the examination may have revealed something that Brad might want to share. He sloughed off the question with a measure of impatience.

"Yep. I told you he said I'm just fine," he said, softening the harshness of his answer with an invitation. "Listen, why don't I get some Chinese for dinner tonight? It'll be simple and then we can spend the evening together." The euphemism was not lost on Josie. She reached for his hand and subtly pulled it to her rib cage just under her breast. "See you later, big boy," she said, grinning. Brad climbed into the car and had left the driveway before she opened the front door to the school. She turned to wave but he already had disappeared from view.

Brad had every intention to stop at home, pick up his clubs, and spend a pleasant afternoon on the golf course. He drove several hundred yards beyond the stark white Archangels guarding the cemetery before the residual image of them caused him to pull to the side of the road. He hooked a quick U-turn, his tires spinning in the gravel on the shoulder of the road. Within a minute, he stood looking down once again at the INFANT inscription on the cold stone, a few stray leaves shielding some of the letters.

"I've got to start somewhere, right, Brad Jr.?" He said the words aloud, then sheepishly glanced around the grounds, relieved to see no one else in sight. The words of Dr. Simms rang clearly in his head. He wasn't alone in his rage at the unfairness of life. The doctor had corroborated what Brad believed to be his right. Controlled rage and even-handed justice should prevail. His history lessons overflowed with examples of this philosophy. Isn't that what brought about revolutions and change? He saw himself in a perfect position, a position from which he could keep his rage focused and morally right.

"I'll see you later, little Brad, he said. "I've got an appointment with your mom's doctor. Perhaps I'm not so weird after all."

Dr. Steve Capaldi

"Whatever houses I may visit, I will come for the benefit
of the sick, remaining free of all intentional injustices"
The Hippocratic Oath

The Covington Country Club, only three miles from the hospital, had the
perfect layout for Brad's plan. While he was at home picking up his golf
clubs, he called and asked for a tee time, knowing that he wouldn't need
one on this midweek afternoon. His name appearing on their list would
be a major help should anything go awry. He found a few twenty-penny
nails rattling around his tool bench and decided that they would be the
perfect length. Stuffing them into his pocket, he bound up the steps,
grabbed his clubs from the living room closet, and was off for his nine
holes of golf.

The course was practically deserted. Brad parked his car as close
to the ninth green as he could and watched while a twosome teed off on
the first hole. He stepped from the car and looked around. Unless someone came roaring in, he could register and manage to get on the course
by himself. He lifted the clubs from the car, still glancing around. The routine of preparing for a round of golf is ingrained in most golfers and he
was no exception. He unzipped the compartment in his bag holding his
golf shoes, ready to put them on as usual. Instead, he put them in the
trunk and slammed it shut.

An uncharacteristically noisy entrance into the pro shop attracted the attention not only of the pro tending the desk but also of the attractive young woman hovering just behind him. As many people as possible
should remember that he had been there.

"Think I'll have time to get in the full round before dark?" Both
the pro and his assistant looked at him as though he was crazy.

"Depends how you play. You by yourself?"

"Yep. Sort of playing hooky from school. You folks won't tell, will you?

The bantering continued until Brad ended it. His identity was firmly established, but he still wanted to be sure that he got off by himself.

"I was in such a rush that I even forgot my golf shoes," Brad said, acting embarrassed as he retreated toward the door after paying for a full round.

He played the first nine holes in just under two hours, purposely lagging behind the twosome ahead just enough so that they wouldn't ask him to join them. His swing was as relaxed as it had been in years as he constantly smiled and talked to himself, thoroughly amused at how juvenile this first act of revenge was going to be.

"Damn Capaldi, he should have known," he said as he retrieved the ball from the cup on the ninth green. Taking care not to be seen leaving the course, he threw his clubs in the passenger side of the car and half crouched as he walked around to the driver's side. One final glance satisfied him that as far as the pro shop was concerned, he played a full eighteen holes of golf and probably didn't finish until early evening.

*   *   *

Lincolns, Cadillacs, and Jaguars filled the reserved parking lot at Covington County Hospital. With a minimum of effort, Brad found the bright red Ford Galaxie 500 convertible he'd seen Steven Capaldi driving on several occasions. The car was parked between two long Continentals, one midnight blue and the other black. In a strange, implausible way, the rows of expensive cars infuriated him. He compared the teachers' parking lot at Hartford West: an automobile junkyard surrounded by a tall, rusting cyclone fence covered with windblown litter of every description.

He brought his Fairlane into an empty space, several rows down from the red convertible. The mid-afternoon sun combined with a hint of nervousness caused a small stain of sweat in the middle of his back. He got out of the car slowly, leaving the door open. With a phony indifference, he walked to the rear and lifted the trunk. Staring in as though expecting something to jump out, he reached into his pocket and extracted the nails. The sharp tip of one of them pricked his finger. The pain startled him and he returned to the open door on the driver's side. He sank down on the seat. The sting from the prick of the nail put a plethora of conflicting thoughts and emotions into motion.

"What in the hell am I doing? I must be nuts." He started the car and looked over his shoulder to begin to back out. "Damn, the trunk. . . ." He slipped the shift into neutral, pulled on the emergency brake and exited the car, squinting in the bright sunlight. Once again he looked around, the nervous pocket of sweat on his back spreading out even further.

"Just slam the friggin' trunk and get the hell out of here," he commanded, as if speaking to a third party uninvolved in his dilemma.

He put both hands on the deck of the trunk, ready to bang it closed. Instead, he stared into it and a vision rose from the darkness. BRADFORD J. WALLACE, JR. INFANT formed on the dark mat at the bottom of the truck. Brad recoiled as the words seemed to leap out at him.

"Oh, God, I really am going crazy here," he said. He shoved his hand deep into his right pocket and felt the cool metal of the nails. "OK, little Brad, we'll do something; nothing drastic but something."

He walked toward the shining red convertible and slipped between it and the huge blue Lincoln. Taking one last look around, he crouched down next to the right front wheel. He pulled a nail from his pocket and wedged the pointed end between two rows of tread at the front of the tire as the head leaned against the concrete. Duck walking around the front of the car to the other side, he repeated the process, this time wedging another nail behind the other front tire. He pulled himself up, using the Lincoln for support. There still was no sign of anyone in the entire lot. A few seconds later he closed the lid of his trunk, averting his eyes away from the rubber mat in the yawning darkness.

*　　*　　*

Brad drove the scenic route home from Covington County Hospital. The autumn colors dappled the taller hills of the Berkshires, and he was sure that a drive through this natural beauty would have a calming effect. The image of Dr. Capaldi tying to change a tire on one of these desolate country roads–possibly even in the dark–vied for Brad's attention with the glorious sun-drenched hills. He speculated whether the good doctor would have driven forward to puncture the right tire or backward to puncture the left. He stretched the usual twenty-minute drive into a half-hour and gave a cursory salute in the direction of his son's grave as he passed the cemetery.

"Not much, but something. Right, Brad?" He said the words loudly, as if convinced that Brad, Jr. might hear.

*   *   *

Brad's afternoon of golf and other activities put him in a positive frame of mind. He had just finished mixing a pitcher of martinis when Josie opened the front door. He swished the pitcher one more time and put it in the refrigerator to stay cold. Josie had one arm out of her jacket when he met her in the hall. Facing the hall closet with her back to him, she started to ask the typical wifely question as she struggled to get her other arm out.

"So, how was the golf game?" She hadn't finished the last word when Brad reached his arms around her waist and squeezed so tightly that "game" came out in a wheeze. She didn't turn around and without protest let him continue exploring her body with his hands while he kissed the back of her neck.

"Wow, what a welcome home," she said, becoming aroused by Brad's passion with each passing second. Finally, he eased his grip and turned her toward him, still maintaining the pelvic pressure but helping with her jacket. He dropped the jacket on the floor, took her hand and led her to the bedroom.

"I'm kind of grungy from a day at the salt mines; why don't we jump in the shower real quick?" Josie's suggestion was made only half-heartedly, as she was absorbed in the heat of the moment.

"I've been thinking about this ever since I saw you at lunch, Jos." Then, giggling like two teenagers, they fell onto the bed, removing only the clothing necessary to make love. The spontaneity of the occasion heightened the eroticism and their senses responded. In a few minutes, they lay exhausted but satisfied in each other's arms. When Brad rolled over and lay on his back, he heard Josie giggling again.

"Just look at us, Brad." Her skirt was pushed up, exposing nothing but nakedness from her waist down. Brad's pants and underpants were rumpled around his ankles, the toes of his white sneakers barely showing and the tail of his golf shirt just covering his pubic hair.

"You're wonderful, Josie, and I love you. Now why don't you get that shower? I'll order Chinese and get the drinks ready."

* * *

The Chinese take out dinner that evening went exactly as planned. The Wallaces' urgent sexual encounter before dinner increased their awareness of each other in other ways. The dinner conversation ranged from political issues to educational philosophy to their personal plans for the future. A sketchy description of his afternoon on the golf course satisfied Josie's inquiry about the remainder of Brad's day after she had seen him. Still euphoric over his accomplishment of the day, he dismissed the slight pang of jealousy he felt as she talked about lunch with the remaining members of the magnificent seven.

"We eat together as often as possible, but it never seems as though we can all get together at the same time. Rich and I are the only two who are always there because our schedules are the same," she explained.

The dinner extended well into the evening with Josie finally saying that she needed to work on her papers and lessons for the next day. Brad settled down for a mindless evening of watching television, extracting a promise from Josie that she would finish in time to watch the local news at ten o'clock with him.

* * *

They sat together on the sofa, snuggling, a soft sensuousness enfolding them. The television news hummed in the background but neither paid much attention as they directed their energies toward each other.

"Been a long time since we made love twice in one night," Josie said softly.

"Should I douse the TV?" The flickering of the television created an eerie blue strobe light effect in the darkened room, a unique but sublimely distracting atmosphere. Josie gave Brad a slight nudge for her response. He grudgingly removed his left hand from under her nightshirt and stood, promising to return quickly. With their attention momentarily diverted, the volume of the news seemed to increase. Brad had taken his first step toward the television when the newscaster somberly informed his viewers of a hit and run accident. His finger froze on the switch when he caught the name "Capaldi" mentioned. He glanced back over his shoulder as the wavering light splashed over Josie. She sat straight up, her provocative lounging position left behind.

"Wait a second, Brad. Don't turn it off." He returned to the couch, reached for her hand and sat down heavily beside her. They listened in mesmerized silence and strained to piece together the story from the remainder of the on-the-scene news reporter's clipped description. Each stared at the screen, troubled but for different reasons.

In the one minute or less that the story occupied in the newscast, any romantic notions the Wallaces entertained had disappeared. To Josie's relief, the reporter ended his story with the prognosis that Dr. Capaldi was expected to recover fully, fortunate to have been struck just a glancing blow by the speeding car. They sat in silence, stunned that they actually knew someone who was the subject of a television news broadcast. Brad's active imagination, using the sketchy information of the newscast, had no difficulty reconstructing the accident. Apparently, the doctor had a flat tire on his way home from the hospital that day. His car was not entirely off the quiet country road and, as he struggled to change the left front tire in the dark, a passing car had struck him, the driver not aware of what had happened until well past the scene. Brad smiled thinly.

"Must've backed out." The words came out loud enough for Josie to hear and he wanted desperately to suck them back into his mouth.

"I'm sorry, hon, what did you say? I was kind of daydreaming." In a well-lit room, Brad's relief might have been obvious but his guilty smirk evaporated in the flashing darkness.

"Oh nothing, I was just thinking out loud. What a shame but at least he's OK." He continued to gaze at the screen, the ghostly environment hiding his insincerity. Later that night, as he stared blankly into the darkness listening to Josie's soft breathing, he turned on his side and whispered to himself.

"Bastard got what he deserved; worked out better than I could have imagined."

*　　*　　*

The story of the hit and run accident received front-page coverage in the Covington County Daily News the next afternoon. Brad customarily stopped at the corner Seven-Eleven to buy the paper on the way home from school. The headline caught his attention and he didn't move from the parking lot until he read through the entire story twice.

Doctor Struck in Hit and Run

Doctor Steven Capaldi of Waterford received minor injuries last night when struck by a car while changing a flat tire on Route 14. According to Dr. Capaldi, who was conscious and alert when the police arrived, the hit-run driver never slowed as he approached and Capaldi paid little attention to the car as he struggled to loosen one of the lug nuts. Fortunately for Capaldi, the impact was a glancing blow.

The article continued with an extensive quote from the policeman who interviewed the doctor at the hospital. His description of the scenario confirmed Brad's image of what had happened.

The flat was on the left front so the doctor must have backed his car out of the space, the nail cleanly puncturing the tire. Enough air remained for the car to travel the few miles into the country. Apparently, the doctor had never changed a tire before, a fact that made Brad smile as he read it.

> *Dr. Capaldi's condition is not serious, his injuries confined to bruises and contusions. He is expected to be released from the hospital in a day or two. The doctor could supply no description of the car or driver. Anyone with information about the accident is encouraged to contact the Covington County Sheriff's Department.*

He closed the paper and threw it on the seat next to him. "Lucky bastard," he hissed through gritted teeth.

"I'm Just A Kid"

"The only way to win and hold the love of a child is to be frank and simple and honest."
Elbert Hubbard

The day after his successful operation on Steve Capaldi's car, Brad left Hartford West as quickly as was allowed by contract, waiting uncomfortably in line with many of the "time clock" teachers. When the minute hand on the official school clock finally clicked to 3:10 p.m., Joan Potter whisked out the STAFF AVAILABLILTY ROSTER and placed it on the counter with a flourish. Her icy stare flitted over the teachers waiting, softening when she saw Brad. The secretary, whom most were convinced could run the school herself, knew that he was not usually one of those who would be out of the building before the students if they could. When he got to the front of the line, he scrawled his initials in the OUT block, noting at least five red lines through IN blocks on this page alone. Joan kept an accurate count of those red lines, each one indicating that a staff member had not arrived at school before 7:15 a.m., when she swooshed away the sheet. Three red lines meant an official letter of reprimand for your file and an unpleasant consultation with your supervisor. He smiled at Joan, still standing at the counter as though supervising the signing out process to make sure that no one signed more than one name.

"Have a nice evening, Joan," he said as he scribbled his name in the degrading process. "Only in our profession," he muttered to a colleague as he went through the door.

Traffic was still light, the rush hour still an hour away and the trip to the cemetery went quickly. Soon he stood over the gravesite of his infant son. The unusually warm late afternoon sun heated the ground enough for him to kneel by the engraved stone.

85

"Well, we did something about you, and it worked out better than we had planned," he said aloud. His black periods continued to evolve, their form taken from his emotional needs at the time. They covered a spectrum from rage-filled despair to calm reminiscences, from depression to euphoria. He could immerse himself in memories almost as a baptism, a spiritual renewal. He studied enough psychology to know that mental illness could be rooted in childhood, and he relished the task of determining what had happened to him. The success of the Steve Capaldi venture allowed him to settle into one of his comfortable periods, and two unforgettable incidents from his younger days came to mind.

*   *   *

Barnstable Elementary School was just three blocks from the Wallace's home. Brad, a precocious and persuasive seven year old, convinced his parents that it would be safe for him to ride his bike to school.

"I promised I would walk the bike across the two intersections," he said to the stone marker in front of where he knelt, speaking in a conversational tone as though Brad Jr. was sitting on his knee in a typical father-son pose.

By the third day of the bike riding adventure, Brad gained enough confidence to try a short cut to school. As he passed the police and fire departments, he turned into the first of the two driveways that led to a vacant field behind the three story brick structures. A well-worn path crossed the field diagonally toward the rear of Barnstable Elementary. The two drives paralleled the buildings on either side, one specified for entrance only and the other for exit only. Turning left off of Station Avenue, he paid no attention to the EXIT ONLY sign, blissfully unaware as children riding bikes to school so often are. He passed the three large garage doors on his right and cast a sidelong glimpse at the glistening fire engines poised in their bays. The exit drive was quite wide, allowing sufficient space for the engines to maneuver and he rode close to the buildings on his right. Coming to the corner of the police station, he looked across the parking area and set a course directly toward the field.

Harry Thompson, aide to the mayor and impressed with his own importance, saw a flash of movement to his left as Brad appeared from behind the corner of the building. Even though his car traveled slowly, the collision with the bicycle sent the young boy sprawling across the gravel. The left front wheel on the huge black Packard came to rest on Brad's bike, now just a twisted mass of metal. By the time the overweight Harry climbed out of his car, Brad had picked himself up. His pants had a gaping hole in the knee and a bright red strawberry already showed through the rip. As he brushed the gravel and dirt from the front of his shirt, the tears of fright had already made their way to his chin.

"I'm really sorry, Mister. I didn't see you." Brad looked at Harry, who appeared ready to explode like the Hindenburg. His face had turned scarlet and he struggled to breathe normally.

"I'm going to back the car off your bike then you get it the hell out of the middle of the driveway." Harry's sharp breaths caused the words to come out in short phrases. "I'll park the car and then we're going to the police station."

He walked back to the driver's side of his car, the door still open. Brad, terrified, watched him turn and arrange his position so that he could plop down into the seat. The Packard's engine started with a roar and the car slowly moved backward. Brad flinched at the crunching, cracking sound of snapping spokes as the huge tire crushed the rear wheel of his bike. Harry guided the car around the wreckage and parked in the first available space. The young boy walked back to his decimated two wheeler, grabbed the bent handlebars, and pulled the bike toward the brick wall of the station, trailing bits and pieces of the thin spokes behind. His hunched shoulders and drooped head only seemed to inflame Harry Thompson's rage further as he waddled toward the door.

"You get your ass in here, boy. I'm not getting any blame for this and you're going to tell 'em what happened."

Brad stood there, staring down at the rubble at his feet.

"Yes, sir," he mumbled in a shaking voice. "I'll be right there." Under his breath, for the first time in his life, he referred to someone as a bastard, a word that was meaningless to him other than he knew that his father reserved it for people he didn't like. It was also a word he dared not say aloud under any circumstances.

The scene in the police station was one that could not be forgiven nor forgotten. Brad would neither forget nor forgive. His face, smudged by a mixture of dirt dampened by tears and highlighted by bright red cheeks and a quivering chin, made him look like a ragamuffin. He had barely entered the station, cowering just inside the doorway, when Harry Thompson was pulling him by the shirt. The desk sergeant stood behind a long counter, well scuffed at its base by years of nervous feet standing in front of it. The chipped tile covering the top of the counter met with Brad's eyes. Thompson rudely yanked him toward his first ever confrontation with the police. As he watched the approaching pair, the sergeant vacillated between the necessity for political wisdom and his empathy for the young lad trembling before him.

"This is the kid, Jimmy. He'll tell you all about it. Let me know if you need me." Harry finally allowed his grip on the shirt to loosen and Brad escaped his grasp. "I'll be upstairs in my office."

The sergeant, a lanky, redheaded Irishman with a friendly devilish twinkle in his eye, waited for Thompson to clear the room. He walked to the end of the counter and pushed open the swinging gate. He motioned for Brad to join him and together they went to his paper-covered desk.

"Have a seat, kid. I need to know exactly what happened." Brad stuttered and stammered his way through the story, fighting back frightened tears. When his story ended, the policeman offered to call his mother. Only after a few seconds of considering his options, Brad decided that it would be best to have his mother come get him. Hopefully his father would have left for work by now; he dreaded the prospect of explaining the whole thing to him that evening, but the thought of having his father see him like this was even worse.

"I'm really sorry this happened to you, son," the sergeant said, "but you need to be more careful on that bike of yours." The image of the useless, mutilated bike leaning against the wall outside made Brad shudder with the frustrated and futile anger of a seven-year-old. The crushing reality of being helpless in the face of the adult world caused his small hands to ball into fists as he again whispered to himself. "Bastard! I'm just a kid."

* * *

After a severe tongue lashing about stupid bike riding from his father the night of the accident, Brad accompanied his father to the police station early the next morning. Harry Thompson, aware that he had overreacted and fearful of any political backlash at his mean-spirited treatment of Brad, agreed with John Wallace that the boy should have a replacement bicycle. After delivering a stern lecture about responsibility and the privilege of riding a bike, Harry handed Brad a ten-dollar bill. Brad understood little of his lecture, but knew ten dollars would not come close to buying a new bike. He looked up at his father, expecting some strong reaction. Instead, he saw the two men shaking hands and smiling, as though they had just closed a lucrative business deal.

"You should thank Mr. Thompson, Brad. He's being quite generous considering the accident was your fault."

"Yeah, sure, Dad." He choked back his disappointment. He could have been as mutilated as his bicycle. He looked up at his father once more but any glimmer of hope for justice vanished when he saw him still smiling.

"Thank you, sir," the boy said, as softly as he could.

The memory receded but the face of Harry Thompson remained clear even now after twenty years. Brad straightened up from the resting position on his haunches and knelt by the gravestone.

"I'd have been a good father to you, I know it," he said. The desolation of his father's perceived betrayal washing away the image of Harry Thompson. His immersion in the innocent rage of childhood continued.

"There was a time, Brad, my boy, when your dad found an antidote for childish anger," he whispered to the grave, as though sharing a special secret.

The vision of Harrison Peaslee, a neighbor of the Wallaces in their first house in Darien, formed in his mind. The burgeoning suburban neighborhood contained the typical melange of housing styles, and the Wallaces considered themselves fortunate to have found a small bungalow within their price range. Large two and a half story colonials dwarfed the house on both sides, each one occupied by rather eccentric neighbors. A local psychiatrist lived in the always-darkened house. On the rare occasions when Brad saw him, he greeted him with a cheery wave and received a positive response most of the time.

The other neighbor, Harrison Peaslee, was obsessed with keeping his expansive lawn and gardens in pristine condition. Brad and several of his friends regularly played the sports in season in the small side yard and on any number of occasions, he would call or wave to Mr. Peaslee. After being rebuffed time and again, he gave up and simply ignored the bitter old man. An evening dinner table conversation between John and Sandra Wallace told Brad that Harrison Peaslee had been a widower for quite a number of years and lived a solitary life.

On Brad's ninth birthday, John surprised Brad with a small mongrel puppy. When he came into the house and set the excited dog down on the floor, it skipped right to Brad, its entire body wagging. The dog was immediately dubbed "Skippy."

Several days later, as Brad and Skippy chased each other in the side yard, old man Peaslee was outside working as usual, raking around the small goldfish pond in his back yard. Skippy, seeing another human being that would love to pet him, set off across the lawn heading directly for Peaslee. He paused briefly at one of the spreading yew shrubs edging the Peaslee property and prepared to mark his territory. Brad and Mr. Peaslee arrived at the bush almost together, but the old man got there first. As Brad hollered "Skippy, come here!" he saw the old man deliver a solid, heavy booted kick into Skippy's side. The kick raised the dog off the ground and rolled him over. The force of the blow sent the small dog back onto the Wallace's property. Brad rushed over to him. As Skippy whimpered in the background, Harrison Peaslee thundered. "Keep that God damned dog off my property. I'll shoot him next time."

"Yes, sir, sorry about this," Brad said, summoning up his most polite, well-mannered tone of voice. He scooped up the dog and looked up at Mr. Peaslee, standing over him with his hands on his hips and a threatening scowl on his face. For what must have been a full minute, he just stared at the man, searching his face for a clue to explain such outrageous behavior. When he found none, a fierce anger welled up, causing his eyes to defocus. He finally turned away and walked slowly back to his house, his entire body slightly hunched.

"Bastard," he snarled. "He's just a puppy."

*   *   *

Brad stood from his kneeling position and brushed the few pine needles and bits of grass from his knees. He felt a slight shiver crawl down his back, unsure if the cause was the late afternoon air or the memory of Mr. Harrison Peaslee.

*   *   *

The teams that wonderful fall Saturday were evenly divided. The small side yard of the Wallaces became the home of the New York Giants, and Brad and five of his friends enjoyed the camaraderie of a touch football game as they imagined themselves playing before a packed Yankee Stadium. Skippy was tied firmly to the large weeping willow in the front yard, well out of reach of their game and Mr. Peaslee's yard. Wisps of smoke from a number of neighborhood leaf burning fires permeated the air. Peaslee, as always, was flitting around his yard raking every leaf, almost catching them as they fell.

His was the only house in the neighborhood with an outside stone fireplace specifically built for burning leaves and rubbish. A solid stream of smoke showed it to be burning steadily. The only attention he paid to the game going on next door was an icy glare every time Skippy barked at a passing squirrel or chipmunk.

Brad's team had just scored and as the best athlete and kicker of the group, he prepared to kick off to his friends. From where he stood, Mr.

Peaslee appeared in his peripheral vision just enough to distract him as he dropped the small rubber football toward his foot. He kicked mightily but the ball slid off the side of his foot. He saw it heading well out of bounds to his right, toward the ever-raking old neighbor. As though in slow motion, all six boys just watched as the ball bounced on the concrete driveway. Collectively holding their breath, the boys waited, hoping for a Wallace bounce back toward their field. Instead, the ball went sailing end over end after it struck the drive, picking up speed with each bounce until it smacked hard into Peaslee's shin and came to rest at his feet.

The six friends stood exactly where they had been since the kick-off, frozen to the spot as they watched with nervous curiosity to see the old man's reaction. He bent over and picked up the ball, examining it as if it were an alien object just fallen from the sky.

"Sorry, Mr. Peaslee," Brad shouted, still rooted to the spot. "Just throw it back, please."

Without a word, the old man, now an acknowledged adversary, turned his back on the six boys and flipped the ball into his stone fireplace. Within seconds, there was a loud pop as the ball exploded. Stunned, the boys moved toward the center of their field in silence, looking back over the shrubs at Harrison Peaslee, who had begun to rake once more.

After his friends left that day, Brad decided that Mr. Peaslee needed to be taught a lesson. He asked permission to use some of his allowance to buy a model airplane at the local Five and Dime and walked the few blocks into the downtown area. He picked out the least expensive model he could find. With his remaining allowance, he bought two large bottles of Clorox bleach at the local supermarket, hiding them under the back steps of his house for use at a later time.

Mr. Peaslee's goldfish pond contained some of the largest and oldest goldfish known to man. After he lost his wife, raising the fish became an obsessive hobby and the pond consumed much of his time and attention. Brad watched from a distance many times as the old man cleaned the pond. Even though a young boy, he noticed the subtle difference between the harsh demeanor and body language of Peaslee as he worked around the house and the gentler, tender treatment of the fishpond.

Brad waited for two more weeks before putting the bottles of Clorox to use. A parent-teacher conference night provided the ideal cover for his operation. Each conference was scheduled to last one-half hour which meant Brad's parents would be gone for at least forty-five minutes. He spread his books out on the floor in front of the radio, retrieved his pillow from his room, and arranged his space so that it would appear that he had never left the spot. As the car left the driveway, he slipped out the back door, hesitating just a moment to make sure that they wouldn't be returning for some forgotten key or paper.

The Clorox bottles remained in the hiding place beneath the stairs. He crawled into the small opening, feeling his way to the bottles through the darkness. With one bottle in each hand, he backed out, dragging them across the dirt floor under the steps. He inched through the opening and sat leaning against the railing, the only light filtering to him from the living room of Peaslee's house. He pictured the old man kicking Skippy and casually throwing his football into the fire. The images focused his attention on what he was about to do.

"Really sorry, little fishes," he said. His hands were steady as he stood, a heavy gallon jug in each hand. In the semi-crouch of a soldier sneaking up to an enemy pillbox, he crept to the edge of their property. His eyes grew accustomed to the dark quickly and he found his way to the shrub line separating the two houses. At the first shrub, he dropped to his knees and crawled the last few yards to the pond. Even in the blackness, the gold of some of the fish swimming toward the top of the pond shone through the water. Brad assumed a prone position, carefully unscrewing the cap of one of the jugs. Holding it over the pond so none of the powerful bleach would spill on the ground, he tilted the jar close to the surface of the pond to avoid any splashing sound. It emptied faster than he expected and he soon was repeating the process with the second bottle. He screwed the caps back on the bottles. His mother had issued dire warnings about the poisonous dangers lurking in the laundry cabinet and the skull and crossbones on the bottles of bleach indicated the potential for disaster. His plan had to work.

The journey back to his house went quickly and Brad proceeded directly to the garage with the two empty bottles. Removing several layers of trash from one of the metal cans, he mixed the bottles in as well as he could and then threw the rest of the rubbish back on top of them. His young man's fascination with trash trucks had taught him that trash collectors were not interested in analyzing anyone's junk and in just two days, those bottles would be lost at the bottom of a dump somewhere.

When Sandra and John Wallace returned from the conference, full of wonderful reports about their son, they found him in his pajamas, asleep on the floor by the radio.

Brad started out for school promptly at 8:15 every morning. The cooler weather prevented him from riding his bicycle but he kept to the same time. As he left the house the morning after his secret mission, he couldn't resist looking across the yard toward his neighbor's property. When he saw Mr. Peaslee standing by the fishpond with the long-handled net he used to remove debris from the pond, Brad slowed his gait to watch. He was removing things from the pond but it was not debris. Each time the net dipped into the pond, Peaslee came up with a gold, flaccid carcass, which he would then drop onto the lawn. As Brad passed his house, he slowed even more. The man's back was to him and he seemed oblivious to everything around him. Before the corner of the house eliminated the old man from view, Brad noticed that Peaslee kept wiping his face with the sleeves of his jacket. It wasn't until he came into the schoolyard that Brad realized what Mr. Peaslee had been doing.

* * *

The lasting image of the old man wiping his nose and eyes on his sleeves dissipated as Brad began to come out of his black period. "So, junior, that's how you change people. You just supply an important, mind-bending emotional event. Old Mr. Peaslee moved shortly after that and never bothered us again. And I was just a kid."

The Nail

"Even if you're on the right track,
you'll get run over if you just sit there."
Will Rogers

A week later after his accident, Dr. Steve Capaldi returned to work for the first time. The early morning sun angled sharply across the lot and as he turned into his assigned space, he noticed a bright reflection shimmering off a shiny object toward the front of the space. He stopped short, stepped out and walked around the car. Kneeling down, he studied the glimmering object before picking it up.

"I'll be damned," he whispered as he studied the nail he held in his hand.

*   *   *

Detective Parker Havenot was saddled with a surname he constantly had to remind people was pronounced with a long "O" as in Havenote. In keeping with the times, he allowed his sandy blond hair to grow well beyond what was acceptable for the regular force, laying well over his collar but not quite hippie length. His slim build belied his rugged strength, developed through years of weight training. Cheek length sideburns framed his sharp facial features and deep-set blue eyes highlighted his disarmingly friendly face. His colleagues looked to him as a role model, an intuitive and instinctive investigator and his reputation in the Covington County Sheriff's Department was without equal.

The department's investigation into Steve Capaldi's hit and run accident had gone nowhere. When the doctor phoned the office with a rather asinine story of finding a nail in the hospital parking lot matching the one in his tire, the other detectives in the precinct rolled their eyes and agreed that this was a case for Detective Havenot. The captain, following

95

the lead of his corps, assigned Parker to investigate.

"His wife probably tried to run him down," Parker announced to anyone who would listen as he left the captain's office. With a cynicism born of years of police work, Havenot suspected the worst from conjugal mates first. He pictured a handsome young doctor who did nothing all day but examine women who lay on their backs, naked, their legs up in stirrups, and spread as wide as possible. While it might be difficult to generate much sympathy for this guy, his professionalism demanded that he approach the case properly and without bias.

A cursory examination of the Capaldi file piqued his interest. Over the years, he had investigated and assisted in prosecuting more than his share of murders and robberies and the case of Dr. Capaldi intrigued him with its lack of witnesses and evidence. Entering the Covington County Hospital, he was anxious to get started on solving the puzzle.

Parker approached the information desk and the young receptionist looked up at him over the reading glasses resting on the tip of her nose.

"Dr. Capaldi's office, please. He's expecting me. Parker Havenot." He smiled down at the young lady, whose attention seemed riveted just below his belt buckle.

"Just follow the blue line to the East Wing and go through the double doors. I'll call and let him know you're coming, Mr. Havenot." She blushed ever so slightly. She hadn't been very subtle in assessing the handsome visitor. "He's in Suite 5," she called after him.

Parker followed the blue line, a garish stripe down the middle of the glistening tile hall. The double doors at the end of the hall were emblazoned with EAST on the left and WING on the right in the same offensive blue color, as if anyone could miss the room after following the blue line to its conclusion. He pushed through the doors, opening both of them. They didn't click shut behind him until he entered Suite 5.

"I hated to bother you with this, Detective, and it's probably a waste of time." Steve Capaldi disarmed Parker with a genuinely apologetic smile.

"Not a problem for me, Doctor. So what's this about a nail?"

The doctor leaned across the enormous mahogany desk that occupied more than half of the square footage in the room. The two nails rested on a glass paperweight inscribed with the initials SSC, one of them with a small piece of tape around it. He handed the nails to Parker with yet another sheepish apology.

"Here's the reason for your trip," he said. "The one with the tape was in the flat tire. The other one I found in my reserved parking space in the hospital lot."

"Not to be wise, Doctor, but I'm not exactly sure what you are suggesting." Parker had taken an instant liking to Steve Capaldi. The doctor's discomfort with the situation was obvious. His quick movement from behind the barricade of the desk provided Parker with all the body language he needed to know that the doctor was regretting ever calling the police.

"I'm not even sure what I thought. It just seemed odd that an identical nail would appear in my parking space. I figure it probably was just a coincidence. Look, I'm really sorry to have bothered you. Why don't we just forget this whole thing?" Capaldi stood and crossed his arms over his chest in that unique way doctors have of letting patients know that the consultation is over.

"OK, Doctor, whatever you say. I should tell you though, that I've been assigned to your hit and run case so you won't be totally rid of me for a while. I'm not sure that we're going to find any connection between these nails and your accident but one quick question, if you don't mind?" Parker paused, waiting out of courtesy for the doctor's affirmative nod.

"So tell me, where exactly did you find the second nail?"

When Steve finished describing the location of the nail he found in the lot, the investigator in Havenot still was not satisfied. "OK, really, just one more question," he said with a smile. Capaldi leaned on his desk, quite happy that this detective seemed to be truly interested in the nails, perhaps enough that his credibility had not suffered as much as he thought.

"Just one more, Detective. I really must get back to my ladies, you know," Steve said. Parker looked at him and they both smiled. Their comfort with one another was obvious.

"What side of the car had the flat?" Parker knew the answer but his logical mind performed better when listening to someone actually say the words instead of dredging them up himself.

"The left front tire," Steve said. "Do you believe in fate, Detective? You know, if the flat had been on the right side, I wouldn't have been nearly killed that night."

"I'm not sure if I'm a true fatalist, Doctor. Way too complex a concept for me. But, you know what, I don't believe in coincidences either. I'll take these nails with me if it's all right with you." The two men shook hands, sensing the bond that had formed so quickly between them.

"Hey, find that guy that hit me, will you?" Steve called as Havenot reached the door.

Parker stopped and, in a conspiratorial tone, whispered back. "How do you doctors do it, anyway, spending all day in places most guys are daydreaming about?"

Steve Capaldi grinned but said nothing.

"Yeah, I know. It's a tough job but someone has to do it," Parker said. They shared a hearty laugh and then the detective was walking briskly along the blue line and out the door to his car, the two nails clinking together in his pocket acting as a focus for his thinking.

The case certainly would present a challenge to him but, as always, he was confident that he would find the driver of the car that struck Capaldi. A much more intriguing mystery was the possible sabotage of the tire on the doctor's car. At first glance, it looked as if someone might have set out to flatten at least one of his tires, taking great care to assure success. Even his hardened policeman's cynicism had trouble with that one.

As he drove back to the precinct, the perplexing questions resonated over and over again. Who would want to pull such an adolescent stunt and why choose Dr. Capaldi of all people?

Very interesting, he thought, and then turned his mind to other things.

It's Preposterous

*"There's a mighty big difference between good,
sound reasons and reasons that sound good."*
Burton Hollis

"It's preposterous, Parker. Absolutely preposterous."

Havenot, in his calmest, most persuasive voice assured him that it likely was.

"Just humor me on this one. I've got nothing better to do, OK?" Parker laughed lightly at his own attempt at humor and Steve Capaldi answered with a chuckle at the other end of the line.

The doctor delivered an average of fifty babies a year. In addition to those patients, he treated another three hundred women for various conditions and diseases. Parker Havenot's request for a list of present and former patients who might have reason to be the least bit unhappy with his treatment over the last year seemed easy at first glance. Parker's interest in his case was gratifying, but he couldn't buy into the implication that anyone would have intentionally tried to run him down. He could not remember any patient who had expressed disapproval until he sat at his desk after his last appointment for the day, pouring over the list of names prepared by his nurse. It was indeed preposterous.

For fifteen minutes, Steve scanned down the list of patients. His nurse had marked any that had asked for their records to be sent to another doctor for reasons other than moving. At his request, she placed a check next to the name of any patient who experienced a problem during their pregnancy. At each name, Steve found he could resurrect a face, and if needed, could have provided an anecdotal record on the patient from memory. The list he would be giving to Parker Havenot would be a short one.

A second perusal limited the choices even further. He glanced at the clock on his desk, opened his desk drawer, and pulled out the detective's card. "Call me any time you want," he had said. He picked up the phone and dialed.

"Havenot here," Parker answered in his best detective manner.

"I've got just a few for you, Parker," he said, without introduction. "I must be a pretty damn good doctor. Very few problems and everyone loves me."

"Right, Steve, and you're humble as well. I'll stop by tomorrow if it's all right and pick up names, addresses, and problems. Did any stand out, you know, any irate, jealous husbands or obsessive, unrequited crushes on their handsome young doctor?"

Steve laughed loudly and glanced down the list in front of him once more. The patients were listed in chronological order beginning with the most recent and descending to the previous year. His eyes quickly dropped down through the names to the bottom of the list.

"None really. There was a patient who lost an infant and the husband wasn't too happy with how I handled everything, but she is still my patient and that was over a year ago now. So no, nothing that I can see. You sure that you don't think this is too much of a stretch?"

"This is my job; it's how I spend my days so I'll see you tomorrow for the names. Have a good night. What was that patient's name, anyway, the one with the unhappy husband?"

*   *   *

Josie heard the phone ringing as she rooted through her pocketbook for the key to the kitchen door. For whatever reason, a ringing phone has a strange effect on most of the human race. Josie responded predictably, practically dumping the contents of her purse in frantic pursuit of the elusive keys so that she could get to the phone before it stopped.

"Sorry to bother you, Mrs. Wallace," Parker said to the breathless Josie. "This is Detective Havenot of the Covington County Sheriff's Department." Josie's first thought was of Brad, who should have been traveling home from school at this very moment.

"Yes?" she said, and waited. Parker had made his share of bad news phone calls in his police career and recognized the panic in her single word response.

"Everything's fine, Mrs. Wallace." The calmness in his voice meant more to her than his words and Josie felt the tightness leave her throat. "I just wondered if I could drop by and speak with you and your husband for a few minutes this evening. Just a routine thing; won't take more than ten minutes, tops."

Josie, relieved to hear that Brad was not splattered over a highway, didn't hesitate, agreeing without asking any further questions.

*   *   *

Brad's reaction to the news that a detective from the sheriff's office was paying them a visit was a little unsettling. While she remained interested in the detective's visit but only vaguely curious, Brad adopted a haughty, unjustly accused citizen stance. He was quiet and introspective during their cocktail hour, doubling his normal martini intake as he let her carry the burden of conversation.

"I mean this is pretty intrusive, don't you think? I can't figure out why you didn't ask more about why he'd want to come here," Brad said as they sat down to dinner. His voice had a harsh edge to it, a sharpness far beyond what the occasion warranted. They ate dinner in virtual silence, the high pitched scraping of their forks on the plates the only sound bouncing off the kitchen walls. When Josie stood to clear the dishes, she felt the need to say something to ease the tension, still uncertain why there was any tension to be eased.

"Why don't you just relax, Brad. He probably just wants to ask about a neighbor or something at school. I'm sorry I didn't get the particulars; I was so relieved that nothing had happened to you that I didn't even think. You're acting like we're being visited by the IRS or something." She looked at him, still sitting at the table, staring through the wall across from him. She abandoned her attempt to draw him out.

Fifteen minutes later, Detective Parker Havenot sat on the second hand sofa in their living room, deftly putting the Wallaces at ease. Both of them expressed surprise at the reason for his visit; the accident involving Dr. Capaldi had occurred several weeks before and Josie needed to be reminded of some of the details.

"This is all very routine, Mrs. Wallace." Parker answered the question before either of the Wallaces could phrase it. "We're simply eliminating things as possibilities."

His strength as an investigator lay in his uncanny ability to elicit responses without asking questions. As he related the events of the accident, including the possible sabotage of the doctor's vehicle, he observed every aspect of the Wallaces' reaction.

Brad stared at the detective as he explained the conspiracy theory in forthcoming fashion.

"Sounds really bizarre but, trust me, I've seen some bizarre things, even here in quiet Covington County. We're just talking to any of the doctor's patients who may have had problems they could blame on him. Once we eliminate that possibility, we'll know that it was just a freak accident and probably'll have a hard time finding the person responsible. I'm not sure what your situation was, Mrs. Wallace, doctor-patient confidentiality and all that, but I'm sorry for it anyway." Brad leaned forward in his chair, a brooding expression clouding his face. His lips lost their fullness and tightened into a thin slit.

"We lost our son at six months, Detective, and I'm sure that Dr. Capaldi did everything possible. We both remember rather vividly what we were doing on the night the doctor was hit." Brad looked directly at Josie and saw a faint glow come into her cheeks, either from pleasure that he remembered or embarrassment at the suggestive inference. "The nail thing is very peculiar; sounds like something a kid would do."

"Yeah." Parker stood abruptly. "I can't imagine what it must be like to lose a child. I'm truly sorry for your loss and sorry to have bothered you. Just part of my job. . . ." His voice lowered and trailed off to nothing as Josie lowered her eyes and turned away. "Thanks for your time. I can find my way out."

Brad waited for the door to close, then went to Josie and embraced her. "Well, that was painless enough," he said.

"Pretty weird world we live in isn't it? How long do you think it will take to get over this, Brad? It's been over a year and I still think of him. Just imagine, we'd have a nine month old bouncing baby boy right now, looking forward to Christmas." Josie rested her head on his shoulder, bit her lip hard and kept her tears to herself.

*   *   *

Parker Havenot reconstructed every word, every gesture, every nuance of voice intonation and every expression from his brief meeting with the Wallaces. A single phone call to Chris Howard at the Hampton Village School District office the next morning confirmed his impressions. The Wallaces could never be considered suspects for any sort of crime. Their dedication and integrity were absolutely above reproach. Parker determined in his rational mind that his intuition, usually reliable, must be mistaken. Yet the disquieting reality was that Brad's alibi for the night of Steve Capaldi's accident was just that–an alibi for the night, not for the afternoon. He picked up the phone and asked the dispatcher to get Hartford West High School for him.

The Summer Home

"You are never given a wish without the
power to make it come true."
Richard Bach

The Wallaces had spent summer vacations on Lake Winnipesaukee every year since Brad was three years old. When Brad married Josie Campbell in the late summer of 1966, his father celebrated by fulfilling a life long dream.

"I'll be damned if I'm doing that any more, Sandra. We're going to have ourselves a retirement spot right where we want it," he announced to his wife, leaving no room for discussion or argument. By his calculations, he could have bought the camp three times over with the rent he paid out over the years.

A second mortgage on his Connecticut home financed the purchase of a small camp nestled in the pines on the northern shore of the lake. On the big lake, the natives called virtually every structure that was not lived in year round a "camp," particularly those with frontage on the water. Waterfront property was finite, and John had the foresight to be sure that he obtained adequate frontage on the lake for future docks, beaches, and seclusion. The building sitting on the property fit the true description of a camp. Like so many that dotted the lake, it had grown in bits and pieces after a humble beginning as a one-room cottage with a traditional one holer outside, complete with a flimsy wooden door featuring a crescent shaped cutout. When the Wallaces first saw it, two other rooms and a bath had been added to the original, tacked on like unnatural appendages, the mismatched roofs and siding an obvious giveaway. The inside, completely done in knotty pine paneling and equipped with pine furniture, enveloped anyone entering with the delightful scent of a dozen freshly cut Christmas trees. With a well-constructed stone fireplace and a

105

small kitchenette area in a corner of the living room, the camp served the vacation needs of the Wallace family well. Although the building itself was small, expansion possibilities abounded. John Wallace imagined all sorts of potential in the two hundred and fifty feet of lake frontage and over an acre of land. His plan worked to perfection. Brad and Josie spent several weeks at the cabin the first summer. Josie turned from winter white to a delicious summer brown while Brad helped his father add yet another bedroom at the rear of the building.

The second summer, the summer of Josie's pregnancy, produced even more frenzied property improvement. John was intent on improving the beach area so that his grandchild could use it the next summer. When Josie gently reminded him that his grandchild would only be about six months old the next summer, he brushed her chiding aside.

"It's never too soon to get a kid used to the water," he said, with an authority reserved for grandfathers. By the end of that second summer, the family was in complete agreement. The camp purchase had been one of John Wallace's best decisions. The house and the beach were ready for the first visit from the grandchild and, hopefully, in the future, other grandchildren as well.

The tragedy of losing their grandchild the following fall struck the older Wallace family hard. The necessity for a partial hysterectomy to save Josie's life intensified the devastating situation. In the late spring before the third summer, both Wallace couples found the initial visit to open the camp difficult. Unable to shake the happy memories of the summer before, the first few days were spent in a subdued dilemma. Everyone went through the motions of enjoying the cottage while fighting the melancholy of reality that there would be no children bringing renewal and their unique vitality into the family. Gradually, the summer warmed and the horrid New Hampshire black flies thinned enough so that it was possible to leave the house without being attacked by swarms of them. The pleasure of visiting the camp increased by the resiliency of human nature allowed the pain of their loss to become a dull ache for the Wallaces. When John and Sandra joined Brad and Josie for their annual vacation surrounding the Fourth of July holiday, the camp once again became a place for making family memories. The gravesite back in Connecticut faded into the out-of-sight but not quite out-of-mind category.

*   *   *

In June of 1970, Brad was named as successor to the retiring Ron Scott as Department Head. The length of his new contract tempered his excitement at the appointment because his time spent at the lake would be seriously affected. When he told his father of the promotion, whining at the added days that allowed only a one-month vacation, he was prepared for the response.

"So, you finally got a full time job," John chided. The usual heated discussion followed, Brad contending that teachers only received pay for days worked, with no paid holidays and no vacations.

"I'm laid off in the summer; I should be able to collect unemployment." John Wallace's reply to this argument was so predictable that when he offered it, both father and son laughed.

"You might as well; you guys only work part time as it is and live off us poor taxpayers to boot."

"Yeah, sure, Dad, and none of us pay taxes either." The debate ended in the usual friendly stalemate and the discussion then turned to the camp.

"I'll probably only be able to take two weeks up there this summer. Josie might spend more than that but I want to save a week at Christmas and some other days during the year." He would miss those warm summer evenings with Josie, the privacy of the camp allowing them to make love on the deck under the stars.

"I've got a few two man projects lined up for this summer so we'll need to coordinate when you'll be there."

"Sure, Dad, we'll work it out," he said. The image of Josie and him on the deck on a warm summer night faded into nothingness.

*   *   *

In the spring of 1970, Kent State provided all the discussion material

Brad's Current Events class needed for a full month. When the National Guard fired on the demonstrating students on the campus, the shock rattled across the country and his students, motivated by their young teacher, plunged into the subject. The shootings sent Brad reeling, and he visited Mountain View Cemetery regularly for one week. The one-sided, therapeutic conversations he had with his dead son's marker released bursts of anger and hostility, enabling him to return to a world of light feeling refreshed and cleansed.

Late one afternoon, one month to the day after Kent State, he sat in his new office pouring over his department budget when the phone rang. He flinched, startled by the sound. Having a phone available on his desk was a luxury in education and a ringing telephone was not yet a familiar sound. How many times as a teacher had he stood in line waiting for an available telephone to call a parent or arrange a field trip for his class. He smiled as he picked up the receiver.

"Hartford West Social Studies Department, Brad Wallace speaking." After a pause, Josie's quavering voice replaced the low hum of silence.

"Brad. . . ." then more silence.

"Josie. Hi!" A muffled sound came from the receiver. "Josie, what is it?"

Between sobs, Josie told her story in bits and pieces.

"I'll leave right away, Josie. I'll come straight there." For the second time since he had moved to Hartford West, he raced to Covington County Hospital. The late afternoon rush hour traffic had just begun and Brad, flashing his headlights, tried to maneuver through it but was stymied at every turn.

An hour later, Josie greeted him at the entrance to the emergency room.

"Oh, Brad, I am so sorry," she stammered as she threw her arms around him. "They're gone, Brad, they're both gone!"

She had waited for him to arrive to go through the official formality of identifying the bodies and accompanied him into the cold morgue with Dr. Linderhoff, the emergency room doctor. As the doctor slowly pulled the covering from his father's face, he felt his knees buckle and acid rise in his throat.

"That's my dad," he whispered as Josie held his hand.

"Sorry, Mr. Wallace, I know this is difficult but we need you to identify your mother as well." Linderhoff closed John Wallace's drawer while unlatching and pulling open the drawer containing Sandra.

"I can't do this, Josie. It's inhuman, for God's sake." Brad's complaint was lost on the doctor who already had pulled the cover from Sandra Wallace's face. "Jesus, yes, it's her," he cried out. Then the drawer slid back into place and closed with a loud and final click. Brad fell apart.

"All that work on the camp, oh shit, Josie! What the hell happened?" He buried his face deep into her shoulder and sobbed.

The Sanctuary

"Within you there is a stillness and sanctuary to
which you can retreat and be yourself."
Hermann Hesse

Josie knew nothing about the accident and Brad's emotional state on the
way home from the hospital would not have allowed for much discussion
anyway. She insisted that she should drive and Brad agreed with only minimal argument. The first half of the ride was silent, as if both of them were
afraid to intrude on the others thoughts. Brad finally broke the silence about
a mile from their house.

"Here's a weird question for you, Jos. What do think has happened
to Mom and Dad's thoughts, all those little electrical impulses flitting
around their brains?" They were passing Mountain View Cemetery as Josie
turned her head to answer. Brad stared out the window, his right hand resting softly on the glass. In that instant, she was sure that she saw his hand
slide back and forth in a tiny waving motion. She turned her attention back
to the road.

"I believe they still exist, Brad, you know that. They're just somewhere else, that's all." They had passed the cemetery. The last few blocks
were again encased in the deathly silence.

Josie guided the car into the drive and came to a stop. She looked
over at Brad. His cheeks were damp and he rubbed his eyes to clear them.

"That's all complete, unadulterated bullshit, Josie, and you know it."
Then he was out of the car and slouching toward the house, his entire body
drooping.

He went immediately to the liquor cabinet, extracting the large
shaker they used for making martinis for a dinner party of four. He had
added the gin when the doorbell rang. Josie hollered from the bedroom that
she would answer it. A few seconds later, as he added a light touch of

vermouth, she called over her shoulder.

"It's the sheriff's department, Brad. You'd better come in here."
Taking a large sip directly from the pitcher, Brad swallowed hard and came
into the living room as Josie escorted Detective Parker Havenot into their
living room.

"Really sorry to bother you now but I thought you deserved a
report about what happened today," he said as he reached for Brad's out-
stretched hand. "I'm Parker Havenot from the Sheriff's Department."

"We've met before, Detective. The Capaldi thing, remember?"
Brad shook his hand without enthusiasm.

"Of course." Havenot moved directly to the reason for his visit.
"They sent me over because it looks like there probably was criminal negligence in this case and I'll be the investigating officer."

The deputy from the Covington County Sheriff's Department who
came to the house to take Josie to the hospital had been assigned by radio
and knew only a few details of what happened. As Havenot described the
accident, he deliberately avoided graphic details and she was grateful for
that. Her memory of his last visit was all positive and his compassionate
attitude under these horrible circumstances reinforced her impression.

"Apparently, this guy worked the 6-2 shift at the Corning
Fiberglass plant and had spent a couple of hours in a bar," Parker said.
Then he came to the most difficult part. Parker knew that families in this
type of circumstance prefer to believe that forces beyond anyone's control
had taken their loved ones away, not some idiot who should never have
been on the road.

"He must've never seen the stoplight; he was probably going
about sixty. They never knew what hit them, Mr. Wallace." The last comment, intended to be comforting, sounded like any of the dozens of other
cliches offered as condolences, meaningless words that were better left
unsaid. "Again, I'm sorry for your trouble; there just aren't any good
words. . . ."

When Havenot finished his story, the room filled with a deafen-
ing silence except for a quiet ticking from the kitchen clock. After an

awkward moment, Brad broke through the intense quiet.

"So, this guy killed my folks with his stupidity, right?" Josie recognized the malevolent tone.

"I know how you must feel, Mr. Wallace but rest assured, we'll nail him." The detective stood, his duty fulfilled.

"I'll walk you to the door, Mr. Havenot." While Parker's formal "Mr. Wallace" indicated a genuine courtesy and respect, Brad's emphasis on the "Mr." had an unintended hostile edge to it. "I'm sorry if I haven't been very gracious; this is pretty tough, you know?"

"Understood. I can't imagine it myself. You two have had your share for sure." Parker extended his hand and the two men shook hands. "By the way, we did get that hit and run guy, you know, with Dr. Capaldi. Never found the kid who flattened his tire though. I did hear that you played hooky from school that day, even fit in a round of golf." Brad reacted at what seemed to him an inappropriate subject for the situation.

"I've never played hooky in my life, Detective. I had a physical that day and it was too late to get back to school." Brad heard his own voice sound as if he were one of his students caught with a crib sheet up his sleeve. There was no reaction from Havenot.

"Just trying to lighten things up, Mr. Wallace. Stupid of me to bring it up. I know all about your reputation. This is all very difficult. Call me if you folks need anything." As he walked toward his patrol car, he glanced over his shoulder at the house. Brad remained at the door, watching through the sheer curtains as he left.

"That is one very complex man," he said as he drove off.

* * *

The summer of 1970 turned from a summer of anticipation to a summer of sadness and mourning. Brad's new position allowed precious few breaks and he visited the camp on the lake only occasionally. After the Wallaces' funeral and burial in Mountain View cemetery, just a few rows from their grandson, Brad and Josie undertook the sorting of the Winnipesaukee cabin first, using it as a practice session for the monumental task of the large home in Connecticut. For several days over the Fourth of July holiday, they worked at the painful process as every inch of the camp, inside and out, wailed out memories of John and Sandra Wallace. Josie, who had loved the quiet and solitude of the camp when she was alone there, now wanted no part of it. Brad tried to convince her to stay for a few extra days after the cleaning had been finished but she refused, saying that she would return only when she was accompanied by him or perhaps another friend or two.

It was quite a different summer than they had planned but it still passed by as fast as summers typically did and Labor Day weekend loomed on the horizon. Brad announced to Mike Costello that he had worked hard all summer, well beyond the usual expected for department heads. Furthermore, as a reward for being prepared for the opening of school weeks in advance, he was taking the week before the long weekend to enjoy the camp on the lake. Hampton Village High School, on a different schedule than Hartford School District, scheduled a teacher orientation day on the Thursday before Labor Day, preventing Josie from accompanying him. Rich Lane and Jess Grogan accepted the open invitation to any of the magnificent seven to come to New Hampshire for the weekend, agreeing to drive up with Josie on Friday.

"Are you sure that you want to do this, Brad?" Josie's concern was founded in her own trepidation about being at the camp alone since the death of the Wallaces, but he laughed at her apprehension.

"I think I'll enjoy it, Jos. I'll miss you, of course, but I feel like it is the right thing for me to do. Maybe provide some closure or something, whatever the shrinks say is the purpose of confronting stuff like this." He didn't have to remind her during the few times they had been alone up there that summer, they had not made love, on the deck or anywhere else.

"I just don't think it's appropriate," she had said. "It feels like we're violating some sort of memory or something."

"It feels as if, not like, Jos. You're an English teacher." She didn't take to his humor well and he let the matter drop.

*　*　*

Early Tuesday morning, Brad packed up the car. As he drove through Hartford, he detoured past the high school and dropped in for messages and memos. A quick scan of his mailbox revealed nothing important. Joan, the ever-efficient secretary, did say that a Detective Havenot had called that morning to tell him that the trial for the driver who killed his parents would be starting the following week.

"He called your home but you had already left," she said. He was sure that anyone who came into school that day would know about the trial via Joan's verbal gossip column.

Three hours after leaving Hartford West, Brad arrived at the camp on a bright blue New Hampshire day. He reached into the rear seat and grabbed his gym bag full of swimming paraphernalia and walked around to the front of the cabin. The beach which his father had worked so hard to perfect reflected the warm sun. At least a dozen truckloads of sand had been dumped there. "So all of our grandchildren can build castles," his father had said.

"I hope this is not a mistake," he whispered as his eyes watered.

There had been no hurricanes to stir up the cold water from the bottom and no chilly nights to cool the lake from the top so most of the summer warmth remained. Brad removed his sneaker and sock from his right foot and splashed some water with his toes. On a spontaneous whim, he moved back toward the deck and reached into his bag for his bathing suit. He removed his shorts, pulling his underpants off with them. Both items caught briefly on his left sneaker as he balanced on one foot. For a moment, he was completely naked from the waist down, his T-shirt coming up short of covering anything important. "Josie would be embarrassed and Mom would have laughed," he thought as he struggled to step out of the shorts.

"Oh, shit and be damned," he said, his eyes watering again, this time to the point of leaking down his cheeks. He yanked his bathing suit on and walked into the water to thigh depth before he dove beneath the surface. The tears mingled with the water and vanished into the crystal clear lake.

Late that night, he turned out every light in the house and sat on the deck in the total blackness, looking out at the lights dotting the shoreline across the lake. Any boaters had long since disappeared, and the lake stilled to a calmness that allowed the stars to reflect in it. The presence of his parents, which he had feared would be palpable after the emotion of the morning, was nowhere to be found. Instead, there was only the ever so gentle lapping of the water on the beach. A calmness came over him. It was Tuesday evening; Josie and her friends would not arrive until sometime Friday. This would be a marvelous sanctuary, a place without fear of discovery. As much as he liked his sessions at Brad's grave, there was risk involved.

The image of the two drawers opening at the morgue like filing cabinets containing lifetimes of memories encroached on his consciousness and the quiet of the night.

Then he began thinking about the drunk who had killed his parents.

"That bastard," he said, lifting his face toward the heavens.

Labor Day

> "Believe me, every man had his secret sorrows,
> which the world knows not; and oftentimes we
> call a man cold when he is only sad."
>
> Henry Wadsworth Longfellow

During the pre-Labor Day orientation day, Josie Wallace, Jess Grogan, Rich Lane, and Jack Hopkins sat together at one of the heavy, oblong library tables, entertaining themselves during the tedious meeting by passing notes back and forth. The four veteran teachers mastered the techniques of many of their students, tricks that made it appear that they were serious and involved while passing the time in various other ways. An occasional outburst from their table earned them a glare from the administrators and an envious glance from their colleagues, jealous that they could be having so much fun.

Much of the talk around their table concerned the weekend. Early in the day, Josie, Jess and Rich prevailed on Jack, forcing him to change his mind and join them at the camp. The group spent their post meeting gathering at Pete's finalizing plans and after several beers, Jack and Jess left, leaving Rich and Josie alone. The bar menu at Pete's left much to be desired but they decided to order a sandwich to soak up the beer gurgling in their stomachs.

As they waited for the greasy cheese steak and onion sandwiches to arrive, Josie directed the conversation to an area other than school.

"Could you do me a small favor this weekend, Rich? I don't want to put you in a spot or anything and, if you're uncomfortable, that's fine."

Rich, who generally could not be serious for even a minute, resisted his impulse to throw out a one-liner or some other smart response. "Hey, you're talking to me. Of course, whatever you need."

"This is going to sound strange but could you please just watch Brad for me. If you get him alone, ask him if everything is all right. There's been a lot of stress in our lives, you know, and. . . ." She paused, wondering how far she could go with this before losing control.

"I'll do the best I can, but I'm sure he's OK. He's the most level headed guy I know."

Josie lowered her voice. "You're right, I'm not even sure what I'm talking about here. If you could just pay attention to him for me, that's all."

The waitress arrived with the sandwiches and they ate in the comfortable silence of two good friends who didn't feel the need to fill every moment with conversation. The meal went by quickly and afterward, as they walked to their cars, he assured her again that he would pay close attention to Brad.

"I'm not nearly as perceptive as you, but I'll try." Josie waited for the inevitable joke that always followed anything serious but Rich disappointed her. "I'm looking forward to this trip, Jos. It'll be nice to be around you . . ." he corrected himself, ". . . umm, both of you for a whole weekend."

"You're sweet, Rich, and I appreciate your friendship." She embraced him in a warm hug and kissed him on the cheek. "I'll see you tomorrow morning," she said as she closed the car door. She, too, was anticipating the weekend.

"A long weekend in a cabin on the lake with four handsome men; a girl can't do much better than that," she said as she drove away, a rare occasion of having the final word with Rich Lane.

* * *

Sitting on the deck on Friday evening, the five watched as several boats continued to pull water skiers around the bay until well after dusk, vacationers filling every possible moment of the last weekend of summer. They spent most of the first evening of the weekend reminiscing about their first year at Hampton Village High School, a mixture of hearty laughs combined with poignant moments when the conversation turned to Tyler Spence and Harriet Long. Josie was the first to leave the warmth of the camaraderie, inviting Brad to retire early with her.

"You two haven't seen each other for four days. We'll stay out here for an hour or so and give you time to catch up on things." Rich grinned and winked at Josie, who blushed at his teasing. She waited for Brad to react and was happy to see him stand, ready to follow her inside. His quick-witted retort that came with a wide smile made her even happier.

"Five minutes should be plenty of time, fellas. That'll be about right, don't you think, Jos?" Josie blushed a deeper scarlet and turned away toward the door.

"You guys are incorrigible and always have been." She opened the screen door and called back. "I'll see you in bed, Brad," she purred with affected sensuousness. Her friends on the deck applauded her attempt to keep up with their bantering and laughed as Brad followed his wife into the camp.

"And keep that screaming down, Josie. We don't want to alarm the neighbors." Rich's last salvo was lost on Josie and Brad but not on Jess and Jack as the three men shared a last laugh at the Wallace's expense. Jack got up, went to the cooler, and replenished the beer supply for the three of them. They turned their aluminum lawn chairs toward the lake and watched the lights from the boats gradually diminish until the lake quieted completely. Their discussions for the remainder of the evening revolved around the usual male topics of sports and women, especially the two attractive new language teachers at Hampton Village. As the night passed and the stars' reflection danced across the ripples on the lake, the men stopped talking, admiring the serenity and beauty of the surroundings. Rich was the first to break the mesmerizing effect of the lake by standing and announcing that he was going to bed.

"Brad seems to be doing pretty well, don't you think?" He waited for a response and both grunted positive answers in unison. Only Jack expanded on his grunt with a comment about how fortunate Brad was to have a woman like Josie.

"Yep, he sure is a lucky guy, all right," Rich said.

* * *

The atmosphere of the lake cabin, with its privacy and intrinsic natural-ness, encouraged a range of uninhibited behavior that Brad found some-what stimulating. Josie and he had not taken advantage of the privacy this summer, the crushing loss of his parents blocking out any romantic incli-nations before they had even the slightest chance to blossom. But this evening had been different. As he watched Josie interact with her col-leagues and the memories of the first days of their courtship flooded back, his yearning for her increased with each passing minute. When she invit-ed him inside, he never hesitated, passing up a night of beer guzzling with the boys.

After he took a quick shower, he padded down the short hallway to their bedroom with a towel wrapped around him. He found Josie lying on top of the blanket on the bed, the large beach towel she had used after her shower lightly covering her from the neck down. He closed the door behind him, approached the bed and sat down next to Josie.

"It's been a while," he said huskily. Then he slowly removed her towel as he pulled his loose. With their three friends less than thirty feet away, they made love in the camp for the first time that summer, a pas-sionate and spirited session that lasted well beyond his five-minute joke.

Later, as they lay with Josie's head resting on his bare shoulder, Brad felt the dampness on his skin. "What's the matter, Jos?" he asked.

He pulled his shoulder out from under her and sat halfway up, leaning on his elbow.

"Nothing, it's really nothing. I'm just happy right now, that's all. I need us to be happy." Josie put such strong emphasis on the word need that Brad reached up and flipped the switch on the reading lamp over their heads. The sultry, smoky eyes of passion just a few minutes before became pleading eyes of concern, clouded with worry and begging to be reassured.

"Not to worry; all our bad luck's behind us." Soon afterward, Josie fell into a deep sleep. Brad followed close behind, his relaxed state of mind coming not only from the just ended time with Josie but the wonderful black periods of the last few days at the camp.

* * *

Saturday of the weekend turned slightly cooler as the late summer days so often do in New Hampshire. Josie found no takers for her offer to drive into Wolfeboro, billed as the oldest summer resort in America by signs at each end of the town line. A shopping expedition, even in a quaint New England village, held no magic for the four male friends, and within minutes after Josie left, they were filling John Wallace's boat with all the gear necessary for a day's outing on the lake, including the necessary cooler full of Budweiser.

Brad had taken his father's boat out only once before during the entire summer, more as a test of his own emotional stability than a genuine desire to cruise the lake. Josie offered to go out with him but he asked her to stay behind, unsure how the first ride without his father would go and not wishing to upset her. He failed the test miserably and was back at the dock after a two-minute spin around the bay. The simplest tasks on the boat became unbearable. The new hunter-orange floating key chain that his father had bought just days before he died hung from a nail by the front door and Brad compelled his hand to reach for it and slide it off its hanger. His father surely had been the last one to touch it. Untying the front line brought with it an intense memory of his father showing him how to tie a bowline knot and its vividness dizzied him.

His friends and their constant bantering were such a wonderful distraction that little time was left for self-indulgence. Before he knew it, they were out on the lake and Rich Lane was in the water, calling for the skis to be thrown overboard to him. Brad spent much of the day behind the wheel as Rich, Jack, and Jess skied until their arms drooped and their legs wobbled. It was four in the afternoon when they approached the camp and watched as Josie waved. When she met them at the dock, a jocular angry forefinger made its rounds to each of them.

"I felt like I was on a widow's watch or something, you guys. Didn't you get hungry out there?" Rich held up the cooler, a lone can rolling around in the few melting ice cubes and water at the bottom.

"Who needed lunch?" he said, a slight slur running the words together.

Leaving Jess to help Brad finish securing the boat, Rich and Jack walked back to the cabin with Josie, toting the almost empty cooler and odds and ends of skiing equipment. Once inside, Rich suggested that Jack be the first to shower since the others all agreed that he smelled the worst. Josie just shook her head and laughed. As soon as Rich and Josie were alone, she came closer to him.

"So what do you think so far?"

"It's kind of as I thought, Jos. I mean, he's the same old Brad as far as I can tell. We've just been having a hell of a good time."

"That's really good, Rich. I'm glad to hear you say that. Last night was even like old times." The words escaped as if they had a life of their own. "Oops, oh God, Rich, I'm sorry, I mean. . . ." She hadn't salvaged much of her dignity before Brad and Jess came in from the boat.

Rich looked at Josie, serious for an instant but quickly moving into his clown mode.

"Hey, Brad, Josie's just been filling us in on your performance last night."

"I give up," Josie said and they had yet another laugh at her expense.

*　　*　　*

The boys needed to give the beer from the day's outing a chance to drain through their system, and they convinced Josie to begin the cocktail hour later than usual that night. As they finished their hearty dinner of spaghetti and meatballs, the September sun was just settling into the lake, fash-

122

ioning yet another spectacular display of God's creation. The white puffy clouds spreading across the horizon gradually adopted the blazing red of the sun, turning from a light pink to rose-colored and finally reflecting like crimson rubies. At Josie's suggestion, they adjourned to the deck, carrying whatever was left of their dinner with them. During the ten minutes it took for the brilliant colors to fade into the gray of dusk, the five remained silent, sitting and inhaling the scene.

Jess Grogan broke the silence with a simple "Wow" and the others indicated their assent with a varied combination of murmurs and nods. The show was barely concluded when Josie stood and announced that she was retiring to the bedroom to read, avoiding any sign that she expected Brad to join her. Rich noted the lack of subtlety in her message and could not resist adding his usual jibes.

"Well, Brad, I guess that tells us a lot about last night. I suppose she expects us to clean up after ourselves, too. The kitchen's a mess, Jos, and that's women's work." Josie sent a glaring smile in his direction, not wanting to encourage him any more but appreciating his good humor just the same.

"I'm sure that four of you can manage the cleanup. I just feel like reading a bit. Good night and I'll see you in the morning." She picked up two empty dishes on her way in and the sound of them clinking together carried through the screen door as she set them down.

Later that night, after Jess and Jack trundled off to bed with the complaint that doing all those dishes had tired them out, Brad and Rich sat on the deck watching again as the Saturday night boat traffic finally grew quiet. Another night with no wind gave the lake a chance to calm itself from the craziness of the last holiday weekend of the summer.

"So, how in the hell are you handling all of this. It's got to be tough, even after almost three months." Rich's sympathetic tone made it impossible for Brad not to respond. He hesitated and picked his way through the emotional minefield that an answer would spread out before him.

"I'm really doing pretty well but thanks for asking. It's just such a waste, you know? I mean, two good people like that gone from the planet because of some first class jerk." His voice rose as he finished. The minefield became more treacherous.

"When's the guy go on trial?" Rich asked, working hard to peel away some of the minefield defenses. "I mean, it's got to be pretty straightforward, right? Probably just a question of how many years he gets?"

Brad answered in a clipped monotone. "Funny you should ask. The detective investigating the case left a message yesterday morning that the trial starts at the end of next week. Not exactly as straightforward as it should be either. Plea bargains and all that shit." His answer stopped there.

Rich tried another question.

"Can you be a witness at the sentencing, assuming he's found guilty? The damn guy made you an orphan, if you think about it." Brad peered through the darkness, trying to discern the expression on his friend's face. Rich had pushed the right button.

"He'd better be found guilty," Brad hissed. "Then they should cut the bastard's balls off and lock him up for life." The anger welling up in him made his eyes water. He stood in the middle of the minefield now, searching for a way out. "It's just another shitty, unfair thing about this whole world." He was no longer responding but was lost in delivering a soliloquy to the quiet lake spread out in front of them. He verbalized the images appearing one after another before his eyes, as if reciting a pastor's prayer in a church service. "Brad, Jr., Tyler, my parents, the Kennedys, Martin Luther King, Kent State, my God, it never ends."

Rich's voice intruded and interrupted his train of thought. "Hey, it's OK, man. I didn't mean to upset you. I know it's got to be hard. You've had your share of the crap, that's for sure." His calm voice pulled Brad back from an edge, a place Rich could not identify but found frightening anyway. He would have a report for Josie but at that moment had no idea what he would say.

"Have you ever noticed how people say things like they know how it is or they know what you're going through or they know it's got be hard? I don't mean to be harsh but most of the time they don't have any idea what the hell they're talking about." A symbolic curtain was drawn around the conversation, separating it from anything that preceded it and anything that might come after it. "I didn't mean to get carried away, but being here at this camp is pretty stressful sometimes. So let's just forget it and have a good time for the rest of this weekend, OK?"

A Letter from Harriet

"Nothing can stop the person with the right attitude from pursuing his goal."
Paul S. McElroy

A chilly, dreary day dampened the enthusiasm of both students and staff preparing for the first day of school at Hampton Village High School. After the long weekend on Lake Winnipesaukee, the four friends agreed to meet an extra fifteen minutes early for coffee and donuts to motivate each other for the new start. Josie arrived first and had the coffee prepared by the time the others drifted into the faculty lounge. Jess and Rich came in together, sharing a cheerful good morning. They each gave Josie a welcome to the new year hug and when Jack came in a minute later, the process was repeated, the men shaking hands all around. Then they sat around the table and relived what had been a restful and relaxing weekend. The group munched on their favorite donuts and talked about the first day's schedule, their excitement and nervousness surpassing that of the students just arriving. Long before the first warning tone sounded, the four left the lounge and picked up the volumes of memos, directives, forms, and other mail stuffed into their miniscule mailboxes in the main office. Rich and Josie walked together toward the English Department wing, skimming the mail they balanced in their arms. They hadn't been alone for a minute after the Saturday night that Rich spent with Brad at the cabin. Josie's classroom came first and they paused at the door.

"I guess I need to talk to you sometime about my conversation with Brad last Saturday. If it's OK with you, I'll drop by your room after school today. We could do it at lunch but I think it might be better if we were alone." The disconcerting urgency in Rich's voice was passed off as the first day of school jitters.

127

"Sure. I do appreciate your trying to help." The second warning bell sounded and what had been a murmur emanating from the students waiting in the cafeteria became louder as they were released into the halls. The chilly rain didn't inhibit the exuberance of the students, reuniting with friends in the comfortable environment and safe haven of Hampton Village.

"Well, here we go again. Have a good day, Rich," Josie called as Rich was swallowed by the hordes of excited students pushing their way through the halls. She moved behind her desk, idly sorting her mail into smaller piles, every third or fourth item flipped into an ancient metal trash can, its gray paint cracking and peeling. Her new homeroom students hadn't yet begun to filter in, preferring to stand in the hall delaying the official entrance into the fall semester as long as possible.

"Good morning, Mrs. Wallace," a youthful female voice called just as Josie extracted a letter from the memos and directives stacked on her desk. She looked up and returned the greeting to her first student of the year. She glanced down at the letter again, having just enough time to absorb the return address before a rush of students tumbled through the doorway, clamoring for her attention.

"Harriet Long, Assistant Professor of Education," Josie said under her breath. "Impressive!" She set the letter aside.

"Let's take our seats, ladies and gentlemen," she said a few minutes later and the new year had begun.

*   *   *

The first day of school traditionally closed with a brief faculty meeting designed to address any unexpected crises that may have arisen during the day. The administration, in a rare display of compassion, kept the meeting to just under thirty minutes

"A new record," Rich Lane, self-appointed keeper of such trivia, announced as the meeting ended. "I'll meet you in your room in an hour," he said to Josie.

The weekend on the lake had a refreshing quality to it, at least from her perspective, and Brad's behavior couldn't have been more normal. An unexplained anxiety distracted her lesson plan review for the next day while she waited for Rich's arrival. The letter from Harriet remained open but unread on the upper corner of her desk. She reached for it as Rich tapped lightly on the door but put it down when he entered. The opening paragraph, as far as she had gotten, indicated that it might be more of a sympathy note for Brad. She would take it home for both of them to read.

Rich dragged a student desk from the front row and sat down across from Josie. She tried to read his expression but gave up, waiting for him to begin the conversation.

"You wanted an impression, right, Jos?" When she nodded, he launched into a detailed recounting of his conversation with Brad the previous Saturday night. She didn't interrupt; her attention focused on what he was saying.

"At first, he was the old Brad but when the subject turned toward his parents' deaths, he just seemed like a different person. We've all seen him get pretty riled up before, but I have to tell you that his intensity was a little scary." He paused, noticing Josie's white knuckle grip on the edge of the desk.

"Look, Josie, I don't really think it is anything. It's just Brad, that's all," he said, trying to diffuse the concern in her eyes.

"Do you really think so?" she asked. Rich moved from the desk and came around behind her. He placed one hand on each shoulder and patted her gently.

"Ah, but yes, my dear," he said in his finest Clark Gable imitation. She smiled. "Same old Brad Wallace as always, in my professional opinion."

She reached her right hand across her chest to his left, still resting on her shoulder. With a reciprocal pat followed by a squeeze, she said softly, "Thanks a lot, Rich. You're a special friend, for both of us."

"Not a problem; what are friends for, anyway?" He started for the door and paused at the threshold. "I just know that if I were that drunk driver, I surely wouldn't want to be alone in the same room with him," he said.

Josie's initial relief at his reassurance disintegrated as he closed the door.

*　　*　　*

Brad arrived home first from a day of staff meetings and preparations for the opening of school the next day in Hartford. His first year as department head would be quite strange. At his insistence, the administration allowed him to continue to teach one class, his favorite Current Events, but most of his duties would be supervisory. The countless hours spent in evening preparation time and paper grading would be no more. When Josie walked in the door, he had already completed any schoolwork for the next day and even started dinner, a tuna noodle casserole so simple that "even I can do it," he told Josie.

Josie, after a quick hello and automatic hug, handed him the letter from Harriet. "Catch that title," she said as she went to the bedroom to change. Brad looked at the return address, neatly printed on a label in the corner of the envelope.

HARRIET E. LONG
ASSISTANT PROFESSOR OF EDUCATION
UNVERSITY OF CHICAGO
CHICAGO, ILLINOIS 45029

Brad had read the first page of the letter and was starting on the second as Josie came out of the bedroom, looking quite attractive in her pink lounging pajamas. As she passed by him, he reached out and pulled her down onto his lap. After a minute or two of groping and light kissing, she extracted herself and stood up.

"My gosh, what in the world have you been thinking about today?" she asked, catching her breath.

"Actually, I thought a lot about last Friday night if you must know." He grinned as he handed her the first page of Harriet's letter. "Sounds like Harriet's doing quite well for herself."

Josie sat on the couch and for a few minutes, they both read the letter. The first paragraph consisted entirely of an expression of sympathy for Brad on the death of his parents. The second paragraph was a lengthy apology for abandoning her old friends at Hampton Village, a no excuse sort of repentance and plea for forgiveness. Then she filled them in on the last year.

Harriet's move to Chicago, as she had hoped, turned out to be the best career move she ever made. The first year of her teaching fellowship under the illustrious biologist, Dr. Marcus C. Hightower, accorded the opportunity to see that brilliant scientists do not automatically make good or even adequate teachers. She loved the stimulation of the academic world and sat for hours in the offices of the science department listening to the hypothetical discourse and profound debates among the faculty, including Dr. Hightower. With increasing regularity, as his professional respect for her knowledge grew, her professor permitted her to teach one of his basic classes.

"There was practically a revolution," Harriet wrote. "The under-grads didn't think they (or their parents) were getting their money's worth having a neophyte for an instructor but I showed them. It was like Hampton Village all over again."

The first year of her teaching fellowship ended with a nomination for an assistant professorship in the Education Department. She had earned only a Master's, but even the surprised full professors admitted that she had a unique talent and drive. Better to keep her at the University of Chicago than allow her to take her talents elsewhere.

"Once I get my doctorate, I'll be one of those movers and shakers that people come from all over to hear," she said. As Josie read the letter, she could visualize Harriet's face and expressions as clearly as if she were in the room with them.

Much of the professional information lay hidden between the lines of Harriet's modest description but no decoding was required when Josie turned to the second page. Harriet had met a wonderful man, a doctoral candidate in the computer science department, and they were planning a wedding for the following spring at Harriet's home church in Vermont. Invitations would be forthcoming in the spring and her fervent hope was that the magnificent five would be able to attend. Before the evening was over, Josie, remembering the sadness when Harriet left Hampton Village, answered the letter, happy to have her old friend back in her life.

A Nail of a Different Sort

"People seem not to see that their opinion of the world is also a confession of character."

Ralph Waldo Emerson

"Unless something weird happens, the sentencing will be next Tuesday at 3:00 p.m. When this stuff happens, we're relieved of any responsibility to be present so I'm pretty sure that I won't be there. I'm hoping he'll get what he deserves but I'm not going to bet on it." The disappointment was evident in Parker's voice.

Brad could not believe what he was hearing. "What'll he get, do you think?" His keen interest lay beneath a facade of placidity as though his stake in the case no longer existed.

"I'll predict that Judge Walker is going to be bound by similar cases that've come before. It's Snyder's first offense and people are forgiving of someone having a few drinks and driving. Most people can relate, you know? I think he'll get loss of license for a year, probation for a couple more and a ninety-day jail sentence, all of it suspended. Now, aren't you sorry you asked?" Havenot, curious, asked if Brad would be there.

"I doubt it, Detective; I mean, what's the point? My folks are dead. Nothing's bringing them back, especially not bitterness and hatred, so I guess I'll just let justice prevail."

"Hell of a good attitude, Mr. Wallace. Surprising, too. Good luck." Then he hung up.

Brad drew a red felt tip marker from the conglomeration of writing utensils stuffed into the pencil holder on his desk. A large appointment calendar lay open on his desk, and he circled the Tuesday date with bold strokes until the red bled through to the next page.

133

*   *   *

Robert J. Snyder considered himself a victim. The system failed him so often in the past that he saw no reason to think anything would be different this time. When the bailiff opened the side door leading to the judge's chambers, he jumped, startled by the loud creak coming from the hinges of the huge door.

"All rise." His lawyer nudged him twice before he finally stood, his anger at the formality of the entire process clearly etched on his face. Nate Lamar, an overweight buffoon who doubtless would have lost his case anyway, stood beside him, breathing heavily from the exertion of simply rising from his chair. The plea bargain was not Robert's idea but after watching Nate present his opening arguments, he decided that there really had not been a choice. Before the second day of the trial started, the counselor persuaded him without too much difficulty to plead guilty to two counts of vehicular manslaughter, the lesser of any number of other evils. Under the best of circumstances, he might receive a short jail term, suspended, and a long probationary period. It would be a combination of luck and the judge's opinion, neither of which were in his control. Luck was a commodity sadly lacking in Robert's life to this point, and the judge's opinion was often a whim of mood and attitude. To his credit, Nate had coached his client carefully in exactly what to say when the judge asked him to confirm his change of plea after the recess the day before. Robert performed his act admirably, mixing just the right amount of remorse and sincerity with a small dose of humility, promising that given a chance, he could become a model citizen.

Judge Robert F. Walker, known for his calm demeanor on the bench, stared icily at Robert, knowing that precedence in cases like this one established firm guidelines for sentencing. As a finale to his act, Robert dropped his head and allowed his shoulders to sag. The vehemence of the judge's next pronouncement surprised everyone in the courtroom.

"We will take a ten minute recess," he bellowed. "I will see the defendant and counsel in my chambers immediately." He stood and was out of the courtroom before the bailiff finished his "All rise" command, his black robe flowing behind him.

The few spectators sat down again as the need to stand disappeared behind the side door. Brad slumped unnoticed in the last row, absorbing the courtroom environment. The building had been built toward the end of the nineteenth century. Everything in the room was either stark white or a sharply contrasting dark mahogany. The highly polished wood railing that separated the spectators from the participants in the drama reflected the light from the tall windows lining both sides of the room like a concave mirror. Discolored patches of white and a few specks of flaking paint around the windows and in the corners indicated the battle that the maintenance crews likely had in keeping the old plaster walls covered. The imposing judge's bench rose like an impregnable fortress at the front of the room, its almost black wood finish adding to the illusion of invulnerability. The announcement from the bailiff interrupted Brad's observations.

"All rise," the bailiff declared once again. Brad noted that the ten-minute recess had stretched into fifteen. Judge Walker strode to the bench and climbed the three steps leading up to his perch above the courtroom. Like a preacher in a pulpit, he was raised physically and, more importantly, symbolically above everyone in the room.

In keeping with ritual, the bailiff announced permission for all to take their seats but his pronouncement came too late for most of those in the room who were seated already, their reaction timed perfectly with the judge. Brad assumed his innocuous invisibility in the back row of benches. The other spectators seemed oblivious to his presence. As promised, Detective Havenot had not appeared for the sentencing.

"The defendant will rise." From Brad's perspective, Judge Walker's head and shoulders looked like part of the bench itself.

"In the case of the State of Connecticut versus Robert J. Snyder, the court rules that his plea of two counts of vehicular manslaughter is hereby accepted." In a public reprimand, Judge Walker summarized what had taken place in his chambers. "Mr. Snyder has been informed that I consider his actions criminal and without excuse or reason. He is now publicly admonished and warned that this finding is placed on file with law enforcement. It is further noted that any future arrest for any reason, whether a vehicular infraction or so much as a littering misdemeanor, will result in the most serious consequences."

The tone of the judge's remarks bore an amazing resemblance to many high school disciplinarian's lectures Brad had heard over the years. He recognized the recalcitrant student's defiant body language from behind, the straightening of the shoulders and jutting of the jaw obvious even from the back row. Robert J. Snyder was playing the system. He didn't even need to hear the rest of Judge Walker's spiel.

"You are sentenced to ninety days in the county jail, seventy five days suspended. The fifteen days may be served on weekends, said time to be completed within six months. Additionally, your driving privileges are suspended for one year, commencing as soon as official notification is received from the Connecticut Department of Motor Vehicles. A fine of one thousand dollars is assessed and shall be paid before you leave today." Judge Walker, with his most dramatic flair, pounded his gavel twice.

"Court is adjourned."

Brad lingered for the obscene spectacle of Nate Lamar and Robert Snyder congratulating each other at the front of the courtroom. A few minutes later, he was sitting in his car waiting for his parents' killer to come out of the building.

*　*　*

For Snyder, the deadly accident had at least one positive outcome. The insurance policy on his Chevrolet Impala contained no hidden clauses that could allow the company to renege on replacing the car. The dark blue replacement, the same model but a year older, had much less mileage in it. Brad watched as Snyder shook hands with his lawyer on the courthouse steps and walked toward his car. His path brought him past the front of Brad's car, the glaring sun backlighting him so that his face showed no features. He continued down the row and then weaved in and out of several rows to get to his car. Brad waited for Snyder's door to close before he started his car and slowly pulled ahead. He looked back over his left shoulder and saw the Impala start toward the exit. With an unobtrusive maneuver, Brad turned and followed a short distance behind, memorizing the five-digit number on the license plate.

Covington County sprawled over sixty square miles; the rural countryside was dotted with a few large farms and a number of housing sub-divisions but primarily was nothing but forest and a few small towns like Hampton Village. The automobile commute to Hartford, the insurance capital of the world, took less than an hour from most locations and a visionary, well-developed commuter rail system served a large population west of the city. Many business executives combined the luxury of country living with the lucrative city job market and the county was growing at an astounding rate.

Bob Snyder's home was less than a twenty-minute ride from the courthouse. The town of Covington, large by county standards but quaint and quiet to urban visitors to the Berkshire's, disappeared in the rear view mirror as Bob's Impala sped out of town on County Road. Brad initially followed directly behind but once out of town, he pulled over and let two cars pass, using them as a buffer. County Road, one of the few straight roads in the western part of the state, allowed Brad to stay a good half-mile behind and still follow the progress of the blue Chevy. One of the cars between them turned off and he closed the distance. Snyder's left turn signal came on and Brad slowed, waiting for him to complete his turn into a small development of one story pre-fabricated ranch houses.

As Brad made the turn, a dilapidated sign to his right announced his entrance into Waterford West, "The Affordable Alternative." The paint on the sign was faded and peeling, it's shabby appearance made more evident by the fact that it couldn't be that old. Snyder's car was no longer in sight. The small houses on either side of the main road into the project were separated by no more than ten feet, so close that the occupants had to hear their neighbors' toilet flushing. Each seemed to be surrounded by a variety of rusting swing sets, bicycles with flat tires and broken training wheels, and plastic toys, their bright colors faded by exposure to the elements.

"Alternative to what?" Brad muttered, surveying the neighborhood.

A series of cul de sacs branched off of Pineland Road, the main street without a single pine tree in sight. A quick look down each of these side streets revealed nothing, only reminding Brad of a satirical novelty song about this very type of housing development. "Little boxes on a hillside, little boxes full of ticky-tacky," he said quietly. Pineland Road ended in its own cul de sac and as he approached the end of the road, he saw the blue Chevy. A hasty parking job left the tail end of the car overflowing into the middle of the turn around and he slowed to a crawl to squeeze past it. The motor was still chugging, puffing small clouds of carbon monoxide into the air. The Snyder household lacked the ticky-tacky of most of the neighbors and the house actually appeared well maintained. The drive-by appeared nonchalant as he glanced around at the other houses as though looking for a particular one, but he noted the gold reflective numerals on the Snyder house.

"202 Pineland Road," he said, committing the address to memory. He retraced his route toward the main road and parked in front of an unoccupied house, a realtor's sign planted amidst the tall grass and weeds comprising the front lawn and waited to see where Robert might be headed next. He reached across the seat, grabbed his soft leather briefcase and rested it on the steering wheel. Unsnapping the flap, he reached his hand in as though searching for something, watching his mirror for any sign of movement from the Snyder household. Soon after, Snyder bounded out of his house and jumped into his car. The enthusiasm was insulting. Brad accepted it as a sign that he was gleefully putting the trial behind him and getting on with this life while his parents lay rotting in their graves. As soon as the Chevy passed him, he put aside the briefcase and followed Snyder down Pineland Road to the intersection.

Brad again allowed several cars to come between his car and Snyder's as they turned left out of the development. Two miles from the intersection, the right blinker on the Impala started to flash. Brad absorbed the whole scene in a fraction of a second. Snyder's car turned into a small mini-mall with several stores, bookended by a Stop and Shop at one end and the Sunset Tavern at the other. He slowed further and by the time he was passing the mall, Snyder was out of the car and walking toward the Sunset Tavern. Parker Havenot mentioned the Sunset Tavern in one of their conversations and a sickening realization settled into the pit of Brad's stomach. The bar he was passing was the very place that had sent Snyder out on the road several months before in such an inebriated state that he had no idea where he even was. The location came clearer to Brad. The deadly intersection with Route 2 lay three miles to the north of the Sunset Tavern, in the opposite direction from Snyder's house. Had Bob Snyder turned in the direction of his house, the accident would never have occurred.

"That bastard, going into that place now, today. GOD DAMN HIM!" He slammed his right fist on the steering wheel. As he drove by slowly, his passenger side mirror reflected Snyder's entrance into the tavern. He turned into the parking lot and faced his car toward the establishment that began the chain of events he still could not bear to think about. After staring at the marquee over the door for several minutes, he drove the three miles to the intersection. Approaching the stop sign, he imagined how it must have been on that afternoon. At moments such as these, it is impossible to avoid wondering about fate or destiny or whatever one would like to call it. He inserted the catalog of "what if" and "if only" on the scene. What if his parents had been two seconds later; what if Snyder had turned toward home; if only John Wallace had driven just a bit slower or a bit faster.

He stopped at the intersection, unable to comprehend how Snyder could possibly have driven through the stop sign at such a high rate of speed. For a few seconds he conjured up the accident scene in his mind and replayed it over several times. The one image that kept coming up, the one he could not let go, was of his mother in the last second of her life. He could see her face clearly, looking to her right as Snyder's Impala bore down on their car. Whatever does one think about in that final second of consciousness? In an effort to avoid slipping over a desperate edge of some sort, Brad forced the image of Sandra Wallace's last conscious second on this earth to evolve into the photograph he had on the mantelpiece at home, a close up showing her sparkling green eyes and wide, vivacious smile. The pleasant picture brought a slight grin to his face but a loud blast of a truck horn erased it in a second, startling him into a quick glance in the rear view mirror. He had been sitting there for at least a full minute. Route 2 was clear to cross but he needed a little more time. Winding the window down as he inched his car over to the side of the road, he extended his left arm and motioned the driver in the pickup to pull around him. The truck stopped exactly opposite him and the driver leaned over the seat and shouted through the closed passenger window.

"Are you OK, Mister?" The question, intended to be a friendly inquiry into the welfare of a fellow traveler, sounded more as though the youthful truck driver had grave doubts about Brad's sanity. Brad nodded and waved, sending the truck hurtling across the highway, the driver shaking his head in frustration. With no other cars in sight, he backed his car until it was fully on the shoulder of the road, stopped and climbed out. He walked into the center of the intersection, standing where he thought the crash probably occurred. An eerie sense of time and place settled over him. Josie and he often discussed *The Time Machine,* an H. G. Wells novel that was a favorite unit in her English class. The fascinating story described a time machine that stayed in one place but carried its traveler forward and backward in time at that very spot. Here he stood, perhaps at the exact place of his parents' death just months before. The confounding philosophical complexities of time travel whirled through his head, as he remained mesmerized by his surroundings.

"What if there were such a machine?" The concrete beneath his feet vibrated with the rumble of a heavy vehicle approaching, breaking the spell and sending him scurrying back to the safety of the gravel shoulder. He stood there as a logging truck, likely illegally overweight with its cargo of oak logs teetering above the sidebars, thundered past. The breeze created blew dust and dirt into his face, forcing him to turn away. When the swirling debris settled, he started for his car, taking one last look back at the intersection. From this different angle, he noticed faint tire marks, barely visible but becoming clearer as he focused on them.

The configuration of the black smudges was unmistakable, as though whatever vehicle they had come from had been pushed sideways across the highway. The fading black lines had been made by his parents' car after Snyder's Impala smashed into them. He stood there staring across the intersection to where the smudges disappeared from view. Another image, equally as compelling to him, became superimposed over the tire tracks to oblivion. He continued to gaze, fascinated as the black streaks from the wheels of the stretcher carrying Josie across his kitchen floor melded into the marks etched onto the concrete of Route 2. Several cars sped by in quick succession, shattering his fascination with the scene and dispersing the images in a flurry of noise, flying dirt and highway litter.

Brad returned to his car, slid behind the wheel but made no effort to move. His legs shook as surely as if he had narrowly avoided a head-on collision himself. When he finally regained sufficient composure to start the car, he made a U-turn and retraced his route down County Road, driving slowly past the Sunset Tavern. The sight of the Chevy Impala still in the parking lot caused him to tremble slightly, his anger morphing into a controlled rage. He glared at the car as though it had assumed the persona of its owner. Two miles later, he turned into Pineland Road and drove past the Snyder house once more, this time at a quicker pace, then he headed for the cemetery and Brad, Jr.

*　*　*

There really was no choice; something had to be done about this horrible malfunction of the wheels of justice; they were not grinding slowly and certainly not exceedingly fine. From his perspective, they had come off the cart. The usual soliloquy delivered to his son at the gravesite clearly defined his expectations. Robert J. Snyder needed to be taught a little humility.

*   *   *

The pattern was easy to analyze. Several weeks of intermittent observation on his way home from Hartford led Brad to an unmistakable conclusion. Robert Snyder broke the law every single day. His blue Chevy Impala continued to be parked at the Sunset Tavern every workday afternoon. Apparently he put little faith in the ability of the Covington County Sheriff's Department to patrol the particular two mile stretch of County Road, and he regularly drove straight from his house to the tavern without his license shortly after his coworker at Owens dropped him off.

Brad waited for the perfect opportunity to mete out his own brand of justice. With the worrisome but pleasurable flush of adolescent excitement, he left school in Hartford on the first Wednesday after Daylight Savings Time expired, driving a route that would take him west on Route 2. At the intersection which by now was all too familiar, he turned left and proceeded to a planned rendezvous with Bob Snyder's blue Chevy.

At four o'clock in the afternoon, the sun had already dropped just below the treetops. Long shadows from the utility poles surrounding the parking lot leaned on the front of the Sunset Tavern. Brad turned in and cruised slowly around the lot. On his second circuit, he pulled into a space on the right side of Bob Snyder's car, so close that his door opened only enough for him to squeeze out. He reached in his pocket for the small tool he had since his childhood bike riding days. A few turns and the valve popped out, the air rushing from the tire with a loud whoosh. He stuffed both the tool and the valve into his pocket and squeezed back into his car just as another vehicle moved through the lot. The driver, intent on finding a parking space, didn't notice him at all. He waited and watched as a tall, attractive woman hurried from her car and disappeared into the tavern.

Confident that the first part of his plan had worked, Brad drove to the far end of the mall, parking as close as possible to the telephone booth near the Stop and Shop. Snyder was certain to be fuzzyheaded enough to not notice a flat on his right rear tire until he was well underway. The blue

Impala was clearly visible from his vantage point; and he waited for the next scene to unfold.

A full hour later, well after the sun had set and the parking area had succumbed to being a poorly lit, shadowy environment, Bob Snyder came weaving out of the Sunset Tavern carrying a brown paper bag. As soon as Brad saw him, he got out of his car and walked straight toward the phone booth, digging through his pocket for a small piece of paper that contained the number of the sheriff's department. He watched as the headlights came on in Snyder's car and the car left the driveway, the rear end visibly wobbling. When he was sure that the car was headed for home, he dialed the number.

"Covington County Sheriff's Department, Deputy Wilkins speaking." Brad attempted to disguise his voice even though his old friend, Detective Havenot, didn't answer.

"I just passed a guy with a flat on County Road; he looks like he might need some help. He's in a pretty dangerous spot, I think." Brad, in a succinct monotone, described the location and explained why he could not help himself, his wife "being ill" and needing him at home.

Deputy Wilkins thanked him profusely, congratulated him on being such a good citizen, and assured him that they would send a car right away. Brad hung up before any more questions came his way. He left the phone booth, looking around as if expecting to see someone who had guessed what he was doing. A few people trundled out of the Stop and Shop but none paid any attention. He crossed the lot to his car and waited long enough to give the police a chance to respond to his attempt to earn a Good Samaritan award. He left the parking lot and not a quarter of a mile ahead, the flashing blue lights of a sheriff's cruiser on his side of the road brightened his spirits. The police car straddled the white line separating the pavement from the dirt shoulder, forming a protective shield from oncoming traffic. He slowed as he passed an agitated Snyder standing by his car, waving his arms as though trying to ward off a cloud of vicious mosquitoes. The right rear of his car tilted crazily and as Brad went by, he could see that Bob hadn't realized he had a flat tire until he had run it off the rim.

"Justice is served," he said quietly as he continued past the scene.

* * *

After a quick visit to the cemetery to bring Brad Jr. up to date, he went home, arriving before Josie even with the lateness of the hour. Disappointed in coming home to an empty house, he mixed a double martini and sat down to wait for her. "Wish some of my staff would work half as hard as she does," he murmured into his glass before taking the first sip.

The phone rang just as Josie came through the door and she raced to answer it, beating Brad's dash handily. She smiled at him and softened her lips before picking up the receiver. By the fourth ring, she had greeted him with a warm kiss, the greeting filled with warmth and sincerity.

"More where that came from," she said as she answered.

"Wallace residence, this is Josie." Her face tightened then relaxed again. "You gave me a scare, Detective," she said, her voice squeaking into a higher octave. "It's for you," she said to him. "I'll go start dinner unless you've made it already."

Brad took the phone nervously, the events of the afternoon plot still fresh in his mind. "Hello," he said quietly.

Detective Havenot, not given to boisterous demonstrations, answered in a loud voice that took Brad by surprise.

"Well, your boy will be doing his ninety days after all, Mr. Wallace. DWI, violation of probation, driving after license revocation . . .what a dumb ass, if you'll pardon the French."

"What the hell, I mean, when did all this happen?" Brad asked, knowing the answer before Havenot responded.

"Pretty weird, really. We got a call to assist a guy with a flat tire over on County Road and when the deputy arrived, there was Snyder, two sheets to the wind. He got real upset when he was asked for his license and registration, and it didn't take long for us to check him out." The satisfaction in Parker Havenot's voice was obvious. Bob Snyder was getting what he deserved. "The deputy contacted me from the car while he drove to the county jail. He thought I'd be interested and I thought the same about you."

Havenot finished his story with his visit with Robert Snyder in his holding cell and the subsequent look at the car.

"Snyder usually was a pretty mellow drunk as I recall but not tonight. He wasn't in the most pleasant of moods, ranting and raving about the new tire that went flat. I calmed him down by promising that I would check into that." A shot of nervousness fluttered through Brad's stomach. "An awful lot of coincidence here but probably just that," he continued. "You know, the flat, the call, his drinking. Anyway, his tire went flat because the valve was missing."

The detective's words tumbled out in stream-of-consciousness fashion. "Unusual but not impossible. He drove for quite a distance and probably blew the stupid thing out somehow. Hey, I'm really rambling. You don't need to know all of this. I just thought you might be happy to know that Mr. Snyder is in a lot of trouble. You had such a great attitude but maybe this all makes things seem just a trifle fairer?" He raised his voice as he ended his monologue, as though some response was expected.

"Yeah, it sure does. I really do appreciate the call, Detective." Brad waited, wondering if Havenot had more that he wanted to say.

"Not a problem; I'll keep you informed if anything new develops. Sure was strange about how he got that flat, though. Good night, Mr. Wallace. Oh, by the way, you didn't by any chance play any golf today, did you?" Parker Havenot chuckled before closing the conversation for good. "Just kidding. Have a good evening." The phone clicked in Brad's ear as another wave of nervousness churned through his stomach.

Detective Parker Havenot

"Failure to hit the bullseye is never
the fault of the target."

Gilbert Arland

Parker Havenot drove to the Covington County Court House wondering what frame of mind Robert Snyder might be in as he faced Judge Walker. Surely, he would be somewhat chastened after a night of drying out in jail. The hearing was scheduled for 9:30, a full half-hour before the regularly scheduled docket began, and Havenot guessed that it wouldn't last much beyond 9:35 if Judge Walker's normal pattern prevailed. The judge's renowned reputation for treating repeat offenders with little patience and clear disdain would have Parker heading back to the sheriff's office in short order. He wasn't sure exactly why he chose to attend the hearing. The sentence imposed for violating probation was automatic, and his presence in the courtroom would have no bearing on the case whatsoever. As he walked toward the imposing courthouse with its two story white pillars flanking an enormous fresco of Justice above the double doors, the question of why he was here was answered as clearly as if someone had screamed in his ear.

"So simple and yet so profound," he whispered under his breath. "So profound yet so corny. I'm just a damned police office who needs to see justice done." He looked around but the few people in the area appeared not to notice that he was talking to himself. He entered the foyer outside of the courtroom by way of a side entrance, unnecessarily flashing his badge to the guard at the door. Every policeman in the county knew Detective Parker Havenot.

* * *

With Hartford a painless commute, just forty minutes to the east,

Covington County experienced one of the first true real estate booms of the decade during the early sixties. Most of the towns comprising the sprawling county fit nicely into the description of "bedroom community," priding themselves on visionary expansion and long range planning. Town fathers scurried to incorporate zoning regulations into town ordinances, an effort previously anathema to native farmers. Now the same farmers counted their riches as housing developments sprouted as readily as their corn crop used to on the farm. The expansion created the inevitable demand for additional government services, especially police protection for the local citizenry. Few of the small towns could afford their own police departments, but enough of them banded together into a consortium to apply the necessary political pressure on the county commissioners to expand the county sheriff's department. At times, even the commissioners themselves were unable to explain exactly what the county taxes accomplished, and increasing the sheriff's personnel had an attractive, tangible quality about it. After several months of wrangling between the sheriff and the politicos over how best to accommodate the expansion, a compromise was reached. The commissioners, anxious to allay the fears of former city dwellers moving to the country, argued that one of the three new deputy positions to be added to the force should be a fully trained investigative detective. The sheriff, at first intimidated by the idea of having such a knowledgeable person working under him, relented. A nationwide search unearthed three viable candidates who were willing to come to rural Connecticut. Parker Havenot was one of them.

The most cursory scan of the three resumes revealed that Havenot should be the choice. His training and experience in the field was extensive and his references corroborated his ability. The harshest questioning during his interview came from the deputy representing the lower echelons of the department, most of whom could not understand his willingness to sacrifice a ranking detective's position on the Philadelphia Police Department to come to Covington County for a reduction in pay and in status.

Parker Havenot was more than ready to escape from the city. Careers in law enforcement demanded a unique type of individual, especially in the city, and marrying a police officer required an equally unique kind of woman. Hannah Havenot was an incomparable woman but in ways unsuited to support Parker's career.

For two years following his graduation from Temple University in 1958, Parker pursued Hannah Rancourt. He first met her at an alumni reception following a crushing defeat of Temple by the visiting Delaware Blue Hens. She had attended the university for two years before tiring of the deadly courses in education required to graduate as a teacher. She loved to say that she left Temple for "a real job," opting to work as a secretary for a small architectural firm in Philadelphia. An extremely attractive blonde, Hannah had left a trail of broken hearts behind when Parker Havenot arrived in her life. He exuded self-confidence and had a borderline fanatical belief in what he did. Like most women, she found him deceptively handsome, with the kind of good looks that become more apparent with each meeting.

One of their first dates was a trip into Center City to see *On the Beach,* a film based on the novel about nuclear war. Several times, she caught him wiping the tears from his cheeks as one after another of the characters came down with radiation sickness. His refreshing sentimentality and genuine compassion impressed her. They were attributes she had not found in most other men. The graduate courses in criminal justice that Parker loved led to many fascinating discussions with Hannah about the noble profession of lawyer versus the life of a criminal investigator. His persuasiveness finally convinced her that his choice of police academy over law school was all right with her. After all, Parker reasoned, there are far fewer men capable of directing a wide-ranging criminal investigation than there are lawyers able to thwart justice at every turn. His logic won Hannah over and in the summer of 1960, they were married.

Within two years, Parker felt things beginning to fall apart. His intuition and competence as an investigator led his chief to automatically funnel most of the difficult cases in his direction, leading to an ever-increasing workload. One warm, late summer night, they sat at each end of the sofa in their still sparsely furnished apartment watching a rerun of an old Dick Van Dyke show on a small television screen embedded in a large RCA console. The loud ring of the telephone on the end table next to Parker startled him. As he reached for the receiver, he felt Hannah's eyes on him. He turned toward her and saw a look that was all at once pleading, pathetic, angry, and defiant.

"Havenot here," he answered. He turned away from Hannah, hunching his shoulders as if to protect the phone from her cold, glaring stare.

"Yeah, but give me a few minutes first, OK?" For the third night in succession, he was being called out in response to a possible homicide.

Hannah recognized the signs and stood up.

"No, Parker. I don't want you to go again," she said with no indication she was ready to compromise. The expectations at the beginning of a marriage often conflict with the eventual realities, and Hannah saw her expectations disintegrating with each day. She wasn't even sure she remembered what they had been, even after just two years.

"Must be a damn full moon this week, or something, Hannah. You know I don't have a choice right now. We'll have to talk about it when I get home." The flickering light of the television reflected the excitement for his work in his eyes; the sparkle tempered this time by what was possibly a watershed moment in their relationship. Without another word, Hannah went down the hall to the bathroom and closed the door behind her with an unmistakable "Don't bother me" finality.

For months after the incident, Parker kept resurrecting the subject of children, often a despairing attempt to stabilize a shaky marriage. Hannah, initially excited about the prospect, cooled to the idea quickly and the marriage remained childless. Whenever the subject was broached, she skirted the issue as though marking time until making a permanent decision of some sort. The disenchantment increased in direct proportion to the constant and, to her, unreasonable demands of Parker's position. Her boring secretarial job and the evenings spent alone eventually combined to drain whatever interest she had in preserving her marriage. Finally, out of desperation, she decided to return to school and finish the requirements for a teaching certificate.

"If you're going to be out gallivanting around the city all night, I might as well do something myself," she said. Parker, the astute, observant police detective, saw through the charade several months later when it became clear that his Hannah really wasn't his Hannah at all, perhaps never had been.

Four years after it began, the marriage was over, a victim of the problematic relationship so common in law enforcement. When she finally made it official, announcing that that she was finished with him, she said it in just that way, as though throwing away an old, unwanted piece of furniture. The finality of the divorce bought about an intensifying dedication to his job as if allowing it to consume him might lessen the pain. Disillusioned and alone, his efforts were fruitless. Everything about the city reminded him of his failed marriage. When the position available notice in Covington County came across the police information wire, he never hesitated, forwarding his resume the very next day.

*   *   *

Parker looked around the courtroom, expecting that Brad Wallace might be present for this occasion. Nate Lamar already sat at the defendants' table, fidgeting in his seat and staring at a blank legal pad in front of him. Parker chose to lean against the back wall instead of sitting. An ornate antique clock ticked quietly on the wall above his head and he took a step away from the wall to confirm the time. It matched his watch to the minute and he resumed his position against the wall. If Wallace happened to come in, he would join him but unless he came within the next ten minutes, he likely would miss the whole event. The side door that opened onto the hallway leading to the jail creaked open and two guards entered with Robert Snyder between them. For reasons that Parker could not fathom, he remained dressed in the street clothes from the night before, looking as ragged as a castaway after days on some lonely island. The smaller of the guards escorted him to the table and he plopped down wordlessly in a chair next to his lawyer. Observing them from behind, Parker thought they could be complete strangers to each other if he didn't know better.

"All rise." The familiar command echoed through the nearly empty courtroom. Judge Walker processed in with all the ceremony of a church choir on a Sunday morning and assumed his place on the bench.

"You may be seated," the bailiff announced, his last word cut off by the judge's booming voice.

"Don't bother being seated, Mr. Lamar and Mr. Snyder. Please approach the bench." His tone was not lost on Nate Lamar, whose subtle body movements distanced him ever so slightly from his client, a comportment noted by the ever-alert detective at the rear of the room. It was as though drawing away an extra inch or two would ease his increasing embarrassment at being associated with Bob Snyder. After a whispered sidebar conference which lasted no more than one minute, lawyer and client returned to their positions behind their table. Snyder started to sit down but Nate grabbed him rudely by the arm, reversing his movement until he was standing straight again. The sidebar apparently had established some specific guidelines for Lamar to follow and he performed his duty in perfunctory fashion.

"Have you anything to present here, Counselor?" Judge Walker might as well have framed the question in the form of a statement, something like "I assume you have nothing to present or to say, Counselor."

"If it please the court, Mr. Snyder would request that his probationary status be kept in place as his actions of last night were just an error in judgement, an error which he admits and regrets. He likely will lose his job and suffer other consequences which would outweigh his offense." Nate Lamar was looking at the door as he finished speaking and Parker would have sworn that one foot already was pointing in that direction.

"Thank you for your representation, Mr. Lamar. This court finds that the defendant, Robert J Snyder, did willfully disregard the terms of his probation and is hereby remanded to the Covington County Jail to serve a full ninety day sentence as indicated by his previous conviction. This court is adjourned." Judge Walker stood, again leaving the courtroom before the bailiff could complete his ritual.

Parker watched as Nate Lamar picked up his blank legal pad and stuffed it into a worn leather briefcase that looked as if it had never been new. He turned his back to his client as the larger of the two guards ushered the prisoner out of the room. Havenot cast an amused roll of the eyes to Nate Lamar as the lawyer huffed his way past him. He waited for everyone to clear the room then looked at his watch.

"Seven minutes, give or take a few seconds; not too bad but longer than I thought," he said to the guard at the door. They shared a brief snicker, both happy to see someone receive at least a portion of what they deserved for a change.

Parker left the courthouse with full intentions of returning to his office immediately but instead decided on a whim to spend an hour or so touring the county. A call to the dispatcher cleared his way. There were a few possible leads on minor robberies and assaults but nothing that couldn't wait for his return. The day was fast becoming one of those bonus days in late fall, a day where the temperature soars into the sixties and the bright sun beckons everyone to seize the moment before winter casts its grayness over everything.

First, a visit to Robert Snyder was in order. He would be safely back in his cell by now, hopefully wearing something other than the same clothes he had worn all night. Now that he had a legitimate jail sentence, he should be issued some regulation prison garb. The jail had its own parking lot but there was no point in moving his car. He walked the short distance to the jail and in minutes was looking down at a crestfallen Snyder sitting on the prison bunk, staring across the cell at the pitted blank wall opposite him.

"So, you've got a private room, I see," he said but Snyder wasn't in the mood for anything approaching light-hearted.

"What can I do for you, Detective? Nice of you to visit but, you know, I'm really busy here." The words, amusing on the surface, were encased in bitter sarcasm.

"Not much and I won't stay long, trust me. I was just curious about that tire." Parker's interest sparked a curious response from Snyder.

"There is no way I should've had a God damned flat tire. Those tires were like new," he said adamantly. He'd done some thinking about the tire.

"The tire was missing its valve. Probably lost by your driving on it, right?" From Snyder's reaction, this was the first time he heard about the valve.

"No shit. That's pretty hard to believe. How do you know all of this? I mean, Christ, don't you guys have anything better to do?" Fifteen minutes had passed since Bob Snyder found out that he would be spending the next ninety days in jail, and the detective could see that the reality hadn't quite made it to his rational consciousness.

"All I had was a piece of shit luck. I've had plenty before and probably plenty again." Snyder faltered a bit. "The fucking valve. Those things don't just come out; you've got to screw them out."

Parker suddenly didn't want to be with him anymore. "One last thing if you don't mind."

Snyder chuckled. "If I don't mind! You got the floor, man. What else can I tell ya?"

"Is there any way the tire might have been flat before you ever left the Sunset lot?"

"The car handled funny but they always do when you've got a few drinks under your belt. Truth? I don't have no idea and I don't really care."

Parker motioned for the cell to be opened and left without another word.

"What an absolute jerk," he said as he and the guard reached the exit door. They shook hands and Parker thanked him for his trouble.

The visit with Snyder used up some of his touring time but he still wanted to take advantage of the day and the time to himself in the car to think. He turned the black unmarked cruiser onto County Road and drove toward the scene of the Wallace accident and an interview with the bartender at the Sunset Tavern.

Euphoria

"It is better to suffer wrong than to do it."
Samuel Johnson

Parker had never been inside Hampton Village High School. He timed his surprise visit to coincide with the afternoon dismissal and made every effort to be inconspicuous, entering through a side door as the students were piling out toward their busses. The ALL VISITORS MUST REPORT TO THE OFFICE sign was partially torn away, enough of an excuse to pretend he didn't see it. He found his way to Josie Wallace's classroom by asking directions from a knot of male students crowded around a bulletin board outside the gymnasium. They looked at him with interest at first but that quickly waned as they went back to scanning the initial cut list from the basketball tryouts. No wonder some of the boys looked so dejected.

He found his way to Room 102 and poked his head in.

Josie bustled around her classroom pushing and pulling the one-piece desk-chair combinations into the U shaped configuration she planned to use the next day. She blanched when she looked up and saw Parker standing inside the door.

"Everything's fine, Mrs. Wallace. Really." His quiet voice and demeanor calmed her and she relaxed.

"Sorry, Detective, you just gave me a start, that's all. Can I help you with something?" Concern overrode her apparent calm.

"I thought you and your husband would like to know that Robert Snyder is in jail. It came out just as I thought it would when I spoke with Mr. Wallace last night. He's serving the full ninety days and won't be driving for a long time." He looked at Josie, who had stopped moving her furniture and come to the front of the room. A confused expression remained locked on her face.

"So, why did you come in person, I mean, I appreciate it and all but you could have called us. I'll have to confess I was frightened when I saw you. It's not often I get a visit from the police, let alone in school."

Parker disarmed her agitation with his most engaging and apologetic smile. "Probably a bad idea. Just the latest in a long line for me. I was driving by and thought I'd just drop in. I'm really sorry and I'll let you get back to work. Need any help with these desks?" He smiled again and Josie moved closer.

"I'm fine, thanks. I do this all the time. I'll be sure to fill Brad in when he gets home tonight and thanks again for coming in. Sorry for my reaction. You know us women." It was her turn to smile.

"Actually I don't know women, that is. Anyway, thanks for passing the information on. I've admired your husband's attitude through this whole thing with Snyder and his parents. It had to be hard but he seems like a pretty stable guy." He watched her closely for any reaction. She turned her head toward the window, moisture forming in her eyes.

"We miss his folks a lot and yes, he is maddeningly stable most of the time, Detective." She extended her hand and Parker shook it as firmly as he would a man's. "Thanks again for coming and drop in any time. I'll try to be more cordial the next time."

*   *   *

Brad's reaction to the news could only be described as euphoric. He never questioned why the officer would have come to Josie's school, a fact Josie discounted as his simply being excited at the prospect of Robert Snyder getting his just due, whatever that cliché might mean. The subject consumed most of the early evening conversation. Brad pressed for every detail about the sentence and anything else that Havenot may have said. His euphoria reached new heights of giddiness when she mentioned the compliment about his stability and the detective's admiration for him. Brad's overreaction puzzled her and after dinner she was ready to ask him what was going on in his head when he insisted that they make love. After an extended period of potent sexuality, Josie assumed that the news about

Snyder had tapped into a hidden energy source in Brad.

As they lay exhausted on the bed, Josie turned to Brad and asked an obvious question. "What in the world got into you tonight; not that I mind, you understand, but you seemed to turn everything up a notch." She chuckled lightly. "And I mean everything!"

"It worked, Josie, that's all. It all worked out." The enigmatic answer added to her confusion and it showed. "I mean, my prayer that Snyder would get caught doing something worked out, Jos. It's hard to explain but I think maybe it is possible for the world to be a better place if we work at it, you know?"

"I guess so but why don't we solve all the world's problems some other time? You wore me out tonight." She kissed him and was sound asleep in seconds.

The next morning, Brad arrived at school ten minutes later than normal, having turned into the cemetery to bring Brad, Jr. up to date on the success of his mission with Bob Snyder. To a casual observer, Brad could have been saying a prayer at the foot of his son's grave.

"It is so easy to separate the two worlds," he said. "It's all about perception. The perceptions people have of you in the white world can eliminate any possibility of them ever thinking of you in the black world. Even the clever detective admires my courage and fortitude and sees me as the paragon of stability and virtue. I'm thinking that I might be able to correct other problems like I did with Snyder and Capaldi. Something's on my side and I have a duty to use it."

Harriet's Wedding

"Fellowship in joy, not sympathy in
sorrow, is what makes friends."
Friedrich Nietzsche

Western Connecticut experienced an early spring in 1972 and when the invitation to Harriet Long's wedding arrived, the robins were already pulling worms from the Wallaces' front lawn. As e.e.cummings so aptly put it, the world was "mud-luscious" and the momentum of another school year at Hampton Village High School sputtered in the face of adolescent hormones and spring fever. The timing of the wedding of Harriet Long and Paul Stanton over the long four-day Easter weekend would be perfect for any number of reasons. It was coming at a time of the year when any break from the school routine was welcome, even for the most dedicated educator. The magnificent seven, sans Tyler Spence, could look forward to a pleasant, rejuvenating reunion, and, of course, Harriet would be getting married.

Since Harriet's letter of the previous fall, Josie and she corresponded faithfully and the short void in their friendship filled back in. She couldn't wait to meet Paul Stanton. Harriet devoted half of every letter to describing how wonderful he was. Comparisons of their life styles and situations were inevitable. Josie couldn't avoid the small twinges of jealousy as she thought of Harriet's academic success and now her marriage to a man whom she rated just below God. When these upsetting thoughts would creep in, she reexamined how fortunate she was; a sound marriage and a stellar career should be enough. Yet, there seemed to be something lurking, an unpleasant edge creeping into her relationship with Brad. Most of the time, the feeling was set aside, but at other times, the sad events crowded into her six-year marriage formed a thunderstorm off on the horizon, approaching on an unpredictable path. She prayed that the

159

storm would pass by, and a long getaway weekend among her friends at a country inn in Vermont might help to redirect it.

The evening the wedding invitation arrived, Josie, with Brad's blessing, called her three male colleagues, all of whom had received the invitation the same day. The same evening, the reservations were made at the Stonington Manor, less than a mile from Harriet's church. The schedule called for the five of them to arrive on Thursday night for the whole weekend. After the arrangements were made, Josie called Harriet, outlining their plans and setting up a dinner date for six of the magnificent seven to have a reunion, certain that the seventh would be there in spirit.

*   *   *

In the four days before they left for Vermont, Rich, Jess, Jack, and Josie spent most of their lunch break planning the trip. All agreed that they were happy about Harriet's wedding, giving them an excuse for a whole weekend of partying. Josie, with the familiarity of a professional colleague, co-worker and long time friend, teased all three of the men about their lack of girlfriends.

"So, you guys can't even dredge up a girl willing to come with you to this gorgeous inn? She said this in different ways every day for weeks before the trip. Rich Lane, the unofficial spokesman for the group, answered in a variation of the same words every day as well.

"Why would we want a woman telling us what to do all the time? Boys just want to have fun and girls get in the way." The three men would wait for Josie's inevitable reaction.

"I give up. I absolutely give up. You're all hopeless." She would throw her hands up in frustration then they would share the intimate kind of laugh that strengthens the powerful bond among friends.

On Thursday, "getaway day" as they called it, Josie announced that she and Brad would have to meet them on Friday night because of a budget meeting in Hartford, an emergency meeting he could not miss.

"We'll just get there as soon as we can and we'll find you. I have no doubt it won't be hard. The inn has a very attractive lounge." She tried

160

hard to hide her disappointment but her friends weren't buying it.

Rich reached across the desk and took her hand.

"Look, Jos, why don't you come with us and Brad can drive up tomorrow. I mean he let you ride with us to Lake Winnipesaukee. Do you want me to write you a note and pin it to your lapel?" He smiled at her.

"Yeah, come on, Josie, we won't bite, I promise," Jess chimed in.

Josie, torn between her desire to see Harriet and her fear that Brad would be miffed if she left that afternoon, agreed to call him and see what his reaction might be.

"I'll let you know ASAP, OK? What time are you leaving?"

"ASAP," Rich said, mimicking her use of the acronym. "Seriously, as soon as we can get ready after closing up here."

"I'll let you know." She left them eating while she went to the cafeteria to get change for the pay phone next to the office. She returned in five minutes, frustration evident in face. "I couldn't get him, but I left a message that I was going with you guys. I'll leave a note at home explaining everything and hopefully he'll be all right with it."

*   *   *

After classes were dismissed for the day, Brad left his office for the ritual of checking his mailbox. One of the major irritations of working in education was its total lack of sound business practices. Teachers were expected to contact parents on a regular basis without availability of telephones, and any messages that might come in during the day were stuffed into mailboxes that most of them couldn't check except before and after school. A crisis of monumental importance had to be occurring for any secretary to be moved to contact a classroom while school was in session. While Brad now had the privilege of a phone in his office as a department head, he still had to make the trek to the office to retrieve messages about calls he may have missed.

He wrapped both hands around what felt like a ream of paper in his mailbox and the small pink telephone message fell out, floating to the floor. He knelt and picked it up, balancing the mailbox contents in one hand and frowning as he saw it was from Josie.

"Damn!" he said, loud enough so Joan the super secretary overheard. "May I use your phone, Joan? I'll reverse the charges."

"Of course." Joan acted as though there was never any doubt about using her phone when in fact there always was.

Brad dialed the operator and asked that she call his home number, collect. He listened as the phone rang at least ten times.

"Shall I keep trying, sir?" the operator asked, impatience clear in her voice. Without answering, he put the receiver in its cradle, holding back from slamming it down and left the office without a word.

The note at home was full of apologies but to Brad the single most important aspect of it lay hidden between two innocuous lines. "Rich convinced me that you wouldn't mind," and "I really wanted to spend some quality time with Harriet before the frenzy of the wedding." There could be only one interpretation as far as he could see.

"She'd rather be up there with them than home with me tonight," Brad said to the piece of shaking notepaper in his hand. He set the note back on the kitchen table at the same time as he reached for the door to the cabinet holding their liquor supply. He carefully mixed his double martini. The first few sips of his drink calmed his nerves and he made his way to his chair in the living room.

"I must make a trip to see Brad, Jr. before Vermont," he said to himself. Then the telephone rang and he returned to the kitchen to answer it, taking his martini with him.

"Hey, you're not mad at us for kidnapping your wife are you?" It was Rich's voice. Brad, switching from black to white, answered quickly.

"Oh, I hadn't noticed that she was gone." He snickered, happy to get the better of Rich. "Of course not. You tell her. . . ." He paused. "Why isn't SHE calling me?"

Rich handed the phone to Josie before Brad finished his sentence.

"Hi. This is Josie," she said and Brad actually held the phone out at arm's length and looked at it.

"No kidding, Jos. I don't know why you thought this might be a problem. I'll get there as soon as I can tomorrow. Miss you 'til then," he said in his smoothest, whitest voice. "Have a great time with Harriet and the boys."

"Thanks! I'm sure I will. Love you and see you tomorrow." The click of the receiver in his ear created a stab of pain like an earache. For the second time that evening, he balanced his martini without spilling a drop on his way to his chair. He sat down, savoring the blackness that enveloped him.

*   *   *

After a pleasant and amusing dinner of reminiscences, the group moved to the lounge. When the three men began to slip into their raucous beer-guzzling mode, Josie and Harriet excused themselves, their exit barely noticed by their male friends, now engaged in a competitive dart game. They strolled back to Josie's room, and she opened the bottle of upscale red wine she had intended to share with Brad. She poured it into the only glasses available in the room, small bathroom tumblers made of cheap plastic that crinkled under the slightest finger pressure.

In the daytime, the room had a marvelous view of the valley and surrounding rolling hills, and the two friends turned their wooden chairs around to face the window, watching for a minute in silence as the lights of the small town twinkled below.

The two years at the University of Chicago plainly agreed with Harriet Long. She had let her hair grow and it flowed over her shoulders to the middle of her back. The few pounds shed following a rigorous workout regimen had fallen away in the right places, emphasizing a movie actress figure. Her hazel eyes were as dark and compelling as ever, radiating confidence.

It was then that Harriet confided that she had been diagnosed with ovarian cancer and had to have a hysterectomy.

"I can't believe you wouldn't have told me about something like this." Josie said.

"Please don't be angry, Jos. I just didn't see the point of worrying everybody back here. It really went well and everything's OK now. It was just a bit of bad luck but I'm lucky they caught it now."

"I might've been able to help you, you know. I mean I'm sort of in the same situation. I didn't have a complete hysterectomy like you did but so much of my insides went with Brad, Jr. that I might as well have." She pushed the chair back and turned it to face Harriet.

"What about Paul? Is he all right with this?" Josie caught herself. "Hey, Harriet, I'm sorry. I shouldn't be prying like this. It's just so sad." She stood and went to the window, staring out into the darkness.

Harriet rose and came to her, gently touching her shoulders. Josie turned and when their eyes met, the raw emotion of burdens shared overwhelmed them and they embraced, their sobs muffled as each buried her face into the other's shoulder.

"It's OK, Josie. It really is," Harriet whispered when she caught her breath. "You're the one who's had it tough. I wanted to call you a hundred times but couldn't do it. You didn't need to relive that again and I'm sorry that you are now."

Josie pulled away and turned again to the window.

"Damn it, Harriet, We're only twenty nine years old. We don't need this shit already." She started to giggle suddenly. "See that, you made me swear twice in the same breath." They joined in a cathartic laugh through their tear-stained faces.

"OK, so, are you going to answer my questions?" Josie asked.

By the end of the evening, the bond from Hampton Village was firmly reestablished, strengthened in just a few hours with a confidence that comes from absolute trust. As the two women heard Rich, Jess, and Jack shouting and lurching through the hallway bouncing off the walls on the way to their rooms, they just looked at each other and laughed.

"Those guys haven't changed a bit, have they?" Harriet said. "I really need to be going but thanks and sorry again for keeping you in the dark about the cancer thing. It's like you feel embarrassed, as if it's your own fault that God decided to smack you across the face. Anyway, no more secrets. I've missed you, Josie"

"Me, too. I can't wait to meet Paul tomorrow. Sounds like you are one lucky girl." They reached the door and Harriet was the first into the hall, glancing to her right at the three men still fumbling for their keys. Josie leaned out to look as well and the three responded predictably, led by the irrepressible Rich Lane.

"Well, how about that, boys. Two young ladies looking for companionship."

"In your dreams! Good night, gentlemen." Harriet said, sharing a final hug with Josie. "See you tomorrow. And you too, boys, if you ever wake up." Josie closed the door, wishing that Brad had been there for the reunion, but most of all to share her bed that night.

Josie undressed. True to her tradition, she had not brought along any sort of nightwear; a tradition shared by Brad whenever they stayed together in a hotel room. After a cursory brushing of her teeth, she slipped under the covers of the enormous queen sized bed, enjoying the touch of the cool sheets on her bare skin and revisited her time together with Harriet.

Paul Stanton seemed, from Harriet's description, to be a saint on earth. The admiration she had for Harriet grew as she listened to her matter-of-fact description of the decision that she and Paul had made concerning children.

"There are thousands of kids around the world who need parents," Harriet had said, "and Paul and I want to be parents so we will be. Babies start out pretty young, you know, and they're not too discriminating about their parents at first." Remembering Harriet's genuineness and positive attitude dampened her eyes, and the inspiration struck so sharply that she sat straight up in the bed.

She and Brad had discussed adoption after the loss of Brad Jr. and its subsequent result, but at the time neither could deal with the possibility realistically. The subject became one of those that most couples have, a subject that is tucked away on a shelf, far from the mainstream of their existence and only rarely rediscovered and exposed to the light. Perhaps with Harriet and Paul as inspiration, they could remove the issue from the shelf and dust it off like some long forgotten box of Christmas decorations. She wiggled back under the sheet and pulled the polyester quilt up to her neck. She was more anxious than ever for Brad to get there.

The barely perceptible knock on the door penetrated Josie's consciousness. She peered at the clock with its faded hands and numbers that had long since lost their luminescence. The knock grew louder more insistent. She reached above her head for the light switch and gathered her wits enough to realize where she was and that it was two o'clock in the morning. Something must be terribly wrong. Her first thought was fire and she threw back the bed covers, grabbing the slippery quilt and wrapping herself in it. She stumbled toward the door, fighting the instinctive urge to panic. She opened the door fully, expecting to be told to run for her life wrapped in this nondescript hotel-style blanket. Instead, a smiling Rich Lane greeted her. An incipient anger replaced her relief and she closed the door until just a crack remained. She moved behind it modestly.

"You look lovely, my dear," Rich said, his voice still thick with the remnants of what must have been quite a night of drinking.

"Rich, what in the hell are you doing? It's two o'clock in the morning. You scared the devil out of me." She regained her composure somewhat and, recognizing Rich's condition, softened. "So, what's going on?" she asked, just her head peeking out from behind the door.

"Can I talk to you for a second, Jos. It won't take long," he implored. "Please?"

"I don't believe you. Just wait out there for a minute while I get dressed in something beside this stupid quilt. I'll come get you."

"I think you look just fine," he said as she pushed the door closed, leaving him standing in the hall.

She opened the door and invited him in. "This better be good and it better be short. I'm not accustomed to entertaining men other than my husband in a hotel room in the middle of the night." Josie looked at him with the expression of a teacher trying without success to be angry at a student's harmless and funny prank.

166

"OK, Jos. Here it is and don't think this is the booze talking. This is your old friend, colleague, companion, and confidant, Rich Lane speaking." He laughed and Josie joined him. "I've known you for going on seven years now and we've been through a lot together, right?" He looked at Josie, waiting until she nodded before continuing.

"I decided that in all fairness, I should let you know how I feel about you and this seemed like the perfect time." Josie shifted in her chair. An attractive professional woman, she had disposed of many passes in her life, ranging from innocent flirtations to salacious attempts at seduction. This would be a good time to interrupt.

Standing up, she said, with a calm, understanding tone, "I really think you need to go back to your room and get some sleep, Rich. We'll continue this in the morning if you'd like after you give it some more thought." She lifted his arm and he followed her lead, slowly rising out of the chair.

"Could I just finish this, Josie? I mean, it took an hour of thinking about it before I came over here." He paused and when she did not respond he plunged ahead into dangerous territory. "What I wanted to say is that you are really special to me. I could easily be in love with you if you'd let me. Actually, I am in love with you, have been for years." He drew a deep breath. "There, I said it and I'm glad. Now I'll leave."

"I think you'd better, Rich. We will talk about this again but for now, know one thing. I love my husband, I'm committed to him and I'd do nothing to hurt him." She escorted him to the door as she spoke. "A second thing. You're special to me and very important in my life. Let's try to forget you ever came here tonight." They were at the door. Josie gave Rich a warm hug, carefully avoiding any pelvic contact. "I love you, too, Rich, but I'm not in love with you. There's quite a difference. Good night." Rich left without saying another word.

*   *   *

Most of those attending the wedding opted for staying at the Manor for the weekend, enjoying the convenience of being at the center of the festivities. The rehearsal dinner was served in a magnificently decorated private room off the main dining room on Friday evening, and the reception on Saturday following the wedding was perfectly orchestrated by the Inn. Even the bride and groom spent the night in the bridal suite at the Inn, risking the possibilities of juvenile pranks but deciding that in the end, the chance was worth the convenience. Harriet, knowing the history of the magnificent seven, danced with each of the men of the group at the reception, threatening them with dire consequences if anyone did anything foolish with the new couple's belongings. In the end, she needn't have worried as Rich, their ringleader, spent most of the weekend somewhat subdued after the first night at the Inn.

Brunch at The Stonington Manor attracted full houses every Sunday even in the middle of winter and with the promise of a warm spring day, the crowds began arriving early. Harriet had reserved a table for seven on the veranda overlooking the several acres of sweeping front lawn, its lush spring verdancy punctuated by several well-manicured circular gardens of blossoming daffodils. Much to the delight of their friends, the couple arrived downstairs ten minutes late, allowing for several Henny Youngman type one-liner newlywed jokes from Brad and Jack before Harriet suppressed them with a withering stare. Rich Lane remained in his pensive mode, a quietness that was ill-suited for a gathering of this group. Josie made a substantial effort to draw him out without success.

The buffet was so sumptuous that it finally inspired Rich to come to life, quipping that he "could eat breakfast, let it settle, eat lunch, let that settle then return for the dinner course all in the same day." After a Bloody Mary salute to the memory of Tyler Spence, the group began their trips to the buffet. Much later, long after the trips to the table became too numerous to count, they began to say their good-byes. Josie, after a weekend in the presence of Harriet, was rejuvenated. As the meal went on, the melancholia she experienced when Harriet went to Chicago gradually permeated her cheerful disposition. She dreaded saying goodbye to her. The intensity of their friendship had an unexpected rebirth this weekend and each swore to the other that they would not degenerate into Christmas card friends again. When Brad, who seemed to have had a wonderful time once he settled in on Friday night, suggested that it was time to check out, Josie reluctantly agreed. The ritual of the hugs began, the emotion building with each one. Paul Stanton joined in freely, his age and personality remarkably similar to Tyler's. As the friends slowly drifted toward their own destinations, the "Parting is such sweet sorrow" myth washed over them. None could deny the sorrow part, but it surely was not sweet.

*   *   *

Josie anticipated the lengthy car ride home with the excitement of a child anticipating Christmas. As soon as Brad arrived on Friday night, the weekend became one extended party. The getaway weekend turned into just that for them, and they made love on three different occasions, the unique environment of the room at the inn providing more than sufficient romance and eroticism to stimulate even the most staid of couples. She knew that any discussion of her plan had to wait for an uninterrupted block of time, and the three hours alone in the car would be a perfect opportunity. The worry over Brad's reaction to her going alone on Thursday with Rich and the boys proved to be superfluous. A successful budget meeting and an early start to the weekend on Friday put Brad in a good mood and he never mentioned her early departure. Josie was relieved that Rich's ebullient spirit had been inhibited by his alcohol-enhanced admission on Thursday night. No matter how positive his frame of mind, Brad would not be prepared to take jokes about his wife alone with three men in an inn overnight.

The Manor hadn't yet disappeared from the rear view mirror when Brad started the conversation.

"What in the world was going on with Rich this weekend, anyway? It was so noticeable. Did he say anything on the way up there?" The genuine concern in his voice impressed Josie so much that she started to tell him the truth.

"He was having a hard time with some stuff and he talked to me about it Thursday night."

"Really? I'd like to hear about it. I knew he wasn't himself and I felt bad for him. So tell me all about it." The whole scene with Rich flashed through her mind and she tried to picture Brad's reaction if she really told him the whole thing. Deciding that "discretion is the better part of valor," she launched a diversionary story.

"It was just a problem he was having at school with some of his athletes; you know, typical kind of stuff that teachers are forever running into," she said. Then, with a deft twist, she switched the subject, hoping that he might not return to it later.

"Something came up with Harriet and Paul that I'd like to talk to you about, if that's OK?" She took his silence for approval and proceeded to lay out her plan including Harriet's idea about the critical need for foreign baby adoptions. Brad listened without a single interruption, staring at the road ahead as though driving through a thick fog or a heavy snowstorm, ignoring the glorious spring afternoon. She had turned to face him, looking at his profile for information, clues that would expose his reaction clearer than any words might. She felt the flush on her cheeks from her increasing excitement as she pushed deeper into the subject, waiting for any positive movement. During her entire monologue, she saw no recognizable response. There was not a nod, a smile, even a glance in her direction. She finished with her most dramatic flourish.

"I think we should do it, Brad. It'd be good for both of us and a valuable humanistic thing to do." She paused, waiting through a proverbial pregnant pause, but Brad continued to drive through the fog. "So, what do you think?" The question dribbled out, her passion for the subject exhausted.

His face remained free of any expression. The question screamed for an answer and she waited another few seconds, unnerved by his manifest apathy.

"Brad, I asked what do you think. I'm beginning to feel a little foolish here. Help me out, will you?"

For the first time since the adoption conversation started, he flashed a glance at Josie, just as quickly turning back to the road.

"You didn't give me a straight answer about Rich and I'm sure as hell not going to talk about some wild adoption scheme at this point. Let's let it go for now and we'll talk about it again later. You need to think about what it would mean to Brad Jr." He looked at her again, seeing the disbelief in her eyes.

"I mean, you know, his memory. Look, let's just let it go for now. We're both tired, and it's not something to be discussed when people aren't at their best. Really, Jos, just let me think about it. It's too much right now."

"Sure, if that's what you want. I just thought that maybe. . . ." She stopped. He had entered the fog again.

"You need to know this is not going away," she said. He didn't need to see her face to know that the words were spoken through clenched teeth. Neither said another word as they let the scenery and the warmth of the spring sun absorb them for the rest of the ride home.

Best Friends

"Life's simplest things are love and kindly friends"
Ripley D. Saunders

Clearing the air, as Rich euphemistically put it, consumed several afternoons of chatting after school. With Josie's realistic advice and practical approach, he succeeded in transcending the gender intrusion on their friendship. By the end of the week after Harriet became Mrs. Paul Stanton, Rich was back to his quick-witted, bantering self, his profuse apologies about coming to Josie's room accepted and understood by both parties.

As the summer vacation approached, the remaining four of the magnificent seven at Hampton Village arranged a spontaneous Friday meeting at Pete's to celebrate its proximity.

"A pretty lame excuse," Josie said to the suggestion.

Jess and Jack had other commitments for later that evening and downed two beers in near record time before excusing themselves, promising that they would leave the next Friday open for a more extensive celebration. Josie and Rich sat alone in the booth and ordered a second beer. He smiled at Josie across the table.

"This is how it should be," he said. "A couple of old friends having a beer." With the "Stonington Fiasco" behind them, he navigated the conversation toward what he thought was certain to be safe waters.

"So, how's Brad doing? He surely seemed to be fine at the wedding; no ill effects from your leaving him alone for a night?" Josie fidgeted on her seat and sat straighter.

"Why do you ask? I mean, he's just fine; things are just fine." Rich watched her closely. He waited, puzzled by the defensive tone of her answer yet sensing that more was coming. "I'm a little worried, that's all," she said after a minute of silence.

Rich continued to look at her without answering. The safer

waters he hoped to be entering were alive with emotional alligators swimming just beneath the surface. He struggled with turning the conversation once more, but Josie continued before he had the chance.

"I don't mind that he doesn't want to adopt. That part's OK with me." Josie stared at her empty beer bottle on the table as if it were a crystal ball, her eyes filled but not quite overflowing. "We're in some sort of role reversal here. You probably don't remember but he fought me on having a funeral and full burial for Brad, Jr." Rich nodded; he did remember. Josie didn't notice. "Now I feel like I've finally moved on but he thinks it would be unfair to our son's memory."

The alligators swam to the surface.

"All this coming from a man who tried to convince me that Brad Jr. never was a human being. I just don't understand it at all." She picked up her crystal ball and idly started to peel its label with her fingernails. "What do you think I should do about it?"

After drawing the kind of heavy sigh that buys a little thinking time, Rich responded.

"I know that you can talk him into it, Jos. He'll come around; he probably just needs some time to get used to the idea." He looked at Josie twirling the labelless bottle in her hands and knew that his useless response had no impact. She had thrown back her shoulders from the sag of moments before.

"He's adamant and I'm going to have to accept it." She seemed to be talking to herself with Rich in the role of spectator. "It's just that Harriet really inspired me. . . ." Her eyes dried. "Let's have another beer, my old friend. Sorry to have gone off like that."

Rich glanced down at his watch. "You know how much I enjoy your company, especially after my wonderful performance at the Stonington, but it's getting pretty late. Shouldn't you be slaving over the hot stove when hubby gets home?" He smiled, "I'll stay as long as you like but I don't want you to get in trouble." He stifled an overwhelming need to put his arms around her. Her hesitation answered him.

"I'll order the beers on my way to the men's room," he said as he stood and squeezed her shoulder.

*   *   *

The staff held back their enthusiasm for the weekend as long as possible on Friday afternoons, then most of them bolted for the exits a minute or two after the required half hour from the close of school. The quietness that descended on the school in the late afternoon, especially on Fridays, had an eerie quality but it was a peculiarity conducive to a productive work time for Brad, always one of the last to leave Hartford West. He sat in his office, revising and perfecting the final set of required evaluations for the twelve teachers in his department. It was a job that he thought he would detest, but now realized how critical those evaluations were if classroom performance was to improve. Of the twelve, only two of his staff were in minor difficulty, mostly because of their inexperience. Mike Costello wielded his principal power to insure that every evaluation included something negative. At department head meetings, he repeated his credo of "No one's perfect, not even me" at every opportunity and Brad came to accept it, however grudgingly. Even his mentor teachers had a caveat inserted into their year end summative evaluation that indicated that there was always room for improvement. His own mastery of the classroom gave him a solid base from which to judge his colleagues, and none of them minded his recommendations, actually finding his advice helpful. After completing six of the reports, he pushed his chair back and stretched. The ticking of the second hand on the large clock over the door attracted his attention, a sound that seemed to be there only on these late afternoons when everything was so quiet. He looked up, surprised to see that it was almost five o'clock. The thought of Josie, at home by now and doubtless beginning to cook dinner, made him smile.

This weekend he would smooth things out with her. It had been a stressful week, the whole adoption thing the subject of discussion each night. They rarely argued but a few of their discussions became heated enough to fall close to that category. Her unhappiness with his firm refusal to entertain the possibility couldn't be mistaken. As he shuffled the papers on his desk into a systematic chaos and prepared to leave for home, the basic philosophy that kept him sane most of the time echoed in his head.

"This too shall pass," he said to himself. With him on his best behavior, a quiet weekend with Josie was sure to eliminate the tension. They had not made love all week, going to bed each night with the adoption wedge firmly separating them.

Brad spent much of the slow commute home fantasizing in the westbound traffic out of Hartford that snarled about five miles out of the city. On the rare occasions when they had lengthy disagreements, the make up periods were predictably intense. The session that was sure to occur when they resolved the question of adoption promised to be quite interesting. He was confident that if he exhibited only the positive side of his nature, she was sure to come around to his way of thinking. The threat that this "is not going to go away" meant little to him. Time and his persuasive disposition would make it go away. The trip home, often deadly and boring when slowed by jams or accidents, passed more quickly than he expected as he kept his mind occupied with visions of Josie and the weekend ahead.

As he pulled into the driveway, he noticed that Josie's car was not there, a rather unusual development considering the lateness of the hour.

"Friday night and Pete's." The two thoughts collided and he said the words aloud. He slipped the car into reverse and within minutes arrived at Pete's, immediately spotting Josie's car in the lot. He parked and walked briskly toward the entrance. With a groan, the solid wooden door with a small speakeasy type of window cut in the center at eye level swung open from his push. Most of the people in the bar looked in his direction, each for different reasons. Brad glanced in the direction of the magnificent seven's favorite table in the far corner. Josie and Rich sat there, part of the few that hadn't taken notice of his entrance. Whatever the subject of their discussion, it was consuming all of their attention and Brad hesitated before approaching them. They weren't aware of his presence until he stood a few feet away and announced it.

"Hi Josie," he called, interested in how she was going to respond. He was disappointed in a strange way, expecting a cool response to his interruption. Instead, she stood immediately and embraced him.

"Oh, shit, Brad, you're always ruining my fun." Rich had stood also. "You caught us. So what happens now?" Rich smiled, an amused but subtly worried look crossing his face. While Josie's greeting was spontaneous and genuine, Brad filed the image of Rich's smile away for future examination, perhaps during a black period when things like that came clear. When the three sat down at the table again, Rich took a different seat, one that was across from Josie instead of next to her.

"So what's going on," Brad asked nonchalantly. "How come I wasn't invited to the party?" The question sounded rhetorical but Josie felt the need to answer anyway.

"Just one of those crazy Friday things, you know, like the celebrations we always have. Jess and Jack just left. I had a wager with them all that you would start dinner if I wasn't home. I guess I lose." Josie was comfortable so Brad turned his attention to his friend.

"What's new with you, Rich? Josie told me you've been having some problems with a few kids at school. Did you have a better week?" Rich looked at Josie but she didn't meet his eye.

"Yeah, sure. You know me, Mr. Flexibility. I'll handle anything they can dish out." He guzzled the last few swallows of his beer, threw a ten-dollar bill on the table and stood to leave. "Thanks for the company, Josie. See you in school on Monday. Have a great weekend. So long, Brad." Suddenly he had a mission and he hurried toward the door without looking back.

"Well, that was interesting," Brad said. "Why don't we go home and see what we can rustle up for dinner?"

*　　*　　*

Once the jobs were divided, they worked in silence, Brad peeling potatoes and Josie making a Caesar salad. The exchange with Rich about the adoption issue was still fresh in her mind. She determined to face the question with finality and move on.

"Brad, I need to tell you this so we can get it all behind us." Brad stopped peeling and moved closer to her. "I'll make this short but don't expect it to be sweet. Adopting a child would be a huge mistake if we weren't in one hundred percent accord. I can't pretend to understand your reasoning for not wanting a baby but I have to respect that decision. I love you and I've thought a lot about this thing." Brad had wrapped his arms around her waist as she spoke. "I think the excitement of Harriet's marriage and all her talk about getting a baby swayed me. I'm sorry for the pressure I put on you." She turned to face him, and the tears that had dried in Rich's presence welled up again and this time she couldn't hold them back. "I just wish we could have had our son, that's all," she sobbed. "Is that so much to ask?"

Brad squeezed her, as if a tight hug could crush the pain. "No, it isn't and we both know it's not fair," and they clung to each other like survivors in a small lifeboat being tossed about on a stormy sea.

*　　*　　*

During the weekend, most of the fantasies that occupied so much of Brad's trip home from Hartford on Friday came to life, with Josie adding a few of her own. The emotional connections compounded themselves and by Sunday night, as they sat on the front step enjoying the warmth of the late spring evening, the rejuvenation of their marriage was a revelation to both of them.

"And imagine, this whole weekend started with a week long fight," Josie kidded. "Wonder what it would have been like if we had been getting along."

"Not nearly as good; you can count on it." Brad's answer was definitive. They sat for a while longer, holding hands and talking about plans for the upcoming summer. Both agreed that they would love to have the group to the camp on the lake again, this time perhaps scheduling it when Harriet and Paul could come as well. The mention of the magnificent seven prompted him to ask how Rich's difficulties at school were progressing.

"I'd be interested in specifics; maybe I could help or maybe he could help me somehow. I've got some teachers who have problem students for sure."

"Actually, I wasn't exactly telling you everything about the Stonington Manor. It's really nothing; actually, in a way, it's kind of funny." Josie said, suffering from the euphoria of closeness and trust that had come with this weekend. When she finished describing Rich's inebriated visit to her room and his confession of a long-term attraction to her, Brad's attention had turned to a point far away. He appeared lost in the same fog they encountered while discussing adoption on the way home in the car.

"We've got it all straightened out now, Brad. It's just funny, isn't it?"

"Oh, yeah, it's funny, all right." She noticed that he wasn't smiling.

Another Winnipesaukee Visit

"We judge others by their acts but
ourselves by our intentions"
Mirabeau

As happens annually, the school year rushed to its frantic conclusion with final exams, field trips, and graduations. Hampton Village and Hartford West had little in common academically, but both faculties engaged in similar activities to "keep the lid on," as their principals constantly reminded them. The seniors of both schools had one foot out the door as early as Easter. The underclassmen generally lasted another month before they too lost interest, going through the motions while their teachers struggled to keep them entertained.

Mathematics teachers took their classes outside to measure sidewalks or figure perimeters or develop formulas for the number of Fords that would pass the school in a given time period–anything to escape the breathtaking heat and humidity in the school. Science classes scoured the property looking for flora and fauna, much more difficult to come by in Hartford than it was in Hampton Village. English teachers, always the most liberal, sat in the middle of a circle of their students on the lush green grass of early summer, reading poetry while the class searched for distractions. The instructors of history and social studies continued to subject their classes to the forty five-minute lecture, their students pummeled into silent submission by the torrent of words flying at them.

For most teachers, the final few weeks of school were exhausting. Administrative pressure to manage the classrooms as they had the rest of the year, ran counter to the reality of approaching summer. Where students once dreaded the coming of summer as a time of tortuous long hours spent in the fields, now they anticipated a long escape from the stifling environment of most schools. Why not try to begin the celebration early?

With Richard Nixon apparently heading for a second term with a mandate to extricate the country from the maze of killing in Southeast Asia, the summer of 1972 seemed an especially appropriate time for early celebrations. For teachers like Josie Wallace, the final few weeks of school were draining. Keeping her students focused, normally an easy task for her, challenged her innovation and creativity on a daily basis. The long Memorial Day weekend provided a tempting chance for a final break before facing the chaos of the final two weeks of school. The short note she received with a wedding present thank you from Harriet Stanton put the plan into motion in earnest.

The University was sending Harriet to a conference at the Museum of Science in Boston during the first week of June, and she thought that she might come early to spend a couple of days with the Wallaces. The first doubts that Josie had about Brad's reaction to a visit from Harriet turned out to be unwarranted. He agreed without hesitation when she suggested that a return trip to the cabin might give the group just what they needed to finish the school year with a positive flourish. The addition of Harriet only made it better. The capacity of the cabin would be taxed to its limit but they were all long time friends who could be flexible. When Josie floated the idea to her lunch companions the day after Brad sanctioned the trip, they responded with unexpected enthusiasm. Rich's only caveat was a smirking remark about timing of the trip coinciding with the height of the black fly season but his friends hooted him down as a wimp. The notorious New Hampshire black flies, the curse that by tradition came on Mothers' Day and left on Fathers' Day, were known to have ruined many an early summer Granite State vacation for unsuspecting tourists. Josie, who teased her three male friends about their failure to bring some females on these excursions, reassured him.

"They never go near the lake, honest." she said.

"Oh, yeah, and if you don't bother them, they won't bother you, just like wasps, right?" Rich responded, unable to let anyone have the last word. Pesky black flies or not, the lake reunion plans proceeded on schedule.

*　*　*

182

"I think it might be time to exact a bit more revenge, wouldn't you agree?" Brad asked. He had not been to the gravesite since before Harriet's wedding. With the lake trip arranged for the next day, he was determined to leave school with enough time to enjoy a brief visit to the cemetery, searching for validation for his weekend plan.

"Nothing dramatic, you know, just more of the same; create a little havoc here and a little there; make some people hurt just a bit, even if they don't know why," he said aloud in a sing-song rhythm. A pirouette on the stone at his feet might have been fitting, as though performing in a whimsical musical comedy.

"We'll just see what happens. It'll be an interesting weekend." Bidding farewell to the grave, he shunted aside the disconcerting image of what the remains in the coffin might look like by now but not before it made him gag.

*   *   *

Josie and Brad managed an early start on Friday afternoon. It soon became obvious that they weren't the only ones with the idea. Stimulated by a Chamber of Commerce forecast promising perfect weather for the long holiday weekend, the traffic into New Hampshire slowed to a crawl just out of Manchester and stayed that way to the lake. The Wallaces finally arrived at the cabin as the late evening twilight changed to the eerie gray pall just before darkness. True to tradition, before unpacking a single item, they went directly to the beach where the calm lake lapped against the sand.

With just a few days left, May of 1972 was on the way to setting a record as the warmest ever in the Lakes Region. Josie and Brad held on to each other as they shed their shoes and socks. They each dipped a tentative big toe in to the water, finding it the temperature of a baby's bath water.

"It's going to be a perfect weekend, Brad; I can just feel it." With the rest of the group not scheduled to arrive until much later that night, Josie slipped her arms around Brad as they stood ankle deep in the water.

"Why don't we just go in for a while? We'll unpack later." There was no mistaking the invitation.

"I haven't had a shower since this morning, Jos. Do you think you can stand me?" Her answer was to drop her hands to his crotch and give a gentle, insistent squeeze.

"Come on inside and we'll just see what comes up, so to speak," Josie said.

Brad always contended that the lake had some remarkable power to generate primeval urges of all kinds in people, a theory that Josie rejected out of hand. His reply to her provocative invitation before accepting it was simple.

"You know my idea about the lake, Jos? Well, I rest my case." He smiled. More than an hour later, they made their way to the car in the dark to unpack for the weekend.

*　　*　　*

A long letter Harriet received from Josie two weeks after the wedding explained in detail what had happened to the adoption suggestion as far as the Wallaces were concerned. The three-hour ride from Logan Airport in the cramped, "We Try Harder" Avis compact car allowed ample time for Harriet to fret about the sort of greeting she might receive from Brad. She gladly would assume all blame for the attractiveness of the idea but embracing it as a plan for their own life was purely the Wallace's decision.

"Should be an interesting weekend," she said to the tiny windshield in front of her as she crossed the border into New Hampshire. She settled into watching the scenery turn from the flat coastal plain into the foothills of the White Mountains. The final stretch of the trip over the hills between Alton and Stoneham featured glimpses of the huge lake to the west. Several white church steeples pierced the sky in Wolfeboro Bay. Occasionally the white cap of snow and ice on top of Mt. Washington far to the north peeked above the Ossipee Mountains. Inspired by the pure beauty of the surroundings, her anticipation for another reunion with her old friends grew into unbridled excitement.

"This'll be fun," she said, again bouncing her observation off the windshield.

*   *   *

Brad heard the car tires crunching on the gravel driveway.

"She's right on schedule," he shouted through the screen door to the others in the kitchen, taking a much-needed break from swatting the black flies swarming around the deck. He was the first around the corner of the house, greeting her with a warm hug.

"Really great to see you again, Harriet." His smile relieved any apprehension she might have had about his welcome.

"You surely brought some nice weather with you," Josie said from over Brad's shoulder. The other men in the group arrived and all six of them spent an awkward moment arranging a group hug. As they sorted themselves out, the vicious black flies found them and within seconds, all but Brad dashed for the safety of the cabin.

"What do you need from the car, Harriet?" he called through the screen door, wildly waving his arms.

"Just the overnight bag, thanks. Just leave the rest there for now."

An unhurried lunch comprised of a smorgasbord of cold cuts and varied salads washed down with copious quantities of beer lasted well into the middle of the afternoon. Brad suggested that they settle their meal with a leisurely boat ride, then added a sarcastic aside.

"As we all know, according to Josie's theory, the black flies don't go out on the lake."

The day, as the forecasters had promised, was inspirational. The innate coolness of spring had been driven away by the unusually warm weather of the past several weeks, and it easily could pass for a day in the middle of July. There was no breeze but the heavy boat traffic put a permanent two-foot chop on all but the most protected of the bays and coves. Brad's offer to set up the water ski equipment was greeted with thundering apathy by his friends and his wife, the mellowing effect of the luncheon beers quite in evidence.

"It would be pretty difficult out here with the traffic anyway," Brad said, alleviating a small part of Rich's guilt for turning down the host of the trip. "It's supposed to be warmer yet tomorrow so I'd suggest an early morning, actually a very early morning, ski session. What do you think?" All but Rich looked at him as if he had suggested that they all leap from a tall building. "The water's really warmed up already," he said with conviction.

"I'm game for that," Rich said, "and this isn't the booze talking. I'd love to be out here on a nice calm morning." He looked around at his friends, fully expecting that his veiled challenge would be accepted. There were no takers.

Josie glanced at him than back to Brad. Her description of Rich's Stonington Manor confession had included the same phrase about the booze talking. Brad turned to face him.

"OK, Rich, you're on. We'll talk about time tonight after we see what condition we're all in by bedtime. Any of the rest of you are welcome." All but Josie gazed intently at the distant shoreline as if searching for the Loch Winnipesaukee monster.

"Someone's got to go. You know you need an observer, Brad." A hint of concern crept into Josie's voice but Brad and Rich dismissed it.

"The lake patrol is never out early in the morning, especially on a Sunday. No need to worry. We won't go far and we'll stay close to shore." Brad, his voice calm and persuasive, neutralized Josie's worry for the moment.

After an hour of bouncing around the choppy lake, Harriet and Josie commiserated about the effect the beer and the jolting were having on their respective bladders and initiated a minor mutiny against the captain and male crewmembers. Their complaints forced a return to the dock for relief. After dropping the women off, the four men voted with silent nods and Brad assumed a position as spokesman.

"We'll be back in an hour or so. We need to check out something across the lake." Their intent was so transparent that Josie laughed and Harriet giggled. They said good-bye and sped away, the

ABSOLUTELY **NO** WAKE sign and the women waving from the dock rapidly disappearing behind them.

"What is the attraction to having a drink in a lounge instead of at home?" Harriet asked as they hurried up the path to the house.

"There's a place near the public beach over in Laconia that must have good looking barmaids or something. It's like a tradition that they go over there at least once a trip." Later, after the maddening flies spoiled another attempt to sit on the deck enjoying the magnificent late afternoon, they moved to the living room, happy to have some time alone.

"I'm really curious and forgive me if this is intrusive but how in the world did your husband of just weeks agree to let you come out here for this weekend; I mean, I could see the conference but this is different." Josie, generally not so inquisitive, offered a chance for Harriet to sidestep the question. "Really, you needn't answer if you don't want to."

Harriet thought for a minute and Josie was unsure whether she was considering not answering or just contemplating her reply.

"Truth be told, Josie, I hadn't thought about it. Paul just asked if I wanted to go and I said yes. There wasn't an issue, for either one of us, as far as I could tell. Would there have been with you and Brad?"

Josie, taken back by Harriet's redirection of the question, considered it. "I don't think so; he let me go with the guys to your wedding; well, actually I went and he approved after the fact. To steal your phrase, truth be told, sometimes I feel like Brad is two different people but no one else seems to feel that way. It'd sound stupid to try to explain so I won't even try. He's a great guy and I'm lucky to have him." She became thoughtful again.

"He's really understanding though, even when I told him about," Josie stopped. "Sorry, I really need to let this subject drop. I don't want to embarrass anyone, including me."

Harriet, perceptive as ever, changed the subject without ever grasping exactly what the subject was.

"Your letter said that you probably wouldn't be interested in adopting?" Without realizing it, Harriet's lead into the subject reopened some of the still unhealed wounds—pain Josie wasn't ready to revisit on this particular weekend.

"Yeah, we decided that at our career stage, we would just wait a while, maybe later, you know, when Brad figures out where he is going with administration." Her answer severed her side of the conversation and she segued into Harriet's plans. The obnoxious piercing horn of the boat over an hour later announced the return of the men, interrupting Harriet's description of her life's plan, including the dramatic announcement that she and Paul would be adopting a foreign baby, likely Korean, in the next year or two. Josie's ambivalence shuttled between absorbing Harriet's happiness and fighting off the negative energy of jealousy threatening to overpower her.

*　　*　　*

Brad padded out of the bedroom at seven a.m., stumbling into the living room where his three friends slept. Each had agreed that they would sacrifice their individual comfort to share the double bed in the guestroom with Harriet, all of them sharing a leering laugh at her expense.

Harriet had laughed right along with them. "Just like the old days, guys. I really miss being available for you to annoy."

Jess, the smallest in physical stature, won the coin toss and slept soundly on the pullout sofa bed, his head buried beneath his pillow. Jack curled up in a fetal position on the short love seat, completely covered by a quilt so that he could have been mistaken for several pillows beneath the blanket. Rich finished third in the competition, drawing an old army-issue folding cot. Brad smiled as he looked around the room. The early morning sun slanted through the kitchen windows, reflecting from every shiny surface in the two rooms and casting a fascinating variety of shadows over his sleeping friends.

Brad tiptoed across the room, interested in awakening only Rich. As he moved closer, Rich turned over, the lightweight metal cot tipping precariously before settling back on its four legs. He tapped Rich on the shoulder, lightly at first but with increasing pressure.

"Come on, you said you wanted to get an early start. It's seven already."

Rich opened his eyes, glanced around the room with that look that says, "Where in the hell am I?"

"I think I'll change my mind. I mean, this is ridiculous." Rich turned away, muttering.

Brad became more insistent. "Come on, you lunkhead, I got up for you and the boat's all ready. It's a beautiful morning." He shook him again.

"Oh, damn it, OK, give me five minutes." Rich threw off his covers and stood to stretch, scratching all the usual places that men scratch upon awakening. "What about the other guys?"

"I'll work on them while you get ready. Let's just hurry before the lake gets busy."

Rich rummaged through his overnight bag and found a fresh bathing suit. "Be right back," he called as he went into the bathroom. "Work on those guys, will you?" The door closed behind him.

Brad went first to Jess, gently lifting the pillow from his head. He bent over him and whispered. "You're still not interested in going this morning, are you?" he asked, giving Jess the perfect opportunity to mumble a semiconscious but definite "No." He placed the pillow back on his head and moved across to Jack.

Just as he pulled the cover away from Jack's face, he heard the toilet flush. Jack had not moved, his easy breathing indicating the soundness of his sleep. Brad delicately replaced the blanket over his face and moved away. The bathroom door opened and Rich came into the room, looking first at Brad then at his still sleeping friends.

"Sorry, no takers. You're stuck with just me this morning," Brad whispered. "We'll just go for a little while then come back for a big breakfast."

*　　*　　*

Lake Winnipesaukee can behave like the most violent of oceans at times but, as Brad promised, the Sunday morning boat traffic was nonexistent and the great lake adopted the tranquility of Mirror Lake, its small neighbor to the north. Brad eased his Winncraft through the no wake zone in the cove and out into the wide bay. The sun perched briefly on Copple Crown Mountain beyond Wolfeboro before continuing its climb into the brilliant blue cloudless sky. Brad looked back at Rich, who had water-skied for the first time from this boat and in about the same location on the lake. There was one other boat to be seen, about three miles away by Brad's estimate.

"You ready back there?" Brad called over his shoulder. He brought the boat to a stop.

"I guess so; what do you think the temperature is, anyway?" The enthusiasm for this adventure, so high the night before, had waned considerably. Rich sat on the edge of the boat, peering into the water as if jumping in would be suicidal.

"I'm guessing that it's probably about sixty-six so you shouldn't be cold when you come out."

"I'm worried about getting in. Tell you what, why don't you go first and let me know how it is?" With that, Rich dropped over the side.

"Holy shit, this is freezing!" he hollered back. "Throw me the damn skis and let's get this over with." He laughed as he said it.

"I'll take you a few places you haven't been, but remember to follow my signal or you could get in trouble, OK?" Rich gave a thumbs up sign and Brad flipped the skis overboard. Rich drifted several feet away from the boat as he pulled the skis on. He paddled back and caught the handle of the towrope.

"Don't forget that I don't have an observer so don't be getting cute out there," Brad hollered above the idling motor. He waited until Rich backstroked out to the end of the line and turned back to the boat before easing the throttle ever so slightly forward. The controls were as familiar to him as the dashboard on his car and he stood there, looking back at his skier, waiting for the signal.

Rich checked the fit of the orange life belt around his waist, smiling. The first time he had ever skied, he had insisted on wearing a Mae West life jacket as well as the traditional waist belt even though he was a good swimmer. His timidity that time became the butt of many sarcastic jokes from his friends but eventually, as he adapted his outstanding athleticism to the sport, the first time was forgotten.

Brad waved his left hand and turned his palm upward in an "Are you ready?" gesture. Rich responded with another thumbs up sign and motioned the go ahead signal. Brad pushed the throttle forward and within a few seconds, Rich was up, a wide grin on his face. He took his left hand off the handle of the towline and waved enthusiastically, urging Brad to go faster. He had never skied behind a boat without an observer, but the fleeting concern disappeared in the self-confidence that comes with competence and an athletic body.

Brad surveyed the lake. Still only one other boat was in sight, that one well out in the broads, at least two miles away. He completed one circuit of the bay, occasionally glancing back at the now thoroughly warmed up Rich, making long sweeps from starboard and back to port, handling the jumps through the wake with the ease of an expert. An image of Rich professing his love for Josie, in her room, just the two of them, formed in the mist of the spray rising behind the skis as Brad looked back.

"OK, Rich, just a minor inconvenience like Snyder and Capaldi, but it'll make me feel a lot better. Nothing worse than betraying a friend or even trying to." Brad spoke as though conversing with someone else in the boat.

"You are one sick puppy, Wallace," he said to whatever was in the boat with him. Then he signaled backward that he would be increasing the speed and received a spirited wave in return.

The boat responded as he moved the throttle forward slowly. Rich stayed directly behind the boat until it was obvious that the boat would not be going any faster, then started to crisscross the wake again. Brad waited for him to complete several trips back and forth, timing each one. Just as Rich was directly behind the boat heading toward starboard side, Brad waved nonchalantly, an indistinguishable signal. Rich responded with a wave of his own. Brad turned his back to the stern, acting as if something in front of the boat had caught his attention. He counted slowly to three, a count he knew would bring Rich to the limit of his starboard sweep, then he turned the wheel sharply to the right and felt the tow line go slack. Without looking back, he turned sharply to port and felt the boat shudder as the line snapped taut for just a second; then he knew he had lost his skier.

His plan had worked perfectly. Just like Mr. Peaslee years before, the object of his revenge didn't have to know why something happened, as long as he did. This unavoidable accident that had just about yanked Rich's arms from their sockets felt good, a small token of justice in an unjust world. He brought the boat about, expecting to see Rich shaking his fist at him through his usual wide grin. Instead, he floated on his back, buoyed by the bright orange lifejacket, unsettlingly still.

"Oh, Jesus," Brad hissed as he guided the boat toward Rich, waiting for some sound, some movement, some anything.

*　　*　　*

Josie and Harriet sat on the deck, sharing a cup of coffee and the glorious beginning of another day on the lake. The temperature had warmed into the low seventies, enough blotches of sunlight creeping on to the deck from behind the house to warm it as well.

"It'll take about fifteen minutes for the black flies to find us so you might want to enjoy the view quickly," Josie said. The house faced southwest, offering a panorama of the Belknap Mountains and Gunstock Ski Area to the left and an endless variety of coves, bays, and islands straight ahead. They sat in respectful silence at the display as the sun rose behind them, throwing glittering reflections of color and light across the water before them. It was still early on Sunday morning, with just a few boats appearing like apparitions at first, slipping out from hidden cottages on the shore and dotting the far horizon.

"This'll keep you humble," Harriet said, spoiling the silence but not the mood. The screen door opened behind them and Jess Grogan wandered out.

"Those guys actually went out there this morning, right? I don't believe it." Jess's presence on the deck apparently changed the human chemistry and the flies began to swarm. "Damn, these things are a pain in the ass," he said as he began to flap his arms. "Oops! Sorry, Harriet, didn't mean to offend you."

"Apology accepted but let's get inside or we'll wind up like a cow trying to cross a piranha stream in South America; they'll find only the bones strewn over the deck." Their laughter faded when Josie shushed them.

"Quiet for just a minute, OK?" The three of them listened. The unmistakable sound of a boat horn, honking intermittently but in a regular pattern carried across the lake from some distance away.

"What do you think that is, Jos?" Harriet asked, having no idea.

"Someone needs help out there," she said. Her hearty complexion bleached into a pasty white.

*   *   *

"I can't move anything, Brad. Jesus Christ, I CAN'T move!"

Brad, relieved to hear Rich's voice but frightened by the shaky panic evident in it, maneuvered the boat as close as possible and cut the engine. He jumped onto the bow of the boat, grabbed the anchor and threw it overboard. Without waiting for it to hit bottom, he returned to the cockpit, kicked off his docksiders, and ripped off his shirt and leaped into the chilly water. Rich lay limp in the water just fifteen feet away and Brad was there in several strokes.

"It's OK; you must've jammed something when you fell. Just relax. We'll get some help here but I've got to get you back to the boat." He slipped his left arm gently under Rich's chin and reached across, firmly grasping his right shoulder and started to paddle back to the boat.

"Oh shit, man, I can't feel your arm on me, oh sweet Jesus, I'm in trouble." Rich closed his eyes. "I'd really rather die, Brad, I'd rather die."

"Will you shut up about trouble and dying, for God's sake!" They were at the boat. "Now, I'm going to leave you in the water while I signal for help." He untied one end of the stern lines and pulled it into the water, looping it under Rich and tying it loosely around his waist.

193

"Now, relax. Everything's going to be fine. I'm going back in the boat to get someone's attention."

"Fucking easy for you to say," Rich said, momentarily recovering his quick wit.

Brad looked at him. He had never seen the eyes of anyone more afraid. He clambered aboard and started sounding the piercing horn in staccato fashion, sure that someone on the lake would respond. He estimated that they were at least a mile from shore, but the offensive sound carrying across the water certainly would attract the attention of many of the folks sleeping late on Sunday morning in the cottages dotting the shoreline.

* * *

Five minutes after the blasting of the boat horn ended, the wailing sirens of a lake patrol boat echoed through the open windows of the cabin. Jess Grogan and Harriet Stanton braved the insects and dashed from the house to the dock, trying to determine what was happening while praying that Brad's boat would appear in the distance. Jack Hopkins helped Josie finish the last few dishes from the night before, and they, too, made a dash to the dock to wait for the *Educator Express* to return.

"Why do I feel like I'm on a widow's watch here?" Josie asked, her vain attempt at levity only adding to the gathering gloom of concern. Jess had brought Brad's high-powered binoculars to the dock and thought he could see the flashing blue lights of the patrol boats far in the distance.

Ten minutes later, the sirens wailed again, this time trailing off to the northwestern side of the lake.

"How about a report, Mr. Lookout," Harriet said, needling Jess who had not stopped peering through the binoculars.

"I really think there's a boat coming in this direction, fast." The other three tried to focus through the blinding combination of sun, water, and bright blue sky. When Jess finally announced that the boat speeding toward them was indeed the *Educator's Express,* all four of them moved out to the edge of the dock.

"I don't see Rich. He must be down in the cabin or something." It was as though Jess felt a need to keep up a running commentary with no idea why. As the distance between the boat and the dock closed, Jess let the binoculars dangle by their strap around his neck.

Brad roared into the no wake zone without reducing his speed. He deftly guided the boat to a perfect landing at the dock as Jack and Josie grabbed the lines.

"Where the hell is Rich?" Josie shouted, a kind of question that has to be asked even though the answer is one that no one wants to hear.

With four desperate people waiting, Brad's nonchalance in responding was maddening.

"He's on his way to Lakes Region Hospital," he finally said after tying the bow line to the dock and leaving the boat. "He got a little reckless out there and had an accident. I'm going to go over there if anyone wants to come." All but Josie interpreted the calmness in his tone to be a positive sign.

"So, what's he got, a broken leg or something?" Josie asked, the question demanding more details from Brad.

"Not sure. He was having some trouble moving so they had him strapped down pretty well. Anyway, I'm going over there if anyone else wants to come." Without hesitation, all four agreed that they wanted to be there.

"I'll be right up; I just want to finish something with the boat," Brad said. All but Josie started back to the house, subdued enough to ignore the flies humming in their ears.

Brad climbed back into the boat and Josie followed him.

"What really happened out there, Brad? You don't seem too concerned." She watched as he rearranged the ski equipment and busied himself with unimportant details that could have waited.

"I think he'll be fine, Jos, really. He just did a stupid thing. An observer wouldn't have helped, if that's what you're thinking. It'll probably sound awful but I think he may have gotten what he deserved for being so daring and so stupid. Now, why don't you let me finish up here and we'll go check him out." He turned back to snapping the cover over the cockpit, dismissing her.

She left the boat and walked slowly back toward the house, oblivious to the beautiful day and the surrounding environment. When she reached the deck, she turned back and looked down at Brad, still absorbed in his minor chores. A nebulous apprehension shivered through her, as though a chilly breeze had unexpectedly blown in from the lake.

*   *   *

The emergency room at Lakes Region General Hospital was having a typically slow Sunday morning until the report of a water skiing accident came in. The staff monitored the radio conversation between the ambulance and the lake patrol boat with concern. The statistical information flowed smoothly but the underlying tone of the emergency crew on the boat indicated that the patient was alive but not much more than that. The patient, an unidentified male in his early thirties, remained on the edge of going into shock, despite strong vital signs and being able to respond to questions. He had no feeling from the neck down and was totally immobilized on the stretcher until his exact injuries could be determined. The emergency room staff prepared for the worst.

In between exchanges about the condition of their patient as he was being transported, the officer in charge of the patrol boat tersely informed the nurse that they would want to interview Brad Wallace if he appeared. As the driver of the boat, they had a few routine questions to ask about the accident and would appreciate him staying available until they could speak with him.

By the time Rich's five friends arrived, the preliminary diagnosis had been made and he was well into the process of being prepared for transport to Boston. The emergency room doctor, a youthful man who might have passed for one of their students, escorted them into a conference room and introduced himself.

"I'm Doctor Richter," he announced in a strong voice that immediately hushed as he continued. "I wish I had better news for you." All six people stood behind the chairs at the conference table as though sitting down would only prolong the suspense and the agony along with it.

"Mr. Lane appears to have suffered severe trauma to his spinal cord. The force of the fall apparently twisted his neck; in laymen's terms, he broke his neck. We have tested nerve and muscle response of all extremities, and at the present time he has no feeling or movement any-where except for his head and upper neck." The doctor performed at his professional best, doling out the worst scenario first then extending the possibility of an incorrect diagnosis.

"It is possible that the cord is not so severely damaged but it will take the experts at Brigham and Women's in Boston to determine. We just aren't equipped for that." Josie was the first to allow a stifled sob to escape, followed quickly by Harriet.

"Can we see him?" Jess asked in a low, quivering voice.

"I'll check on that for you; I know he's stabilized and alert and I think is just about ready to go. We wondered if any of you would be going with him?"

The unexpected request caught them all unprepared but Harriet, always the quick thinker, said immediately, "I'll go. I've got to be in Boston on Tuesday anyway and you guys can arrange to get the rental car back to me, right?" Taking his cue from her unsurprising selflessness, Jess joined in.

"No problem, Harriet, Jack and I'll figure it out," he said. The doc-tor excused himself but returned before they had an opportunity to dis-cuss anything among themselves, just his head showing through the con-ference room door.

"If you're ready, I'll take you in. He said he would like to see you."

Josie reached for Brad's hand and held it tightly as they walked down the corridor, trailing the doctor and their three friends. When they reached the room, Dr. Richter opened the door and stood aside, letting them file in and stand awkwardly looking across at Rich, his stretcher sandwiched between two nurses looking like asylum matrons protecting a fragile but menacing psychopath.

Rich's head lay encased in protective padding and he was strapped onto the gurney without any hope of moving even if he

197

could. He sensed their presence in the room and spoke, his voice strong and clear.

"Well, come on over here." They followed his invitation and, with the exception of Brad, moved as one body to his side. Brad stayed behind, able to see him only if he looked between any two heads, like someone straining to get a better view of the screen in a movie theater.

"I suppose you're wondering why I've called you all together," he said, the familiar Lane glint in his eye. Josie let a faint, barely perceptible sigh slip out. The others, having sucked in their breath without realizing it as they approached the wheeled stretcher, followed her lead. From their angle, it was difficult to tell if the sparkle in Rich's eyes came from his teasing or if they were simply watering.

"I've called you here to tell you that my friend Brad, the one hiding behind you, could have killed me today." Brad tilted his head slightly to peer over Josie's shoulder, anxious to see his friend's face. Instead, his attention was drawn to the rapid movement of his Adam's apple, as if he was gulping for air but with no other sign of distress. Then the reason for the sparkle was clear; the wetness dribbled down his cheeks. Harriet fished in her pocketbook for a Kleenex and was the first to move. She gently dried the stains on his face.

"Can't even dry my own fucking tears. Sorry, Harriet, but I'm allowed to swear in this predicament, aren't I?"

Dr. Richter came in, observed the situation and just stood back, waiting for them to finish.

"Brad. Please come closer." Josie and Harriet moved apart to let Brad through, his hesitancy painfully clear.

"How could you let me be so stupid, Brad, how could you?" He closed his eyes tightly, as if doing so could shut out the brutal realities surrounding him.

"Jesus, Rich, I'm so sorry." Brad dropped his eyes to the floor as Dr. Richter moved into the group.

"We've got to take him now. Who's coming?"

Harriet rested her hand on his shoulder as the two nurses assumed

198

their stations at each end of the gurney and started to wheel him out.

"Don't be too hard on yourself, Brad. It wasn't your fault," Rich said as he started to roll away, his eyes flitting from side to side as he strained to see everyone. Other than the cover on his chest rising and falling with each breath, his eyes were the only part of his body moving.

Brad pulled a well-used handkerchief from the back pocket of his shorts and covered his eyes with it, keeping his head down. Josie moved closer and put her arm around him as Rich and his entourage disappeared around the corner. She squeezed him, a motherly type of squeeze that drew them closer together. Jess Grogan came to them, enfolding both of them in his arms. He leaned his head on Josie's shoulder like a little boy who had just narrowly escaped from the local bully.

"I should've gone with them, Josie," he said, as though Brad was not part of the small group hug. Jess's startling sob brought Jack into the group and the four of them stood together as though frozen to the spot.

"I should've gotten my lazy ass out of bed and gone with them," Jess said, "God damn it." His voice began angry and ended barely audible.

Brad, physically still in the middle of the group but emotionally not part of it, broke the horrible tension descending on them.

"I think the patrol guys are waiting to talk with me." As if on cue, one of the nurses who had wheeled Rich out came to the door.

"I'm sorry to interrupt but there is a patrolman here wanting to speak with Mr. Wallace. He said he'll meet you in the waiting room down the hall." She assumed her professionally sympathetic nurse expression. "Sorry about your friend," she said and then was gone.

Brad extricated himself from the tangle arms holding them together and stuffed his dry handkerchief back in his pocket. "This shouldn't take long. I'll see you all outside."

"I think I should go with you," Josie protested. "It'll be hard to talk about."

"They're not going to arrest me, for goodness sakes, Jos. They'll just want to confirm some stuff, that's all. It's not going to be hard to talk about; it's just something that happened, an unfortunate accident, as they

199

say. You go ahead with your friends and I'll be along shortly." Afraid that his attitude had slipped into the slightly cavalier, Brad kissed her on the cheek.

"Thanks for your concern but really I'll be fine. I'm the eternal optimist, you know. I'm sure Rich's prognosis will change in Boston."

The four of them happily escaped the sterilized environment of the hospital emergency room with its overpowering antiseptic smells and array of frightening equipment lining every wall. The ever-present nurse directed Brad to the right and the others walked toward the exit off to the left. After stepping out into the warm sunshine, the three took a collective deep breath, inhaling the fresh New Hampshire air. Jack Hopkins was the first to speak.

"What the hell's he mean, go with your friends, Josie? I thought we were his friends too. What gives?"

*   *   *

Brad's interview with Patrolman Gordon Tibideau was over in ten minutes. He described his effort to avoid what he feared might be a rock just below the surface, guiding the boat hard to starboard. Rich, gaining enough confidence to become reckless, had cut across the wake from the port side. At this point, Tibideau interrupted his narrative.

"I don't mean to be harsh, here, Mr. Wallace, especially with the serious injury to your friend, but if there had been an observer in the boat this may not have happened."

"I guess that if I believed that, I think I'd be going crazy right now." He paused for effect.

"Do you believe in fate, Officer?" Brad succeeded in redirecting the patrolman's feelings toward compassion.

"I guess I do to a point, like everyone else, I suppose. You must be pretty upset, I'm sure, but I've got to do this." Tibideau looked away as Brad swallowed hard and rubbed his eyes.

Brad paused again, as if having difficulty gathering his thoughts.

"I really don't think an observer would have helped. Everything happened so fast and Rich couldn't be alerted to what was going on. I straightened out as soon as I saw him out there but by that time, he had let the line go slack. As I said, call it fate or destiny or whatever, the timing was just bad." He composed himself for what had to come next. "I've seen this happen before, you now, plenty of times. All that usually comes of it is a bruised ego and a snootful of water. This time was no different, observer or not." A positive finality closed his analysis of the accident.

The patrolman, despite his youth and inexperience, had seen enough arrogance and reckless behavior on the lake to place this event in the category of skiing mistakes coming from either stupid or naïve judgement.

"Well, Mr. Wallace, I've got no choice but to give you a citation for the observer infraction. The fine is minimal and you can just mail it in. I'm sure that this'll be all the action we'll take. I'm truly sorry about what happened and I'll be praying that Mr. Lane will be OK." He reached out and shook Brad's hand. They walked together down the hall and exited the building, relieved to be out of the suffocating ambience of a hospital emergency room. Josie was waiting for them on the concrete steps leading down to the sidewalk. After an introduction to Patrolman Tibideau, they crossed the parking lot to the car. It was just after ten o'clock and still quiet on the streets surrounding the hospital. Most Sunday morning activity for the residents and tourists consisted of finding a morning paper and a cup of coffee. The town was just coming to life, an ironic fact not lost on the four people who piled into Brad's car. The incredible event they had experienced assumed a surreal quality, easily denied if it didn't continue to slap them emotionally in the face on the trip back to the cabin. They could have been any one of the other carloads of tourists, getting warmed up for a Sunday on a long holiday weekend. Instead, the mountains, the lake, the weather, the very air they breathed blended together into a mist of sorrow.

"What are we going to do, Brad? I mean we've got to let his father know. Oh, God, he's going to be devastated." Jess, the mathematician, the logician, the most grounded of any of them, choked on his words. "His father is such a great guy; a wife and son in a two year time span. My good Christ, I can't believe this." He stared out the window, seeing nothing but a blur.

"Look, Jess, he's going to be all right. He's not dead, for God's sake." Brad's agitation surfaced with a vengeance. "We'll probably get a phone call to come get him tonight so let's not overreact."

Josie erupted. "How can you say that, Brad? Do you know something that we don't? I believe he's in really bad shape and we'd better start calling people."

The two men in the back seat leaned forward and Jack tried to ease the tension. "Come on, kids, fight nice, please. Things are bad enough."

Brad softened. He removed a hand from the wheel to rub the back of his neck and tried to squeeze the tautness out of the hard knots that had formed in every muscle. "Look, everybody, I'm sorry but I guess I've got a little defense mechanism going here. I have to believe that he'll be OK; that's all there is to it." He let his shoulders sag just enough so that the others would notice.

Josie was the first to reach across to him, putting her hand on his thigh and squeezing gently. In turn, each of the men in the back seat leaned forward, patted his shoulder and reclined again. The wind whistling through the partially opened driver's side window was the only sound in the car for several minutes.

Josie finally broke the echoing silence. "We got to have a plan here, guys, so let's work on it."

The plans were not quite completed when they arrived at the cabin and after each took a quick trip to the bathroom, they reconvened on the deck. The late morning sun, high in the sky with the approach of summer, discouraged but didn't entirely dissuade the clouds of flies. The inconvenient intrusion on the gathering was hardly noticed, their thoughts centered on how best to go forward with the awful task before them. Jess, Mr. Logic personified, listed all that needed to be done on the first sheet of the yellow legal pad he managed to produce whenever the need arose. The list became like a job jar for a large family, the unpopular chores being divided equally among the members.

Josie agreed to call Rich's father, after insisting on collaborative advice as to what she should say. The general consensus was simply telling him that his son had been injured and taken to Boston for evaluation. No details need be provided. If she waited to make the call until they packed everything, they could be at Brighams to meet him. Jack Hopkins, whose complexion had been a pasty white ever since he found out about the accident, swallowed hard and said that he would inform Superintendent Chris Howard. The mention of the Superintendent's name in this context evoked a disturbing vision in Brad, one that made him visibly blanche.

"Tyler Spence," he said loudly. The association of the tragedy of Tyler with Chris Howard was unfortunate but one that would never be erased for Brad.

"What'll you tell the Super? I'd suggest not much until we have more to go on." Brad's suggestion seemed appropriate and Jack latched onto it as a relatively easy out for him.

The question of packing Harriet's clothes and arranging to drive her rental car back to Boston fell to Jess while Brad, by an ironic process of elimination, became responsible for all of Rich's belongings. The divvying of the chores completed, Brad suggested that they break the unwritten but strictly observed commandment, "Thou shalt not consume alcohol before noon."

"Why don't we have a drink, right here on the deck to spite the flies, and then get to it? We can be in Boston in a few hours, say hello to Rich and his dad and be back in Connecticut by nightfall." He smiled, as though the crisis was solved and all was well.

"I hope it is that simple when we get there," Josie said. "I have a feeling we might be there for a while."

*　　*　　*

Harriet sat in the waiting room and saw Josie walk by the window. She jumped up and called after her. The expression on her face shouted that the news was not good. The colorful waiting room with its modernistic splashes of bright shades of red and yellow clashed with Harriet's somber mood. Josie stood by the door until the men came down the hall then all huddled to hear about Rich's condition.

"Well, there were several surgeons waiting for us when we got here. I guess the nature of his injury attracted a lot of attention. Anyway, they were all set up to do their tests and diagnosis so it didn't take long.

"Will you get to the point, Harriet. Jesus!" Jack Hopkins' complexion changed from chalky white to a noticeable pink as he voiced his frustration.

"Sorry, it's just hard to get this out. This type of injury does not repair itself. All their preliminary stuff indicates total paralysis from the neck down. The nurse told me that spinal cord injuries attract the best neurological surgeons because of the challenge, but they sure weren't very hopeful."

"Have they told Rich any of this yet?" Brad asked.

"They wanted me to tell him but I couldn't, at least not until you all got here. What about his father? I remember him being a wonderful man."

"Chicken shit doctors; what is it with them anyway? It's their job to tell people stuff like this." Brad felt Josie staring at him.

"What about chicken shit boat drivers or chicken shit water skiers? I just don't understand you sometimes, Brad. Can we just deal with our friend's problem here, please," she said, anger and frustration and choking sadness spewing out. She turned to Harriet.

"To answer your question, his father's on his way; I think we should wait. How do you feel about it?"

Brad retreated to a corner of the room and sank into an overstuffed chair that seemed ready to swallow him. The others nodded agreement. In silence they moved toward the varied chairs around the perimeter of the room. Josie sat as far away from Brad as she could. They waited for Mr. Lane to arrive, all lost in the private world of their own thoughts. To a passerby glancing in the window, they could have been assorted patients sitting in a doctor's office, all perfect strangers to each other.

Another Havenot Visit

"The mass of men live lives of quiet desperation."
Henry David Thoreau

Josie and the rest of the staff and students at Hampton Village High School spent the last two weeks of school trying to convince the world that everything was normal. They observed every ritual, attended every customary event, and played every senior prank. The traditions became mandatory, as if going through the motions would erase the pain of Rich Lane's absence. She forced the lunches with Jess and Jack to continue, even though at times the sadness made it impossible to speak.

Josie kept up with Rich's progress at the hospital through a daily phone call, timed to the minute so that a nurse would be available to hold the phone to his ear. The tenth and final full day of his stay, he laughed as Josie asked him the standard question about how he was doing.

"Wait 'til you hear this, Jos. And you must know that this is a direct quote from the head of my crack neuro team. 'You've got a clean bill of health,' he says. So I said, 'You mean except for the minor detail about not walking or feeding myself or wiping my own ass?' Don't you just love it? I think he must mean that I'm able to breathe."

Josie paused, her chuckling indistinguishable from choked back sobs.

"You are really too much," she finally said.

Rich came home from Brighams late on Thursday afternoon, to even the most optimistic observer, just an amazing eleven days after the accident. The weather had turned cool for the middle of June. As the ambulance driver and an assistant lowered the stretcher to the pavement, the wool blanket covering him slipped to the ground. His father, watching from the porch, noticed that his son did not react at all to the cool breeze blowing across him. He turned away, fighting a wave of nausea. Ever since he arrived at the hospital on the fateful Sunday and watched another piece of his comfortable world crumble, a quiet desperation assumed control. All aspects of Rich's care became personal missions.

In the short time available, he arranged for every imaginable kind of technological assistance to be installed at his spacious country home. With Josie's help, most of Rich's clothes and personal effects were moved from his apartment to a first floor room that had been his father's study. A temporary ramp, somewhat steep but still negotiable, covered the four steps leading to the front porch.

When the gurney was secured and the blanket picked up, Richard Lane Sr. rolled the heavy-duty wheel chair down the ramp and to the side of the stretcher. The driver cradled Rich's head and the two men lifted him gently into the chair. After seeing that he was strapped in properly, the two attendants placed the rolling cart back in the ambulance and closed the door.

"Thanks a lot, fellas," Rich said. His father, still recovering from the blanket scene, mumbled a perfunctory thanks before the men climbed into the vehicle. He watched as it pulled away, the similarity between the delivery of a new refrigerator several weeks before and the delivery of his son today crashing in on him. The short trip up the driveway and the ramp into the house was silent and came close to undoing him again. The fragility of human existence makes us all prisoners, one way or another.

"I'm glad your mother isn't here to see this," he said as they reached what was to be Rich's room. He came around to the front of the wheel chair and knelt down, his head bowed as if in prayer.

"We've got full time help coming starting tonight," he said to the carpet. Then he looked up at his son, the pain in his eyes palpable.

"I love you, Rich, and I don't know why this had to happen." He studied the carpet again. After a few seconds of silence, both men cried together as they had just two years before when Rich's mother died.

*   *   *

Rich convinced his father to take him to Hampton Village High School for his first visit since the accident on the final day of school for the staff. The half-day teacher workshop schedule would allow him a chance to have lunch with his friends while avoiding any contact with the students. Josie and Jess were his most faithful visitors and could handle the problems attached to mealtime for him. Arrangements were made and Josie was waiting in front of the school as the specially equipped Econoline van pulled up. Rich's father had mastered the vagaries of the power liftgate and Rich was out of the van in a few moments. Josie took over, pushing Rich toward the picnic table where Jess and Jack were to meet them for lunch.

"Give us about an hour or so, Mr. Lane," she called back. With a wave, he climbed back into the van and drove off.

"So, what's new?" Rich laughed at Josie's usual opening question.

"I've got a new good looking nurse but she's only temporary. Doesn't that just figure? Other than that, I'm doing all right." After arranging his chair at one end of the table, she locked the brake and straddled the bench so she could face him. The question took on a life of its own, as though she had no power to control it.

"The prognosis hasn't changed but we didn't expect that it would, did we?"

The padded supports on either side of his head made him look as if he were wearing large black earmuffs that were too tight for him.

"Are you comfortable with those things on?" she asked.

"You should see my head wobble when I get excited if I don't have them holding me. I asked Dad to put them in place because I knew I was seeing you and you know how that affects me." His smirk told her that there was no need to answer.

"You're still utterly incorrigible." She laughed and Rich laughed with her.

"I'm sure not very dangerous now, as if I ever were. That Brad is one lucky guy and I hope he knows it."

207

The welcome distraction of Jess walking toward them allowed Josie the excuse to end this troubling part of the conversation.

"I'm sure that he does. At least I think he does," she said.

Rich peered at her. It was as if all his senses had combined to make his eyes their focus, making them more penetrating than ever.

"You're going to get a lot of company. I hope that's OK," Josie said, wilting under his gaze.

"Oh yeah, sure, that's great." He continued to stare at her as she stood to greet Jess, watching until she moved out of his range of vision.

Over an hour and dozens of well-wishing teachers later, Richard Lane drove into the circular drive in the van. Rich's back was to his father and he became aware of his presence by way of Josie's greeting.

"My heavens, Mr. Lane, has it really been an hour already?" she asked. A few of the staff remained, including Jack Hopkins, but they drifted away when they saw Rich's father approach. For these few, especially Jack, seeing the indomitable Rich Lane as a quadriplegic had been quite enough for one day. Watching his father approach led to a series of mumbled apologies from their colleagues. Except for Josie, none of them were prepared with the pain that was sure to follow. Soon, she and Rich sat alone at the picnic table with his father.

"Could you stay a few minutes, Mr. Lane? The cafeteria's desperate to get rid of everything today and I'm sure I could find something." Josie asked.

The early summer afternoon stretched out before him. He promised the day nurse that she could have the afternoon off, and they had at least two more hours before the second shift arrived.

"Sure, why not, if it's OK with you, Rich." He expected a flip answer and Rich did not disappoint him.

"Oh, shoot, Dad, you promised to take me golfing today, but I'll forego that for a few more minutes with my friend here." Rich winked at Josie.

Several minutes later, Josie came out of the school balancing a cardboard tray overloaded with two ham sandwiches, several snack packs of potato chips, and a Coca-Cola. Since Rich was a favorite with all the school support staff and cafeteria workers, they were pleased to send as much as they could.

As she returned to the picnic table with the overloaded tray, she noticed a third person hovering around Rich and his father. Her surprise blossomed into concern when she moved close enough to see who it was.

"Detective Havenot. Is everything all right?" she asked, her voice a raspy, worried gasp.

"Didn't mean to worry you, Mrs. Wallace, but yes, everything is just fine. I read in the papers about your friend's accident a couple of weeks back and I've meant to drop by to see how you were doing. Quite a coincidence to meet Mr. Lane here. I thought it'd be OK with this being the last day of school and no kids around. I hope you don't mind."

Josie continued to be nonplussed, caught off-balance by his thoughtfulness.

"No, not at all. It's just that I didn't expect you and, to tell you the truth, anytime I see you it's usually for something unpleasant."

Parker laughed and the two Lanes joined in.

"Great reputation you've got there, Detective," Rich said and Josie noticed the familiar impish twinkle in his eyes.

"Unbelievable," she said. The three men looked at her as if searching for an explanation but when none was forthcoming, they let the comment drop.

Richard Lane devoured the two sandwiches while Josie, Parker, and Rich talked about the weather, sports, and any other subject that avoided mention of the accident. By the time he finished his lunch, Rich admitted that he was beginning to get tired. His father, with the subtle, loving attention reserved for parent-child relationships, tucked the light covering around Rich and checked to make sure he was strapped in the chair properly.

"Great lunch, Josie. Good to meet you, Detective." Richard moved to Josie and gave her a warm, unexpected hug.

"Thanks for your support, Josie; it means more to me and Rich than you could know."

Josie went to Rich and kissed him on the cheek.

"You take care and I'll talk to you soon." Rich looked at her, all pretense of his strong constitution leaving him.

"See you," he said, helplessly nodding his head to signal his father to start rolling the chair. "Thanks, Josie." His eyes filled and he bowed his head. Without another word, Mr. Lane turned the wheel chair and pushed his son toward the van.

Josie and Parker observed the entire process of loading the chair and its wasted human cargo, standing in a solemn silence reminiscent of watching a casket lowered into the ground at a graveside service.

After the van drove off, Parker broke the heavy silence.

"Damn, that is tough. Pardon my French, Mrs. Wallace, but life can be pretty shitty, if you ask me."

"Yes, it surely can," was all she answered. The tired tone in her voice touched the seasoned detective more than he was prepared for.

"I guess I'll be getting along. I know you've been through a lot and didn't need this. If I can be of any help, please give me a call." After a moment of awkward quiet, he started across the front lawn toward his car. She called after him to come back, surprising him.

"Thanks for coming by, Detective; please don't think I didn't appreciate your concern. You just surprised me, that's all. If you've got the time why don't you sit for a minute?" He spun on his heel and came back to the table.

"Only if you call me Parker," he said, smiling.

"That's a deal, Parker, but only if you'll stop calling me Mrs. Wallace."

*　　*　　*

"One of those damn 'another place, another time' things," he said loudly, his comment echoing through the car as he drove back to the station. Parker couldn't deny enjoying his visit with Josie, even under the trying circumstances of seeing Rich Lane.

Her compassion, her strength and an unassuming yet robust

210

beauty impressed him. He knew that with Josie Wallace, he'd better follow his personal creed, a belief that had kept him out of trouble with women since his divorce.

"Feelings can't be controlled; actions can be," he recited to himself. "Attraction does not have to lead to action."

With that out of his way, the conversation with Josie came back in detective preciseness and he decided that he'd like to talk with Patrolman Tibideau up on Lake Winnipesaukee. Josie's casual mention of Brad's insistence on speaking with the officer investigating the accident alone bothered him although there was no clear reason why it should. There was nothing here but a tragic accident and water-skiing was well out of his element. Returning to his office, he indulged in the luxury of sitting with his feet propped on his desk as he sat looking at the phone. Finally he picked it up, asking the dispatcher to contact an Officer Tibideau of the Lake Winnipesaukee Lake Patrol in New Hampshire.

When the dispatcher inquired innocently about what was going on up North, he said "Probably nothing, just for curiosity, mostly," and added under his breath, "Maybe for Josie, too."

Late that afternoon, the return call from Tibideau came through to his office. Parker regretted yet another intrusion into the lives of Josie and Brad Wallace but the feeling was not strong enough to have him cancel the call.

"Havenot here."

"This is Gordon Tibideau, returning your call." From the youthful voice, he pictured the patrolman as barely of shaving age.

"I've got a friend who was involved in that skiing accident a few weeks ago up there. I wondered if you'd mind if I asked a couple of questions?"

In five minutes, Parker had all the information he wanted and thanked the young man for calling back. He started a doodle on the well-worn blotter covering his desk as he reconstructed the accident in his mind. Gordon was adamant on two points. First, this type of accident was relatively common, but the outcome was rarely as sad as in Rich Lane's case. Second, an observer may or may not have prevented the accident.

"These things happen so fast that the driver of the craft usually can't respond to the situation quickly enough," Gordon said.

"Just for the sake of argument," Parker asked with a blasé disinterest. "How difficult would it be for someone to duplicate the conditions of this accident?"

Gordon Tibideau answered quickly.

"I'm not sure why you'd want to but it's easy to do. That's why it's so common." As he described the circumstances of the accident, Parker continued his doodling on the blotter.

"Call if I can be of any more help, Detective. I hope all the folks involved down there are doing OK," Tibideau said before hanging up.

"Nice young man," Parker thought as he looked at his doodle on the blotter. It was a boat with a stick figure water skiing behind it.

The Blackest Period

*"When we cannot find contentment within ourselves,
it is useless to seek it elsewhere."*
La Rochefoucauld

After administering justice and destiny to Rich Lane, Brad did not visit the gravesite for more than four weeks. The official school year had ended, but his department head duties kept him trekking to Hartford for an additional two weeks. Josie had enrolled in an evening summer class at the Danbury Campus of the University of Connecticut, a six-week course that meant two westward trips a week. Every Tuesday and Thursday, Brad was left to his own devices for dinner. On the second night of her course, he mixed a powerful martini, retrieved a folding lawn chair from the porch, and walked toward the cemetery.

The route he selected took him past the elementary school. The squeals of the children coming from the playground area slowed him down. He stopped, putting the chair down and leaning on the short cyclone fence. Four or five groups of children ran from one amusement to the other, their parents unable to keep up with them. The tallest set of swings sat at the far end of the playground and the loud laughter coming from them caught his attention. Two fathers, engaged in friendly competition, pushed their young sons higher and higher, the boys laughing with the nervous twitter that separates fun from fear. Brad Jr. would have been four years old. He picked up his chair and continued toward the cemetery, with the pressure of a steel band pulled tightly across his chest.

The early summer growth of grass spilled over onto the stone, touching but not covering the inscription. He set up the chair then dropped to his hands and knees. He pushed the grass back to the edge of the stone and, using both hands, trimmed his way around the stone. He removed his handkerchief from his pocket and dusted the dirt from the

213

marker until there was no evidence of any overgrowth.

Several rows away, an elderly couple stood clinging to each other, staring at a large granite headstone. The woman's shoulders shook but there was no sound. They paid no attention to him but he waited until they exhausted their tears and walked away. No one else chose this night to mourn, at least as far as he could see.

He positioned his chair so that when he sat down, he would have to straddle Brad's stone with his feet. He stood reverently for several minutes before sitting down. When he bowed his head, he looked straight down at it.

"Well, let me tell you what I've been up to, my boy," he said loudly then dropped his voice to a whisper. He welcomed the descending blackness.

"I handled everything just fine," he said. He recounted the details of the accident, interspersed with asides. "You probably could have been calling him Uncle." And a few minutes later, "He might have been your Godfather, for Christ's sake." He concluded the tale with his voice raised once more.

"Best of all, Fate stepped in to decide the punishment so I know that what I'm doing is right. Some things are meant to be, that's all." He stood, careful again not to disturb the grass or dirt around the stone. He snapped the folding chair together and tucked it under his arm.

"Good night, son, and thanks." The darkness lifted and he began the walk home.

Harriet's News

"Life moves on, whether we act as cowards or heroes."
Henry Miller

Richard Nixon made good on his campaign promise to extract the United States from the deadly conflict in Southeast Asia. In January of 1973, a peace treaty was signed and by March, the last of the United States troops had left Vietnam. Less than two years later, the American President resigned from office under a siege of a different type, a crushing humiliation after a special prosecutor's office amassed enough evidence of criminal activity and cover-up in the Watergate scandal to drive him from Washington.

Against this backdrop of historically depressing news, Harriet called Josie two days after the resignation of Nixon with what she said was some good Asian news for a change. A final adoption agreement had been approved and a little Korean girl was already on her way to Chicago. Harriet's infectious excitement practically sent sparks through the line. Josie's melancholy caused by Brad's apathy toward adoption returned.

"I want you to be her godmother and we're asking a friend of Paul's to be her godfather." A slight twinge drained some of Josie's happiness. It would be nice if she and Brad could be godparents together but Brad had not been one of Harriet's favorite people since Rich's accident. The slight, if it were noticed, would at least be understood. Brad hadn't handled himself well in that situation two years before.

"It sure has taken a long time but this is so exciting, Jos. Maybe when Brad sees her, he'll change his mind," Harriet said. The chances of that happening, she knew, fluctuated between slim and none.

Josie disconnected with her finger, the phone still in her hand as she dialed Rich's number. His nurse answered, her professional tone softening when she heard Josie's voice.

"Hi, Josie. Hold on a minute and I'll get the phone to him. He's just watching more of that dumb Watergate stuff. What he gets from that I'll never understand. All these post mortems are driving me crazy. He'd do a lot better with a soap opera."

Josie laughed. She could imagine Rich sitting there waiting for the phone to be hooked on his head, gritting his teeth for patience. Nurse Becky was cute and efficient but insufferably opinionated.

"Hey, Josie, what's up?" Rich asked, his cheerful voice already erasing some of her edginess. "Can you believe this Becky; she gets away with murder just because I love to see her bend over to tuck me in." Josie was certain that Becky would be standing there blushing but enjoying every minute of it.

"Harriet just called. They're getting a Korean child." Rich responded exactly as she knew he would.

"That is so wonderful, Josie. We could use a lot more people like her and Paul in this world. They're really special. I'll give her a call as soon as I'm finished with you." Rich's enthusiasm for the world had not diminished. For two hopeful months after the accident, he followed an aggressive rehabilitation schedule prescribed by his doctors, his inherent optimism taking control. After seeing no improvement and with the finality of his predicament obvious, Rich made a conscious and courageous decision. He simply refused to allow his "inconvenience" to affect his personality and his outlook. Josie found it ironic to hear him speaking of how special the Stantons were. The world needed more people with attitudes like Rich Lane.

"I'm still here, Josie," he had said when the doctors faced the absolute permanency of his condition. "As I see it, I don't have a choice. It's a bad hand to be dealt but that sure as hell doesn't mean that I've got to throw it in."

Within minutes after disconnecting from Josie, Becky had Harriet on the phone. She set the phone so that Rich could speak and hear without effort and then left the room.

"So, Harriet, Josie just phoned with the news. I want to hear all

216

about everything." The natural animation in his voice blended with such sincere empathy that Harriet drew a deep breath before answering.

"OK, I'll tell you everything but first you have to tell me. How're you doing? I mean, really, how are you doing?" she asked, emphasizing each word of the question. "I think of you all the time."

"Oh, my gosh, I hope you don't tell your husband." They both laughed. "I'm doing pretty well, honest. Ups and downs but the ups outnumber the downs and I guess we'd all like to be able to say that, right? Now, come on, tell me about this little girl you guys are getting."

Harriet related the details of the Korean baby who was on a plane as they spoke. When she finished, it was Rich who took the deep breath to keep from weeping.

The baby had been left on the steps of a textile factory in Seoul by a mother apparently too poor or too embarrassed to raise the child. The damp cold of the night penetrated the tiny basket, making the light blanket covering the child useless. Severely weakened by pneumonia when discovered early in the morning, she was taken to the Adventist Hospital in Seoul, where doctors held little hope for her survival. At this point in her story, Harriet paused.

"Do you remember a deep philosophical discussion we had about that Thorton Wilder idea, the one from *The Bridge of San Luis Rey*? It was one of those Fridays at Pete's and after several beers you English teachers were holding forth as usual." Harriet was sure that he would remember.

"Of course I remember. I've got a mind like a steel trap. Something like either we live by accident and die by accident or we live by plan and die by plan. I sure have a different perspective on that right about now." His soft chuckle astonished Harriet once more. "What's that got to do with your little girl, anyway?"

"Everything. I think it has everything to do with her. She should've died and now she's coming to me. It's got to be part of the plan."

Harriet finished her story. The baby, whether by plan or by accident, miraculously survived the pneumonia. Through a series of coincidences, the baby was moved to a caring foster home and spent six months there before the adoption was arranged through an international Christian agency.

"I'll send you a picture, Rich. She is just precious. We feel so blessed."

Rich drew in another deep breath, forcing back the choking lump in his throat.

"She's blessed to have you two and, by the way, I don't really believe in coincidences."

*　　*　　*

Josie spent much of the day wondering how Brad would react to Harriet's news. She admitted to Harriet that the chances of changing his mind were not good. She had set herself up for disappointment in the past and did not plan on repeating that mistake again. This would be a simple informational session, with no hidden agenda, no clinging to hope allowed. She waited until they sat on the front porch, enjoying the early evening in the neighborhood with their well-iced martinis.

"I had a call from Harriet today," she said, praying that it sounded as nonchalant as she intended. "Their adoption is finalized and the baby will be with them within two days."

"That seems awfully quick," Brad answered without looking up from his newspaper.

"They didn't tell anyone until the last minute; didn't want to jinx anything. It's a Korean baby."

"That's really nice, if that's what they want. I hope they don't regret it. It's the kind of decision people sometimes regret, you know what I mean?" The answer to his question was a loud slurp as Josie gulped a large mouthful of martini.

"Well, how was your day, dear?" she asked, another question that needn't be answered. Earlier she had wondered about his reaction to the Stantons' child; now she wondered if there were married couples who spoke nothing but cliches to each other twenty four hours a day. *It's probably true,* she thought as she slurped her martini once more.

Havenot's Vacation

"Live Free or Die"
State Motto of New Hampshire

Western Connecticut provided as much country living as Parker Havenot desired. He accepted Gordon Tibideau's kind invitation to visit Lake Winnipesaukee to observe what the lake patrol did, mostly as a matter of professional courtesy. He had not taken any sort of vacation since joining the Covington County Sheriff's Department, and Gordon's insistence to spend a few days in the Lakes Region exposed him to an area that he now used as a haven at every opportunity. Several informative phone conversations about Rich's accident created a bond of mutual respect between the two, and Parker's curiosity about the lake and Rich's accident was piqued enough to follow through with the visit.

Gordon originally invited him to spend the long Fourth of July weekend with them but Parker begged off, thinking that he would rather spend his first trip to the lake in a slower mid-week period. When he announced that he would be taking several days off, his colleagues at the sheriff's department were incredulous.

"Only one possibility here; it's got to be a woman." John Lockhart, Parker's closest friend in the department, led off the joking and the others around hopped aboard.

"Don't I wish." Parker responded with an inadequate comeback in the face of the teasing. "Actually, I just want to get away from you guys for a while."

*   *   *

Parker planned on taking a leisurely drive on his first trip and four hours and several minor detours later, he found the small town of Mapleboro. After several more dead-ends and dirt road frustrations, he found the

219

Tibideaus just in time for lunch. Gordon had volunteered to take the three to eleven shift that day, anticipating that Detective Havenot might want to ride with him. The warm hospitality and instant rapport with the Tibideaus put him at ease immediately and Parker immersed himself in the good company and the awesome scenery. When Gordon stood up, announcing that he needed to prepare for work, his parents and their guest were shocked that the two hours passed so quickly.

"What should I wear out there, Gordon? I'm kind of new to this, you know."

"Just don't look like a damned flatlander, even if you are." When they all laughed, Parker joined them, uncertain why he did so.

"Don't mind him, Parker. He has to deal with all sorts of unusual things on the lake and a lot of times it's tourists who cause 'em. You can wear whatever you want. I don't expect you'll be going in the water." They all laughed again at Mr. Tibideau's little joke.

A half-hour later, they arrived at the large town dock in the neighboring town of Stoneham. The lake patrol boat Gordon would be piloting hadn't arrived at the dock yet.

"I usually run across the street and get a sandwich to take with me for dinner. What would you like?" Parker agreed to walk with him and see what might be available.

The summer warmth and sunshine enticed most people to stay on the beaches longer than usual but the quaint downtown shopping district still bustled. Tourists and local vendors tending their sandwich and snack carts mixed with a smattering of natives, a breed difficult to find during the summer in any of the lake side towns. Vehicular traffic crawled through the area and Gordon stepped into a crosswalk, in front of cars coming in both directions.

Parker reacted instinctively, grabbing his shirt from behind.

"They have to yield, Parker; this is New Hampshire, remember?" Gordon laughed at the puzzled look on his new friend's face.

Parker reacted with typical city logic. "Maybe the sign says so but I wouldn't want to be arguing from a prone position with tire tracks running over my chest." He smiled and shook his head as they continued through the crosswalk, the cars stopping to let them pass.

The local grocery store, minuscule by most supermarket standards, was well stocked and Parker enjoyed people watching as they meandered through the aisles until Gordon finished his shopping. As they approached the express checkout line, Parker heard one of the baggers, an older man with a confident air about him, clear his throat, a sound intended to catch someone's attention. His policeman mentality and training required absorbing details at both a conscious and subconscious level, and he had given up trying to put aside this ingrained aspect of his nature. He looked at the throat clearer and saw him nod, directing the attention of another older man bagging on a second checkout aisle toward the entrance. His instincts told him that these were two retired gentlemen filling the their time with a mindless job that enabled them to interact with people on a stress free level. He followed their gaze to the entrance, fully expecting to see a young woman with exhibitionist tendencies flouncing through the door. Instead, he was stunned to see Josie Wallace, looking beautiful in a sleeveless but modest summer dress. The eyes of the beholder supplied any unintended sexiness. She stopped her cart just past the entrance at a shelf filled with newspapers, pausing to glance at the headlines. Parker was at her side before she had the *Boston Globe* in the child's seat of the cart.

"Mrs. Wallace, what in the world are you doing here?" The coincidence shocked him at first but his discussions with Rich Lane about coincidences had led him to believe that there likely aren't any such things in this life

Josie, surprised also but quickly recovering, looked at him.

"I thought we had a deal, DETECTIVE HAVENOT," she said, emphasizing each syllable of his name.

Parker fumbled through an awkward response. "Sorry, Josie, I just have trouble with that after calling you Mrs. Wallace for so long." She interrupted him.

"It's all right, PARKER, I'm just teasing a bit." She smiled and he turned back toward Gordon to hide what he was afraid might be a flush rising in his cheeks. He was grateful when Gordon joined them.

"Mrs. Wallace. I saw you at the hospital but never had the chance to meet you. How's your friend doing?" Gordon's sincerity touched her and she stumbled ever so slightly with her answer.

"As well as can be expected. It's all pretty sad and we still can't believe it." Josie directed her attention to Parker. "I'm up for two weeks at our cabin. I should ask you the same question. What are you doing here?"

Parker paused. He felt his voice shaking when he answered.

"Gordon here invited me up. I've never been here before. I thought I'd try to get a taste of the real country." He was fumbling again. "I'm just here for a few days. The boys back at HQ can't get along for too long without their crack investigator." His attempt at humor failed miserably and Gordon rolled his eyes.

Several customers squeezed by before the three of them realized that they were blocking two thirds of the small entrance aisle. "Listen, we've got to run. It was good to bump into you, Mrs. Wal. . ."

"Good to see you again, too, Parker," she said, coating his name with the same good-natured sarcasm she used earlier.

As the two men walked through the first exit door, Parker turned around and caught a last glimpse of Josie before she turned the corner of the first aisle. His glance was enough to divert his attention and he crashed into the edge of the second door that Gordon held open.

"Well, that was fun. Are you going to be OK, Detective Havenot?" he asked, mimicking Josie's voice. Parker laughed, a vain attempt at covering his embarrassment.

*   *   *

Parker's respect for his new young friend grew with each passing minute as their patrol boat cruised through his assigned territory. Gordon Tibideau carried himself with the confidence of an experienced, hardened state trooper. He could supplant a friendly wave with an angry glare in an instant if the occasion warranted it. A few minutes after leaving the dock and weaving their way through the water skiers spreading out around the bay, Gordon noticed a speeding boat cornering around Cobb's Point. Pine Cove, a quiet development of expensive houses, lay just beyond the point. Most of the homes were second or third residences but during the summer the occupancy rate was high. He called back to Parker who was leaning back on the rear seat, craning his neck around like a first time visitor to New York City.

"Hold on, Detective, I think we might have a violation here." He smiled, as if proud to show off a bit for his visitor. The boat responded to his command instantly, forcing Parker's head back as it lurched forward. They rounded the point and Gordon flipped on his blue light. Parker's interest moved him to the front of the craft. The offending driver looked back over his shoulder and brought his boat to a stop, the high wake behind diminishing to a ripple.

Parker, still wondering what crime had been committed, watched as Gordon eased his craft next to the other boat and motioned with a finger drawn across the throat for the driver to cut his engine. As the rocking of both boats gradually subsided, Gordon reached out and grabbed the railing, pulling them together.

"What's going on, Officer?" The driver appeared honestly perplexed. Parker moved to the side, enjoying the role of observer.

"You were going a might fast for this area, don't you think? The residents are used to peace and quiet in the cove." Gordon's tone of voice indicated that he wasn't as angry as he seemed; there would be no issuing of citations. He let go of the rail and removed a clipboard from a hook by the wheel.

"I could cite you for careless operation but I'll just give you a warning." The boats had begun to drift apart. Gordon wrote something on his pad and then dismissed the other driver. "Just use your common sense, OK? Don't do something stupid that could ruin your vacation. Now you have an enjoyable rest of the day."

"Thanks a lot and sorry for your trouble." The other driver, relieved, started his engine and pulled away slowly, tossing a tentative half salute in Gordon's direction.

"Isn't there something in the Hippocratic oath about doing no harm?" Gordon said. "That's my philosophy sometimes. If I give that guy who's just being a little careless a citation and get him all ticked off, he develops an attitude that we're the enemy. This way, he might think about what he's doing and see us in a more positive light. I'm not always that easy, Parker."

Parker looked at him and nodded. People in law enforcement understand each other and communicate as well wordlessly as verbally. Nothing more need be said. Gordon's handling of the relatively minor incident told Parker that he was in the presence of a quality officer.

Activity on the lake quieted in the late afternoon and Gordon piloted his guest to the location of Rich's accident, demonstrating as well as he could how he thought it had happened.

"People fall on skis all the time, Parker. You wouldn't believe some of the crazy stuff I've seen out here. This was just one of those avoidable but tragic things, you know? It's so damned sad, that's all. Life changes in seconds and all the regrets and postmortems can't do a thing about it." Gordon elevated himself another notch in Parker's perception as he looked at the mountains in the distance, his eyes glistening. Then he turned to him.

"Somebody once said that life is like licking honey from a thorn," he said, his voice barely audible over the noise of the engine. "Well, poor Rich Lane found a whole rose bush full, didn't he?"

Parker's afternoon with Gordon gave him enough confidence that he could raise the evocative question, knowing that it would stay right there in the boat with them.

"This is probably going to sound pretty stupid under the circumstances but you know how policemen are. Do you think Rich's accident could have been caused deliberately, or at the very least, by a sort of intentional negligence, if there is such a thing?"

"You're right; it does sound stupid," Gordon said, but with a smile. "What the hell is an intentional negligence, anyway? But yeah, sure, a good driver could easily create that situation. Suppose Rich was clowning around and Brad Wallace got a little annoyed and decided to teach him a lesson by dumping him; he could've intentionally let that rope go taut. Interesting idea, Parker, but these guys have been good friends for a long time, haven't they?"

"Yep, they have and I'm sure it's just as you said, nothing but a damn tragic accident," Parker said, putting aside his cynical police investigator background for the moment.

He changed the subject.

"Anyway, you've got a great job here, Gordon. I envy you."

*   *   *

Gordon had convinced his parents to let Parker rent one of their bedrooms for his first stay on the lake. The three older adults in the household formed a remarkably quick friendship, the kind of instant kinship that people use as an argument for believing in reincarnation. From the moment they met, it was as though they had known each other for years. They had even discussed it on the second night of his stay as they sat in the pine paneled living room, watching through a wide picture window as the sun set. The spectacular exhibition of nature inspired reflective discussion.

"I've met a lot of people as you might imagine," Parker said, sipping a cool gin and tonic. "I guess I believe that there are just some people who you've got a natural affinity for. Who knows where it comes from."

He was going to like New Hampshire.

Brad's Promotion

"Watch for good times to retreat into yourself."
Thomas a Kempis

The two years of course work passed quickly for Brad Wallace. He loved the intellectual stimulation that came from mixing with colleagues from other districts in high-level postgraduate classes. His role as a department head in a large high school dovetailed perfectly with both the theoretical and practical aspects of most of the courses. His pragmatic experience in budgeting and finance combined with the more ethereal areas of curriculum, methodology, and teacher evaluation made him a welcome addition to any class discussion. The Master's degree in educational administration offered through the University of Hartford was designed to be completed in three years since most of the students were working full time in various educational positions. Brad convinced Josie that the best plan would be to compress the required courses and get it over with as soon as possible. His graduation coincided with the announcement by the Hartford City School District that a new position was being added to the bureaucracy at the upper echelons of the system. The title of Assistant Superintendent appealed to him and he made the decision to apply, ignoring the protest from his principal.

"How the hell can you be an assistant superintendent when you haven't even been a principal?" Mike asked when Brad informed him of his decision.

"It's just an exercise in futility, anyway. You know I'll never get the job. There are way too many people in the district with seniority and, shall I say, a degree of insider influence. Not to worry. You'll be stuck with me for a while yet but could I at least count on your recommendation should they ask?" Brad was certain that he could. Mike was as straightforward and honest as any administrator he had ever met.

"You know you can but why are you putting yourself through this? You've got such a good situation here. I guess I just don't understand, but it's your life." The conversation ended there.

One month later, Brad was looking around his office, planning how best to attack his packing chore in preparation for a move to the central administration building in downtown Hartford.

"Peter Principle be damned," he said as he disconnected the call with his finger, keeping the receiver cradled between his shoulder and his ear. He dialed the internal number for Mike Costello's office.

"Hey, Mike, I may have reached my level of incompetence. The Super just called. I got that job."

"I know. He called me first. Good luck, Brad. I just hope it's the right thing for you.

The newly established position held little attraction for others in the district. Moving into the upper levels of administration meant giving up the security of tenure in previous positions and the salary, while a substantial increase for Brad, was not inviting enough for most others to take the chance. His competition for the position consisted of just one other local candidate, an assistant principal from Hartford East High School, but Brad's job performance in the district made him the clear choice. If the tenuous nature of the position meant that he was out of a job in a year, so be it. He was a commodity in demand; there would be many districts out there ready to bring him on board, and at his compensation level as well.

He called Josie and told her to prepare a special supper.

On the way home, he turned into the cemetery. In the two years since Rich's accident, the visits to Brad Jr. had been infrequent. He welcomed the period of relative calm in his life and the visits he paid to the grave were positive. There seemed to be no need to escape the light of the world.

He parked the car and walked to Brad's marker, searching for a reason for stopping on this particular day. The stone was showing signs of age, the coloring of the carved letters beginning to blend in with the surrounding granite. For some reason, the phenomenon saddened him. He stared hard at the marker, as if trying to see through to the casket and the contents that lay beneath it. If the stone were aging, imagine what must be happening to his son below it. A chill flitted across the hair on the back of his neck in spite of the warmth of the early evening. It was as if a butterfly had brushed its wings against him.

Then he knew why he had turned into the cemetery.

"I made a mistake," he said as the blessed blackness enveloped him.

Laura Janice Stanton

"One joy scatters a hundred griefs."
Chinese Proverb

At least once a month, the Wallaces received a letter from Harriet and Paul Stanton, ostensibly to keep them informed of their remarkably busy academic lives. Not much imagination was required to see through the facade to the real reason for the correspondence. Each letter included a recent photograph of Laura Janice Stanton, their beautiful daughter with the penetrating black eyes that shone with a vibrancy that even the flat, two dimensional image couldn't disguise. The formula to most of the letters became predictable. The first third would outline the successes of the Stantons in their respective academic circles with the remainder describing each of little Laura's growing steps in vivid, endearing detail.

Josie loved the letters, vicariously experiencing her goddaughter's progress through the sitting up, crawling, walking, baby food to table food, and teething stages. She initially shared the letters with Brad by reading them to him before dinner, but after one particular incident she began to leave the letters available for him to read by himself.

The Stantons had celebrated Laura's six month birthday, and Harriet ended her lengthy description of the party with what Brad interpreted as an admonition, almost a scolding.

"You don't know what you're missing," she said. "Laura is an absolute blessing in our lives. She's added more than you could imagine. If you change your mind, I'll be glad to help you connect with the people who handled ours."

When Josie finished reading that section, Brad stood and moved into the kitchen. She followed him, letter in hand, prepared to continue reading.

He turned to her as she trailed after him, glaring at her intrusion.

"I really don't want to hear any more, Josie," he said sharply. "It's all well and good for them but it wouldn't be right for us, and I think it's pretty damned presumptuous for Harriet to keep putting the pressure on me. I mean, we made our decision and that's it, right? I'll read the rest of the letter when I damn well feel like, OK?"

Josie left the room without a word. Brad stared after her for a moment then added more gin to his martini without toning it down with vermouth. He followed her into the living room and they drank their cocktails in silence.

The letters continued to arrive and Josie and Harriet spoke regularly on the phone. When Brad received his promotion to Assistant Superintendent, Harriet was one of the first to call with congratulations. It was one of the few times they had spoken since Rich's accident two years before.

"Josie's not home right now, Harriet. Sorry but I'll tell her you called." His icy response to the call sent an obvious message. Harriet's natural exuberance disappeared and she went directly to the point.

"Actually, I called to talk to you anyway. Congratulations on the new promotion," she said, her enthusiasm dampened by his reply. Curtly, he thanked her for calling and ended the conversation. Later, when he mentioned the call to Josie, she asked how Laura was doing. Brad had no answer; he hadn't asked about the child.

"Sometimes, I'm not sure that I really know you anymore, Brad," she said.

"Well, if it's any consolation, sometimes I'm not sure that I know myself," he mumbled.

It wasn't.

The Cop and the Quadriplegic

"Friendship needs no words; it is a loneliness relieved of the anguish of loneliness."

Dag Hammarskold

Rich no longer had any doubts about the truth of part of Thorton Wilder's premise: human beings indeed do live by plan and die by plan. After his coincidental meeting with Detective Havenot just weeks after his accident, he needed little convincing. Parker, fascinated by Rich's courage, contacted him several times in the ensuing weeks after meeting him at the school. At first, the detective seemed obsessed with the accident, focusing most of the conversation on that. The third time he dropped by to visit, Rich finally balked at talking about it any more. Parker was chagrined.

"I'm really sorry, Rich. I didn't mean to be such a pest about it," he said. "It's just that I'm interested, you know, a typical cop who needs to know everything. Actually, I find your attitude totally amazing. I've got to admit that you are a revelation to me."

Rich, touched by such a tribute, sloughed it off with one of his trademark quips.

"I've been called a lot of things in my life, especially by my students, but a revelation is certainly not one of them. I appreciate that. I'd give you a hug if I could." He smiled and Havenot laughed out loud.

Friendships often begin in the most unlikely settings and circumstances, and Rich's father, who observed the bantering and developing bond with interest, said quietly, "I guess you aren't going to arrest my son so I'll leave you two alone. You seem to be getting along just fine."

Parker became a regular visitor, scheduling his visits late in the afternoon so he could give the nurse a break and share a cold beer with Rich before dinner. On a number of occasions, he was visiting when Josie Wallace dropped by after school. Several months of long conversations and thoughtful discussions led to the clear realization that the two men had much in common. When Josie arrived one day around Christmas, she found the two friends engaged in a typically male conversation about women.

"You're just in time, Josie. We're having this discussion and you can clear something up for us," Rich said, his most devilish look making Josie smile.

"Here's the question. Parker here thinks that there's one right person for everyone and if you find that person, you're set for life. I say that there're thousands of right people out there for everybody. What do you think?"

Josie hesitated, glancing back and forth between them.

"I guess I need to think about that before I answer. I'll get back to you." Her comment redirected the conversation and she stayed another fifteen minutes before excusing herself. Parker stood with her and Rich couldn't let it go.

"Oh yeah, Parker, make me look bad. Standing up like a gentleman and here I sit." They shared a minor giggle and Josie left.

"Great woman, isn't she?" Parker said.

"Sure is; I had, actually probably still do have, such a crush on her. I can't believe I'm telling you this. It's a pretty foolish thing to admit but I'm feeling confident that you're one of those trustworthy cops, right?" Rich's eyes filmed over as he finished his confession. "Once, when I had had too much to drink, I told her that I was in love with her."

"You're kidding! What did she say?" Parker's interest level soared.

"She gave me a typical English teacher's lesson in semantics. I love you, too, but I'm not in love with you, she said. It was like being told by a high school sweetheart that she just wants to be friends. Verbal castration, I call it."

Parker smiled but did not let the subject drop. "Did Brad ever find out? I mean, does he know how you felt about her?"

"It feels a little like you're talking about me in the past tense, Detective. Let's have none of that. She did tell him about the incident but passed it off as being entirely harmless. From what she said, I guess Brad did also. We've shared a lot over the years; you know, really good friends, so we just transcended that little bit of stupidity on my part and got back to normal. Hey, I'm rambling here. Back to your original question; she is a great woman. I'm just glad Brad didn't kill me when she told him." Rich smiled, the thoughtful haze in his eyes slowly dissipating.

A puzzled concern flashed across Parker's face. "What a funny thing to say." His comment ended the conversation about Josie Wallace but not his interest in knowing more about her.

Brad's Mistake

"Most of the learning in use is of no great use."
Benjamin Franklin

The official title of the new position in the Hartford School District heaped an unaccustomed dose of credibility on Brad Wallace. Mike Costello presented him with an inscribed nameplate for his new desk on his last day at Hartford West High School. The second line, under Brad's name, read ASSISTANT SUPERINTENDENT FOR SPECIAL SERVICES, PERSONNEL, HEALTH, PUBLIC RELATIONS, ETC.ETC. The gift drew loud laughter from the rest of the staff and Brad accepted it with good humor. The truth of the situation was that the description for Brad's new job encompassed any responsibilities that the other upper level administrators wanted eliminated from their own.

With the new contract effective July 1, the prospects for spending any time at the Winnipesaukee cabin during the summer appeared grim. After his first meeting with Superintendent George Metcalf, the slim chances vanished all together.

"We need to have coverage here, Brad; I'm sure you appreciate that. You've been around education long enough to know about coverage. We all choose our vacation times in January so July and August are pretty much taken. Next year, you'll be mixed in with the rest of us. As the new kid on the block, no one will expect you to know too much but we do have to show our public that their central command is always on the job. I'm sure you'll handle it just fine." When Metcalf finished, Brad agreed, having no choice whatsoever.

The little speech made him want to gag. His superintendent certainly had taken his course in Educational Jargon and Cliches seriously. Josie would just have to go to the lake by herself if she wanted to, especially if "Central Command" was expected to be on duty on weekends as well. The prospect of a weekend commute between Connecticut and New

Hampshire in the summer was not too exciting anyway.

As he had done from the start of his professional career, Brad resolved to make the best of this new position, confident that the empowerment that came with the title could broaden the scope of his influence. He would make a difference in the lives of the children of Hartford.

*   *   *

Josie's experience over the years proved that the last week of July and the first week of August were usually the best of the summer at the cabin. The water in the lake held its warmth, even in the face of an occasional cool night. Yet, the approaching autumn drove any lingering summer humidity away. She would miss Brad, she told Harriet in a letter but admitted to a small dash of guilt when she talked about anticipating the quiet aloneness more than she should.

Brad escaped from the office an hour early on the Friday that Josie left for her vacation at the lake. His first few weeks on the job had been a blend of eager excitement and disappointing reality, the nagging feeling of having made a mistake hovering as palpably as a thunder cloud on the horizon. He imagined the Superintendent's office as a veritable beehive of educational innovation and visionary thinking. The truth was that most of his work thus far involved tedious state reports, bland paperwork and little intellectual stimulation. When Josie asked him to drive to New Hampshire when he finished work to spend the first weekend with her, he protested but only mildly. A weekend at the cabin with Josie might revitalize his enthusiasm.

"I'll make it well worth your while," she told him, her sensuous smile easily winning him over.

The extra hour that Brad squeezed out of the afternoon simplified the trip. He was through the Hookset tollbooth a few minutes before five o'clock, feeling like a vehicular surfer staying just ahead of a monstrous wave of traffic closing behind. When he arrived at the cabin, Josie had their martinis mixed and cooling in the refrigerator. After a warm greeting, she took his hand and led him out to the deck.

"You sit right down here and relax. I'll be right back." Brad did as he was told and surveyed the lake as he waited for her return. The water paraded its varied colors as the early evening sun glanced off of it. The physical and emotional tension of the workweek and the long drive easing. He heard Josie kick the screen door open and she appeared with a delicately balanced tray of cocktail shaker, glasses, and a bowl of peel and eat shrimp with two different dips on the side.

"Now, if you want, you can tell me about your day. Whatever you'd like to do is fine with me." As she poured the first batch of drinks, Brad's attention moved away from the tray to Josie. She had changed into a short terry cloth beach cover that accentuated every curve of her figure. She finished pouring and sat down.

"Cheers," she said, smiling and leaning slowly toward him to clink her glass with his. The green robe, pulled by her movement, opened at the top and rode up her thighs.

"God, you're beautiful," Brad said. It was over an hour later before they had their first taste of the shrimp and martinis.

*   *   *

"I wanted to try out this idea with you, Brad, but don't answer until you have a chance to think about it, OK?" They sat in the darkness on the deck, absorbing the light caress of a warm breeze blowing in from the lake. The evening could not have been more perfect.

"I'd like to invite Rich up for the second week that I'm here. I could see if one of his nurses could come. It'd be sort of a vacation for her, too. I just think it would do him a world of good." The words were tumbling out so fast that she was short of breath. "I thought you could bring them up in the van next Friday and drive my car home. Then I could go home with them at the end of the week. Is this a crazy idea or what?" She tried to read his face in the darkness.

The silence lasted longer than it should have. Just as Josie was about to continue, Brad spoke.

"Sounds as if you've got it all figured out, Jos. I bring a guy who's admitted to being in love with my wife up here to spend a week with her in a lakeside cabin. That makes a lot of sense. I'd be really worried if he weren't dead in the water."

"Brad, he's our good friend, OUR good friend and he's a quadriplegic, for God's sake. I can't believe you said that about him." Josie was glad to have the darkness as cover for a face flushed with anger.

He continued in a much softer tone, as if he had trespassed over an invisible boundary of some sort and needed to backtrack quickly.

"Of course, I'd be glad to do that. Why don't you call tomorrow to try to arrange everything?" His response met only silence. "Josie, I said I'd do it. What else do you want from me?" Josie recognized his question as rhetorical. He didn't want it answered.

"Nothing else, Brad, nothing else at all. Thanks." She stood. "I'm really bushed. Thanks for a wonderful evening. I think I'll read for a while."

"I'm just going to sit out here a while longer. Good night." Josie kissed him on the back of the neck but he didn't respond.

"Good night, Brad." Another small piece of the fabric of their relationship had ripped.

* * *

Brad's urgency for a visit with Brad, Jr. became a compulsion soon after he listened to the conversation between Josie and Rich on Saturday morning. She was more animated than the situation called for and in ten minutes, the trip was arranged, including having his favorite nurse, Becky, come along.

"Well, that wasn't too difficult, was it?" Brad asked. "I'm going for a boat ride. I don't suppose you'd like to come along?" The question was framed as more of a statement that he would rather be going alone.

"I think I'll stay here and relax a bit, if that's all right with you," Josie said.

Brad shrugged, saying that he'd be back in an hour or so. She walked out the deck with him and hugged him, a hug that he returned

240

without enthusiasm. He followed the path to the dock and she watched as he prepared the boat. As he pushed away from the dock, she called out.

"Be careful, Brad." Her words never reached him, overpowered by the engine roaring to life. She watched until the boat disappeared in the distance, a knot forming in her stomach.

"I've got to do something about this." The words came out like an announcement she might have made to one of her classes, startling her as they reverberated around the deck.

* * *

The sky still had a faint tinge of light left when Brad turned into the cemetery. Using the excuse that he wanted to beat the traffic heading south on Sunday evening, he had left the cabin and Josie late in the afternoon, promising to call upon his safe arrival at home. For this visit, he felt he wouldn't need much time.

"I need a little help, son. It seems that we still have a problem with Mr. Lane, even though we pretty much rendered him useless. So, what do you think? Do we need to worry?" Brad paused for effect, as though waiting for an answer to his question from a thoughtful but still reluctant student. The darkness was coming fast. He looked around and saw that he had left his headlights on. He waited for another moment.

"I agree. That's all settled, then. We've got nothing to worry about. I'll bring the affable and now harmless Mr. Lane to your mom for a visit." He turned and walked back to the car.

* * *

Brad had what could only be described as a hellish week of work. Just he and the business administrator were on the job, the rest of the staff off in exotic places on vacation. George Metcalf was the only one who left a phone number where he could be reached, but he also left no doubt that the circumstances had better be dire if he were to be bothered. Determined not to contact the Superintendent, Brad handled one crisis after another, each a stern test of his ability as a problem solver and as a tactful arbitrator. By Thursday, he had felt more heat in a single week than in all of the previous years of his career combined. Deadlines for four teacher grievance responses fell during the Superintendent's absence, an incredible lapse of professionalism on his superior's part, but Brad was able to research enough information on each case to move them along. He fought the rising resentment and tried with limited success to allow George Metcalf the benefit of the doubt.

"You know how it is when people are getting ready to go on vacation. They can get into a very self-centered mode." Harry Klause, the business administrator offered his limp defense of his close friend, Metcalf. But Brad remained agitated.

On Thursday morning, two sets of parents arrived to complain about the placement of their child in an unpopular fifth grade teacher's class. Brad sat at the small conference table in Metcalf's office, not daring to use his mammoth desk to do his work. The buzz of the intercom startled him and he asked the secretary for a minute before sending them in. Brad moved behind the well-cushioned chair pushed tightly against the desk as if guarding against any intrusion and flipped back through the pages of Metcalf's calendar to the present week. "Vacation" was scrawled across both of the pages, the word spanning the center crease. The last two letters ended on Thursday morning, interfering with but not hiding what was written beneath them. The names Ketterer and Mobley were written in at 9:30 a.m.

Six or seven file folders lay neatly overlapped on the right side of the desk, giving the appearance of a well-organized, detail-oriented person. He scanned the tabs of the file folders on the desk and found one with the two names on it. The single letter in it was a simple request for a meeting to discuss class assignments of their children.

"I'll be damned," he whispered. "He knew they were coming and never even told me." Requests of this sort rarely reached this far up the chain of command. With no evidence explaining who these folks might be, he spoke into the intercom.

"Send them in," he said. When the parents entered the office, the four faces held matching expressions of anger that told him why they had not been redirected somewhere down the line. They hadn't been satisfied so far and he had no idea how to diffuse the situation. Brad tried every persuasive technique with as calm and rational a tone as he could muster but the Keterers and the Mobleys were not buying. After a half-hour of venting their frustrations with each step of their climb up the ladder of bureaucracy, the parents realized that this person could do nothing for them. He didn't even know the teacher in question.

"I'll pass your concern on to Dr. Metcalf; you may count on that," Brad said. He meant it. As the four proceeded from the office in single file, Brad saw Metcalf's secretary standing at her desk, her shoulders in mid shrug and her eyes rolling at him. He walked to the door, closed it behind him, and leaned heavily against it.

"That bastard; I think he set me up," he said. He wouldn't have been surprised to see Alan Funt jump out from behind a curtain.

That afternoon, Brad left the office at exactly four o'clock and one hour later had mixed one of his patented martinis, disguised it in a plastic coffee cup and walked from his house to the cemetery to discuss the events of the week.

Another Week on the Big Lake

"No man is an island, entire of itself;
every man is a piece of the continent."

John Donne

Rich Lane's new van was equipped with much more innovative gadgetry than the one Brad had seen two years before. The comfortable ride and easy handling made it a joy to drive. The lift gate on the side of the van deposited Rich and his wheelchair into a firmly locked position facing the picture window side of the vehicle. It was one of the few features that allowed for no flexibility.

"I really hate this part of it," he said as they got underway. "Everything just goes by in a blur and I can't really see either of you." Becky Turnbull had heard this poignant complaint numerous times but it went unnoticed by the other passenger. After the first hour on the road, Brad convinced her that he should be driving since he knew exactly where they were going. She reluctantly agreed, pulling into a rest area just over the Massachusetts border to switch seats. After some initial bantering, a quiet pensiveness settled over Rich and when the driver exchange took place, he became subdued and within a few minutes, he was asleep.

"I'm not sure what's bothering him," Becky said, confident that he was sound asleep. After two years of forty-hour weeks spent nursing him, she knew Rich's habits as well as her own. "He did mention that he was a little nervous about returning to the scene of the crime. Maybe that's it."

"That's what he called it?" Brad asked. "He actually called it the scene of the crime?"

"He's always joking; surely you know that. He is a good friend of yours, right?" The question commanded his attention. He looked at her.

"He's always saying that God should be indicted for crimes against humanity; the worst of the mass murdering war criminals." Becky smiled. "It's not sacrilegious though, just being realistic." It was Brad's turn to laugh.

"Not sacrilegious, huh?"

"No, really; he doesn't blame anybody, even God, for what happened to him. He just says there's a lot of shitty stuff that happens. That's a quote; I don't usually swear. Anyway, can we talk about something else?"

"OK. How about politics? I say that if the best the Democrats can come up with is Jimmy Carter, we're all in big trouble." Rich's voice drifted over from the rear of the van.

"Thought I was asleep, did you? Invoking the name of Jimmy Carter would awaken anybody. And there is a lot of shitty stuff that goes on, Brad. And, as you know, I do swear." Rich's voice was strong and clear. "I'll admit that this trip is a little nerve wracking for me but I'll try to be my usual witty, incisive self from now on. Don't want my favorite nurse worrying about me."

*   *   *

The Wallace cabin was not designed to be accessible by wheelchair. After an affectionate hug from Josie and an anxious look down the dirt path to the back door, Rich quipped that perhaps he should sleep in the van. Nurse Becky assumed a leadership role and began barking orders like a drill sergeant. The short trip down the path was an adventure as Brad did the navigation from the handles of the chair and Becky and Josie stood at each side, guiding it over the short but rock-strewn path to the door. Once inside, the irrepressible Rich had them all laughing again.

"Son of a bitch," he said, "I cheated death again, no thanks to you guys."

The weather, rarely a factor that ruins any plans in New Hampshire in late July, turned sour on Saturday. The scattered light showers predicted by the National Weather Service inundated the Lakes Region all morning, drenching the area with as much rain as the entire summer

246

had produced to that point. When the sun finally broke through several hours later than promised in the afternoon, the four occupants of the cabin had long since tired of playing Scrabble. Rich was the first to suggest a change of scenery.

"What would you say to taking a ride into town while everything dries out around here?" he asked, sounding like a child who had been cooped up with his parents all morning.

The other three readily agreed, their patience with being housebound exhausted. Nurse Becky, on her first visit to the Lakes Region of New Hampshire, was especially anxious. Within minutes, they were again negotiating the path with Rich and his wheelchair, pausing regularly to gain adequate footholds in the dirt turned mud from the rain. The strong sun was rapidly drying the moisture. The droplets of rainwater on the van turned into puffs of steam rising from the heated sheet metal as they loaded the chair.

"This is just beautiful, isn't it?" Rich said to no one in particular as he was pushed through the door. Josie just shook her head in wonder.

"Yep, it sure is. Where in the world do you get your enthusiasm, Rich?" she asked.

He didn't answer until she climbed into the rear seat behind him. The bench seat allowed her to slide against the far side of the van where Rich could see her with a slight turn of his head.

When he could see her face, he spoke so softly that Becky and Brad in the front could not hear him.

"It's not something that I get, Jos. It's something I'm desperately trying to keep." Then he stared straight ahead through the large window.

"So let's get this show on the road," he said boisterously, drawing a verbal curtain around himself and his melancholy.

Becky guided the van into the Stoneham A & P parking lot, following Brad's directions to proceed to the far end where they could cross over two spaces and get Rich out with a minimum of trouble. The weather, so gloomy and wet at the start of the day, assumed a shirt drenching humidity and breathtaking heat, again uncharacteristic of New

Hampshire. Becky and Brad unloaded Rich and both were sweating when they finished. Rich made a conscious decision never to apologize for any inconvenience or discomfort his condition caused, using what to him was an accurate analogy by saying that it would be like a bridge partner apologizing for not being dealt a good hand.

"Why ask forgiveness for anything that lay completely beyond your control?" he would say whenever the occasion warranted it.

As Brad rolled the chair off the lift, he searched his pocket for a handkerchief. Finding none, he lifted his untucked shirt to his face and wiped the sweat away.

"Let us wash that shirt for you when we get back, OK? Becky's very good at laundry." Rich winked at her. It was as close to an apology as he would get.

"So, what would you like to do?" Josie directed her question to Becky. "Brad and I are going to pick up some things at the A&P and we can meet you somewhere."

Rich answered for both of them. "We're taking a walk down to the dock, aren't we?" Becky smiled and started pushing the chair across the lot.

"I guess we'll be down at the dock," she said over her shoulder, without the slightest rancor in her voice.

"We'll come find you," Josie called after them. "We won't be long."

*　　*　　*

"That's where it happened. Out there, just around where that piece of land juts out." Rich's attention was riveted on the lake, as if straining to see across to some distant shore. He had not prepared himself for the impact of this first visit. He watched as a water skier stretched the towline behind a boat as it disappeared around the bend.

"See that, Becky? It was just like that. So God damned stupid!" Becky set the brake on his chair and came around to face him. She crouched in front of him, the simple exertion raising beads of perspiration on her forehead.

"Do you want to tell me about it? I'm a pretty good listener when I really try to keep quiet."

"Hell, no. What's the sense? Water under the bridge or over the dam or wherever in the hell water goes. I screwed up, that's all. Or at least somebody did. As I said, it was all just so fucking stupid." He looked at her. She put her hands to her cheeks as if she had been slapped. "Oh, shit. I guess I never used that word with you before."

"It's not that, Rich. It's just that I've never heard you so bitter before." Becky came out of her crouch and turned back to the lake.

"I suppose I didn't know what being so close to the scene of the crime would do to me," he said to her back. After a long pause, he said, "I'm human, you know, even if I don't feel like it most of the time."

Becky worked her way back to the handles of the chair, carefully avoiding any possibility that she might embarrass him by looking directly at his face. She waited until she was sure that his tears had stopped before reaching around and gently dabbing at them from behind with a Kleenex.

"I never cry, damn it. Well, at least almost never. Thanks."

"I know you don't," she said, " and I've always wondered why."

*　　*　　*

Shortly after lunch on Sunday afternoon, Brad began to prepare for his trip back to Connecticut. Three days spent in constant companionship with one of his victims acted as a battering ram to his senses. The first blows were sloughed off but the constant reminders eventually began to extract a vengeance of their own. By Sunday, he needed to escape the psychological punishment, the silent reprimand that Rich's physical presence screamed at him. However unintentional the final outcome had been, the ram was wearing him down.

" I thought you weren't leaving until after dinner," Josie said when she found him in the bedroom throwing his clothes carelessly into a suitcase.

"I'm just thinking about the traffic and getting organized for tomorrow at work, just the usual stuff. It's not like we would be having an afternoon to ourselves. You have plenty of company." He turned the excuse into a plausible reason for his hurry to return home. Josie didn't press the issue.

"How about having a beer with us on the deck before you go? An extra half hour isn't going to make that much difference." Her expression announced that she truly wanted him to stay.

"OK, I'll be right out." She left him to explain to the guests why their host was leaving so early.

Brad drank the beer in the hurried fashion of a man whose wife has just called the bar looking for him. He seemed to be leaning toward the door the entire time. He sat on the edge of the chair, as though he was preparing to sprint at any moment. Fifteen minutes later, he stood up.

"I've really got to be going. Sorry to rush off but I'm sure you guys understand. It's a long drive. . . ." His voice trailed off to a mumble when he realized by their nodding that Josie had already explained his upcoming departure. He crossed the deck to Becky and extended his hand which she accepted as she stood. She gave him a light hug.

"Have a safe trip and thanks a lot for bringing us up here." She watched as he turned to Rich, who appeared amused as Brad struggled with his goodbye. He stood in front of the wheelchair as if at attention, finally backing up one step.

"Have a good time, Rich," he said, stumbling through the stupidity of the words. "I mean, enjoy the fresh air and hospitality." He was backing toward the door like an embarrassed child searching for a graceful exit from a room full of fawning adults. Josie saved him.

"I'll walk you to the car. Do you have everything you came with?" She opened the door and Brad bumped into her as he went through first. He grabbed his suitcase from the middle of the kitchen floor and was at the car well ahead of Josie.

"Drive carefully, Brad. Remember you're driving my car," she said, trying to lighten the farewell but unable to disguise her concern. "What was that all about in there, Brad?"

"What're you talking about? I'm anxious to get started, that's all." An emotionless, tight-lipped kiss was his final goodbye as he opened the

car door. "I'll see you sometime Friday night. Have a good week." He started the car before the door closed behind him. Josie threw a futile wave at
the back of the car as it left the driveway. She stood there watching as the
dust settled and the sound of the car faded in the distance then turned her
attention to her guests.

*   *   *

Brad could not have stayed at the cabin another minute. The sensation of
claustrophobia in such an open environment was illogical and strayed
frighteningly close to being psychopathic yet he couldn't deny it. After
three days of watching Becky and Josie fawning over Rich Lane, he wanted to scream. The whole weekend he felt as if he were trapped in a jetlin-
er speeding toward a crash on takeoff with no chance of escape.

"Might as well be in a giant silver bullet," he commented to a seat-
mate on one of his trips. "It's that hopeless if anything goes wrong." The
uneasy feeling that something was going to go wrong pervaded the entire
weekend. As often as he told himself that Rich ultimately was the one at
fault here, he continued to be suffocated by his presence. He needed to get
away.

As his car left the drive, a powerful rush of relief washed over
him, causing him to tremble. After setting a new time record for the trip,
he drove directly to the cemetery, anxious to form a suitable plan for Dr.
Metcalf, who needed a small inconvenience for placing him in such
untenable positions the week before.

"Here's how I see it, son," he said. "It's all pretty complicated but
simple at the same time. All my little pranks do is start things in motion;
then, some higher power takes over and decides how serious everything
will get. Fate and destiny, that's what it's all about.

"So I figure that we'll try the nails out on another doctor and
watch what happens. Let's see what kind of destiny Dr. Metcalf has laid
out for him."

The welcome blackness enfolded him.

*   *   *

251

After Brad's hasty departure, the afternoon passed quietly. Josie, immersed in her book but still aware of her environment, noticed again the subtle gentleness that Becky lavished on Rich, somehow avoiding being obnoxious.

"You would have made a wonderful elementary teacher. You've got that inexhaustible patience," Josie said during a dishwashing stint in the kitchen. When Rich wanted to read, she sat next to him, turning the pages of the book on the small folding music stand mounted on the arm of his chair.

"An invention born not of necessity but of a father's love," he called it.

The chicken barbecue dinner Josie prepared that evening was delicious. None of the vague tension present earlier at lunch was evident, Brad apparently having carried it off to Connecticut with him. After the women completed what Rich kept calling their "womanly duties" in the kitchen, Josie assured Becky that she could handle Rich's needs for a while. The nurse took advantage of the offer for a long twilight walk on some of the many trails through the woods surrounding the property, ignoring Rich's dire but comical warning to "watch out for moose and bears."

Rich and Josie sat on the deck alone watching another flaming Winnipesaukee sunset. They enjoyed one of the many characteristics of true friendship, the uniqueness of silence. Most acquaintances could not sit together in total silence for long without feeling the need to say something. As Rich had said on another occasion, they transcended that feeling, comfortable in each other's silence as they observed the colorful phenomenon filling the sky before them. Josie finally broke the spell.

"Brad would say that if you've seen one sunset, you've seen them all. I've never agreed with that. Even if they were all identical, we'd bring a different mood to them, like watching a sitcom on television after hearing that a friend is seriously ill can color your perspective on what's funny." With the silence interrupted, Josie floated the question that had been on her mind all afternoon.

"So, what do you think was bugging Brad today?"

"Wow! That's the most philosophical question you can come up with in the face of this humbling sunset?" He smiled, his ever-present impish nature revealed by the glow in his eyes.

"First of all, he spent the whole weekend looking at someone like me. Then add in a measure of responsibility and, just like that, you've got a man who wants to go home early. Period, end of story." He pronounced this with a finality that said he was finished with this particular issue.

"OK," Josie said. "Let's go back to watching the sunset."

"Does this mean no more talking? I did have something else."

Josie chuckled. He was going to keep going anyway.

"I didn't tell you this, especially while Brad was here. Parker Havenot is not one of his favorite people but I wondered if maybe we could get together with him. He's up here for a few days this week staying with Gordon Tibideau."

"Parker is up here? He hadn't mentioned he was coming up the last time I saw him at your house." The connection between Josie and Parker remained in the highly restrictive professional interest realm. Josie hesitated before answering. She hadn't experienced a social occasion with a police officer before.

"No pressure, Jos. It's just that he's become a special kind of friend, probably the only new one I've developed BC. Kind of takes me like I am."

"What is BC? And of course we could invite him over if you'd like." How could she refuse?

"Before Crippled and thanks a lot," Rich said.

*   *   *

The first few moments of Parker's initial visit to the Wallace's cabin were awkward. Josie greeted him at the door and ushered him quickly through the house and out onto the deck where Rich and Becky waited. After the usual greetings, Parker sat down.

"Before I get your drinks, could I ask a favor?" She didn't wait for a reply. "I'd like to ask that we not talk about anything dealing with police things, especially present company stuff. I've never had a policeman to dinner so I wasn't sure how to handle this but I don't feel like answering questions." A full-fledged blush reddened her face when all three of them exploded into laughter. Rich was the first to respond.

"Did you check your heater at the door, Detective. No police stuff in this house." He laughed again. "I believe Parker came to dinner, not to arrest anyone, Josie." Her blush went from red to a wonderful shade of crimson.

"OK. I'm being stupid. There's one other rule then; no more laughter at my expense." She smiled and the awkwardness vanished. For an occasion she had anticipated with a fair share of trepidation, the remainder of the evening was enjoyable.

"I left my 'heater' at home, Josie," Parker said with a grin as she walked him to the door at the end of night. It was the first reference to anything even vaguely connected to police work since Josie's gauche beginning to the evening.

"I'm a little embarrassed. No, actually, I'm a lot embarrassed. Thanks for understanding and thanks for coming. Perhaps we can get you and Rich together again before the week is out. Good night." She stood at the door and waited until he had climbed the path to his car then flipped off the outside light.

At Rich's insistence and with no quibbling on Josie's part, the group, including Parker once again, spent Thursday cruising the lake on the Mt. Washington, a large vessel that traveled through five major ports from one end of the lake to the other. They completed the day with a take out Chinese dinner and a lengthy game of Scrabble on the deck of the cabin. The ten-hour day spent in the company of Becky, Rich, and Parker fit into Josie's comfort zone quite well.

As the evening came to a close, Rich started bemoaning the fact that the time at the lake had gone by so fast.

"Are you fishing for another invitation, Rich?" Josie asked. "I think it's worked out really well. I'm sure we'll be able to arrange something before the fall season ends," she said, her voice softening as she looked at him.

"I'd be happy to bring him up, as long as Nurse Becky here comes along for company and the Tibideaus aren't getting sick of me," Parker said, drawing everyone's surprised attention.

"I had heard you were a workaholic, Detective," Becky said, "but I'd be glad to come any time."

"We always have some extra room here if Gordon's parents are tired of you," Josie said. An involuntary giggle escaped from her and she caught herself. "As long as it's all right with Brad, of course."

They arranged to meet the next morning for breakfast and to form a two car caravan for the drive home. Parker went directly to the wheel chair, placing one hand over Rich's and the other firmly on the back of his neck. "I'll see you tomorrow. You behave yourself with these two beautiful women tonight."

Rich laughed while Parker made a hasty retreat to the door. Becky and Josie looked after him, dumbfounded.

"I'll see you all tomorrow and thanks for a very pleasant day. I appreciate your letting me tag along. I really enjoyed it." He closed the door behind him as he said the last word, as though not wanting to expose any more vulnerability than he already had.

"He's an awfully nice guy," Becky said after he was gone. "And quite attractive to boot."

"Don't you go getting any ideas. You know that you're my girl," Rich said, the usual gleam twinkling in his eyes.

"I just hope that he doesn't think I'm foolish. I sure pulled a few stupid tricks this week," Josie said. Her concern was more profound than the situation warranted.

"Everybody pulls stupid tricks," Rich said. "You think the detective has never seen people look foolish?"

"Well, thanks a lot for that vote of confidence. I'm going to bed. I'll see you in the morning."

*   *   *

As a relatively attractive and interesting member of the male species, Parker had his share of relationships since his divorce but none had lasted. The divorce ranked first on his list of life's adventures that he did not want to duplicate. He adapted several theories about women into one that suited his needs and spent most of the short drive back to the Tibideaus reciting his personal philosophy as though it were a catechism lesson memorized in childhood.

Feelings can't be helped but attraction does not have to lead to action, he thought at first then repeated it aloud. His wariness showed in any burgeoning relationships and likely kept things simpler. The last few days in Josie's company had been pleasant, and he dismissed her troubling image from his mind with yet another repetition of his philosophy.

"Wouldn't that complicate things?" He scolded himself for thoughts and feelings that couldn't be helped.

Metcalf's Destiny

"Do one thing every day that scares you."
Kurt Vonnegut

School began with the usual optimism at all levels. Dr. George Metcalf delivered his annual motivational message to the staff with the effortless grace of a polished politician. The palpable enthusiasm of the gathering in the huge auditorium would spread to the students the next day during the first day of classes. The momentum of opening day could carry for weeks before reality set in. Brad would watch for signs that the momentum needed refurbishing. Metcalf introduced the new staff in his office, including Brad Wallace as his all purpose assistant, predictably falling back on an old administrator's joke that used new employees as the foil.

"If you ever have any compliments, I'll be glad to take them. All complaints may be directed to Brad." Most of the staff chuckled under the duress of a quip told by the boss while others groaned and sat on their hands. All of the teachers from around the city were present. Brad's experience as a classroom teacher told him that most of them were anxious to be released with so much preparation required for the next day. When Metcalf finally wished everyone luck and dismissed them, a few of Brad's colleagues from Hartford West made their way to the front of the auditorium to shake his hand.

Brad first felt the indisputable change that occurs so often in education as he was fixing his coffee that morning in the cafeteria before the meeting. The greetings he received from the milling groups of teachers were muted and cool. It was as though joining management automatically made him a turncoat. Even the few of his former staff who made the effort to see him, hurriedly shook his hand and moved on, usually with downcast eyes. He was experienced enough to recognize what was happening but the disappointment still hurt. As he watched the last of the teachers leave the auditorium, he felt a hand on his shoulder and turned around. It was George Metcalf.

"I know what you're thinking, Brad, my boy, but don't let it get to you. You've changed sides here and unfortunately you've got to shift some loyalties. It's not like being a department head or even a principal. We work for the city and our salaries depend on that. You'll see what I mean when we get into contract negotiation time. They probably feel like you're a traitor. But you know what? They're probably right. Just don't forget on what side your bread is buttered on." He slapped Brad on the back, a gesture as annoying as the worn out cliches that flowed so naturally from George Metcalf.

"I'll see you back at the office. I've got a few jobs for you to do."

Brad stood there, looking around at the empty auditorium. The only sound to be heard was the clacking of Metcalf's heels on the wooden floor as he walked up the aisle toward the door. He waited until the door slammed shut before gathering the stacks of leftover staff handouts strewn across the empty stage behind the podium. A rueful smile formed on his lips as he remembered times when eager to please students would help him straighten his room at the end of a school day. "Mr. Wallace's lackeys." He jammed the papers under his arm and picked up his briefcase.

"Dr. Metcalf's lackey," he said. "Shit, I've made a mistake."

*　　*　　*

The spaces in the parking lot of Hartford School District Central Administration Building were numbered and assigned.

"Probably in descending order of importance," Brad muttered to himself as he pulled into slot number 20 even though his was the first car in the lot. He reached into the glove compartment and gathered the nails from among the maps and napkins and pens. He slipped them into the side pocket of his suit jacket and reached across the seat for his briefcase. The key he had been given was not for the front door.

"Five years minimum before you get a front door key," Metcalf

258

had joked but he was probably right. His route to the side door took him past parking slot number 1 at the end of the front row. It was the only spot that had a sign in front of it, an arrogant over-sized sign reading RESERVED FOR DR. GEORGE W. METCALF. Brad hesitated, looking around as his hand found the nails in his pocket and jingled them. The familiar rush of juvenile excitement washed over him.

I've got to be nuts but this one will be fun. In the brief time he had worked at the central office, he noticed that Metcalf always left for lunch between twelve and twelve thirty. Brad had two meetings in separate elementary schools that morning, meaning that he would be walking past the Superintendent's car four times. With any luck, at least two of those times it would be possible to plant a nail or two in a tire then be able to enjoy Metcalf's grousing after lunch. The anticipation of creating a small bit of fate equaled the expectancy he felt over his spending his first real school day on the job. He continued toward the side door with a slight smile on his face. He worked for over an hour before he heard another person enter the office.

George Metcalf was the last of the staff to arrive, blustering his way through the office with loud, mostly off color remarks to the secretaries. Brad sat in his office and cringed. When the Superintendent leaned his head through Brad's door, he jumped to his feet. Brad slapped his hand against his side, stilling the nails rattling in his pocket.

"How was your weekend?" Metcalf asked. Brad started to answer but the Superintendent was already gone, greeting someone else down the hall with the same question. Brad looked at the clock. It was almost time to gather his materials for his first meeting with a principal of an elementary school several miles away. He organized the papers in his briefcase, reached into his pocket and removed all but two of the nails. The rest he placed in the only desk drawer that locked.

Before leaving the building, he tapped on George Metcalf's partially closed door.

"Come on in," the Superintendent bellowed. Brad was taken back and hesitated.

"Come in, I said." The voice showed some impatience. Brad inched into the room.

"I just wanted to let you know that I'll be at Paragon Elementary for an hour," Brad said. He would never have considered leaving the building without first getting permission from someone.

"Hey, you're in the big leagues now. Long as the secretary knows where you are in case we need you, just go. No need for authorization."

"Sorry to have bothered you but I'm not used to that. Must be my teacher background. We could barely use the bathroom without permission. Just something I'll have to work on." Brad was backing out of the door as he finished, embarrassment coloring his face. He alleviated the foolish feeling settling in his stomach by jabbing his free hand into his jacket pocket, drawing comfort from the point of one of the nails as it poked into the tip of his index finger.

"See you in an hour, then," he said as he drew the door back to its original position. Hearing nothing but silence from the other side, he walked away.

Standing by the post that held the obnoxious parking sign, Brad looked back at the building. A full flight of granite steps led to the front door. The high windows on the front side of the building prevented a clear view of the parking lot unless someone made the conscious effort to walk to the window and look down. Brad moved to the left front of George Metcalf's huge black Lincoln Towncar that any funeral director would be proud to own. When he was close enough to the wheel, he bent as if to tie his shoe, setting his briefcase aside. Unlike his Capaldi caper, he needed to place the nail on only one side of the tire since Metcalf could only back out of his spot. He wedged the nail between the tire tread and the black top and stood up, shaking his pant leg as if to smooth it out after tying his shoe. Picking up his briefcase, he proceeded to slot number 20, satisfied that if he could not manage to place one more nail, the first would do the job.

An hour later, Brad passed by the Superintendent's car once more, this time on his way into the building. As he reached the right rear panel of the Lincoln, he stopped and looked up at the windows. He crouched again, disappearing between Metcalf's car and its neighbor in slot number 2. In a single deft motion, he had the nail out of his pocket and jammed into place. He stood and casually walked toward his new quarters, confident that Metcalf was going to join the ranks of Brad Wallace's destiny riders. There was no need to press his luck. Two flat tires would provide enough space for Fate to step in if She were so inclined. He hadn't anticipated an afternoon quite as much in a long time.

*   *   *

Melissa Harrington, principal of Paragon Elementary School, waited until all of the children would be seated at their tables in the cafeteria. The call from George Metcalf had surprised her. Even in the most well-organized and smoothest running schools, the first day with students required the full attention of the administration and staff. George was at his most insistent and assured her that she had trained her assistant well enough to cover for just an hour. Turning into the cafeteria through the open double doors, she noted that her expectations for student and staff conduct during the lunch recess were being met. She breezed through the room, smiling and addressing student after student by name, moving to the front where Nancy Cotton stood by the microphone, ready to announce the marching orders for each table.

"I hate to do this to you, Nancy," she whispered, holding her hand over the microphone, causing an ear piercing feedback squeal. "I need to leave the building for an hour or so. It seems as if you've got everything under control here."

Nancy smiled. "Is this a test? Three years as your assistant and you've never left me alone on the first day. Is everything OK?"

"Yeah. I just had a call from the Super and he needs to see me. Probably something that Brad Wallace told him about from this morning. I'll be back as soon as I can. Thanks a lot." She zigzagged among the tables, nodding in response to the enthusiastic greetings from her students.

The warm September day exaggerated the peanut butter and jelly aroma of the elementary cafeteria and Melissa drew a deep breath as she stepped outside. As she walked the three blocks to the usual meeting place, the sidewalk and the tall buildings lining the street radiated the absorbed heat from the late summer sun back toward the crowds of pedestrians spilling from the offices for their lunch hour escape. She loved blending into the anonymity that the city provided. She couldn't deny the excitement of her involvement with George Metcalf and their agreement that discretion was the highest priority suited her just fine. For the last three years, they scattered the business lunches and afternoon meetings far enough apart that no one would question them. Today was unexpected but spontaneity often was George's style. She would see what kind of plan he had in mind this time.

*　　*　　*

George Metcalf discovered the small state park at the beginning of a weekend trip to Mystic Seaport with his family. As they passed the sign on the interstate, he made a mental note that it might be an interesting place to take Melissa for one of their luncheon meetings. A drive through inspection the following Monday confirmed that the park was virtually empty during the week.

He met Melissa at their usual corner. He had estimated that the drive might take ten minutes, leaving a nice block of time for whatever may happen. The wide Lincoln navigated the first road into the park with no difficulty but as George turned toward an isolated picnic area through a narrow dirt road, the tell-tale squeal of bushes scraping the side of his car made him stop. They both turned to look out the back window and decided that this was a fine place for privacy.

Forty minutes later, after an especially creative session on the front bench seat of the car, George and Melissa spent a few minutes straightening out the various pieces of clothing that had been pushed up or pulled down or just shunted aside. George started the car and began to back slowly toward the main road. As he turned the wheel to maneuver, he felt the unmistakable wobble. He threw the shift lever into the park position.

"Hold on just a minute, Melissa. Let me just check something." She watched as he exited and walked to the front of the car. "Shit! Can you believe this?" Melissa stopped putting on her lipstick and flipped the mirrored visor up. She opened the door to get out and noticed a slight tilt of the right rear of the car.

"You've got a flat tire back here, George." Metcalf looked at her as if she had announced a death in the family. In three strides, he crossed in front of the car and stared at the offending wheel.

"Son of a bitch; two fucking flat tires. What the hell are we going to do?"

*　*　*

An enervated Brad shared the entire story with Josie during their cocktail hour. She listened quietly, interrupting only once to ask how the car could get two flat tires at the same time.

"That's really not the point, Jos." An agitation showed in his voice. "Metcalf can claim innocence all he wants but there was a lot of snickering and whispering going on in that office after he got back with that story. A lunch meeting with a female principal in a deserted park? He got caught; fate takes a hand, as they say. I love it!"

"I need to tend to dinner," she said when he finished. She offered no comment on the George Metcalf incident during their meal, instead directing all discussion to areas that disguised her concern for Brad's gleeful reaction.

*　*　*

As Josie arrived at Rich's house for her first visit since the opening of school, she recognized Havenot's car parked in the driveway. She shifted into park without turning the engine off. She sat looking up at the house, sifting through reasons for her hesitation in proceeding. Finally, she decided that Rich expected her and she had no choice but to continue. As soon as Becky opened the door, the unexplained nervousness subsided.

"Hi Josie! It's good to see you." Parker stood and was the first to greet her as she entered Rich's room. Her nervousness returned with a vengeance. She accepted Parker's firm handshake and then crossed to Rich, kissing him on the forehead.

"Are you all right?" Rich asked. "You seem a little agitated or something."

Josie flushed. "I'm fine, really. Just the usual Friday afternoon decompression from the first full week of school. You remember how that is, right?" She sat down heavily in her normal seat with Parker following her lead.

After Becky returned from the kitchen with tall glasses of iced tea for all, Rich asked how the "hot shot assistant superintendent" was doing.

"A really funny thing happened." she paused. "Well, Brad thought it was funny anyway but I'm not sure if I should tell you."

"Hey, we're all friends here and we can always use a laugh." Parker's smile and lightly phrased encouragement had Josie embarking on the tale of the Superintendent and the principal in the park, a story her friends found almost as funny as her husband had.

"Two flat tires; can you imagine that kind of luck?" Parker shifted from a slouch to a straightened up, leaning forward posture in the over-stuffed armchair.

"Just curious, Josie. Do they know what caused his flat tires? I mean two flat tires—that's pretty unusual." Parker leaned further forward in his chair.

"I asked the same question but Brad sloughed it off. He just said the other night when I asked him about it again that they think Metcalf picked up the nails at a school construction site he had stopped by that morning. As I said, incredibly bad luck."

Parker resumed his slouch, sinking into the soft cushions again. He gazed at Josie until she turned away. Shortly afterward, he abruptly stood to leave.

"I've got to get on my way, Rich. I'll be in touch and stop by again soon. Good to see you again, Josie." Parker abruptly stood to leave.

"Was it something I said, Detective?" Rich chided. "Only teasing.

Thanks for coming by and for leaving me alone with these good looking women." He threw Parker's line back at him with a solid laugh.

"Good to see you, too," Josie and Becky said, almost in unison.

"Hope to see you here again sometime," Josie said and instantly regretted it.

"Thanks." Parker muttered his response while looking down at his feet like an embarrassed adolescent.

*   *   *

Two phone calls on Saturday morning were all Parker needed. The desk sergeant in the South Hartford precinct gave him the name and phone number of the towing company that the state park authorities called if a visitor had car problems. His good luck intact, Parker's second call to the Patterson Service Center connected with the driver of the tow truck who had brought in the hapless Towncar. After a hearty laugh at the Superintendent's predicament, the driver confirmed that they had found one twenty penny nail still lodged in one of the tires while the other tire had a puncture that likely was caused by a similar nail.

"How could the car be driven with the nails in the tires?" Parker asked, being fairly sure of the answer.

"The park isn't that far from town, probably about ten minutes. He easily could have driven that far before the tires went flat. Of course, just sitting in the parked car having his meeting. . . ."The driver doused the word "meeting" with a heavy coating of sarcasm. "The air would just seep out and he would not have noticed; you know, being engaged in his meeting and all." A final leering chuckle filtered through the receiver to Parker.

"Thanks a lot for the info. I'm just following something up for a friend out here and appreciate your help." Parker set the receiver lightly on the cradle.

"Better keep an eye on this sucker," he said to the sketch of the water skier stuck into the corner of the blotter on his desk. A red flag fluttered wildly in his head.

*   *   *

Parker's favorite instructor during the intensive training in police investigation spent considerable time discussing what he called the naturals, those police officers who possessed a level of intuition far above average.

"They'll see red flags where other investigators see nothing but black and white," he had said. Parker dismissed the theory, feeling that every profession had its outstanding people and its average people. Not everyone can be at the top of the class.

To his colleagues in the field, first in the city and now in rural Connecticut, Parker represented one of those naturals. To him, he had no special gift, only doing his job and doing it well. That was what one was supposed to do.

Laura's Angel

"A happy family is but an earlier heaven."
Sir John Browning

Jimmy Carter's election in 1976 shocked many people around the country but no one more than Brad Wallace. If ever there might be an occasion for the saying that certain events cause some people to spin in their graves, Brad was convinced that his father certainly was spinning in his on November 4, 1976. The four years of the Carter administration had, in the eyes of virtually every Republican and a surprising number of Democrats, been a disaster for the country. Inflation, gas and energy shortages, an Iranian hostage crisis, and a variety of perceived domestic and foreign policy failures lay strewn at the doorstep of Jimmy Carter's White House. While Carter's reputation spiraled downward, Brad's career in the upper echelons of the Hartford Administrative Team was ascending.

The small internal scandal provoked by George Metcalf's luncheon meeting at Whispering Pines State Park with Melissa Harrington appeared to have chastened his boss somewhat. Brad found the Superintendent to be quite a capable administrator when he paid attention to his job and Brad congratulated himself on his role in the turnabout. Every time the Superintendent delegated an additional responsibility to Brad, he was rewarded with an exemplary performance. Brad envisioned his professional life as being directly on track. His personal life, meanwhile, seemed to be derailed. Parker Havenot and his flat tire story surely compounded his problems in that area. There could be no doubt of that.

*   *   *

Josie never tired of hearing news about her goddaughter from Harriet. One of her teaching strengths was her ability to demonstrate to her students the art of specificity in writing. She often used Harriet's letters as examples of the theory of specificity, the capability of delivering vicarious experiences to readers in such vivid terms that they became real. Harriet would describe Laura's exploits, from potty training to writing her name for the first time, in glorious detail, a detail broadened by her deep love for the child.

Brad had stopped reading the letters. His perception was that they had become nothing more than propaganda designed to spread layer after layer of guilt on him for refusing to agree to the adoption route that Josie so desperately wanted. No sooner would the wedge of tension caused by the disagreement be cast aside than another letter would arrive from Harriet, opening the wound again.

Late in October of 1980, Brad's euphoria over the likely election of Ronald Reagan was obvious. "Someone's got to save us from that bumbling and incompetent Jimmy Carter," he said on numerous occasions to whomever would listen. He believed that the nation needed a savior and Reagan would ride into Washington on his white horse to be just that.

After a particularly satisfying day overseeing a teacher-training workshop in late fall, Brad arrived home to find Josie sitting in her favorite chair clutching a damp handkerchief in one hand and a letter in the other.

"What's wrong, Josie? What is it?" Brad quickly imagined the worst.

"It's nothing, Brad; just something that Harriet sent along about Laura. You really should read this but don't feel that you have to for my sake." The edge was unmistakable.

"Maybe later. What makes this so special?" Brad matched Josie's edge.

"You'd have to read it yourself, that's all," she said as she left the room.

His interest and curiosity aroused, Brad picked up the three-page letter. Only the first few lines were from Harriet, describing what followed, a transcript of Laura telling her story to a tape recorder.

A Special Angel
The baby was only six months old. She came all the way from Korea and was picked up by a woman who became the baby's mom and special angel.

The little baby was fed and loved and held by her special angel for many months. The baby grew up protected and loved by her angel. Once she got very sick and couldn't sleep but the angel rocked her in her favorite rocking chair for hours until she fell asleep. Her angel read to her every night and she learned about Santa and God and the Easter Bunny and Halloween and her birthday. The angel worked very hard to raise the little baby. Soon the little girl asked a lot of questions like why she looked different than other children. The angel gave her a hug and told her that she was the prettiest girl in the whole world. Her angel pulled out a round plastic ball with all kinds of shapes and words. The angel spun the ball and stopped it on a small black dot on a small shape. The little girl looked up at her angel. "This is where you come from," she said. "Some day we'll visit Korea so you can see where you were born and what it's all about."

The little girl thinks about Korea and how things must have happened every day. Things must be all right because the little baby grew up to be healthy and strong. Every night before she goes to sleep, her special angel flies through her door and tucks her in. The little girl wonders how she was so lucky to have such a beautiful angel to take care of her. Then the light clicks off and the angel flies away into the darkness.

Brad read only as far as the title. "Maybe later," he said, putting the letter down on the coffee table.

The next day, Josie requisitioned a tape recorder from the audio/visual department. The transcript of Laura Stanton's story provided an excellent example for a spontaneous lesson in storytelling. She carefully explained to her class that at Laura's age her speaking vocabulary far exceeded her writing vocabulary but the feelings and emotions of the young girl could not be denied. Then she told them that the special angel was a former teacher at Hampton Village High School. She didn't mention that she would give anything to be one of those special angels.

A Wallace Family Crisis

"If you truly love and enjoy your friends, they are a
part of the golden circle that makes life good."

Marjorie Holmes

Josie saw Parker standing at the doorway of her classroom. "What a pleasant surprise. What brings you to my classroom on this beautiful fall day?" She reacted without alarm to this visit.

"Do you have just a few minutes? Rich thought I should talk to you and I guess I agree and if it's all right. . . ." He was struggling.

"Calm down. As long as nothing is wrong, we can chat for a few minutes." Her well-composed demeanor eased his tension. Josie sat at her desk while he squeezed awkwardly into a one-piece student desk in the front row.

"So, what's up?" Josie asked, no concern showing in her voice.

"I'm not sure exactly where to start but you can chalk this all up to a cop's paranoia if you'd like." Parker straightened in the chair as though he was about to testify in court.

When he finished his monologue, Josie had a single word reaction, one Parker had heard before in different circumstances.

"Preposterous!" she exclaimed.

"I know it all sounds bizarre but . . ."

Josie interrupted. "I'm sorry. This is just too absurd for words, Parker. I'm sure you're thinking of me but this is truly out of the question.

"OK. I've done my duty according to Rich. Let's forget it. I told him it would sound stupid but I had no idea how stupid. I'm sorry for even bringing it up. Just a bunch of silly coincidences, even if there are no such things." Parker abruptly began talking about the rain due that night and within a minute was excusing himself.

"I've got to get back to the station. I'll see you later, Josie." He paused. "That is, if you ever want to see me again." He started for the door, not expecting an answer.

"Of course I'll see you. Thanks for your concern." She waved to him as he stumbled from the room.

When Parker returned to his office, the first thing he noticed as he plunked down in his chair was the sketch of the water skier, yellowing slightly from age.

"No way I could bring that up to either of them," he whispered. "Absolutely no way I could even hint at it."

*   *   *

"I had a visit from Havenot at school today," Josie began. Brad let the evening Hartford Courier drop to his lap.

"So what did the esteemed detective want this time?" Brad asked, his face masked with a nonchalant expression.

"He wanted to let me know about a number of coincidences that he was aware of, most of them about flat tires of all things." Josie watched intensely for his response.

Brad picked up the paper from his lap, as if ready to begin reading again. His question, while caustic, was not hostile.

"I'd be interested in hearing about them. Did he say you could tell me?" As she described the incidents that Parker had told her, Brad kept one eye on the paper while nodding and grunting in response.

"So what did you make of the whole idea?" he asked when she finished.

"I told him I thought his coincidences were just that. So you happened to know some people who had car trouble. So what?" Brad put the paper down and looked directly at her.

"Thanks for your defense, although I don't think I needed it. Detective Havenot does seem to find reasons to visit you, though. Have you noticed that?"

Josie recoiled ever so slightly. "No, I've really not noticed that but he's become very good friends with Rich and I think that's pretty special. Rich needs all the support he can get."

Brad tossed the paper on the coffee table and stood up. "That is special and I admire him for it. As for the other stuff, perhaps you could tell him something the next time you see him." He paused, as if struggling to stay in control. "I'm sure he'll come to visit you again and when he does, mention to him that I'd appreciate hearing about his coincidences in person rather than second hand through my wife. Now, would you like another drink, my dear? I think I've had enough of this conversation." Without waiting for an answer, he left the room.

*　　*　　*

Brad avoided Rich Lane's house as if it were posted with a quarantine sign for some horribly contagious disease. He waited for three weeks after Josie told him about the detective's curiosity before calling Nurse Becky and arranging the visit. Brad complied with the social amenities and apologized profusely for not coming to visit more often. Rich, with a gentle good humor, reminded him that he had never come to visit but that he wouldn't hold it against him. Eventually, Brad squeezed in the question about Parker Havenot's "crazy coincidences."

"That's a policeman for you," Rich said. "Conspiracies and evil plots are lurking everywhere. Actually, when he told me about them, I said it all seemed like so much happy horseshit to me."

The answer relieved him and Brad quickly moved on to a self-absorbed detailed description of how important his job in Hartford was. He changed the subject when he realized how obnoxious he was sounding.

"We'll have to get you up to the camp on Lake Winnipesaukee again. Josie said that you seemed to enjoy it." Brad's body language gave him away.

"Yeah, we'll have to do that. Parker said he'd be glad to drive me up there sometime as long as Becky came along." Brad waited for a hint that would give him permission to leave but none was forthcoming. He stood up.

"Does Havenot know where our camp is?" he asked, trying to sound disinterested.

"Hey, Brad, you really don't have to hang around. Becky will be bathing me pretty soon and that's kind of a private thing," he said laughing. "Oh, yeah, Parker's been to the camp quite a few times as I recall; I'm surprised Josie hasn't told you."

"She probably did; you know how it is with married couples—a lot of halves. They mean half of what they say and hear half of what their other half says." Brad said goodbye from across the room and let himself out, a sigh escaping as he closed the door behind him.

A solid hour of daylight remained in the late fall sky and he was grateful for that. The flat tires didn't appear to be an issue any longer but a trip to the cemetery on the way home might be helpful.

*   *   *

"Parker Havenot; what the hell are you doing in my life?" he said through clenched teeth as he walked toward the gravesite.

Brad stood by the marker, lightly scuffling his right foot as if practicing the shuffle step in an elementary tap dance lesson. He wasn't surprised by the outcome of the visit to the gravesite. The detective represented a threat to him but also posed a difficult challenge to his standard operating procedure of administering justice. He waited for an answer to come to him, just as it always had. It was not what he expected.

"Nothing! There's absolutely nothing you have to do about Parker Havenot right now. Put that thought out of your head!" The severity of the reprimand startled him. His embarrassment showed in the hunched shoulders and downcast eyes as he shifted his weight back and forth from one foot to the other. His body language imitated an insubordinate but chastened student.

"OK, Junior, you're right but I'm not letting this go forever. He's interfering with my life now and something's going to be done. Timing is everything, as they say, and some day the timing will be just right. I'm in no hurry but our good detective needs to back off a bit."

Brad straightened up, all vestiges of embarrassment draining from him. "See you later, Bradford, Jr."

Josie Campbell Wallace, Professional

"No one should teach who is not in love with teaching."
Margaret E. Sanger

Josie Wallace entertained no desire to be more than she was. From her perspective, she could not have been more satisfied with her teaching career. Other colleagues seemed to be constantly searching for the perfect position in the perfect school, a daunting, hopeless search worthy of Don Quixote but she concentrated on providing her students at Hampton Village with the best and most innovative teaching she could. Others, including her husband, searched for courses that would add to their total of graduate credits so they might move up the salary scale. Josie trekked to small, meaningful workshops all over the state, programs that she felt might improve her effectiveness in the classroom. After twenty years at Hampton Village, her status on the salary scale had moved only to the Bachelor Degree plus ten graduate credits.

Brad, her husband of eighteen years, had stopped his sarcastic ridiculing of her lack of ambition. His supervisory position over hundreds of instructors in the Hartford School District finally convinced him that Josie was correct in her assumption that taking college courses doesn't necessarily improve one's teaching capabilities. He had visited enough classrooms to know that the best teachers used most of their energies figuring out ways to perfect lesson plans, squeezing the most learning possible from each classroom minute. Others, including some with advanced degrees, had one great year of teaching and then repeated the same lessons every year until their retirement. These were the classrooms that seemed stuck in a time warp, only the clothes and hairstyles of the students changing as the lessons stagnated over the years.

*   *   *

"Of course I'm not the same guy I was twelve years ago. What the hell do you expect, being subjected to Richard Nixon, then Jimmy Carter, and now Ronald Reagan? My God, Josie, it's enough to send anyone over the edge." Rich Lane's humorous edge had not been lost. His retort came after several minutes of verbal sparring with both Josie and Parker. The detective obviously had received a phone call from Becky as well.

Becky, now composed, joined them in time to hear Rich ask about the coincidence of both of his favorite visitors arriving on the same day at around the same time. Rich, his sensory perception of his environment infinitely sharper than that of the average person, caught the involuntary glance that Becky shared with the other two. "So, you're all in cahoots. Why'd you do this, Becky?"

"Come on, Rich. She's just concerned about you and thought we could alleviate some of her worry," Parker chided but with a gentleness born of love for his friend and compassion for his predicament.

Becky, visibly affected by her plan being discovered and flustered into a crimson shade of red, backed one step and moved behind Josie's chair.

"All right, I'll admit it," she said as she stepped out from behind the chair. "You've been different lately, Rich, and frankly it's frightening me." Rich's response was unexpected. He laughed as if Becky had just told a joke with a perfectly timed and quite funny punch line.

"How about a game of turnabout, folks. They always say that turnabout is fair play so let's do it." His smile disarmed their trepidation as he continued. "First of all, Becky, I do appreciate what you do for me. I don't know what I would do without you. Back to turnabout; if you think it's frightening for you, how do you think it feels from my side? Imagine being trapped in a huge container with just your head showing for twelve years, so long that you forget that you ever had the rest of your body. Here's what's wrong and I'll keep it simple for those of you who are slow on the uptake." Rich smiled again, the famous Lane smile that his friends always told him could charm the pants off a fifty-year-old virgin.

"Here it is in the proverbial nutshell, my friends. I'm going through a stage where I'm scared to death that I could live another few decades like this. What if I did? What if you weren't here for me? My dad's sadness crushes me every time I see him. What the hell am I doing here, nothing but a parasite draining everyone's energy?" He stopped, short of breath. "I'm just tired of being trapped. I've got no hope of getting out of my container and it's really been bugging me lately." He dropped his head, his chin touching his chest. Parker was the first to reach him, putting his hand gently on the top of his friend's head. The colorful flowered Hawaiian shirt already showed an expanding damp spot.

"Damn it, Parker, now I'm really embarrassed." Josie and Becky could have been choreographed as they acted in tandem, each kneeling on one side of the wheel chair, putting one arm around Rich's shoulder and laying the other hand on his forearm. Rich slowly picked his head up. The tears now were rerouted down his cheeks, creating another broadening damp spot on his shirt. He looked from one to the other, all with eyes glistening. Becky and Josie felt the muscles in the back of his neck tighten as he straightened his head even further. The four of them exchanged expressions ranging from anguish and distress to despair and sadness. Rich, his cheeks rapidly drying, broke the silent eye conversation.

"Well, you've got me surrounded. What happens now?" His entire turnabout monologue and the resulting group hug consumed not more than five minutes but the cathartic effect on Rich enveloped the room. With only one part of his body capable of providing clues to what he might be feeling, he drained the tension from the three mesmerized people around him. "No need to worry, folks, the next forty or fifty years will pass by very quickly and then you'll be off the hook." Becky stood and put her hands on her hips, looking like a mother about to scold a three-year-old who had broken a plate while trying to help her dry the dishes.

"For weeks I've been worried about you but you probably were just enjoying it, weren't you?" The others shook their heads in agreement.

"Would I do something like that to my friends and my nurse? I'm hurt that you would think that." Rich laughed and the relief around the wheel chair was palpable. "Seriously, this was all a test of your loyalty and you passed with flying colors. And while I'm throwing cliches around, I must admit the 'becoming a burden' thing was beginning to bother me."

Josie couldn't resist.

"Becoming a burden! It's been twelve years, Rich. Check your tense usage here. Becoming doesn't usually take that long. Have become might work better." She smiled, having gotten the better of Rich Lane, a memorable occasion for her. She caught the appreciative and attentive gaze of Parker Havenot and a warmth spread into her cheeks.

Going Through the Motions

*"We must realize that life is a voyage and
we are sailing under sealed orders"*
Elbert Hubbard

In quiet moments of desperation, Brad Wallace traced the beginnings of the demise of his stellar career to an insignificant incident brought about by insignificant people. At the time, he passed off the whole matter as unworthy of the effort for gaining a measure of justice. It was so unimportant that it didn't even require a trip to the cemetery for a revitalizing black period. Like a tiny pebble tossed into a small puddle, the ripples spread and it wasn't until those small undulations touched the edges of the puddle that he grasped their importance.

Unlike George Metcalf, he studiously avoided any involvement in the political circus of the city, instead devoting his energies toward the improvement of instruction for his students. When Melissa Harrington contacted him with a request to observe one of her veteran teachers who seemed to be developing some bad habits, Brad agreed. An interview with Melissa, whose discreet connection with George Metcalf continued despite the infamous flat tire meeting episode of years before, revealed that the ability of the teacher in question had been suspect since her first day on the job over ten years before.

"So why is she still here?" Brad tilted back on the legs of the straight chair opposite her, almost losing his balance. "It seems as though the principal before you and now you have questioned her capabilities yet the summative year end evaluations are average and above. We can't fire someone without sound documentation; you know that as well as I do, Miss Harrington." Melissa squirmed at the formality of his approach and didn't correct his error. She had been married two summers before.

"I'm thinking of our kids, Brad, that's all. You do know who she is, right?"

He didn't.

"Fill me in if you don't mind." His first months at work flashed through his mind and with it an obscene picture of the woman opposite him splayed across the front seat of a Lincoln, intertwined with George Metcalf.

"Well, it's just that George thought we needed to keep her but I'm feeling pretty guilty about it now, if you must know. You begin adding up children and in ten years over two hundred have been subjected to her." Melissa's nervousness showed but the fierce dedication of an elementary school educator to her students kept her going.

"That's why I'm hoping that you can help."

The phrase "subjected to her" brought the front legs of Brad's chair clumping back to the floor.

"I'm still not hearing who she is." Brad's impatience raised Melissa's anxiety a notch.

"Donald Shaw's niece; actually his wife's niece which makes him not really related to her at all, technically. Anyway, she's always been a favorite of his and I guess the United States senator from the great state of Connecticut wants his niece by marriage continuing her teaching career. He can always say that he identifies with the large educator voting bloc if he has one in the family. You know how that goes." She stopped speaking abruptly, as if a grape or a piece of hot dog had slipped down her throat.

"It really shouldn't matter. End of story, Miss Harrington. It's good to see you advocating for your students but, not to be a smart-ass, what took you so long?" Brad caught Melissa's flinch and the harshness drained from his voice.

"Let's get to solving this little problem, shall we?"

"Little problem, huh?" She chuckled without humor. "I see that you haven't crossed any serious swords with George Metcalf yet. I would've thought his philosophy might have rubbed off on you by now. You pick your battles and win them but make sure that you win them against people who can't hurt you afterward." She looked directly at Brad, searching for a sign that she had not said too much.

"This is a professional conference, Melissa, and we need to be candid. I appreciate your concern but I'll be glad to try to help. I'll need every particle of information about Mrs. Agnese Desmond," he said, adding a caustic aside. "Of the Hartford Desmonds, of course. I'm actually looking forward to watching her performance in the classroom. Maybe I'll learn something." His face relaxed and he winked at her.

Melissa understood the deliberate use of her first name, as though something had transpired in the last few minutes that had moved her to his side of the fence. They were partners now, charging at two of the most difficult windmills to be found in education and likely in any other field as well: despotism and incompetence. Each is difficult in its own right but when woven together, the problem becomes far more formidable.

"Thanks, Brad. I'll put together a file for you and let me know when you'll be scheduling the observations." She looked at him directly once more. "I'm not sure you realize how hard this is for me." She didn't expect any answer but received one anyway.

"Oh, but I do, Melissa; I really do. Let's just let fate take over here and we'll see what happens." With that, he stood and left her office.

* * *

Brad couldn't remember seeing George Metcalf quite so upset. The Superintendent slammed his office door so hard behind him that the breeze ruffled Brad's pants. Metcalf strode behind his enormous dark mahogany desk, which now presented a rather imposing protective barrier. Brad stood just inside the door waiting to be asked to take a seat. The offer was not forthcoming. From the other side of the desk, Metcalf bellowed across the room.

"You've got to be fucking kidding me, Brad. Agnese Desmond! There've got to be better targets for your obstinate professional performance requirements bullshit." Metcalf paced back and forth, careful not to venture out behind the edges of the desk, as if the lines on the rug marked a safety zone in a game of tag.

The ferociousness and the surprise of the attack moved Brad back half a step. He was practically leaning against the door. While he struggled to recover, Metcalf continued but in a more subdued tone.

"There are some things and some people that are off limits. That is the reality of the situation, Brad. I'd have thought you might have learned that by now. Agnese Desmond is a more than adequate teacher and I won't support your request for putting her on probation. Her evaluations simply do not warrant it. And I'm curious why you are involved anyway. It's a principal's call and Melissa hasn't seen any problems that I've heard about." Metcalf stopped pacing, as though he had made his point and the discussion was concluded.

"With all due respect, Dr. Metcalf, I agree about the principal's call but she did ask for some assistance in evaluating Mrs. Desmond, a request that I thought was certainly within her purview. I do have some responsibility for personnel, I believe." George Metcalf leaned forward and slid several file folders aside on his desk then put his hands down as if preparing to do a series of pushups.

"I'm well aware what your responsibilities are, Mr. Wallace, but you can't go getting involved in evaluating the entire staff of Hartford. If the principal doesn't have the guts to do it herself, maybe she's the one who should be put on probation."

Brad, not usually one to be rendered speechless, fished for an adequate response while his boss glared at him from his bunker across the room.

"The principal is a good one and I thought she deserved some help here. I've observed Mrs. Desmond on three occasions and interviewed her twice. I think we're hurting kids and something needs to be done." Brad remained on his heels, unhappy with his response.

"Here's what we're going to do and we'll solve the problem. First of all, kids survive an occasional poor teacher, assuming Mrs. Desmond is in that category, which I'm still doubting. I want all documentation that you've gathered about Mrs. Desmond in my hands by this afternoon. If it will make you feel better, you can write a cover-your-ass memo saying that you thought I should get involved since this is a ten-year veteran we're talking about. I'll take over from here. I'll also handle Melissa Harrington or Barrister or whatever the hell her name is now. Is there anything else you need to know?" The question was framed as a dismissal notice.

"No sir; I guess you've pretty much made everything absolutely clear. I have to tell you that I don't agree with cover-your-ass memos so that won't be forthcoming. What will be coming is a letter of protest about your handling of this issue with a copy to the Hartford School Board chairman. You realize that I have to do that for my own satisfaction." Still facing George Metcalf, Brad felt for the doorknob behind him as Metcalf straightened up, a cynical smile on his face.

"Of course you do, Brad, and I respect that. I'm sure that the chairman and the senator will appreciate your candor and honesty. We'll probably all be discussing your attributes at our next golf outing or poker game. You do a great job and we're lucky to have you but as the old song says, 'You gotta know when to hold em and know when to fold em.' This is one of those times when you need to fold them."

Brad opened the door just wide enough to slip out and walked briskly through the outer offices. The rage welling up from the pit of his stomach showed signs of spilling over and he avoided the nods and greetings of the secretaries. When he reached his office, he closed the door and sat at his desk. He picked up a manila folder filed with so many papers that the label was partially hidden. Holding it in both hands, he turned to stare out the window. Across the parking lot, he could see the gleaming black top of George Metcalf's Lincoln, partially obscured by the sign announcing the Superintendent's personal parking space.

"You bastard," he hissed, setting the folder back on his desk. The papers in it shifted, revealing the first line on the label on the folder. In bold capital letters, it read DESMOND, AGNESE.

* * *

Mike Costello, Brad's former principal at Hartford West and by far the most effective principal he had ever met, believed that most people resisted change. They preferred to maintain the status quo in their lives until forced to do otherwise. His theory became a credo for most of the teachers who served under him. Brad revisited Mike's theory on numerous occasions during his years under the leadership of George Metcalf, for which Brad coined the word "sleazership." The Agnese Desmond case forced him into examining Mike's theory once again. He had adopted the idea because it fit so well with his belief that truly changing people required introducing an almost cataclysmic event into their lives, one so fraught with emotion that they had to change.

The principal saw the importance of never allowing his teachers to become so entrenched in their teaching assignment that they began to, in his terminology, "ride the wave of mediocrity" by going through the motions of professional life. His answer to the potential problem was simple. Change the assignment of every teacher every five years, whether they liked it or not. The change didn't have to measure up to the significant emotional events Brad felt were necessary. It did have to force them to do something different, to plan new lessons, to deal with different student populations, to climb out of the rut of ritualistic teaching before it became too deep. This would eliminate the well-known phenomenon of the talented teacher who, after two or three years of successful instruction, copied the lesson plan book every year for the next thirty, taking excited students and grinding their enthusiasm into apathy and boredom.

At the conclusion of his fifth year as "Dr. Metcalf's lackey", Brad called Mike Costello and asked for a short lecture to refresh his memory on his "five year plan." The call lasted an hour and inspired Brad to send out a spurt of resumes to school districts closer to home. The first time that Metcalf received an informal call from one of his superintendent friends asking about Brad Wallace, he called him into his office.

"So, you're thinking of leaving us. Was it something I said or do you just want a change of scenery?" Metcalf realized what it would mean to him if Brad left the district. "You're not still pissed off about the Desmond thing, are you?"

"I'm just looking at my options, that's all. It's nothing personal. I'm not getting younger and I think that maybe I'd make a good superintendent." Brad had no idea where the conversation was going. He waited for Metcalf to respond.

"We're very happy with you, Brad. You've got principles and integrity, qualities that are rare around here." Brad's loud chuckle interrupted the Superintendent but he continued. "Plus, you're a damn good educator. We need people like you and I don't want to lose you. Another five to ten years down the road, you'll probably have my job. I'm sure we can work things out. Let me take a look at your contract, see if we could spice it up a bit. I'll get back to you on that but in the meantime, I'd rather not get any more calls from potential employers. What do you say?"

Brad responded with a weak expression of thanks. With surprising ease, Metcalf's little speech moved him toward the rationalization that Mike's five year theory didn't apply in his case. He was not going through the motions; he was making a difference. There were many people in the district who knew that they could depend on him for, as Metcalf had pointed out, his integrity and willingness to battle for principle. Melissa Harrington Barrister might be one who would disagree since she continued to deal with Agnese Desmond's incompetence, but his professional reputation remained intact with most of his colleagues. With a salary that few districts would be willing to match and an increasingly comfortable niche in the central administrative office, Brad set aside Mike Costello's theory. Late in the afternoon following his brief meeting with George Metcalf, he contacted every district that had his resume and requested that his file be placed on inactive status. He would continue to serve the Hartford School District in his role as the paragon of virtue, the protector of professional rights, and, quite often, the savior of his blundering Superintendent from professional embarrassment.

*　　*　　*

Josie was unable to hide her disappointment.

"For the past few years, all you've talked about is how screwed up the central office is. I thought you wanted out of there. Whatever happened to the escape from the hassle and politics of big city education?

I was looking forward to having you closer to home. What changed your mind?" Josie's insistent questioning placed Brad on the defensive.

"Look, Josie, I know what I'm doing. Things are good for me there; I'm making good money with a nice vacation and benefits. Why change just for the sake of change? It looks like you'll be spending your whole life at the same high school so what's wrong with me staying where I am?" Brad asked, with an odd combination of passivity and aggressiveness that Josie attributed to his second *Beefeater* martini.

"I thought you wanted to change, Brad, and where I am has nothing to do with it. I'm happy with what I'm doing and I'm doing it damn well, too. You really don't have to bring my situation into it; it's not what we're talking about here." Her voice was mimicking his passive-aggressive tone and she paused. "Why don't we just drop it for now. I'm happy if you're happy but no more complaints about George Metcalf and his political hobnobbing, OK? Parker thinks they're all crooks up there anyway." She regretted the Havenot reference before the last syllable escaped from her lips.

"And I suppose the detective included me in the category; the old guilt by association trick? What other incisive tidbits has he shared with you about the folks in Hartford?" he asked as he considered how far he wanted to go with the Parker Havenot thing.

"On second thought, I agree." He watched the tension drain from Josie. "Let's just drop it." Brad reached for the paper on the coffee table and raised it like a privacy curtain, closing the discussion and any chance at further communication.

*   *   *

The traditional rubber stamping of the Superintendent's administrative recommendations occurred during the second meeting in April. The agenda for the board meeting included the list of contractual renewals for all administrative personnel along with a summary of the terms of each contract. Brad found his name toward the top of the list and the summary confirmed what the Superintendent had told him in his final evaluation meeting for the year. The substantial raise with an additional week of vacation justified his decision to stay. Scanning down the lists, arranged alphabetically by position, he smiled as he connected a face with each name. He knew all of them and could recite the strengths and weaknesses of each if called upon to do so. After the casual scan, he went back to the beginning of the principal's list to look more closely at each one's salary and benefit package. The second name on the list was Melissa Harrington Barrister. His finger stopped tracing at the first column next to her name. The letters "NR" consumed the whole space. Every other name on the page had the letter "R" in the column.

He grabbed the phone and hit the internal button and #1.

"Dr. Metcalf speaking. What can I do for you?"

"You're not renewing Melissa Harrington," he said without any introduction and neglecting once again to correct her last name. "What the hell is going on?"

"You passed the Desmond problem along to me, remember? I told you I'd handle it and I did. Mrs. Harrington Barrister is first in line for a position in Enfield, a position I suggested that she apply for. A good friend of mine is the super up there and he needed a good elementary principal. She realizes that her leaving was for the best." The silence from Brad's end prompted Metcalf to continue. "She made a mistake getting you involved, Brad. I had made the situation with Agnese Desmond quite clear to her and she should've known better. Sometimes things need to be left alone. I hope you've learned that." He waited again and this time Brad answered.

"And what about Agnese Desmond?" he asked flatly, already knowing the answer but wanting Metcalf to confirm it.

"We're putting Nancy Cotton, Melissa's assistant, into the position and she understands that Agnese will need a little guidance and direction. I'm sure Nancy can iron out any of the minor problems she might have in the classroom. She'll be fine." The finality in Metcalf's voice was unmistakable. "Was there anything else you needed?"

"A little guidance and direction! She's a damn ten year veteran . . . " Brad's voice rose with his agitation. He stopped abruptly.

"I guess you've covered it all, Dr. Metcalf." He hung up, thought for a minute and dialed another number.

"Good morning; Paragon Elementary, where learning is fun. How may I help you?" The sincere enthusiasm in the secretary's voice made the lengthy salutation palatable.

"Melissa Barrister, please. This is Brad Wallace."

Several long silences punctuated the fifteen-minute conversation. Melissa Harrington Barrister had involuntarily joined the ranks of those who were on the receiving end of life altering emotional events. Admitting that her involvement with George Metcalf had been more than professional, she stumbled through an explanation of the choices he offered her. She could fight her non-renewal, with all of the bitterness that was sure to engender, and, with the grievance procedure ending with the school board, she had little chance of winning that battle. Even if she did win, the subtle pressure that a superintendent can apply to principal level administrators would likely destroy her anyway. She could accept what Metcalf called a "gracious offer," another position far from Hartford. Finally, she could simply accept her dismissal and try to find another position on her own, an intolerable option since George Metcalf would be a primary reference.

"I really don't have a choice," she said. "To be crass and crude, he's got me by the short hairs." Brad chuckled at her use of a favorite male analogy then realized that the silence on the other end of the line was interspersed with choked back sobs.

"I love it here, Brad. This is my school with my kids and my staff." Her grip on her composure continued to slip. "I thought you were going to help me with this." Another long silence followed.

"I thought so too, Melissa." He threw in a final meaningless cliché. "My hands are tied on this one. I'm sorry that it worked out this way. Good luck." Brad set the phone down gently.

"George Metcalf and Parker Havenot. There are two people who deserve to be taught some serious lessons," he whispered as he peered from the window at Metcalf's car once again.

He looked down at the manila file folders lined up, waiting for his attention. *The wave of mediocrity and I'm riding it like a God damned seasoned surfer*, he thought. *Just sailing through the motions of professional life.* He gripped the edge of his desk as if to keep from sinking further into quiet desperation.

Going through the Motions-Josie's Version

"A friend is one with whom I may be myself."
Ralph Waldo Emerson

There is a theory that attempts to explain how it is that time seems to pass more quickly with each passing year. When Brad killed the goldfish in Harrison Peaslee's pond, a year represented just one ninth of his young life. To the man approaching middle age at forty-two, the same three hundred and sixty five days had shrunk to the minimal fraction of just 1/42 of his life. In the prime of his professional life, Brad found the years slipping by with astounding speed. The five years since he assumed his position in the Hartford administrative bureaucracy had been financially lucrative but emotionally draining. What Josie referred to as the "Desmond Effect" hovered over him like a vulture circling over a decaying carcass of a deer in the forest. Her contention, one that Brad readily but unhappily agreed with, grew out of her ability to visualize the bigger picture of her profession. In their twenty years in education, both of them observed variations on the "Desmond Effect" many times. Its explanation was as simple as the human nature that inspired it.

Brad had accepted his responsibility and tried to assist in ridding Melissa Harrington of an incompetent veteran teacher. In that single attempt to perform his professional duties the way he saw them, he invoked the wrath of all three of the educational groups in the district.

Inevitably, supporters of Agnese Desmond rallied to her defense, citing her years of service and threatening to activate the grievance procedure for tenured teachers. When the Superintendent cleared the muddied waters by eliminating Melissa from the equation, the building level administrators blamed Brad Wallace for his lack of courageous support. George

289

Metcalf, aware that practicality dictated that he should keep Brad's professional talents available to him, covered his unhappiness for Brad's interference but let it be known that he thought Brad had made a big mistake.

"Pick your battles and win them," Metcalf's advice began. Brad understood only a fraction of its importance as he sorted through the wreckage of the Agnese Desmond case, but the aftermath had the vulture making those sweeping circles in the sky above his head. Even after a battle that he had fought and lost, there were those who would cheerfully hurt him if the opportune time came.

Josie succinctly arranged the entire episode in easy to understand language. "You did your job, or at least tried to. If the others can't see that, they're stupid. But, as we both know, people will always be stupid and they'll find ways to keep fairness and justice from intruding on their stupidity."

*　　*　　*

While Brad proceeded through his motions of life and advanced toward the quiet desperation looming on the horizon, Josie did the same without the desperation. She became one of those rare teachers who spend entire careers in one school with ever increasing effectiveness. The unusual success came from her passion for innovation. While fellow members of her English department used the same ancient filmstrips and records to bore the television generation of students into a daily forty five-minute stupor, she created new methods of inspiration. Believing that engagement was everything, she entered the student's world through their door instead of through the typically narrow entrance reserved for most adults. Every spring her two elective classes in *Shakespeare* and *American Literature of the Nineteenth Century* were filled to capacity before the first day of registration. Parents overwhelmed the Director of Guidance with requests that their children be placed in Mrs. Wallace's senior English classes, confident that they would then be prepared for the rigors of collegiate courses in composition and writing. Josie Campbell Wallace, the ultimate professional, embodied the traits that often made her the target of professional jealousy on the part of many of the weaker members of the staff. After twenty years in the classroom, her gleaming eyes still showed the fiery excitement for her subject and her students as she faced her packed classroom.

*   *   *

Whenever Josie broached the subject of upgrading to a larger house, Brad insisted that theirs was more than adequate for their needs and he would not consider any move that was further away from Mountain View Cemetery where their son was buried. With any hope of children long since crushed by Brad's harsh rejection of adoption, the modest but charming three-bedroom ranch certainly was large enough and it was just under a mile from the cemetery. The surrounding lot, over an acre in size, had allowed for the construction of a large deck off the rear of the house. Brad found that standing in the northeast corner of the deck provided a view of the iron picket fence surrounding the cemetery across the intervening backyards of the neighbors' houses.

As soon as the weather turned warm, Josie and Brad used the deck for their evening winding down cocktail and "How was your day today, dear?" conversations. He usually sat on the railing in that corner facing toward his son's grave, absorbing an indefinable comfort from it.

"I'm not sure what you want me to say, Brad. You've been adamant about not moving away from the proximity of Mountain View. We've been through this so many times. Now you want to move to New Hampshire. Even if you could find something up there, I'm not ready to give up what I have at Hampton." The topic of the discussion was, once again, his desire to escape from the stultifying environment of the Metcalf administration.

"It'd be a trade off, Josie, and well worth it for me. I'm not getting anywhere. I thought I could make a difference in the level of instructional competence in that damn city but George is set on the status quo and it's driving me crazy. Just because he pays me a good salary, he thinks he can just keep me around to do all of his dirty work."

Josie sat on a small lawn chair looking up at Brad as he sat on the corner railing, staring over her head at the iron fence in the distance. They both sipped their martinis, and then Josie tried vainly to interject some humor.

"Would you like some cheese with your whine, dear?" She instantly regretted her feeble attempt. The look she received in return was vicious as his resentment boiled over.

"Things are great for you, Josie, but I'd think that you'd want me to be happy, too."

A silence enveloped them, resounding as loudly as a cymbal player reaching a crescendo. It reverberated for several seconds before Josie recovered.

"My life has been about that, Brad. I mean, for God's sake, it just seems like I'm always giving and you're always taking. Of course, I want you to be happy but I've run out of options for figuring out how to do that." An excruciating pause followed.

"Look, let's just forget this for a while. We're both under a lot of stress so let's just put it aside for now, OK?" Josie adopted her best conciliatory posture, a stance that could be as perceived as weakness.

"I really don't want to forget it right now, Josie. You've got a pretty strong support base with your friends at school and, I've got to admit, a little bit of a worrisome relationship with Rich and that Havenot guy. It's been years since Rich's accident but all of you seem to be still connected. You're what I have; you and Brad, Jr." Brad sputtered to a stop and gazed across at the cemetery, as if asking for some help.

The gaze slapped Josie hard and she stood involuntarily like a World War II veteran at a Fourth of July parade as the colors passed.

"Brad, Jr.! What in the name of God are you talking about?" Her reaction drew clear parameters around the conversation but left him with no place to go. She sat down with a sigh and gave no indication that she wanted to follow her question with another. She waited for him to respond.

"You're right, Jos. Let's just forget it." An enigmatic smile contradicting the content of his words slid across his face.

Unsatisfied with his answer, she pushed onward.

"You made the choices, Brad. You withdrew from the magnificent seven. You had good friends there who cared about you. You wanted to move onward and upward instead of staying where you were. It's all your choice so don't come complaining when stuff doesn't work out. But, more importantly, what's this about Brad, Jr.? He's been gone for years so why even mention his name in this discussion?"

"That was stupid, Josie. I don't know where that came from." He looked down at Josie, his physical position of dominance diminishing in direct proportion to the fury of her anger.

"Using your word, it is stupid. If you remember, you didn't even want to bury him and the next thing I know is that you don't want to move out of sight of the cemetery. There are times when you actually frighten me and I don't even know why." She stood again, this time with her shoulders sagging, the defiance drained from her. "I'm not going anywhere, Brad. If you want to find a job in New Hampshire, go right ahead. I'm staying here."

*   *   *

When Nurse Becky became Mrs. Rich Lane, Josie's deepening friendship with Parker Havenot became a bit more problematic. The unique wedding ceremony that took place at Rich's house had just five people present. Rich arranged for a local pastor to perform the brief ceremony. Josie and Parker acted as Matron of Honor and Best Man respectively, but not before each of them had grilled their friends, their pointed questions similar.

"What in heaven's name are you thinking of, Becky?" Josie asked when she told her about their plans. She launched into a long and not unexpected lecture, knowing that anything she might be saying would most likely be futile.

"I love him, Josie; it truly is that simple. He is the most engaging, charming man I've ever met and we'll be good for each other." She smiled as she watched Josie struggling to frame the difficult question, an inquiry so obvious but so impossible to put into delicate words. She decided to help her.

"It's a non-issue, Josie. I want to be with him all the time and I'll manage the sex thing. There are all sorts of imaginative ways for me to solve my own problems and Rich can compensate. I guess the pros of being loved by a man as special as he is far outweigh the cons of not having the usual sort of sex life." Josie was staring at her with a mixture of admiration and silent interrogation. "Look at your relationship with Parker. I see how much you mean to each other and the lack of sex probably makes it easier and less complicated."

Josie looked away, not wanting Becky to see the serious blush that would soon be working its way up her cheeks. "I don't know what you're talking about, Becky. Parker and I don't have a relationship. We are just good friends. I hardly ever see him except when we're in your company." Her defensiveness exposed her and she knew it. "OK, I enjoy it when we are all together. It's fun like it used to be in the old days when Brad was still at Hampton, before Rich's accident and Tyler Spence and Brad's parents and Brad, Jr. . . ." She stopped and her eyes filled. "Oh, shit, Becky, this was my lecture, not yours. Things happen, people change and the meat grinder of life takes the sirloin and makes it into hamburger. I envy you and Rich and know that you'll pull this off. You're both really special and you, Becky, have more courage than I could ever imagine." Her lecture at an end, she let her eyes dry without wiping them.

Her regular visits with the Lanes and Parker had become her salvation. Friendships often rise and fall when faced with the daunting task of sharing living quarters, and the innumerable trips to the lakeside cabin allowed their connection to move into a realm of intimacy that came only from spending long periods of time together. The ease with which she could share her concerns about Brad's erratic behavior with her three friends was a constant reminder of the importance of what having them in her life meant to her.

* * *

For Josie, the appeal of the cabin on Lake Winnipesaukee heightened with each passing year while Brad's interest in spending time there diminished, his trips reduced to the summer bookend holiday weekends of Memorial Day and Labor Day and an occasional Fourth of July. Her adamant stance on remaining in Hampton Village drained his enthusiasm for New Hampshire. The intensity of Josie's one hundred and eighty five days at the high school left her gasping by the time the summer would come, and she easily sloughed off the gentle teasing from Parker about the part time job that teachers have. Other than occasional weekend visits home, she spent most of the months of July and August at the lake, content to have some free time for recreational reading and mindless activity. Rich and Becky spread their visits out over the two months, timing them carefully so that they wouldn't be there at the same time as Brad. Parker, now totally enamored of the lakeside lifestyle that typified summer in central New Hampshire, coordinated his mid-week visits with the Tibideaus to correspond with the Lanes staying at Josie's cabin. Despite several years of coaxing from Becky and Rich, he couldn't bring himself to actually spend the night at the Wallace cabin.

For the Wallaces and their friends, the approach of middle age solidified their behavioral patterns. With most human beings, habits and routines become so entrenched that only a dire set of circumstances can force them to change. The summer patterns of Josie and Brad evolved to the point that when they did see each other there was an uncomfortable awkwardness, an uneasiness that remained throughout the visit, whether in New Hampshire or Connecticut. When the summer was over and they were reunited, the fall patterns quickly were reestablished and life proceeded as usual. Sadly and guiltily, Josie admitted to herself that the time away from Brad in the summer had become a relief.

The visits from Rich and Becky heightened the relief she felt in the summer. Being with her old friends in such a calming environment as the cabin drained her inhibitions and she shared her concerns with surprising candor. Rich constantly referred to himself as the luckiest man on the face of the earth, humorously imitating the quavering voice of Lou Gehrig when he used the same phrase in his dramatic speech in Yankee Stadium. Josie's respect for Rich, which pyramided as time went by, arrived at a level of admiration and trust far beyond what she would ever have imagined.

One sultry July night, while Becky showered off the residue of the hot summer day, they sat together on the deck listening to the clashing sounds of civilization and nature, the cry of the loon rising desperately above the piercing whine of jet skis and power boats.

"You should have taken me up on my offer, Jos. I mean, look where we'd be now. You could have changed the whole course of history that weekend of Harriet's wedding." Rich could read Josie's face clearly in the closing dusk as the sun dropped into the lake with yet another blinding display of brilliance. His automatic reaction was, as always, an attempt to lighten the tone of the moment whenever somberness or sadness crept in. His eyes exposed his surprise at Josie's answer to his flippant response, forcing him to turn away and gaze at the sunset.

"Had I known then what I know now, I surely might have considered it. But that's the destiny that Brad's always talking about. One choice and the path changes forever." Josie's gaze joined Rich's on the horizon.

"Yeah. Like Yogi Berra said, if you come to a fork in the road, take it." Rich laughed at his own joke and Josie joined in.

"That would've been some fork, wouldn't it? Just think, no accident for you, no life like you have . . ." Josie stopped short. "Oh, shit, I did not mean that."

"Not to worry, Mrs. Wallace. I'm flattered that you'd even think that might be a choice you would reconsider if you could. But then, I wouldn't have met Becky who has made me . . ."

Josie interrupted. "I know, Rich. The luckiest man on the face of the earth." She warbled as she said it and they both laughed.

"He calls what happened to you destiny, you know?" Rich turned his face away from the vista and faced Josie.

"I'm sure he does but I call it the luck of the draw. As the bumper sticker says, 'Shit happens', or something like that. I've heard him talk about stuff like that before. I don't think he would say that a little clowning around on skis deserved this. That's a pretty stiff slap from Fate, I'd say."

"Destiny strikes again, he said." Josie thought that if he could, Rich would've been leaning forward in his wheelchair.

The screen door opened and Becky came out, the terry cloth beach cover clinging to her still damp body, already beginning again to perspire in the unusual New Hampshire humidity.

"But Fate always compensates," Rich said. "That was tough but look what it got me." Becky walked up behind Rich and draped herself provocatively over his shoulders.

Josie silently stared ahead. Rich immediately recognized that his old friend seemed to be holding something back. "So what else do you have to tell me?" Becky removed her breasts from their position on either side of Rich's head and stood up.

"It's really nothing new but lately when he talks about people who have gotten what they deserve, you're mentioned right up with my Dr. Capaldi and the guy who killed his parents and even his superintendent. You've gotten lumped into some company that he has no time for." Becky and Rich stared at her. Becky crossed the deck and leaned against the railing just opposite Josie.

"The accident was years ago; I can't believe that Brad still even talks about it?" Becky ended the statement with a question mark, requiring Josie to respond.

Once in a great while conditions and circumstances combine to allow the natural protective layers of caution present in all human beings to fall away. Sitting on the deck with Rich and Becky in the enfolding haven of their friendship and the natural environment of the lake, Josie began speaking, all pretenses aside. Before the evening was over, most of Josie's fears about her husband found a voice, even concerns she had never faced herself. With Parker scheduled to visit the cabin the next evening, Josie quickly began examining her options before her protective layers could shove them back beneath the surface.

*　　*　　*

Parker anticipated the evening with enthusiasm. The big lake and his escapes to it had become an integral part of his personal quality world, that secret place that psychologist/educator William Glasser proposes is at the center of why humans make the choices they do. Parker listened to so many philosophical discussions between Josie and Rich that he could recite educational and learning theory with the best of them. Dr. Glasser wouldn't have to delve too far into his subconscious to uncover the real reason that he loved spending time at the lake.

Ostensibly, the purpose of his regular visits remained the camaraderie and friendship with Gordon Tibideau and his parents and that served as his consciously accepted rationale. Becky and Rich Lane, both major players in Parker's circle of human contact, saw things differently and spent much of their conversation time speculating on Parker's love life. Their deepening friendship allowed for wide ranging discussions but if there were any women in his life, they remained a well-shrouded secret that made for fascinating speculation. The day after Josie's worrisome revelation of Brad's fatalistic beliefs, Parker visited the Wallace cabin for a quiet dinner and an evening of *Trivial Pursuit,* a game that he disliked but tolerated because of its attraction for his friends. The frustration of always losing to Rich Lane was an acceptable tradeoff for being Josie Wallace's partner. The phone rang just as he finished his shower and he heard Gordon call to him.

"It's Becky Lane for you, Parker." He quickly finished drying himself off, his demeanor having changed from positive to negative in a matter of seconds.

"Shit, they're going to cancel," he whispered to himself. A few more seconds on the phone and he switched back into an even more positive mode than before. Becky asked him to join them on a shopping expedition to Stoneham that afternoon before his visit. He whistled softly as he dressed. It was just a month since the last time he visited and played the game that made him feel like a moron most of the time. He had called Rich a "damned walking encyclopedia" then realized what he had said and amidst fierce blushes, apologized profusely while Josie, Becky and Rich enjoyed one of the heartiest laughs of the summer season at his expense.

He readily accepted Becky's invitation and arrived at the town dock a full hour ahead of the scheduled meeting time. As always on a warm summer day, parking spaces were at a premium but his policeman's luck held and a space in the front row opened just in front of him. After opening every window in the car, he walked leisurely toward the ice cream window of Twiggy's Restaurant, packed with tourists enjoying the view from the air conditioned dining room. As he waited for the ten or twelve customers in front of him to be served, he passed the time practicing his observation skills on the milling crowds around the docks. The young lady serving the ice cream questioned his choice but grudgingly complied.

"A single dip of plain vanilla seems hardly worth waiting for, mister. We've got twenty six flavors." Parker noticed the slight bulge in her right bicep, a sure sign that she had worked here dipping the hard but delicious homemade ice cream all summer. He just nodded and she turned from him, shaking her head. Determined to make her smile, he handed her a five-dollar bill and told her to keep the change.

"I'm on vacation," he said in answer to her quizzical look. He was rewarded with a toothy, wholesome smile and started toward an empty bench in front of the larger public boat slips.

The hour wait for the Lanes and Josie passed quickly as Parker watched with fascination at the varying skill levels of the skippers as they guided their boats into tight slips. He was happy for the warmth of the day as it discouraged the ladies from using their beach covers, and he smiled as they struggled with their lines while trying to keep the often scanty bathing suits from falling off.

A soft touch of a horn caused him to turn around just as the Lane's van came to a stop in the only handicapped parking space in the lot. He stood, scattering the ducks that were gathering by the DO NOT FEED THE DUCKS sign to be fed by several young boys clutching bags of popcorn. The *BiNaY I* was just docking and Parker paused briefly to admire the beautiful blonde performing her sailor's duty in the bow of the boat then he walked quickly toward the van, his stomach fluttering with that annoying nervousness.

"Give it up, Parker," he told himself out loud before he arrived at the van. "A good friend, that's all she can ever be." He climbed into the van to help with Rich and looked around.

"Where's Josie?" he asked. Becky was in a good position to see the disappointment evident in his face.

"She had to stay back at the cabin; I should've told you but I thought you'd come anyway."

"Of course I would. I just thought she'd be here. No big deal." The disappointment faded but slowly.

They extricated Rich and his wheelchair and Becky pushed him toward his favorite place in the shade where he could look out to the bay at what he continued to refer to as the scene of the crime.

"Damn that Brad," he said as Becky set the brake on his chair. "You'd think he'd be a little more compassionate." He stared out at the water. The bitterness that until now had been submerged beneath a layer of good-natured human understanding surfaced. The evening of discussion about Brad's obsession with the fate of others whose lives were intertwined with his had taken a toll.

Parker, not privy to Josie's information of the night before, looked at Becky and was surprised to see her wink and nod her head, indicating that she would fill him in later.

"You don't mind if we leave you here, Rich. I could use Parker to help me carry the packages. I promise I'll come back for you." She smiled, knowing what was coming.

"Just so you know, if something better comes along, I'll be taking it, Becky; lots of women around who can't resist a guy in a wheelchair."

*   *   *

The walk from the park to the small downtown grocery store consumed just a few minutes but it was time enough for Parker to sense that his friend had something she wanted to say.

"Everybody gets stuck in ruts at some point in their lives but most of the time they don't know it or at least refuse to acknowledge it," Becky said. As they entered the store, Becky caught Parker smiling to himself. Moments later she had the whole story of Parker's first coincidental meeting with Josie and his embarrassing sidelong crash into the door as he glanced back over his shoulder to catch a final glimpse of her that day.

"So, it's obvious that we need to talk but this is probably not the place, right?"

Becky nodded affirmatively but said nothing.

"Maybe we can just visit a while before going back to the cabin?"

"It would be helpful if Rich were included for part of it but the other part I'd prefer to have you to myself if you don't mind," Becky said in response.

Parker couldn't conceal his curiosity but tried in vain to cover it with humor.

"Why, Mrs. Lane, you're a married woman. I'm surprised at you, coming on to me like this." It was a lame attempt and he knew it. "Sorry, Becky. It's just that I can't imagine what you're talking about."

"It's a woman thing and I'll bet I can finish my part in the five minutes it will take us to walk back to the park. Now, let's get shopping." They were silent for the rest of the journey through the pleasantly crowded little store, their time divided between shopping and exchanging affable greetings whenever their carriage bumped with another shopper's.

"I'm going to save what we learned about Brad Wallace last night for when we're with Rich but I really want you to know something and I'm probably out of line here and you might think I'm crazy but I think it's important for you to know and . . ." She paused, more than slightly out of breath.

"Good thing we're not with those English teachers, Becky. I think you just violated a whole bunch of grammatical rules." Parker laughed but only half-heartedly. His was curious and wanted her to continue.

"Josie Wallace is a fine person and I don't want to see her hurt." Becky paused again and they both stopped walking to shift the weight of the grocery bags around. She took the opportunity to look directly at

Parker and his law enforcement instinct scrolled words like honest and sincere and compassionate across Becky's face.

"This is what I want to say and then I'm going to leave it. I know you care a lot about Josie. To another woman, your feelings are obvious and I can't believe they aren't to her as well. All I'm asking is that you not give up on her or anything. Situations in life change and one never knows what might happen." Becky rearranged the bags in her arms again and started to walk away.

"Wait a second, Becky. I guess after that you deserve to know this. I'm not planning on going anywhere but I'm not planning on trying to ruin a marriage either. As you say, life's situations can change in a heartbeat but we can't hurry them along to suit our own selfish purposes. Don't you agree?" They began to walk slowly toward the park where Rich waited.

"Of course, I agree and I admire your restraint all this time. It can't be easy."

"No, it isn't; it isn't at all." They walked the rest of the way, both of them relieved but somehow despondent.

*   *   *

When they got to Rich, he was uncharacteristically subdued and not the least interested in staying in the park for another minute. His strong suggestion that they return to the cabin right away left no room for discussion. Parker balanced all the groceries while Becky wheeled him back, leaving no chance for the planned discussion about Josie's concerns from the night before.

That evening, after one round of *Trivial Pursuit* ended with the usual result, Josie's suggestion that they play again was met with what Rich described as thundering apathy, especially from Parker.

"I'm a damn albatross around Josie's neck," he exclaimed after yet another drubbing from the Lanes. His three friends predictably rose to his defense, afraid that eventually his discouragement would lead to a 'no more Trivial Pursuit' stance.

"You're doing fine, Parker, really. You've really improved. You know all the answers; you just can't remember them." Coming from anyone but Josie, he would have taken the comment as condescending but instead he just accepted it.

"Thanks for the confidence, Jos, " he said. "Now, let's take a break and enjoy an evening on the deck with a Grand Marnier or something."

Once they were all seated and sipping the powerful after dinner drink, Parker innocently initiated a conversation that would last well into the night.

"So, Rich, what was going on at the lake today? You seemed out of sorts when we got back from shopping."

"I just got thinking about some of the stuff Josie brought up last night but I'll get over it." Josie responded to his comment with a withering glance that silently framed the question which a second later she verbalized.

"Where are you going with this, Rich? I'm sure Parker wouldn't be interested in my little problems." The gathering darkness prevented her from seeing Parker's face across the deck but she sensed that Rich's remark had drawn his attention. She felt his gaze without seeing it.

Parker tried to disguise his curiosity but fearing that his natural inquisitiveness might offend Josie, attempted to diffuse the tension.

"Sorry, Josie, I wouldn't want to pry. I just thought that Rich might like to talk a bit. I had no idea what was going on." Josie warmed to Parker's naïveté and eased the situation further.

"It's not a problem; I'm comfortable sharing with you as well. I think Rich could tell you what he's talking about if he wants to."

The cathartic revelations of the night slowly began to spill out. Rich started with his disappointment with Brad's apparent indifference to his accident, holding his emotions in check until it was mentioned that Brad thought he "deserved what he got" for clowning on the skis.

"No one in the whole fucking human race deserves what I got and I can't believe anyone could ever say that." Becky pulled her chair next to his and put her arm around him as his voice faded behind choking sobs.

"Must be the damn booze," he said softly after regaining his composure. "Makes me crazy and I cry every time."

Josie stood and slowly paced back and forth on the deck. Only the scuffing of her sandals on the slightly warped boards of the deck as she walked back and forth interrupted the deadly silence hanging over the four of them. Finally, a forceful but melancholy wale of a loon skittered across the lake, reaching the deck like a trumpet sounding to call everyone to attention for a major announcement. Josie seemed to take it as a signal to stop pacing. Just enough of the ambient light from inside the cabin drifted across the deck to illuminate her back as she leaned on the railing and stared out toward the lake. She started to speak almost in a whisper.

"It seems like it all started with Brad, Jr.," she turned toward her three friends. The light cast an eerie glow across her face. Her glistening eyes reflected the dim light as she continued her recitation, an encore soliloquy repeating much of what was said the previous night. Becky tightened her grip around Rich's shoulders and looked over at Parker. This performance was for his benefit.

The litany consumed more than an hour. Parker remembered his assessment of Brad Wallace and as he listened to Josie, he decided that his appraisal had been accurate. Brad was indeed a "really complex guy."

When she finished, Josie sat down, exhausted, looking like she had just been cross-examined by a vicious defense attorney who had made her doubt her own sanity. For the Lanes, the repeat performance was as draining as the previous one. It was like watching Patty Duke and Anne Bancroft playing their exhausting meal scene in *The Miracle Worker* twice in succession. Parker's dilemma lay in separating his strong emotional attachment to Josie from his calculating policeman's perspective that indicated that Brad Wallace's actions showed a man descending into a systematized delusory state of paranoia.

Josie, after spending several minutes in silence, excused herself with a perfunctory "good night" and disappeared into the cabin. The evening came to an unexpected and quick end. Parker, saddened by Josie's sudden departure, saw no reason to stay any longer.

"May I ask you a question, Rich? It's kind of one that I'd like to ask you alone, if that's all right with you, Becky. It's no big deal but it's a man thing, you know." Becky, trying to act angry but not succeeding, acquiesced to the request.

"Let me know when you're ready to come in, Rich. I'll just be inside doing the dishes," than, as an aside, "That's a woman thing, you know." She smiled and left the men alone.

"I'll let you go, Rich, but I'd appreciate knowing just one thing if you don't mind. I know it's been a long time but you told me once that you told Josie you loved her?" Parker used the old detective's ploy of making a statement that became a question requiring a response.

"Yeah, I did; that was back in my wild and crazy days. But she put everything in perspective and we went on from there. That was at Harriet's wedding weekend at the Stonington Manor. Why do you ask?"

Parker, using another tool of his trade, ignored the question and moved on.

"Did Brad Wallace ever hear about your true confession?"

"What the hell is going on here, Parker? You're sounding like a police detective." He grinned. "Yeah, Josie told him and said he took it very well. Then a couple months later . . . I'm not much of a threat anyway."

"Hey. It's been a long night. I'll be taking off now and I'll be in touch tomorrow. Take care, Rich, and congrats on winning yet again at *Pursuit*. One of these days . . ." He gave Rich his customary pats on each shoulder and called through the screen door to tell Becky that he was leaving. It had indeed been a very long night and for him, it was just beginning.

* * *

While he was married, Parker Havenot infuriated his wife on a nightly basis with his uncanny ability to be sound asleep seconds after assuming a prone position. He attributed it to his overnight shifts on the New York City police force when he and his partner could alternate twenty-minute naps in the ten to twelve slot. After that, they had to be ready for the deluge of inevitable emergency calls rolling in as the night deepened and the normal population was replaced by what he referred to as the fourth dimension of New York. Both agreed that they could sleep soundly for two minutes if the occasion warranted it.

After the session at Josie Wallace's cabin, there was no hope of sleep until he interlocked some pieces of the interesting puzzle that was Brad Wallace. The number of his visits to the Lakes Region had increased so much that he was sure that he was an imposition on the Tibideau's generosity, and on this visit had rented a room at the Stoneham Inn, a less expensive but far less elegant hotel than the Wolfeboro Inn. The two inns represented a microcosm of the difference between the two neighboring towns.

Stoneham and Wolfeboro were almost identical in most small New Hampshire town categories but with only half the lake frontage of its sister town, Stoneham seemed always on the short end of any comparison. As he settled in for the night, Parker was happy to have the burden of being a guest in someone's home lifted for this trip and the smaller accommodations were more than adequate.

After a minute or two of rummaging through his briefcase, Parker finally found the faded yellow legal pad, its edges dulled and the corners turned up from being shoved in with piles of other paper work. He folded both of the pillows on his bed and leaned them against the headboard for support, then undressed to his boxer shorts and climbed into bed. After ripping off the first soiled page of the pad and tossing it in the direction of the tiny trash can, he divided the second page into three columns. Across the top of the page he scrawled the words DATES, EVENT, and finally WALLACE, matching each word with a column. Then he let his investigative mind assume control.

Parker used the middle column as the starting point. In his own type of shorthand, he listed contacts that he had with the Wallaces since first meeting them sixteen years before. On the first line under EVENT he wrote *Capaldi* then filled in the date column with 1968. Under the WALLACE column, he simply scratched in a "Y". Drawing from his own memory, he filled more than half of the page. He then let his mind revisit pertinent stories related to Brad Wallace as told through the eyes of his friends and acquaintances. Those carried him to the top of a third page, where he again drew in the three columns and began again. The final category involved the revelations from Josie just hours before. He amazed himself with his memory of what she had said, practically every word of her plaintive catalog coming to him verbatim. A scattering of the events such as the George Metcalf/ Melissa Harrington fiasco were not new to him. Others, including Brad's refusal to consider adoption after losing Brad, Jr., added more kindling to the anger building toward a man who apparently was making Josie Wallace quite unhappy.

After several scans of the notes occupying two pages of the legal pad, the detective side of Parker, the realistic side that refused to accept coincidences, came to a decision and began to wrestle with his more human side as how best to approach some disturbing conclusions.

He looked once more at the "Y's" lining the right side of the pages and slowly shook his head. With the exception of the accident that killed Brad Wallace's parents, every event he listed was followed by a "Y" in the WALLACE column. "The model citizen, exemplary educator, the faithful husband . . . that son of a bitch could have been involved in all this stuff. It's all right there in black and yellow." He realized that he was talking to himself but in most of his best police work he used the same technique. "I'll be damned." Saying things aloud or putting them in writing somehow stamped the words or ideas with additional credibility. Thoughts, no matter how real, remained in a nebulous, slippery world, one that could be lucid and crystalline one moment and vague and misty the next. The phrase "dead in the water" drifted into his consciousness as he skimmed the list and stopped at Rich's accident in the EVENT column.

"That is a rotten thing to say, even about a fucking enemy in that situation." These words came out louder, as if expressing his irritation to a partner in the privacy of a police cruiser. He pushed the pad on the small table next to the bed, knocking the laminated directions for the phone and television use to the floor. Darkness enveloped the room as he switched off the reading light above his head. Unlike city hotels where intrusive outside light could keep a patron awake, the Stoneham Inn lay several hundred feet from the road and a blessed blackness allowed a double-faced image of Josie Wallace to form clearly in his mind. Like the comedy/tragedy masks of the theatre, the images exposed the two sides of Josie. From earlier that evening, he saw the pained mask of sadness etching her face. The contrasting mask showed her wide smile and laughing eyes as they verbally sparred about calling each other by their first names instead of by formal titles. The prone position, the tiring revelations of the evening, and the quietness of his room combined to send Parker into a sound sleep.

Just after daylight, Parker awakened to a loud knocking on the huge poplar tree just outside his window. He threw back the sheet and padded to the window, stretching and scratching himself into wakefulness. A large pileated woodpecker, its bright red crest bobbing back and forth, pounded the upper trunk of the tree, searching frantically for his juicy breakfast of insects. Parker smiled and returned to bed, his dreams from the night taking shape in his mind. He remembered the masks as he settled back on the bed, the textured swirls in the ceiling aiding in the reconstruction of his dreams. Not surprisingly, Josie Wallace apparently was the centerpiece for most of them.

As he showered, Parker found, to his distress, that the images of Josie remained with him, as though one of the masks sat on each shoulder. He would be driving back to Connecticut later in the morning and, as he turned to let the warm water beat some of the tension out of his neck and shoulders, he decided that he would stop by the cabin to check in on his friends. He faced the shower again and allowed the smiling mask of Josie to push the tragic one aside. Now the warm water cascaded down his chest and for just a moment, he dawdled, permitting a disturbing and slightly embarrassing eroticism to take control. Then, with a resolute and willful determination, he forced his attention back to controlling the animosity blossoming toward Brad Wallace, a hostility accidentally intensified by Josie the previous night.

A quick stop at the Tibideaus resulted in a sworn promise that on his next visit, Parker would stay with them. "End of discussion, period, end of story," John Tibideau had announced, leaving no room for an answer. Then, he had a ten minute ride to decide what he might say to Josie, weakly wishing that she might not be home so that he wouldn't have to deal with the powerful feelings that turned his stomach inside out whenever he was in her presence.

"She's down by the dock," Becky said through the screen door. "If you want to come in, you're welcome but I have a feeling you came by to see her."

Parker protested, but feebly. "I wanted to say so long to all of you. I'm heading back today."

"We know," Rich called from inside the cabin. "You told us that last night, and you said goodbye too." He laughed when Parker replied that it must have been the second Grand Marnier.

"You guys give me that expensive stuff to cloud my mind; what do you expect? I'll just see Josie for a minute then stop back for enough ridiculing to last me for the ride home." He walked around the side of the house and found Josie wiping down the inside of the boat.

"Well, this is a surprise, I didn't think you'd ever come back after that performance last night." Josie continued to wipe, looking down as if it required all of her attention.

Parker stood on the dock, awkwardly waiting to be told what to do. Josie took a few more wipes then climbed out of the boat.

"Look," she said. I'm more than a little embarrassed. I appreciate your friendship, but sharing all that was an outrageous imposition on you and I'm sorry." She stared out at the lake, the activities of the day causing a gentle lapping of small waves at the shoreline.

"We go back a long way, Josie. Remember Steve Capaldi and his flat tire? That's when I first met you. So it's OK. Anyway, I'm a cold-hearted police detective; I don't do emotion. I'm just sorry that you. . ." Parker stuttered, searching for the right words. "You just deserve things to be good, that's all I'm saying." He stopped, sure that he just said something completely stupid.

"Thanks, Parker, and things are good. They surely could be a lot worse. The old saying about feeling bad because I had no shoes until I met a man who had no feet is very true. I'm fine but I do appreciate your concern. I'm lucky to have friends like you and Harriet and Rich and Becky. What do people do who don't have that kind of support system?" She was looking at him now, squinting into the morning sun. "What brings you here, anyway? I thought you were taking off today."

Parker held up his hand, casting a shadow that shielded her face from the blinding sun. Absurdly, the brief erotic thoughts he had in the shower about Josie encroached on his mind and his stomach fluttered. "I should be going, really." He lowered his hand and she flinched as the sunlight struck her full in the eyes. "Just stopped by to check on everyone, that's all. Sorry to have interrupted your work." He started off the dock and she followed him.

"Thanks for coming, Parker, and don't take last night too much to heart. As I said, everyone has problems." They walked to his car in silence.

"When are you coming back to good old New Hampshire? I think I'll probably be here most of the summer. It's a really special place and Harriet might even come out for the week before Labor Day."

"I'll let you know but it'll probably be sooner than later. It is a special place." He opened the car door and she lightly touched his arm and turned him around.

"I'll see you soon, then? Drive carefully." She hugged him tightly, so tightly that it caused his whole body to tense. "Will you relax? You really worry too much, you know that?" She laughed as she released him. He climbed in the car, waving to her through the open window as he drove away. Several miles down the road, he remembered that he hadn't even stopped to say goodbye to Rich and Becky, a fact that he was sure they'd never let him forget.

With one hand, he opened the briefcase, which lay on the passenger seat and reached in. His hand found the yellow pad and he pulled it out, laying it on the console between the front bucket seats. The trip to Connecticut seemed shorter than ever as he would glance down, absorb an "EVENT" and let his mind examine it from every conceivable angle.

"Well, Mr. Bradford Wallace, I believe I'll just check out any unusual habits you might have this summer," he announced loudly. "Your wife deserves at least that."

* * *

Parker found Brad Wallace to be a most predictable creature of habit while his wife was at the cabin in New Hampshire. By a simple parolee type of drive-by check of the Wallace house in his unmarked car, he confirmed that Brad had no secret life, at least not in his rural Connecticut life. Unless he was up to something in Hartford, he appeared to be a very average country homeowner, keeping regular sorts of hours at the office and maintaining an immaculate lawn and house in his free time. Within a short time, Parker could predict that he would arrive home by five with martini likely in hand by five ten. A few phone calls to friends in various police stations solidified Brad's position as a man who represented the best definition of the phrase "model citizen" and Parker began to think that his problems with Josie were easily explained. Some couples, just by virtue of living together for an extended period of time, simply grew apart, the disagreements between them not of a vicious nature but rather of old fashioned personality conflicts based on changing philosophical beliefs. Falling out of love with each other often was not the issue; the issue more often was disappointment in the type of person one or the other had become. According to Rich Lane, the quirks in Brad Wallace's personality surely became more evident as the years passed and maybe Josie's unhappiness could be explained that easily.

* * *

Always the faithful and professional policeman, Parker timed his informal observations of Brad Wallace to coincide with other duties in the area so that his motives could never be questioned. Late on a Wednesday afternoon in mid August after going off duty, Parker parked his car on a side street near the Wallace's home and proceeded to work on some required reports while waiting for Brad to arrive, expecting the usual routine. Predictably, at about ten minutes to five, he noticed Brad's car go by. High expectations are rarely met and since he began his observations, his expectations had gone from moderately high to despairingly low. He waited ten minutes, started his car and slowly drove up the side street, startled to see Brad Wallace walking through the crosswalk, a large paper cup in one hand and a lawn chair in the other. Parker stopped, although Brad seemed so intent on his destination that he doubted he would be discovered. Putting his considerable training to use, Parker easily maneuvered through a tail procedure, keeping Brad in sight without arousing any suspicion. When he saw his subject turn through the gates and enter Mountain View Cemetery, he found an unobtrusive observation point and pulled his binoculars from the glove compartment.

"This is nuts," he whispered, feeling like a voyeur. "Man can't even visit his son's grave." He started the car but flipped off the ignition just as the starter reacted. The engine shuddered and quit. His police instincts, ingrained so deeply that he often despaired of ever shucking them, took over. The cemetery was deserted except for Brad, and Parker watched with almost morbid fascination as Brad seemed to carry on an animated and one-sided conversation. He didn't leave his son's grave until a full hour had passed. The reluctant, hesitant gait he exhibited on the way to the cemetery was replaced by an enthusiastic, bouncy stride.

Parker waited for Brad to pass well out of range and then eased toward Mountain View. He parked outside the gate, checked his bearings with his observation spot, and walked toward Brad, Jr.'s grave. As he walked along the paved path, he tried to imagine Josie walking the same path almost eighteen years before but gave up.

Graveyards tend to bring on philosophical fits of self-examination and Parker couldn't resist checking the life spans of the people lying beneath the markers. He was confident that his relief was universal when he discovered that most of the people residing in Mountain View had been older than he was. Every night when he read the obituaries in the local paper, he felt the same way, comforted when the subject was older but disturbed when it was someone younger.

He paused on the path, looking back toward where he had parked his car to observe Brad's bizarre visit. Not far ahead, he was sure he would find Josie's infant son, a son who would have been leaving for his first year in college in a week or two. The inherent gloom of looking across row after row of tombstones can capture even the most hardened human being and bury them under a heavy dose of melancholia. The detective increased his pace.

A short walk later, he was looking down at the slab. While others similar to it couldn't be read as the encroaching grass and weeds covered the inscriptions, Brad, Jr.'s was meticulously trimmed. The **INFANT** inscribed on the stone caught his attention. One of the young patrolmen at the sheriff's department recently lost a six-month-old daughter to Sudden Infant Death Syndrome.

"Guess they could've said she was fifteen months old," he said aloud, then glanced around, happy to see no one watching. He revisited his image of Brad Wallace standing over this marker and speaking almost non stop for an hour.

What the hell could he have been talking about?

* * *

A week later to the day, the scene, with only minor variations in the time frame, was repeated. A discomfiting uneasiness washed over him as he watched Brad from virtually the same place. The next time he saw Josie in a setting that was relaxing for both of them, he would have to tell her what he had seen. Good friends help each other and Josie needed to know this. His motivation was pure; he was certain of that.

Harriet's Labor Day Visit

"Your friend is your needs answered."
Kahlil Gibran

Harriet Long Stanton and Josie Campbell Wallace could be the models for friendships that withstand the ravages of time, distance, and physical separation while keeping the strong emotional bond that lets those impediments fall away at a moment's notice. The slam of the rental car door still echoed over the lake as Josie ran up the hill next to the cabin and pulled Harriet to her in a tight, grasping hug, the joy of seeing her old friend thoroughly dampening her eyes. They separated, looked at each other, and hugged again. Over Harriet's shoulder, Josie saw Laura emerge from the passenger side of the car.

"Oh my God!" The exclamation involuntarily escaped, startling Harriet. Laura Stanton, a stunning young woman of sixteen, smiled at Josie across the roof.

"Hi, Aunt Josie. It's really good to see you." She moved around the car as Josie relaxed her hold on Harriet.

The regular correspondence in the three years since they last saw each other included the usual pictures taken by harried school photographers but no impersonal two-dimensional images could possibly capture the aura of Laura Stanton. After yet another emotional hug, Josie put her hands on Laura's shoulders and gently pushed her away.

"Let Aunt Josie get a look at you," she said as her English teacher background rebelled against the use of such a tired old cliché.

Josie's experience and training in working with adolescents should have prepared her for the changes in her godchild. The Laura standing in front of her differed so dramatically from the thirteen year old child she had last seen that she could only stand there repeating "My goodness" several times before sweeping her into her arms again for another clinging hug.

315

* * *

The merchants in the Lakes Region of New Hampshire referred to the Labor Day weekend as the last fling, their last major chance to encourage the tourists to part with more of their money. While some people were preparing signs to hang on the overpasses of Interstate 93 encouraging the "last tourist leaving New Hampshire to turn out the lights," sidewalk sales and summer closeout specials abounded in every type of business surrounding the big lake.

At Josie's urging, Laura and Harriet Stanton arrived on Wednesday for two days of sightseeing before the onslaught of heavy weekend traffic precluded any activities except enjoying the lake from the Wallace cabin. Their itinerary changed just two weeks before when Brad informed Josie that he would not be making the trip to the cabin for the last big weekend of the summer. His excuse that he couldn't leave work until late afternoon on Friday and needed to get some work done around the house rang hollow. He soothed some of Josie's unhappiness with a promise to spend the Columbus Day weekend with her at the cabin. Without Brad, she decided to issue the invitation to the Stantons to move their trip back to the long weekend and, on a momentary whim, included the Lanes as well.

Rich and Becky were not scheduled to arrive until Thursday afternoon. Josie eagerly anticipated a full day of quality time with Harriet and Laura, disappointed yet relieved that Paul was directing an orientation program at the university and would not be coming to New Hampshire with them.

While her guests settled into one of the newly pine-paneled bedrooms at the rear of the cabin, Josie prepared a cold cut and salad buffet and spread it out on the picnic table on the deck. The chill of the late August nights thankfully sent any insects and bugs back to wherever they went after a summer of munching on the human population. The relaxing and peaceful environment was perfect for enjoying the buffet. The brilliant blue sky highlighting the reflection of the mountains in the water supplied an inspirational visual poetry.

Josie sat in the lounge chair with her back toward the lake. As she

316

waited for Laura and Harriet to join her, she surveyed the property. It had evolved from the Wallace family cabin to one that had much more of a Josie Campbell stamp on it. She had changed the color of the exterior stain and done all the repainting; the porch and the deck furniture were her choices; she planted and tended the flower gardens and a small vegetable garden. Sadly, the years gradually eroded the physical vestiges of the influence of Brad's parents, leaving only dimming memories of their spirit. Her eyes caught a glimmer of white in the far corner of the property, the sun bouncing off a pile of steel poles just beneath the surface of an intertwined layer of weeds and grass. The rusting remnants lay against a portion of wooden stockade fence, the only unkempt part of the property partially hiding a small portion of the swing set that was to have been a present to their first grandchild.

"God, I've got to get rid of those things," she whispered. Laura's appearance at the screen door interrupted the penetration of the pinpoint of light reflecting back at her and into her subconscious. Josie blinked quickly several times and stood to greet her. Laura looked at her, her deep black eyes wide and startlingly beautiful.

"Are you OK, Aunt Josie?" she asked.

Josie, taken back by the question, responded with a stammering "Sure, why do you ask?"

"Sorry, it just seemed like you were upset."

Josie, accustomed to sixteen year olds whose demeanor and speech habits put them solidly in the early adolescent category, was impressed. The young lady standing before her had a presence, a uniquely adult quality in spite of her petite build. The concern registering on her face carried an undeniable sincerity. She glowed with the kind of youthful vitality that kept even the most disgruntled teachers returning to the classroom year after year.

Laura smiled, a smile that drained any tension either of them felt at the moment. Her long black hair glistened in the sunlight, framing her perfect Asian facial features.

"You really are a beautiful girl," Josie said, causing Laura to drop her eyes to her sandals, her cheeks reddening so that she looked like a living China doll.

"So what's to eat?" Laura asked, determined to shift the attention to another direction.

After an extended lunch, Josie offered a boat ride around the lake, suggesting that perhaps Laura would like to try water skiing. Harriet, not usually an overly protective mother, swallowed hard.

"Maybe that could wait for another time," she said, knowing that Laura would accept the offer.

Josie quickly provided an alternative, sensing her friend's concern.

"I know Becky Lane loves to ski so maybe we could wait until another time this weekend when she's here." Laura, always agreeable, thought that would be fine and they spent much of the afternoon cruising around the huge lake, Josie enjoying her role as tour guide for her young visitor.

In spite of Josie's spirited protest, Harriet insisted on treating to dinner that evening. As they sat on the deck sipping their cocktails and waiting for Laura to join them, the phone rang. Josie excused herself and ran into the living room to answer it. Harriet, not eavesdropping but hearing part of the conversation drifting through the open windows, decided from the enthusiasm in Josie's voice that it must be Brad at the other end of the line. During the brief conversation, Laura appeared on the deck, dressed for dinner and looking old enough to be offered a cocktail herself.

"That's great; we'll meet you there. It'll be good to see you." The last part of the conversation came through to the deck clearly.

Josie joined them with news that there would be another guest meeting them for dinner but Harriet was absolutely not to treat him. "Parker's a guy who likes to pay his own way," she said.

*　　*　　*

Josie had cruised on Mount Washington too many times. The three-hour trip around Lake Winnipesaukee seemed to be a requisite for every new tourist to the Lakes Region and she had taken more than her share of visitors on the long sight seeing cruise. With Becky and Rich Lane due to arrive in the early afternoon on Thursday, Josie proposed that she stay behind to greet them while Harriet and Laura took the tour. Her guests, always agreeable, welcomed her suggestion and she drove them to the town dock in Stoneham to board the big boat, promising to be there to meet them when they returned.

In an unusual bit of luck, they found a parking space and Josie walked with Harriet to purchase the tickets while Laura sauntered among the boats filling every available space at the docks.

The cruise was not scheduled to start for a half-hour and Josie and Harriet found an empty bench and looked out at the lake. Harriet cleared her throat in the way people do when they are preparing to say something important.

"So, Josie, what's up with this Parker Havenot?" The question, as straightforward as it seemed to be, allowed room for Josie to answer it in several different ways and she used the easiest way.

"He just a good friend, mostly Rich's friend, actually. You should see him with Rich; he's wonderful. You heard him last night; he thought Rich was coming yesterday. It's pretty uncanny the way he's entered our lives . . ." The deep horn of the Mt. Washington startled both of them, interrupting Josie's faltering explanation. "You'd better find Laura and get aboard; they leave right on time." Harriet let the matter drop for the moment.

"We'll talk more about your detective later." Harriet hugged Josie, muffling her response but still hearing it clearly.

"He's not MY detective," she said. "Have a good day and take some pictures, OK?" She watched as Laura came running toward her mother and took her arm. As they boarded, they could have been mistaken for close girlfriends sharing an adventure, arm in arm and giggling their way up the gangplank. Josie glanced at her watch. She would do her grocery shopping for the weekend when she returned to pick them up. Parker had said he'd stop by at about twelve on his way home and she did not want to miss him.

* * *

The lake already buzzed with an unusually high Thursday boat activity. A couple of jetskis, Gordon Tibideau's "infernal noise machines", ran in circles not far off shore. Apparently many summer visitors extended the long weekend into a longer one to enjoy the expected perfect late summer weather. Despite the racket echoing toward the house from the water bugs flitting around, Josie invited Parker to join her on the deck.

* * *

"It's not normal behavior, Josie. That's really all I can tell you. A guy visiting his son's grave is perfectly legitimate but carrying on a lengthy conversation with himself is a little strange. I just thought you should know about it. Actually, I wish I didn't have to say this but I will. I'm worried about you in that situation."

"I don't feel like I'm in a 'situation,' Parker, but I have to tell you that you're scaring me a bit here."

Parker's expression said that he wished he had never started this conversation. He stuttered to a conclusion. "It's probably nothing. Truth be told, I shouldn't have been following him anyway but after that night you told us all that stuff. . ." He noticed her flinch slightly and bumbled on. "Shit, Josie, pardon the French, but I should never have told you. I just thought there're too many coincidences. I'm sorry if I frightened you but I'm allowed to be worried about a good friend, right?"

She shifted in the lawn chair and gazed out toward the lake. "Yes, you are and I appreciate that. Would you like a beer or something before you go? I'm expecting Rich and Becky any minute and maybe you'd like to hang around until they get here?"

ATTRACTION, NOT ACTION rumbled like a freight train through his head as he looked at her profile. "I really shouldn't. I need to get going."

She continued to stare out to the lake. She might have been talking to herself if Parker didn't know she wanted him to hear.

"He insisted on staying close to that cemetery when we were

looking at houses." Her face, normally so natural and uncomplicated, adopted a touch of Parker's worries. "He always stands in a corner of the deck where he can see Mountain View." A faint shudder passed through her as she stood and started toward the door. "I'm going to have that beer now. It's well after twelve so it's permissible, right? Sure you won't join me?"

Parker looked up at her. "OK, maybe a quick one then I've got to be going." As she passed his chair, he reached out and touched her arm, a movement so instinctive that it startled him. She stopped and waited.

"Josie, I'm really sorry if I upset you. I wouldn't want that. You deserve better, that's all." His hand remained on her arm; she squeezed it hard and smiled down at him.

"Thanks," she said softly and continued on her way. When she returned, they sat wordlessly on the deck sipping their beer from frosted mugs she always kept in the freezer.

Parker drained his glass first, his tapping feet and shifting body language indicated that he was ready to go.

"Rich'll be here any minute. I'm sure they left Connecticut early this morning. He'll be disappointed to have missed you."

"Tell him I'll catch up with him next week. A long weekend combined with a full moon is going to make for a busy time for us poor policemen so I'm going to head out. Thanks for the beer." His irrational urge to leave before seeing the Lanes was pushing him toward the door.

They stood in unison and faced each other. "Let me know if you need anything, Josie."

She moved toward him and embraced him. "You're a special person and I'm glad you're in my life. Now, have a safe trip back and be careful with all those marauding bands of criminals in Covington County this weekend." She kissed him on the cheek and pulled away. Parker realized that he had been holding his breath, an accidental and embarrassingly heavy sigh escaped.

"I'll be careful if you will be. I can find my way to the car." He went down the steps of the deck, looking back at Josie just as he rounded the corner of the cabin. She still looked after him and they exchanged small waves.

Once again, the long ride home passed quickly as Parker reviewed a photo album of the mind, a catalog of years of images of Josie Wallace. The pleasure of the experience was unnerving and much more energizing than it should have been.

*   *   *

The weekend visit with Harriet, Laura, and the Lanes turned out better than expected, a rarity when expectations for a good time are so high. Josie enjoyed Laura's company so much that the others complained about their exclusion, their light-hearted joking taking a toll on Laura, who couldn't always sort out the serious from humorous. During the five days together, Laura learned from Rich not to take everything so seriously and she soon was returning the good-natured insults with a sharpness that rivaled his.

For Laura's entire life she knew she had a long distance surrogate mom in Josie but the long weekend moved their relationship beyond the special occasion cards and presents stage. When they shared a special picnic outing on one of the few uninhabited Winnipesaukee islands, Josie discovered how well-grounded her young godchild was. The three hours spent on the boat and the shore allowed for a variety of conversations that led from girlish giggling to philosophical pondering and back again. The wide-ranging discussions left Josie with a heightened respect and admiration for her friend Harriet. Laura Stanton was as fine a young woman as Josie had seen in all her years in education and it was Harriet's courage that led to the adoption. It was Harriet's compassion that had nurtured the child into an exceptionally caring young woman.

The plan to move out ahead of the weekend traffic meant that the final meal they all had together was an early breakfast on Monday morning. The expressions of gratitude for the marvelous weekend abounded until an innocent comment from Laura sent everyone to their rooms to finish packing.

"The only thing that might've made it better, especially for Aunt Josie, would have been for Uncle Brad to be here." After that, the meal came to a quick and melancholy end but Josie rejuvenated the enthusiasm by offering a repeat performance over the Columbus Day weekend, mentioning that Brad promised to make it to the cabin then. While her guests prepared to leave, Josie poured another cup of coffee and walked down to the dock. A minute later, the screen door slammed and Harriet clumped down the stairs and joined her.

"Thanks for all the time you spent with Laura this weekend, Jos. I know she thinks you are something special." Harriet moved close enough to put her arm around Josie's shoulder. "May I ask you a question that you don't have to answer if you don't want to?"

"I hate when people say that because it sounds as though they're giving you an option when they really aren't." Josie smiled. "Of course you can, you know that."

"OK, here goes. Are things all right with you and Brad? I can't believe he leaves you here most of the summer then doesn't even come up for this weekend. And what does he think of your friendship with the detective?"

"First of all, you said you had a question, not two, but I'll forgive you." Josie leaned against one of the huge pilings holding the dock in place. "Things are OK more than they are not OK. He's always been intense as you'd recall from the magnificent seven days but he's not the same old Brad you'd remember." The screen door slammed again and they both looked up to see Laura starting off the deck. "Sometimes, I'm not sure I even know who he is but other times, he's like his old self." Laura stopped to look at the jetskis that were skimming over the water like giant water bugs, allowing Josie time to finish the interrupted conversation.

"As for the friendship with Parker, Brad would be upset if he knew how much I see of him. Remember the personality conflicts that parents would claim existed in order to get a student removed from a class? I think maybe that's what goes on with Brad. Maybe he connects Parker with too many of the bad things that happened. I don't know but I just don't mention that the detective is often with

Becky and Rich when I am. Just seems the prudent thing to do."

Laura joined them on the dock. "We need to get going, Mom. As you always say, the Fly-By-Night jet waits for no man. I'll see you back at the cabin but we do need to hurry."

"Your smile could light up all of Winnipesaukee," Josie called to her, sending Laura back to the house blushing. They watched her jump from rock to rock with the gusto of a small child.

"There's a lot more to the Brad Wallace story but we'll save that. Our last few minutes are too precious to waste on such morbidity." Putting their arms around each other like old war buddies in a bar, they climbed the small hill back to the cabin.

*   *   *

The two friends didn't see each other until the following spring when the city of Boston hosted the annual New England Association of Teachers of English Conference. Harriet Long Stanton was featured as one of the keynote speakers. The author of several definitive articles on the relationship between effective methodology in the classroom and student success, she had gained some notoriety over the last several years as a critic of the standard lecture method of instruction used in so many high school classrooms. Her pieces in a number of educational journals, including *The English Journal,* struck a positive chord with administrators and a negative nerve with entrenched, self-absorbed teachers. Her satirical programs contained harsh but effective criticism, tempered by humor, of what she called the "I am the font of wisdom and thou shalt learn from me" school of teaching. Josie arranged a professional development day and escaped from Hampton Village to attend her speech in the morning and enjoy an extended lunch with her before driving her to the airport later that afternoon. Much of their time together was spent discussing Laura and the unusual teenager she had become.

Later that evening, Harriet called to say she had arrived in Chicago safely.

"You know what they say about confession being good for the

soul, Harriet," Josie said as she began her side of the conversation. She then proceeded to describe the difficult ride home from Logan Airport.

"First I thought of Brad, Jr. then it was like a stream of consciousness novel, Harriet. Like how he would look, would he have been an athlete, a good student? Then it got into some heavier stuff, like resentment toward Brad. I mean, it's worked out so well for you and I'm really happy but I've got to admit to a few little pangs of jealousy. There you've got Paul and Laura and I've got Brad and a cemetery plot to visit." Harriet reacted predictably, listening quietly. She gave no indication that she was bothered in the least by the content of her friend's railing against the inequities that slap the human race around much of the time. Josie finished her venting, thoroughly ashamed of herself.

"I am blessed, Jos, and surely don't know why. I wish I could say something magical but it's not there." She paused, allowing Josie an opening if she wanted to continue.

"Great speech today, Harriet. I'm proud of you. Thanks for listening. Love you."

"I love you, too, Josie." Her eyes filled as she slowly put the phone down.

Therapy

> "(Life) is a tale told by an idiot,
> full of sound and fury, signifying nothing."
> William Shakespeare (*Macbeth, Act V, scene*)

Brad's need for any extensive black periods had diminished as the agitations in his life decreased in number. His regular therapy sessions with Brad Jr., occurring on an almost weekly basis, appeared to supplant his need for escaping into the deep black periods of the past. There were times when he grappled with the differentiation between those black periods and the therapy sessions of the present but that happened infrequently. Answers to most of his dilemmas came through clearly when he brought them into the open at the grave.

The first of August traditionally signaled a change in the atmosphere in the central administrative offices of the Hartford School District. The softness of the summer schedule was replaced by daily increases in the frenetic pace of preparing for the opening of school. Last minute staff resignations, supply delivery problems, unsettled grievances, and a slew of other problems that existed but were ignored in July suddenly had to be resolved. Brad had framed a calligraphic version of a paraphrased quotation he heard in a time management seminar years before and frequently pointed to it when George Metcalf would rush, uninvited, into his office.

"A LACK OF PLANNING ON YOUR PART DOES NOT CREATE AN EMERGENCY ON MINE" the sign read.

With Labor Day approaching, several problems lurking on the horizon prodded Brad into scheduling weekly sessions late on Wednesday afternoon, the only day when he could escape for the office at a reasonable hour. Even when there were other visitors in the cemetery, the familiar gravesite served as a personal sanctuary, a physical haven where he

327

could shut out the rest of the world. Brad tried, usually unsuccessfully, not to exceed the standard fifty-minute hour in his sessions, as if Brad, Jr. had another client waiting. The subject of the particular session determined the format. Some, like the ones that dealt with his increasingly troubled marriage, would be verbalized, as though speaking aloud improved the chances of finding an adequate solution. With others, like his perception of the ever-present incompetence of his Superintendent, George Metcalf, he would communicate his unhappiness silently, spending his hour thinking through the problem with only occasional vocal outbursts.

An early-August phone call from Josie represented a microcosm of the current state of his marriage. Her insistent request that he come and share the Labor Day weekend with the Lanes and Harriet precipitated a vocal session that spilled well beyond his usual hour. Clearly, the most pressing problem in his life at the moment had nothing to do with his job; it was his marriage.

Knowing that this session might be a long one, Brad balanced his paper cup martini with a folding aluminum lawn chair and, walking at a brisk pace, covered the distance to Mountain View in less than fifteen minutes. He entered his sanctuary as if entering an enclosed space, a refuge sealed off from the outside world. He stared down at the rectangular stone for several minutes, gathering his thoughts as one might prepare a mental list of questions before an annual physical with the family doctor. Finally, he launched into his session, occasionally slipping into a stream of consciousness technique that William Faulkner might have envied.

"Your mom wants me to come for the Labor Day weekend and visit with all of her friends," he began. "But you know what? I'm not sure when it happened . . . I've lost control . . . damned cabin is more hers than mine . . . maybe she's gained control . . ." The pauses between the staccato phrases were like one beat breath rests in four-four time. "I'm real tempted to sell the place . . . might as well be one of her visitors. . . . You know what, Brad? It hardly seems like we're married in the summer anymore." He stopped, took a deep breath and moved on to the next element on his mental list.

"Don't mean to embarrass you but what do you think your mom

does for sex for two months? . . . The few times I see her we do all right but she's a pretty sexy woman . . . never worried about Rich since we fixed him . . . maybe someone up there's taking care of her." A shadow crept over the stone, as if a cloud was passing in front of the sun, even though not a single cloud could be found in the brilliant blue of the late afternoon sky. The image of Josie with someone else caused the encroachment of the black period on the session; there could be no doubt about that.

Unlike the early days, black periods were in his control now; he decided when he allowed them into his life and this session was not going to be overtaken by one. "Couldn't be . . . she would never do that." He smiled as the shadow disappeared. "Moving right along here, Brad."

The remainder of his session dwelled primarily on Brad's frustrations with his job, what he perceived as an incompetent and ineffectual George Metcalf and a potentially crippling teacher strike on the horizon. After a litany of job related problems, he returned to the difficulties in his personal life as the hour came to a close.

"We could've moved to New Hampshire but she nixed it . . . forget about how hard my job is . . . good old Hampton Village High School has its teeth in her . . . she's up there all summer while I'm here covering everyone's ass . . . it just ticks me off, you know? Now, you agree, right? Your mom wouldn't be fooling around?" He stood and stretched, loosening the tightened muscles in his legs after a whole hour in the same position in the lawn chair.

He looked down at the date on the stone, amazed at how quickly life vanishes in a blur, the peaks and valleys of tragedy and euphoria blending with the tedium of everyday existence. He knelt and as he gently ran his fingers across the etched inscription, the troublesome nonexistent cloud cast a shadow over his shoulder once again. A vague image of a face appeared on the stone, coming more clearly into focus with each passing second.

"Parker Havenot! Well, I'll be damned. This is a problem we just might need to address." He folded his chair, poured out the melted ice from his paper cup and walked home at a much slower pace.

The Icing

"Life is just one long process of getting tired."
Author unknown

In retrospect, the long and lonely drive home after the long Labor Day weekend was a watershed event of its own. Heavy holiday traffic extended the trip by over an hour. Brad's apparent lack of interest in spending time with her at the cabin had sown the seeds and the resentment started to blossom. A series of well-constructed scenes arranged themselves neatly in order, a vivid visual essay scrolling through her mind. First, she thought about the unexpected revelations from Parker, surprised, dismayed, and more than a little frightened at Brad's bizarre behavior at Mountain View Cemetery. Next, she pictured the warm and loving relationship between Harriet and Laura, and more blooms of bitterness toward Brad flowered. Then the images of the totally committed and unselfish love in the marriage of Becky and Rich Lane rolled by like the visual movie credits in a James Bond film, leaving her happy and sad at the same time. The combination fed her developing anger. Then, a softening as she pondered the most pleasant but also the most disconcerting of all the memories of that weekend, memories that focused on her friendship with Parker.

A major dilemma, its horns goring her in the depths of her soul, existed and she was still unsure how to solve it as she arrived in the driveway after the exhausting trip home. Confrontation seemed to be the only way. Brad needed help, she was certain of that. She had no idea how to raise the issues she felt needed attention and decided to "wing it," in faculty lounge jargon. There was no need to plan the conversation; surely their years of marriage must mean something and she should be able to mention things that were bothering her.

The perfunctory business of getting reacquainted after a fairly prolonged absence went as might be expected. It was a scene they had reenacted many times before. After sharing a delivered pizza, Josie poured a second glass of wine for both of them and invited Brad to sit with her on the deck.

"I need to talk to you, Brad." Josie said, feeling a quavering in her voice, the kind of nervousness that one feels must be obvious to anyone hearing it but isn't. Brad assumed his regular position in the corner of the deck, leaning against the railing with his arms folded tightly across his chest.

"This won't take long, will it?" He smiled, leering at her in the familiarly suggestive way. "I'd much prefer spending the time in bed. Aren't you just a little horny, Jos?" His look infuriated her.

"I'm just really upset that you didn't come up this weekend. It almost seems like you'd rather be home by yourself than with me." Josie noticed Brad stiffen out of his slouch. "What's going on with you, Brad?"

Brad assumed his defensive posture. "You didn't have any trouble filling the cabin with visitors in my place. I probably couldn't have found a place to sleep."

"I invited people after you said you weren't coming. I would've preferred to be alone with my husband for the weekend but I wasn't going to be alone myself." Josie's composure waffled.

Josie was determined to keep this discussion focused on what was bothering her in the present, refusing to let it degenerate into real or imagined issues from the past.

"I'm worried about you, Brad. I need to know that you're OK. You've got to admit that it's not normal to lose interest in the cabin. We used to have such a great time there. What's happening?"

"Nothing's happening, Josie. We've just turned into the typical married couple; you know, the kind where the marriage survives because they make it a point not to spend too much time together." Brad stared into the distance. Josie knew where he was looking.

"Why are you spending so much time at the cemetery, Brad?" The question came out naturally but Josie gulped. "Winging it" in this conversation was going as poorly as "winging it" in a classroom usually did.

"What in the hell are you talking about, Josie?" Brad asked, incredulously. "Why would you ask something stupid like that?" He left his post in the corner of the deck and approached Josie, his entire demeanor taut and demanding, his fingers curling his fists into loose balls. Josie tried to imagine where this was going but couldn't conjure a picture, certainly not any sort of picture she wanted to contemplate.

"Because I know, Brad. Someone saw you there, talking as if you were carrying on a conversation. It really worries me, if you must know." Josie, to her relief, noticed Brad's fists slowly relax. He looked deflated, as though his plan to deny the accusation had just been pricked, the air slowly leaking from his balloon.

"Sure I spend time there; I'd think you'd want to as well. And I'd be lying if I told you that I'm not disappointed in you," he said, hostility creeping into his voice. "Having someone spying on me while you're gone is not what I'd expect from you."

Josie responded angrily to the insinuation but tried to diffuse the situation that was moving beyond her control. "I'd never do that, Brad, and you know it. It's not something I planned but it just happened. Regardless, I'd like to know how I can help you."

"I don't need any help but I'll admit to being mighty curious, Jos. I mean people don't just happen to spend time watching other people visiting cemeteries. Tell me more about that, will you?" Brad moved closer to Josie's chair until he was standing over her, his hands resting lightly on his hips, looking down at her as a mother would when scolding a small child. "Like mainly who might have just happened by, apparently more often than just once?" Sarcasm drenched every word. "You did ask why I was spending so much time at the cemetery, right? So tell me, Josie, who is your informant?"

The sun was setting behind him, casting an ominous shadow across Josie's face. His dominant position over her compelled her to try to equalize his physical presence and she stood, sliding out of his shadow. He followed as she walked to the corner of the deck and turned toward him. His use of law enforcement terminology dredged a picture of Parker from her subconscious and brought it to the surface. In desperation, she tried to submerge the image, as a flush filled her cheeks. Brad stared at her as though reading her mind.

"Havenot!" Brad exclaimed, so loudly that Josie recoiled, squeezing into the corner railing even harder. "Parker Havenot. That bastard," he hissed. He looked at Josie sadly then turned and went into the house.

The evening eventually turned out the way he thought it might. The mention of Parker Havenot's name and the realization that he was responsible for informing Josie about Brad's visits to Mountain View had a cathartic effect on him. The giddy feeling of having suspicions confirmed and enemies identified allowed him the luxury of hearing Josie's explanations without rancor. She followed him into the house, determined to bring the whole issue to some sort of conclusion and he allowed her to talk. He believed her when she said that Havenot acted on his own and listened with considerable amusement as she described the concern that they all had for his well being. She clearly was being quite selective in what she told him but he asked no questions, operating on the theory that it's often better not to know some things. He remembered an old friend who always called his wife to let her know if he was going to be coming home earlier than expected on the theory that if she had a lover, he didn't want to know about it. If there were more to this story than Josie was telling, he didn't want to know about it.

"Now I know what your detective friend thinks about me but I'd be interested in what you think, Josie. Do you honestly believe that I'm that screwed up?" The phrasing of the question was much harsher than its delivery. Brad spoke softly, as if recovering from an unusually hurtful insult.

"I'd really like to know." He crossed the room as she fumbled for a response. She hadn't answered when he reached her and he gently placed his hands against her cheeks, now dampened by tears.

"I don't know what to think, Brad. I love you and want everything to be all right with us but I just don't know . . ." He moved his hands from her face and reached for her hands, pulling her up from her chair. "I'm sorry; it's just hard to sort this all out."

They shared what began as a tentative and awkward hug. Long married couples follow a pattern after an argument and the hug set the Wallace's pattern in motion. The physical dynamics and the sexual compatibility of their relationship assumed control after a few mumbled apologies from both parties.

"I just want everything to be what it was, Brad," Josie said later that night just before falling asleep. Her relief at sharing her deep concerns with Brad was severely tempered by his apparent disdain for them.

"Everything will be just fine, Josie. Not to worry." He turned away from her without another word.

*   *   *

Josie's light measured breathing told Brad that she was sound asleep. Intrusive vignettes agitated him to the point that sleep was impossible but he forced himself to stay in bed, the importance of Josie thinking all was well was paramount in his mind.

His mind raced through scenario after scenario, all based on what she had told him earlier that evening. He imagined Havenot watching him at the cemetery; he constructed conversations the Lanes, Havenot, and Josie might have had with him as the subject; most upsetting was a scene involving Josie and Parker Havenot at the cabin, alone and discussing his unusual behavior.

Years before, Mike Costello, Brad's all time favorite principal, developed what he called his momentum theory. He had first hand experience with the validity of Mike's theory, reluctantly deciding that it may very well apply to his marriage.

Lying there in the dark, Brad remembered the sad conversation he had with Mike when he returned to Hartford for a visit several years after accepting a superintendency in New York. He had left behind a legacy of exceptional quality at Hartford West High, a school he had made a model for city high schools in the northeast.

"My momentum theory works, you see, Brad," he said after

observing his old school. When leadership changes, any school or institution that does not continue to improve will have the momentum to carry it forward on reputation for a year or two. By the third year, the downhill slide will be apparent. Hartford West High School, the pride of the city under Mike Costello's leadership, had lost the forward thrust that Mike provided, sinking into mediocrity under an ineffective new principal.

"It works with anything," Mike would say, whether it's a school, a business, a hospital, or a small general store. "It's like a locomotive under full steam. Stop feeding it coal and it still runs for a while but eventually, it'll roll to a stop."

Before falling asleep, Brad performed a quick retrospective of his marriage to Josie, gauging how long its forward momentum would last.

*   *   *

Brad couldn't believe that the coming Labor Day would mark the third anniversary of the defining discussion of their marriage. The blending of weeks and months into years continues at a frightening rate in human existence and he and Josie allowed the impetus of twenty years of marital habits and rituals to carry them through the last three. Going through the motions was so much easier than changing the status quo. With intervening summers, their separate lives were easy to maintain. As with most long term, slowly dissolving marriages, they managed to avoid each other with surprising adroitness, facing the finality of failure not worth the effort. Happiness was not the issue in their marriage; it is toleration that keeps the momentum train grinding down the track.

"Let me tell you about what destroys marriages, Josie," he said during one of their discussions. "Ever accumulating acrimony, that's what it is; an accumulation of bitterness, often not even of the partner's making."

He didn't need to mention the subtle invasiveness of Josie's long friendships with Harriet and the Lanes combined with whatever went on between her and Parker Havenot. For almost three years, the relief of the black periods at the cemetery was sporadic. His fear of discovery by the lurking Havenot eliminated all spontaneity. The powerful resentment at the intrusion into his privacy gnawed at him, a constant pebble in the shoe of his life. On days when the hatred was at its worst, he found himself looking in the mirror after his shower, vowing that he would do something about it. Occasionally, ghosts of the past would taunt him, ridiculing his self-made promises.

Just twice since the Labor Day discussion, Brad made the trip to the New Hampshire cabin. Josie pleaded with him to spend the Columbus Day weekend with her the first October after she had told him about Parker Havenot's report. When he accepted, she cancelled all plans to have her friends there with her as well, concentrating instead on getting her marriage train up to speed again. They arrived late Friday night and they took advantage of the Indian summer warm spell to make love on the deck, "just like the old days," Josie said. But it wasn't like the old days for long. By Saturday morning, Brad's disposition turned into a brooding somberness that continued for the rest of the weekend, despite Josie's many attempts to change it.

"I hardly recognize the place anymore, Josie," Brad had said, feebly excusing his moodiness. She ignored the comment, refusing to allow the weekend to degenerate into more of what they were experiencing at home. Brad's second and final visit was the following spring when he went with Josie to help open the cabin up for the summer. They loaded both of their cars with the usual supply of bedding, food staples, and clothing and made the trip in separate cars. Brad stayed only one night, leaving Josie to spend the rest of her weekend alone, getting the cabin ready for the summer and the cycle began again.

Once again, he used the problems at work as a ready excuse.

"Metcalf's on my back about the teachers again. They still don't have a goddamned contract but it's not their fault. I'd better be around in case he needs me." He left the cabin with just a perfunctory wave to Josie.

*   *   *

"Two goddamned years, Brad. It's been over two fucking years," George Metcalf screamed. This was Metcalf at his worst. "I want those bastards to sign the contract; it's that simple." Brad sat across from his boss, bearing the brunt of an irrational tirade directed at the teaching staff of the city. The trickle down theory of Reagannomics failed to provide anything but crumbs for the teachers in Hartford and the union was beginning to use the dreaded "s" word if the representatives of the Board did not offer something other than minimal below cost of living raises. Working without a contract for over two years had drained the patience and loyalty of even the most dedicated of the staff and George Metcalf placed most of the blame for the failure and poor press on the man sitting opposite him.

"You're the guy who's out there among them," Metcalf said. "I would expect that you could get them to be reasonable.

"With all due respect, Dr. Metcalf, I think they've been pretty reasonable. They're just tired of feeling like no one cares." Brad, serving as liaison between the staff and the Board, knew both sides of the story well and he couldn't hide his prejudice toward the teachers' side in this particular battle.

"Just because you've got a wife who's a teacher shouldn't fuzzy your thinking, Brad." Metcalf's mention of Josie caused an involuntary nervous ripple through Brad's stomach. The momentum of that relationship seemed to be grinding to an inexorable halt and he didn't need his superintendent to remind him of the fact.

"She's not in this district and my thinking isn't being 'fuzzied' by anything. What we need to do is figure out how to solve this problem," Brad said, tapping his fingers rapidly on the arms of his chair.

Metcalf, always the politician, retreated. "Sorry, Brad, that was out of line but I don't want a strike; we've got a good thing going here and the national publicity of a city wide strike would not be helpful to our cause. So just solve it, will you. That's why you get the big bucks, as they say." He stood, his personal signal for dismissal; the meeting was over.

Brad looked at him. He estimated that Metcalf must have gained fifty pounds since they first met, most of it threatening to pop the lower buttons on his shirt. An image of him tussling with Melissa Harrington and the steering wheel in the front seat of his Lincoln in his present condition flashed through Brad's mind, causing an internal smile.

"I'll do my best," he said as he left the office.

"It'd better be good enough," Metcalf muttered just loud enough for him to hear.

Brad returned to his office and dialed the number for Jack Montgomery, the president of the teacher's union. The line rang busy, the repeating signal hypnotic in his ear. He cradled the phone against his ear for a long time, staring at a poster on the wall in front of him. The words were superimposed over a haunting dark blue picture of an ocean wave crashing against the shore.

YOU ARE NEVER GIVEN A WISH WITHOUT THE POWER TO MAKE IT COME TRUE, the poster read. The combination of the words and Metcalf's mention of his teaching wife created a flood of memories as the busy signal echoed in his ear. The muddied floodwaters swept through his head, carrying the twisted debris of twenty-three years of marriage. He remembered the rest of the quotation by Richard Bach that was cleverly left off the poster. The exact wording escaped him but it was something like "you may have to work for it, however."

*　　*　　*

Finally, after more than two years of ineffective negotiations, the vote was taken. The teachers overwhelmingly agreed to strike by a six to one margin. In Brad's opinion, the fault for the problem ever reaching this point could be placed on both parties. The militant and recalcitrant negotiators for the teachers clashed repeatedly with the stubborn lawyers representing the Board on what to him were minor issues in the larger picture. The negotiators for the Hartford School Board, harboring the typical lawyer grudge against the teachers who dared place themselves on the same professional level, obstinately refused to relinquish any administrative control over class size and assignment. Teacher empowerment clearly was an issue that held little interest for them or their clients.

Unfortunately for Brad, George Metcalf felt that the blame for this "embarrassment," as he called it, lay squarely with the administrator he put in charge of seeing that everything worked out. As the strike stretched into the beginning of a second week and he was increasingly hounded by parents' groups, student demonstrators camped outside the administrative offices, and members of both the local and national press, Metcalf knew that the time had come to find a scapegoat. The Superintendent, after weighing all his options carefully and meeting with a few key advisors, decided that Brad Wallace had become expendable.

He sat doodling on the yellow legal pad in front of him, the reasons for Brad's termination carefully listed on the first page. The innate timing of an expert politician told him that the rank and file teachers would soon be pressuring their leadership for a solution. Teachers were not teamsters; the natural docility of the group would win out over confrontation every time. The fierce hostility at the beginning of the strike already was waning. He would replace his assistant as mediator, riding into the negotiations like an Indian scout in a John Wayne calvary film, bringing a fair settlement with him and solidifying his reputation with his colleagues and political friends and foes alike. Early in the morning on the seventh day of the strike, he summoned Brad to his office.

"So what's your plan, Brad. Do you think we can work this out or what?" Metcalf asked. From previous experience, he knew that Brad would have a plan.

Brad, sitting on the edge of his chair as if not sure how long he would be staying, reached for his briefcase.

"Actually, I put together a proposal last night that I'd like to present at the negotiations this afternoon, if it's all right with you. No one has seen it yet so both sides would need time but it gives them both an out and a chance to look good to their constituents. I think there're all getting ready to move." He handed Metcalf the thin folder containing just two sheets of paper. Metcalf opened it. It took a full ten minutes for him to read through each item, as Brad remained teetering on the edge of his seat.

There were six major issues involved, from salary and health insurance to class size and teacher involvement in evaluation practices. Under each, Brad included a "give" and a "get" explanation for each side. The proposal was deceiving in its simplicity. Even George Metcalf, used to having his thinking done by his lieutenants, saw that it bordered on the brilliant.

"I guess I don't understand what took so long, Brad. This all makes infinite sense to me but why didn't we get it sooner?" Metcalf closed the folder and mixed it with the folders on his desk.

"The format is different but the content hasn't really changed that much, just enough to give everybody something. Sometimes it's better to let people hash things out themselves for a while first. Makes them more amenable." Brad expected to be dismissed. "I'll let you know how everything turns out this afternoon, Dr. Metcalf. May I have the folder?"

"Actually, there is something else, Brad. I feel a little like Marlon Brando here but I'm going to make you an offer you can't refuse. Why don't you sit back down for a few minutes?" Metcalf straightened the folders on his desk and Brad's disappeared into them, as if it were a card slipped into a deck by a magician. He picked up the yellow legal pad, looked at it for a few seconds then began to speak.

*   *   *

Leaving George Metcalf gaping after him, he returned to his office and picked up his jacket.

"I'm not sure when I'll be back," he said to the several secretaries in the office as he left. "If ever," he added caustically.

A few times a year, Brad rode the train into Hartford, usually because one or the other of their cars was being serviced. With his car in the shop for several days for transmission work, Josie had driven him to the train station several miles from their house that morning. He actually enjoyed the commute by train on those rare occasions when he was forced to do it. It was a mindless activity, requiring nothing of the passenger. After leaving his office, he thought about taking the train back to Hampton Village and walking home but thought better of it. Instead, he walked the streets of Hartford for several hours, finally settling into a dark booth of a tiny bar at noon. A wall-sized mirror behind the bar seemed to double the size of the place and reflected a few obvious business types having lunch, all sipping on a different brand of beer.

"It's been a pretty bad day so far," he said in answer to the surprised expression of his buxom waitress at his request for a double Beefeater martini. She smiled and returned quickly with a frosted pitcher similar to the one he used to make the drinks for Josie and him at home. She bent over slightly to pour the first half of his drink, exposing so much cleavage that Brad looked away. He spent the rest of the afternoon in the bar, spreading his alcohol intake so that he would still be lucid when Josie picked him up at the station yet inebriated just enough to ward off the severe depression threatening to overtake him.

"What in the world is wrong, Brad? What happened?" Josie was stunned by his appearance when she picked him up at the station. The stale aroma of the bar clung to him, the unique pungency permeating his clothes. His level of intoxication was obvious.

"Where have you been?" Josie's concern increased with each second of silence.

"I'll tell you a little now and then more after I visit Brad, Jr., OK?" Josie's anxiety reached a stomach churning level.

Brad spoke in staccato fashion, fitting in the crucial points during the ride home. The depth of his rage was frightening. He recited George Metcalf's one-sided conversation with him in what appeared to be verbatim fashion.

"I've lost touch with my teachers and support staff; my effectiveness as a mediator has been compromised; I've undermined his authority in public to the detriment of the morale of the district; I've not followed the chain of command in decision making. Then, listen to this: the bastard said that I made him look foolish in the whole Melissa Harrington thing. He let one of the most effective principals we've ever had walk out the door and I made him look foolish. I mean, who the hell was groping her in the front seat of the Lincoln, for God's sake? So, I'm an involuntary early retiree, effective at the end of this year. Great package but I'm not even fifty years old. What the hell kind of a career is that? But if I try to fight the whole thing, I get nothing. You know the last thing I said to him, Josie? I called him an ignorant bastard. That shut him up." Josie could only stare at the road straight ahead in shocked silence.

"Slow down, Josie. The cemetery's coming up here."

"Please just come home, Brad. We'll come back together later." He didn't appear to even hear her.

"Stop here, Josie. I'll walk home. This won't take long."

Josie brought the car to a stop at the gate.

"I'll come with you." He ignored her and she raised her voice. "Please, Brad, you're scaring me. Please?"

He got out of the car without a word and went around to the driver's side. Josie had lowered the window.

"Go home, now. I'll just be few minutes. Mix us up a batch of martinis, OK? I can't have you here." She watched him walk up the path toward the gravesite with a gait that announced he was heading toward his favorite place in the whole world.

"Oh my God," she whispered as she slipped the car into gear and slowly rolled forward. The sadness boiled up from the pit of her stomach. She looked one last time at Brad's back as he disappeared up the path. He might as well have been walking off the planet.

*   *   *

After a long tense evening with Josie, during which she made her position clear, Brad slept in his favorite chair in the living room, finally awakening to the sunlight splattering across the room early the next morning. The trauma of the day before floated to the surface of his consciousness. As the sleep cleared from his eyes, a crushing reality filtered in, replacing what he was sure must have been a bad dream.

In robotic fashion, he left his chair and tiptoed down the hall to peek in at the still sleeping Josie. Following a habitual course as if through rote memory, he backtracked to the front door and went out to retrieve the Hartford Courier from the front lawn. For just a moment, he paused on the front lawn and looked around his neighborhood as if trying to commit the scene to memory. As he walked back toward the porch, he slipped the rubber band off the paper, letting it open to the front page. He was on the second step when he saw the headline over a three-column story on the left side of the paper. It froze him and he reached involuntarily to the railing for support.

METCALF ENDS TEACHER STRIKE slapped him, creating a ringing in his ears and for an instant he thought he might be having a stroke. The physical sensation reminded him of the first shocking punch in the jaw he ever received during a playground fight third grade. The subheadline beneath it caused his eyes to defocus momentarily.

SUPERINTENDENT'S PROPOSAL ACCEPTED BY BOTH SIDES. He retraced his steps back toward the living room, slumped down in his chair and read the story. It highlighted the intense bargaining session that culminated with George Metcalf's announcing the tentative agreement just before the paper's deadline at midnight.

"I had to get involved. As Harry Truman used to say, 'The buck stops here.' My proposals made sense and I'm sure that both sides will ratify the agreement quickly. I stepped in because I refuse to let my students be shortchanged." The quote from Metcalf at the end of the story was part of a prepared news release and, in the absence of an official interview, the editor felt obligated to use it.

When Josie came out of the bedroom, she found Brad sitting in the chair staring into space, the newspaper scattered in rumpled pieces on the floor around him.

"I'm not going back, Josie. Can you get a ride to school today? My car should be finished this afternoon but I don't want to wait. I'd like to take a ride up to the cabin, maybe stay a few days if that's all right with you."

Josie wasn't sure what had happened but was transfixed by Brad's clipped tone of voice. His request didn't feel like something she could refuse.

"Sure, Brad, I'll make a call. I'm sure I can get a ride. Would you like a bagel or something for breakfast?" The conversation was so stilted that it seemed surreal.

"No thanks. I'll just throw a few things together and be on my way." He disappeared down the hall and into the bedroom. Josie started the coffee and picked up the paper while she waited for it to finish brewing. She was eating her bagel and cereal with the front page of the paper folded to the article on the strike propped against the box of Total on the table when Brad emerged from the bedroom with his duffel bag.

"I'm not sure when I'll be back but you don't mind using my car for a few days if I decide to stay, do you? I'd appreciate it." He sounded defeated as he removed the key to her car from the hanger by the door. He noticed what she was reading and the frightening hostility returned.

"Some day those bastards are going to pay," he said as he reached for the door. He left without saying another word, slamming the door behind him.

Josie picked up the phone and dialed the Covington County Sheriff's Department. "May I speak to Detective Havenot, please?" she asked the dispatcher.

"Havenot here," Parker answered in his most professional tone, a tone warmed instantly when he heard Josie's voice.

"This sounds really stupid, Parker, but I need a ride to school. You're not by any chance traveling around my neighborhood this morning, are you?"

"Not a problem at all. What time would you like me to come by?"

The tenseness in Josie's neck and shoulder muscles relaxed almost instantly, disappearing before the soothing calmness in Parker's voice.

*　　*　　*

With some hesitation, Parker agreed to leave his office to give Josie a ride to school. Her call rattled his detective instincts, the ones that can identify a voice straining to remain calm and simple words carrying more meaning than they should. Josie stood on her porch when he arrived and before he stopped his car, she was at the passenger door. She greeted him with the usual "How're you doing?" but Parker saw them as just more simple words that she needed to get out of the way.

"Just look at this and I'll fill you in as we go." She showed him the paper, still creased open to the story about the Hartford strike. Havenot glanced at the headline and looked at her, the questions obvious in his eyes.

"It was his plan, his proposals; he said he's never going back." The short ride to school allowed sufficient time for Josie to describe the events of the last twenty-four hours. Parker's only interruption came when she mentioned the stop at the cemetery.

"Holy shit, Josie!" The exclamation escaped before Parker realized it. "Sorry," he mumbled, embarrassed.

"He's gone, to the cabin, he said. I don't know what's going to happen." They reached the school parking lot and Parker swung the car into a space far removed from any other cars. He shifted in his seat and turned to face Josie directly.

"I'll do whatever you want me to do, Josie. We've certainly known each other long enough for you to know that." Her eyes filled as she stared through the windshield as if focusing on some unseen object far in the distance.

"I do know that, and I appreciate it. Right now I'm not even sure what to think, let alone what to do. Bear with me, OK? And thanks for picking me up. I'll be in touch." She leaned across the seat, kissed him on the cheek, and then was hurrying into the school.

Parker waited until the door closed behind her. He started the car and drove slowly from the parking lot, still watching the door expecting that she might return. She didn't and it was four days before he heard from her again.

*　　*　　*

The ride from Connecticut allowed Brad ample time for thinking through his next move and when he arrived at his camp, his decision was made. He spent most of his three days at the cabin looking for property on the other side of the lake, finally settling on a small secluded cottage that sat well back from the shore line. A long, narrow, private drive meandered through the five acres of land that came with the house, leaving no chance for anyone to accidentally drive by. The cottage itself was well maintained, requiring no attention before he could move in. His phone call to Josie announcing his decision was short and to the point.

"I've put an offer in on a place and I'll be moving out as soon as possible. I think it's probably the best solution." A long silence followed on the other end of the line.

"I guess you're right." Josie's voice quivered but yet was firm. "Brad, what's happened to you? Are you going to be all right?"

"I'm fine but thanks for asking. Remember Richard Nixon's speech to the reporters after losing that gubernatorial race? Well, to paraphrase the great Tricky Dicky, you all won't have Bradford Wallace to kick around any more. I'll let you work out whatever needs to be done. I'll come back later this week and trade cars with you and pick up a few things. This place is vacant so I can move in right away as a renter until the papers are passed." His flat voice showed no emotion.

"Why don't you just use our cabin?" Josie asked. "I'll come up and we can talk about this."

"Because it's not our cabin, Josie. It's yours. Besides, it's too full of memories. And there's really nothing more to talk about. It'll be better for everybody if I just disappear."

Josie felt obligated to protest more vigorously.

"You can't just disappear, Brad. There are people who care about you."

Brad's unexpected explosion of laughter ripped through the receiver, startling Josie so much that she almost dropped the phone.

"Really, Jos? I doubt that anyone will miss me. You asked what happened to me. Life happened, Josie and it's just worn me down. But don't worry about me; I'll be fine."

Josie, who had been sitting on the deck during the whole conversation, put the receiver down and walked to his favorite corner. She turned and faced the cemetery in the same fashion as Brad had done so many times before.

What if, she thought as she remembered their numerous conversations about fate and destiny, *what if Brad, Jr. had lived?* The barely visible fence around Mountain View blurred as her eyes filled. She put her hands to her face, unable to stem the flow of tears.

* * *

Brad handled all of the paperwork necessary for arranging the financial details of his early retirement by mail. The uneasy fear of how he would react if he happened to see George Metcalf discouraged him from returning to the office in person. Shortly after Metcalf made the offer that he couldn't refuse, he began his new life as a recluse at the cottage on the lake. The mailbox guarding the entrance at the end of the lane looked like an old picture he had seen of J. D. Salinger's, its appearance more like a subtle "NO TRESPASSING" sign than a repository for mail.

With the generous lump sum payment from the district and his substantial state pension easily supporting his simple lifestyle, Brad Wallace entered a different phase of his life. He was surprised but oddly not all that disappointed how easily Josie accepted his new situation, even respecting his highly unusual request that he be left entirely alone until he contacted her. The mailing address he gave her was a simple box in a small combination general store and post office. When she asked how she would contact him if there happened to be an emergency, he replied icily that "I'm sure that I wouldn't be interested."

The transformation from an upper level school administrator to a lake hermit was easier than he might have imagined. His major regret was leaving behind his son's grave and the therapeutic haven it provided but the new cabin and its isolation would serve his purposes just as well. It would serve as a perfect base of operations for extracting some well-deserved retribution from those he viewed as causing his self-imposed exile.

* * *

One of Brad's favorite amenities of his new but humble cabin was a rocky breakwater that prevented the wind-whipped waves from washing over the dock when the violent but beautiful summer thunderstorms rumbled down the lake. Early in the first summer of what he now dubbed his period of reformation, Brad sat on the last of the enormous rocks forming the breakwater, enjoying a spectacular sunset and observing the diminishing boat traffic. The beauty of the evening brought with it memories of similar sunsets in different circumstances, encroaching on the solitude of the moment and finally forcing him to turn his back.

An unusually loud engine sound approaching from the south attracted his attention. Raising the binoculars that were already a fixture around his neck, he watched as the new addition to the lake steamed around the peninsula that protected his privacy from the intrusive and constant boat activity crisscrossing the lake from the Weirs to Wolfeboro and back. His powerful binoculars zeroed in on the *Winnipesaukee Belle* churning across the lake on its maiden voyage, at least its maiden voyage on this lake. The riverboat-style side paddlewheel was at least a half mile away but the colorful bunting draped over the railings and the passengers milling about on the double decks were easily visible. The music from the live brass band on the upper deck drifted across the water to him and he watched, fascinated, as the boat gradually disappeared behind one of the large islands dotting the lake, the wailing sounds of the trumpets trailing behind even as it went out of sight. The mesmerizing scene piqued his curiosity and effectively made the decision for him to visit the Wolfeboro Public Library the next day to uncover the story of the *Belle*.

The Box

"The man in the street is always a stranger."
Mason Cooley

The cover letter for the package was terse, a mean spirited undertone evident even in its brevity. George Metcalf's secretary framed every sentence with a pervasive negativism, leaving the distinct impression that whatever Brad said when he informed the office that he would not be returning had surely burned every one of those proverbial bridges behind him.

"This box contains whatever personal things we found in his desk drawers. If your husband has any questions, he should contact me, not Dr. Metcalf," the letter concluded. Apparently, Brad had instructed them to send anything to Josie, not to him. She decided to open the box, wondering as she did if she would ever see him again.

The contents looked as if they had been hurriedly and unceremoniously dumped from the drawers. Josie pawed through the conglomeration of used office supplies, a few inscribed paperweights, and various pens and pencils. She was about to close the box again when she noticed the nails that had sifted to the bottom of the box.

* * *

"I know that you don't think it could be coincidence. You and Rich have me convinced of that," Josie said. Parker held the nails from Brad's desk in his right hand. The nails in his other hand came from an envelope he had brought with him.

"The thing with Dr. Capaldi was over twenty years ago. I can't believe you still have them."

Parker laughed. "You wouldn't believe what they'd find in my desk drawers. I know I'd never say to send my stuff anywhere but to me." Josie smiled at him. "To answer your question or at least what sounded

351

like a question. No, I'd bet my reputation on this not being a coincidence. I know all nails kind of look alike, but I'm sure any police lab in the country would confirm that they all came from the same batch."

"So what do we do about it?" Josie asked. "Is there a statue of limitations on flattening people's tires?" This time she laughed and Parker joined her.

"Let's run through an 'If, then' exercise for just a minute. If your husband used the nails to gain a small measure of revenge on Steve Capaldi, then he probably did the same with George Metcalf. If he succeeded with what we'll call the tire capers just for fun, then maybe he did something similar to the guy who killed his parents. If he thought a good friend was trying to move in on his wife, then . . ." Josie's loud reaction stopped him in mid sentence.

"NO! Don't finish it, please. He never could've done that." Josie left her chair across the room and sat cross-legged on the sofa facing Parker.

"Look," she said, her steady gaze so penetrating that Parker looked away briefly before reconnecting. "I know in my heart what you're saying but can we not go any further tonight? I mean, we're talking about an outstanding educator here and a man who still happens to be my husband." Josie's agitation increased with each word.

Parker, sensitive to every nuance of emotion from his years of interviewing crime scene witnesses, retreated.

"Sure, Josie, I'm sorry. I get carried away with myself sometimes. It was stupid. One last thing to think about and maybe this might make you feel better; then we'll leave it alone. Let's change our 'If, then' to 'What if?' He waited until she indicated with a slight nod that she was ready to keep going.

"What if Brad only meant to play a childish prank? How many kids have done something silly, only to have someone get hurt? Haven't you ever had one of your students thoughtlessly pull out a chair from a classmate just as they sat down? It's the same thing. I don't believe Brad thought about the 'what ifs' until later. Now, let's talk about something else."

"Thanks a lot," she said. "You're right. It does make me feel a little better. He really is a good person, you know." She leaned over and hugged him. He returned the hug and for a minute, they clung together, looking like survivors on a lifeboat. Parker was the first to move. Three hours later, after an evening of wide ranging conversation touching on most topics in their lives except Brad Wallace, a more leisurely hug was repeated at the door, both of them lingering, absorbing the warmth. When it began to turn to heat, they parted in a silence.

Parker strode to the car like an adolescent boy after his first good night kiss.

*   *   *

"It would be a snap for me to find out if you all really wanted to know. I'm a detective, after all, but you guys give me no respect," Parker said, feigning indignation as Josie laughed.

"And a good one, too," she said. "We're not questioning that and you know it."

Spending the evening with the Lanes was her idea, one that Parker readily accepted. Rich and Becky needed to know, actually deserved to know, the direction that their relationship had taken and to be brought up to date on the latest news about Brad.

"Anyway, I'm guessing that he must be in the Lakes Region based on the P.O. box," Josie continued. "That's the area he's most familiar with. But he's dead serious about being left alone. He says that he won't be contesting anything. He just seems so damned happy when he calls that I say we should all agree to let him disappear if he wants to."

Rich, who remained completely and naively puzzled by Brad's actions shed his perspective.

"It's too weird, even for Brad. I think we should track him down and bring him to his senses." Josie and Parker looked at each other but neither had the slightest interest in mentioning the unsettling 'If, then' of Rich's accident. Rich, ever alert, caught the eye movements but misinterpreted them. "Come on, Becky, you've got to be on my side."

"I'm on everybody's side but I think that it should be a matter of MYOB as far as Brad is concerned. He's making some strange choices but who doesn't at some point." A mischievous twinkle appeared in her eyes.

"After all, I married you, didn't I, Rich?" When the laughter subsided, Rich acquiesced.

"OK, I'll let it go," he said. "At least for now."

Josie and Parker

"This is the way the world ends:
not with a bang but a whimper."

T. S. Eliot

The love and marriage train of Josie and Brad Wallace derailed short of its silver anniversary. The momentum that carried them through the motions for the last several years ceased, the forever-parallel railroad tracks of life finally converging into a dead end. Josie saw Brad just once after his abrupt move to New Hampshire, a meeting that was heart wrenchingly sad for her, yet she couldn't deny the poorly defined but clearly present feeling of relief.

"I'll be in touch," he had said after flipping her the keys to her car. She watched him leave, struck by the similarity of watching him walk toward the cemetery the day of his dismissal. He had moved beyond her, as clearly as if he were stepping into another world, a place well beyond her reach. To Josie, the few seconds that passed as he walked toward his car were like the traditional seconds just before death, the time when an entire life passes before the eyes. A jumbled montage of events careened through her head and she wondered if she had ever really known Bradford Wallace. The sadness should have turned to bleakness but each step he took seemed to have the opposite effect. When he reached his car, he never turned back. As he drove away, the last scene of the montage evaporated, vanishing into a welcoming mist in her mind.

One of the few lines of T. S. Eliot that her students found comprehensible formed in her head and she voiced it in the low whisper she would use if reciting it in front of one of her classes. "This is the way the world ends, this is the way the world ends, this is the way the world ends; not with a bang but a whimper."

* * *

"I don't have a problem with it at all," Becky said. "They've known each other for more than twenty years."

Rich felt the need to play devil's advocate but only half-heartedly. "It's probably just the incurable romantic in me but I can't believe that Josie and Brad are done. I keep hoping that he'll come to his senses and come back. It's just all too weird. Heaven knows, I love Parker and I want Josie to be happy but Brad's an old friend. I mean, we started our teaching careers together."

"You're assuming that Josie would take him back, first of all. And you've told me you thought he was a little strange then, right? Illogical overreactions, temper tantrums over things he couldn't control, all that stuff? So I see it as a good thing." Becky's argument, proclaimed in her usual calm, convincing manner, was irrefutable. Brad Wallace, making choices that none of them really understood, obviously wanted the curtain to be drawn. His former friends and his wife needed to realize that and move on.

"That's all she's doing, Rich. She's moving on and I can't think of a better man to move on with than Parker."

Rich, happily defeated, agreed. "What's that Frank Sinatra song, the one about love being better the second time around? Maybe there's something to that but don't you go getting any ideas." Rich joshing tone became more serious. "I couldn't handle losing you, Becky." She knelt down on one knee and took both his hands in hers.

"You are never going to need to worry about that," she said, her eyes glistening. "You've given me more than you could ever know." When his eyes also began to mist, she squeezed his hands.

"I love you," she said simply. "Now let's have fun watching the love story of Josie and Parker unfold."

* * *

For months after Brad "disappeared" into the woods of New Hampshire, the comfortable friendship remained just that. Josie, still unsure that her decision to allow her long marriage to just fade away without a fight was the correct one, kept the growing chemistry at bay. Brad's clothes still hung in his closet; his tools still were scattered over the tool bench in the garage; his desk in the corner of the bedroom remained covered with papers. It felt to her as if he could arrive any minute and take up residency again, never missing a beat. Other times, as she sat among the vestiges and ashes of their marriage, she realized how much it seemed as if he might as well have died. This is what a household looks like when a man leaves, fully expecting to return, only to meet with a fluke of fate that permanently removes him from the world.

Two months after they switched cars, Brad drew the final curtain in a typed, formal letter stating that he had signed all necessary forms for the divorce, agreeing to any and all stipulations. She could dispose of anything around the house in any way she chose. The final sentence of the letter reiterated the request he had made on numerous occasions.

"Please respect my wishes and leave me alone." Under the request he had typed in all capital letters the words "BRADFORD WALLACE". The formality of the letter and the closing signature were definitive but painful. Gripping the letter, she walked slowly through the house, following the advice of Emily Dickinson's poem and sweeping up memories that won't be used again until eternity.

The deck was bathed in the late afternoon, mid-November sun. Still holding the letter, she went directly to "Brad's corner" and gazed at the cemetery. She opened a rarely visited corner of her mind, allowing the memory of the day she lost her son and any future hope of other sons to form out of the distant mist. When Brad's crestfallen face appeared at the end of the memory, she closed her eyes tightly, desperately but unsuccessfully trying to erase it. When she opened her eyes again, she blinked back the brightness of the slanting sunlight sparkling in the dampness. With considerable effort, she returned to the kitchen and picked up the phone, dialing Parker's private number.

"How about if I cook you a special dinner tonight? I'm in the mood for something special." She had no doubt what his response would be.

That night, they made love for the first time.

Gordon and Parker

"For now we see through a glass darkly . . ."
First Corinthians 13:12

A year before Josie Wallace and Parker Havenot consummated their relationship, Gordon Tibideau's parents had passed away within two months of each other. Gordon often wondered whether he or Parker felt the loss more. Parker, closer to being a contemporary, adopted the Tibideaus as family and losing them both in such a short period of time proved extremely difficult, even for the hardened police officer. Gordon, on the other hand, was so close to his father that seeing him finally released from the painful and debilitating effects of a wildly spreading pancreatic cancer was actually a relief. He truly was not surprised when less than two months after burying his father, his mother passed quietly in her sleep. While love affairs produce broken hearts, the death of a lifetime partner and soulmate can produce such a profound sense of loss, of irreparable emotional damage that the will to live fades into nothingness. When Gordon found his mother, the serenity of a peaceful death was obvious as she lay there, an 8 X 10 colorized version of their wedding portrait clutched to her chest.

Gordon moved from what his father called his "decadent bachelor pad" over their garage into the large two story New England colonial and rattled around, his sadness at times overwhelming. Never at a loss for female attention, he followed the passionately dispensed advice of his older and wiser friend, Parker Havenot.

"Be sure that it's the real thing. That's especially important for law enforcement people," Parker would say. "It's got to be the real thing." As Gordon searched for the "real thing," he left a wake of disappointed women trailing behind him, leaving his father shaking his head in amazement at his stamina and ability to deftly juggle his array of female companions.

After his parents were gone and Gordon had taken over the house, he anticipated Parker's visits more than ever, the distractions from the family memories a welcome change. The two close friends shared each other's lives more like brothers might and Gordon wasn't surprised with the news that Parker would be staying at Josie Wallace's cottage on any trips to Winnipesaukee in the foreseeable future. The few times over the years that he was with Josie and Parker in social situations, he sensed that the chemistry between them, although muted by reality, exceeded that of just good friends. When Parker informed him of the breakup of the Wallace's twenty five-year marriage, Gordon was fairly certain what would follow.

*   *   *

"You're a cop, Parker. Why don't you just use all those resources out there to find out?"

Rich's question carried the concern of a friend and he was being obnoxiously insistent. "This is an intelligent person we're talking about here. A man doesn't just vanish from the planet and leave behind a whole life."

"Ah, but they do, all the time. I've seen it uncountable times. People just get tired or depressed or just sick of the whole thing and want a change. I really believe that a higher percentage than you could imagine would opt out if they saw the chance." Brad Wallace served as a lively topic of conversation whenever Josie wasn't present. The first New England winter since Brad performed his disappearing act had been exceptionally harsh, and Rich began this particular discussion with his concern that his old friend may not have fared too well if he spent it in New Hampshire. As happy as he was for Josie and Parker, he continued to struggle with what he saw as a completely illogical choice by Brad Wallace.

"You're talking about him as if he were a deer or some poor forest creature grappling with survival. He's fine; I can guarantee it. Josie thinks he should be left alone and I'm not going against her wishes." Parker looked to Becky, grateful for any support she might supply.

"Parker's right. You can't intrude where you're not wanted. As hard as it is, you've got to accept the fact that your old friend has made his choice for now." Becky switched the subject. "When are you and Josie going up to the cottage to get it ready? Maybe we could all go up and help."

"I'll serve in my usual supervisory capacity," Rich said, smiling. "You guys win. We'll just let Brad come to us if he needs us."

"We're planning on going up over Mother's Day weekend to give the black flies something to gnaw on. I'm sure that Josie would love to have you both come along."

Rich couldn't let the opportunity pass. "I'm only coming if you and Josie promise not to make too much noise during the night. No screaming or anything like that, OK?" Becky shushed him, blushing furiously. Parker laughed out loud.

"I'll tell her you made that a condition. And, if it'll make you feel any better, I'll do a little surreptitious checking on Brad, although I can't imagine why you'd care what happens to him." Parker choked on his words. His stupid remark didn't pass unnoticed. Becky and Rich stared at him.

"Why wouldn't I care? What a foolish thing to say." Rich seemed genuinely offended.

In that moment, Parker made a decision. "Could I have a minute with Rich by himself, Becky?"

Rich interrupted Becky's "Of course".

"What the hell is this all about?" The usual jovial mood of any gathering of the three friends quickly disappeared. "Becky can stay. It's pretty trite but we have no secrets." Becky stayed.

Ten minutes later, Parker regretted his decision with every fiber of his being. There had been many emotional times during the years of their friendship and occasions when mutual tears had been shed. Nothing compared to Rich's painful reaction to the possibility that his accident was purposeful.

"Oh shit, all these fucking years in this chair." His voice crumbled beneath the sobs shaking his body. Parker was frozen in place as Becky hugged Rich from behind, trying in vain to absorb some of his anguish. Rich caught his breath and recovered a semblance of emotional balance.

"I think I always knew," he said quietly. "It's like knowing there's a snake under the rock but if you never move the rock, you can pretend it's not there. You just moved the rock, Parker. Thanks."

"There's no proof. . . ." Parker started to say, not sure if Rich's thanks was sarcastic or genuine. Rich shook his head, silencing him.

"Purely circumstantial evidence, Mr. Detective, but, as you and I have discussed so many times, coincidences are all part of the big plan, aren't they? I guess I don't care if you ever find the bastard." He looked up at Becky and smiled. "I would never have met you so it all worked out just fine," he said, tears again welling up in his eyes.

* * *

The Mothers' Day weekend cleanup at the cottage went as expected. The weather cooperated with abundant sunshine warming the temperatures into the seventies every day. Rich sat on the deck, supervising the outside work under the protection of a net head covering that made him look like a space alien while the others waved ineffectually at the clouds of black flies surrounding them. By late Sunday afternoon, most of the work was completed and the two couples were joined by Gordon Tibideau and yet another of his female acquaintances for a season opening celebratory cookout.

Parker used the occasion to have Gordon perform a safety check on the boat and the two men spent the better part of an hour cruising the bay in front of the cabin. The shakedown cruise allowed ample time for Parker to prepare Gordon for some questions that likely would be forthcoming from Rich Lane about his accident.

"Why on earth did you tell him that, Parker? What were you thinking?" Gordon scolded.

Chagrined once again and having no satisfactory answer, Parker just mumbled that it probably was all a huge mistake but it was out there on the table and there was no taking it back. He changed the subject just before they returned to the dock, the boat having passed Gordon's test.

"I'd like to know how our old friend Brad is faring without Josie knowing. How hard would it be for you to check around the Lakes Region and find out exactly where he is? I can give you a post office box number but even Josie's not sure where he's living."

"Shouldn't be a problem. I've got friends in high places, you know," Gordon said, laughing. "Tomorrow is a day off for me. Too bad you're not staying tonight. I'm sure we could be doing a house tour of Brad's place by tomorrow afternoon if he's around."

"I'm off tomorrow. Maybe Josie could go back with the Lanes and I'll hang around if you think it would be worthwhile."

"I didn't say it'd be worthwhile but we could have some fun on the lake anyway. I'm available so let me know."

Most of the conversation during the cocktail hour dealt with water-skiing, Rich Lane asking a series of questions directed at the expert lake patrolman, Gordon Tibideau. As Rich's questions began to sound more like an attorney's cross-examination, Parker felt the need to interrupt. Rich apologized but by the time dinner was served, he had gathered enough information. Parker's circumstantial evidence was correct. His accident should have never happened.

*   *   *

Although disappointed that Parker wouldn't be driving home with her, Josie agreed to his proposal to spend one more day at the cabin finishing some odd jobs that needed to be done.

Shortly after noon the next day, as he finished painting some trim over the kitchen door, the phone rang. Missing the last step on the ladder in his rush to answer it, he turned his ankle. By the time he arrived at the phone, he was breathless and in some discomfort.

"Hey, Gordon," he said, expecting to hear Gordon Tibideau's voice. It was Josie.

"Are you all right? It sounds as if you're out of breath." Parker smiled the familiar warm feeling at the sound of her voice consuming him.

"Yeah, fine; just about broke my ankle though. I miss you and it's only been hours. Where the heck were you all my life?"

"I miss you, too. That's the only reason I called, just to tell you that. And by the way, I've been in your life for a long time but now I feel

363

like a real part of it. I have to tell you that I like the feeling. So you expected to hear from Gordon. How come?"

"He said he was off today and he had some stuff to show me. It won't hold me up, don't worry about that."

"I'll have dinner ready when you get here, maybe something special." She giggled, using a phrase that already was a euphemism in their lives. "Well, something good anyway. Say hi to Gordon and I'll see you later. Love you." Parker did not hang up right away, as if by holding the phone he could prolong the connection. No sooner did he finally set the phone down then it rang again.

"I'll pick you up in ten minutes. I found it," Gordon said, a manifest excitement edging his voice.

*   *   *

In less than thirty minutes, they were driving past the neglected mailbox acting as a sentinel at the head of the long dirt lane to Brad Wallace's cabin. With no logical reason to drive back to his house, they drove past twice in each direction, straining to see any sign of life. With the trees all in leaf and the thick undergrowth eliminating any possibility of viewing even a small portion of the house, Parker asked Gordon to park on the side of the road, less than a quarter of a mile from the entrance.

"What would you think if I kind of creeped in through the woods, just for a peek? My curiosity is killing me."

"I'd say you were crazy but I'm sure you could pull it off. I'd love to be a fly on the wall when you try to explain what in the hell you're doing there if he catches you." Gordon was smiling. They were acting like foolish adolescents.

"The worst that could happen is you'd have to run like you stole something." They both laughed.

"Hell with it. I'm going for it. He'll never catch me. I'll just stay parallel to the lane in and out and be back in ten minutes." He left the car and walked back toward the lane. Gordon watched as he turned into the woods and disappeared about fifty yards from the entrance.

364

Parker picked his way through the woods with all the wariness of a bowhunter stalking a trophy buck, taking small steps and pausing at regular intervals. As the outline of the house took shape through the woods, he looked to his left and found the lane. He moved closer to it and let his eyes follow it to the cabin. There was no garage and the well-worn path showed exactly where Brad's car should have been parked. Parker slowly made his way to the clearing around the small house and paused at the edge. His instincts told him that the occupant or occupants were not at home.

"What in the hell am I doing? This is worse than watching him at the cemetery," he whispered. As he turned to leave, a large trellis encased in roses caught his attention. It was set on the edge of the woods under an enormous oak tree, not far from where he stood. A granite bench sat nearby, facing the canopy formed by the roses intertwined on the white trellis. Parker looked around again and seeing nothing to stop him, skirted along the edge of the woods. In just a few steps, he was at the trellis. The bench had no ornate decorations, although the construction showed a professional flair. He moved behind the bench, noting that the trellis symmetrically framed it. With one last glance over his shoulder back at the house, he stepped over the bench and sat down, the whole scene reminding him of a worshipful grotto to the Virgin Mary.

"Holy shit!" The exclamation escaped loudly as he looked down at the ground directly in front of him. The gravestone sitting directly beneath the trellis was fresh, no more than several months old at best. He recognized it as an exact replica; the stone, the carving, and the font were identical.

BRADFORD J. WALLACE, JR

INFANT

The Wedding and Living Simply

"No worse fate can befall a man in this world than to live and grow old alone."

Henry Drummond

A uniquely designed wedding ceremony on Saturday of Labor Day weekend began two days of partying at Josie's cabin on the lake. Gordon Tibideau's pontoon craft, a boat that resembled a twenty four-foot floating dock with a motor attached, had sufficient room for the limited guest list. Gordon had it decorated as if it were going to be judged in a Fourth of July parade, multi-colored buntings hanging from the railings and brightly hued pennants hoisted up the mast.

After loading all of the guests and a local, chosen at random, minister at the dock, Gordon ferried them to a secluded spot on the lake, the kind of place that only a lake patrolman would know about. Against a backdrop of mountains, a brilliant early fall sky and the sparkling clean water of the big lake, Josie Wallace became Mrs. Parker Havenot, officially closing a long, bittersweet chapter of her life. The actual ceremony was brief but emotional, each of the witnesses and participants bringing their own perspective and memories to the event.

"This is going to sound incredibly corny and trite but you've made me a very happy man, Jos," Parker whispered in Josie's ear after the traditional bridal kiss. The soft aside was heard by everyone in the close proximity of the boat and while the women's eyes glistened and the men looked down at their shoes, Parker and Josie kissed again.

Just before starting the engine, Gordon called to Paul Stanton to assist in unfurling a large "Just Married" banner across the stern of the boat. The informality of the setting permitted the bride and groom to move from one guest to another, greeting them as Gordon guided the boat on a cruise back to the dock, taking a longer and more scenic route. A chorus of deep horns echoed across the lake and enthusiastic waves followed them as fellow boaters noticed the sign trailing behind. After running the gauntlet of their guests, the Havenots stood alone on the bow of the boat, a misty spray dampening their faces.

"You could've had more of your friends," Josie said. All on board except for Gordon Tibideau came from her life.

"The two guys I might have had couldn't have made it anyway. Besides, I'm afraid that like it or not, you're sharing most of this group already. Anyway, it doesn't matter. What matters is that somehow you appeared in my life and, for reasons I can't fathom, fell in love enough to marry me." Parker stared at the shoreline and the cabin closing in.

"I can't fathom it either. Why in the world would I want to change my name to Havenot and spend the first three days in my classes explaining why the consonant and vowel rules don't apply to proper names, especially my new one?" Josie put her arm around his waist and leaned against him. Her joke made him laugh but before he could respond, the Stantons had joined them.

"It's beautiful, isn't it, Dad?" Laura said to her father as she sidled up to her Aunt Josie. Josie had been moved to tears when Harriet called and told her that all three of them would be attending the wedding. Now, as the beautiful young woman stood next to her, the inherent emotion of any wedding, let alone her own, joined with a compendium of provocative memories. She laid her head on Laura's shoulder, the dampness from her tears slowly spreading down the sleeve of her beloved godchild's gorgeous special occasion dress.

"It's OK, Aunt Josie. It's really OK," Laura said as she hugged her tightly, adding her tears to the mix.

Parker's unnerving discovery of the mock gravesite for Brad Wallace Jr. several months before had been temporarily set aside, fading in the euphoria of marrying a woman he loved. He dreaded the day when his discovery would have to be shared with Josie.

Brad's Imitation

"I went to the woods because I wanted to live simply."
Henry David Thoreau

Brad Wallace's life became an imitation that surely would have made Thoreau happy, living his credo of simplicity with a vengeance. Those who lead the simplest of lives appear to form habits most easily. Brad's closest neighbors, an elderly couple every bit as reclusive as he was, retrieved their mail at exactly the same time every day, an apparent highlight of their existence even if the mail consisted of nothing but advertising flyers. Over the first six months of his new found freedom at his isolated cabin, Brad made a daily trip to the local general store for the *Boston Globe,* a trip that assumed ritualistic proportions for him. On Thursday morning, he added the *Lakes Region Register,* the weekly newspaper for the area, to his ritual. He would return with the papers and, depending on the weather, sit on the small back porch or in the knotty pine paneled living room and devour every word, much of the morning often taken up with the "task."

On the second Thursday after the Labor Day weekend, still feeling the strange effects of not returning to school in the fall for the first time since he was six years old, Brad worked his way through to the social pages of the small town newspaper. This section normally provided him with a lighthearted start to every Thursday. The news of the various towns were full of personal tidbits about hernia operations, hangnail sufferers, and who entertained whom on the whirling small town social circuit. This issue had all of the usual items of interest plus reports on several weddings that were celebrated over the Labor Day weekend. In customary fashion, Brad meticulously began at the top left-hand corner of the page, glimpsing at the photos before reading the reports, a pastime he couldn't believe he had adopted. The small one column article at the bottom right of the page might have eluded the average reader's cursory glance, lacking the usual accompanying photo. For Brad, the names in capital letters at the top of the article created a tremor that shook his entire body. WALLACE-HAVENOT headed the report. Brad scanned the report with blurred eyes, anger welling up with each name of an attendant or guest.

"Son of a bitch," he seethed through clenched teeth. He threw the paper across the room, the sections of the papers separating in the air and drifting to the floor. "Bastards!"

He slammed the door behind him as he left, walking briskly directly to the grotto on the edge of the woods.

"You are not going to believe this, my boy," he began.

*　　*　　*

While Brad submerged himself into winter hibernation, Josie and Parker explored the joys of their second time around love. The comfort of over twenty years of friendship made up for the lack of a long official courtship and they adjusted quickly to the intimacy of marriage. With the onset of the next summer season, Josie lost interest in spending as much time at the cabin as she had the last few years of her life with Brad. There simply was no reason to escape from the tension at home any longer. Whether she and Parker were playing cribbage or reading quietly in the same room or making love, she was content, happier than she had been in years.

With the sheer joy of sharing life with Parker, Josie's school year passed as quickly as any she could ever remember. On rare occasions, she would feel the need to talk with Parker about her past, discussions which always ended with Parker lightly dismissing her concern about Brad's health and well being.

"He's made his choices and apparently is doing what he wants to do. If he wants to reconnect, I've got no problem with that as long as you don't. I guess I feel like he had a good thing and blew it, for whatever reason. Not to be hurtful but I have a feeling that he's not interested any more." It was refrain that he used on practically every occasion, only the construction changing but not the content.

During a late winter snowstorm, the kind that so discouragingly deflates the spirit of the oncoming spring, Josie and Parker sat on a blanket in front of the fireplace, the roar from the fire competing for attention with the howling wind outside. The environment exuded sensuousness and their cuddling soon led to a spontaneous love making session. Afterwards, as they sat in the emotional afterglow, soaking in the closeness that always comes after physical intimacy, Parker noticed Josie's tears, the dampness reflecting the flickering flames from the fire.

"What's wrong?" he asked, concern showing in his voice.

"It's really nothing, nothing at all. It's just that I'm so happy that I almost feel guilty. I mean, not all that long ago, I might have been sitting here with Brad but certainly not in the same frame of mind. It's stupid but I still think of him; I mean I don't really think of him but I guess I worry about him."

"That's just you, Josie. It's what makes you so special. It's what I love about you. I know he's doing OK. I've even seen where he lives." She broke free of their close snuggling position, sat straight up and looked at him, the wavering light from the fire bouncing off his face.

"What do you mean, you know where he lives? How did you find out? Where?" Josie's voice moved to a higher pitch. "When did all this happen?"

Parker felt as if the heat from the fire had suddenly cooled.

"Last Labor Day. Gordon found out and we took a ride past; just curious, you know?" He sounded stupid and felt even more stupid. "I should've told you. I'm really sorry, Josie."

"It's OK, but I'd be lying if I said I wasn't disappointed. So bring me up-to-date, even if it is after the fact," she said, deliberately dulling the edge in her voice.

She listened intently as Parker described the cottage, her expression changing from keen interest to a deepening sadness as he told her about the gravestone.

"Oh, my God," she said as she resumed her snuggling position. "OH, MY GOD!"

*　　*　　*

Brad Wallace spent the winter preparing for a summer of final retribution. Even when the snows came and the bitter cold descended on New Hampshire, he made regular visits to the grotto in his back yard, keeping a shoveled path open and the bench and stone clear. Since reading about Josie's wedding to Parker Havenot, the black periods came with increasing frequency but he made no effort to curtail them, instead immersing himself in their healing qualities. If the fine line between genius and insanity, between reality and illusion, even between good and evil exists, by early spring Brad had likely crossed it.

Each of his sessions with Brad, Jr. began with all the solemnity of a sinner's entrance into the confessional at a Catholic church. The theme remained the same even when the content varied.

"I'll just become an agent for justice, son. Someone has to take a stand and at least try to change things for the better. There is just too much that is wrong to ignore it. First we'll wreak a little havoc on some of the wealthy bastards around this lake, the type that want the best schools and the best police protection and all kinds of services but show up at every town and school meeting to vote against spending any money. It'll be like old Mr. Peaslee or Bob Snyder or the good doctor Capaldi or even my favorite superintendent and a former best friend. We'll just start things in motion and see where fate takes them. And, of course, at some point, we'll have to include the wonderful detective on the list." Brad shivered as the light snow became heavier, the wind sharper on his face.

He had opened the Christmas card from Josie, with it's "Hope all is well with you" greeting and signed with an innocuous "Best, Jos" as he walked back up the lane from picking up the mail. It sent him directly to the grotto for a healing. The session had an immediate effect, raising his spirits as what had been a nebulous plan for finally setting some things right formed more clearly in his mind. The heralded upcoming national conference that would solve all the problems in public education could still be the culmination of his efforts. In the meantime, he would practice on some of the folks who deserved to suffer just a little; how much would depend on the vagaries of their personal relationship with Clotho, his favorite of the Greek Fates. She would weave the tapestry of their lives after he supplied the warp threads that would set it into motion.

The snow, coming heavier but still powdery, swirled around him as he sat on the icy bench. The stone at his feet held on to the blowing fluff for the moment but gradually disappeared beneath it. He still clutched the card from Josie in the balled fist of his right hand as he made his way back to the warmth of the cottage, tilting his head for protection against the intensifying storm. After shaking the snow from his coat and hanging it on one of the nails driven into the wall in the mudroom, he kicked off his boots, went into the kitchen and filled a large mug with hot coffee. The steam from the cup rose behind him as he found his way into the overstuffed chair in front of the fireplace. He reached into his pocket and pulled out the rumpled Christmas card, smoothing it enough to reread the curt message.

He rolled the card into a tight ball and threw it into the fire, his eyes watering as the flames consumed it.

The Summer of Discontent

"Do not be overcome with evil,
but overcome evil with good."
Romans 12:21

Unlike the pre-Josie period of his life, Parker now used every available vacation day at his disposal, spending as much time with her at the lake as possible. Although he saw Gordon on a fairly regular basis, the boat sinkings on the lake had not been part of their conversations until early in August, just a few weeks shy of the Havenot's first anniversary.

"First, we've got Bill Yates. The poor guy probably would still be here except for that accident. Seems the stress of it all was just too much. Then, every few weeks, some other boat sinks. It's like an epidemic of rich people with expensive boats who keep finding stuff to run into. It's the damndest thing I seen in all my years on the lake. Most summers we'll get one or two and then a few who'll run aground in the dark because they don't know the lake or are going too fast or have had too much to drink." Gordon Tibideau, the model of professionalism for officers patrolling the big lake, was venting. "I know you don't believe in coincidences but there's no other frigging explanation."

Parker Havenot didn't have to use his perceptiveness to know that his friend was frustrated.

"It's just been a tough summer and it's only the beginning of August," Gordon said. "I can't wait to see what the full moon brings at the end of this month."

"I've got to tell you, Parker, I wonder what's coming next. If you don't mind, I'd really like your take on what in the hell is going on."

The story was as simple as it was complicated.

"We've got four boat sinkings, beginning with the *BiNaY II*. All of them happened with experienced sailors at the helm. They strike some object—a rock or something submerged–and they go down. Simple as that."

Parker's time tested logistic ability surfaced.

"Let's really look at this without your emotion getting in the way," he said, as if speaking with a policeman who had just experienced his first fatal shooting. "First, we eliminate coincidence. Could something reasonable have happened? Is it possible that all of these people could have screwed up? You wouldn't believe how many people I've seen in my life who have done dumber things than sink a boat."

"Don't you dare quote that shit about 'there are no coincidences.' Where the hell did that come from, anyway?" Gordon, the quiet efficient patrolman, was again showing his agitation.

"Gordon, you're swearing like a sailor. I truly am shocked!" Parker assumed his most hurt expression, deliberately overreacting.

"Get off of it, will you? I've got a real problem here." Gordon matched Parker's theatrics with some of his own.

Parker, contrite but relentless, continued his questioning. "Tell me the circumstances again and be patient. I'm not one of your lake seaman who knows every nuance of what you're saying."

"OK, Parker. Here it is in a stupid nutshell. After the Yates's boat went down, another three have done the same thing. All the boaters agree to one common thread. They heard a dull thud, thinking they had struck any one of dozens of obstructions floating in the lake. Within minutes, their boats foundered and then wound up at the bottom of Winnipesaukee. I mean it's like God said let's give these boats a flat tire just for spite. I don't have quite the same belief about coincidences that you do, but I've got to tell you that it seems as though someone's trying to get even with the rich and famous around the lake."

As Gordon's apparently harmless observation penetrated deeper, Parker tried to dismiss it.

"I'd be glad to help if you'd like, only on an unofficial basis, of course." The phraseology about flat tires and God's intrusion into the affairs of human beings clanged through Parker's subconscious like an off-key note from the bass section of a church choir. He remembered

Steve Capaldi's response to his suggestion so many years before.

"It's preposterous," Parker said loudly, startling Gordon, who was still trying to follow his friend's reasoning.

"What in the hell are you talking about?" Gordon asked, then chuckled. "Uh-oh, I've gone and sworn again. Whatever will become of me?" They shared a heartier laugh.

"It really is preposterous," Parker said, the furrow in his brow clashing with the smile on his face. He was causing more consternation than relief for his friend.

"Something's going on in that detective head of yours, I can tell. Come on and tell me what you're thinking." For the next few minutes, Gordon listened, mesmerized into silence by Parker's outrageous theory.

*   *   *

The death of Bill Yates temporarily upset Brad's schedule. He admitted freely during his therapy sessions at the grotto that it was nothing but morbid curiosity that sent him to the funeral and even gave him the audacity to pass through the receiving line in the basement of the small church on the lake. Expecting that attending the service would validate his firm belief in human destiny, he wasn't prepared for the effect that the proceedings had on him.

He joined the huge crowd spilling out the doors of the Lakewood Evangelical Lutheran Church. The funeral for Bill Yates attracted people from all around the state, including many of the most powerful politicians. He had touched a large segment of the population through his success in real estate and active involvement in a variety of community and church projects. His popularity, coupled with the utter tragedy of the accident, made attendance at his funeral a necessity for most of those who knew him.

Brad worked his way between an usher and George Grover, the local police chief, as they stood chatting at the front door of the church, oblivious to the fact that they were blocking the doorway. Every seat in the spacious church was taken; extra chairs were set in the choir loft and several rows lining the sanctuary were already occupied. He found his way to the rear corner of the church, the space behind the last pew filling quickly with others who would stand for what probably would be a lengthy service. The inconspicuous place suited Brad just fine. His well practiced eavesdropping skills should glean some interesting information about how the general population viewed what happened to the *BiNaY II* as he mingled with the others after the service.

He had not prepared himself for the entrance of Nancy Yates and her sons. The side entryway at the front of the church provided a subtle and unobtrusive method to enter the sanctuary. Grieving families and nervous bridegrooms or anyone who wished to enter the church while attracting minimal attention used it. Peering over and around the heads in front of him, Brad watched as Nancy entered, one son in front and the other behind. Her head was bowed and her shoulders had a slight sag, the universal posture of a person who finds that the world has recently become so much more difficult to bear. She did not acknowledge anyone's presence, looking down at the floor in front of her as though expecting to trip on an unseen flaw in the worn carpet. She was a beautiful woman and sadness swept over him. Before his melancholy could turn to remorse, it was gone, instantly regretted. For the next hour, he followed the cultural ritual of paying his last respects to a man he had never known.

The tedious yet curiously uplifting service with its procession of eulogies culminated in the stomach wrenching emotional farewells of Tom and Bill Yates, Jr. The crowded church echoed with muffled sobs as the pastor closed with the traditional Twenty Third Psalm as a benediction, followed by a spirited rendition of "A Mighty Fortress Is Our God" from the organ. The sincerity of the love for Bill Yates was evident and, like so many at funerals, Brad wondered how many would come to his final service and what might be said about his life. His Lutheran background forced his throat to tighten at the sound of a "Mighty Fortress." Each stanza weakened his best effort at remaining detached from the withering emotional power of the hymn. When the organ postlude finally ended, his desperate need for fresh air was stymied as the congregation sat and waited for the Yates family to exit slowly through the side door. The crush of standees in the rear of the church prevented Brad from moving and for a moment, a panic attack seemed imminent. The disquieting sensation passed quickly and he watched as young Tom Yates, the last of the family to leave, pushed the door closed and the ushers began to dismiss the mourners row by row.

After navigating through the crowded activity room of the large white community building attached to the side of the traditional New England country church, Brad stood at one of the windows looking out at the lake. The subdued hum of a variety of conversations bounced off the low ceiling in the room behind him and melted into one unintelligible murmur. If he were to accomplish his purpose here, he had to mingle but he first had to compose himself. The service left him with an unexpected and disconcerting empathy toward the Yates family. The success of any future "missions" depended upon gleaning some information from the gathering in this room. He drew in a deep breath, turned and looked around the room.

George Grover, the police chief, had just completed his turn at running the emotional gauntlet through the line of the grieving family and already was engaged in serious conversation with several other men at the end of the refreshment table. Brad casually maneuvered into a position where he could hear if the chief said anything interesting. Acting as though the large chocolate chip cookies were his main purpose in moving closer to the chief and his group, he positioned himself so that he could hear everything quite clearly. In less than five minutes, he discovered that his first mission had been an unqualified success.

"Course we found the boat, Andy; Gordon Tibideau is an expert in cases like these." Brad edged closer.

"She got a hole on the starboard side big enough to let a school of lake trout through. No way it could stay afloat with that kinda damage," the chief continued. Brad shifted his position around the table, making a subtle move from the chocolate chips to the vegetable tray close by.

"I talked with Nancy but she's pretty torn up. She's gonna try to take me out to where they were but really isn't sure she could pinpoint exactly when or where it happened. She did hear it though–passed it off as a log or something."

Another man whom Brad did not recognize joined in. "Just really rotten bad luck for Bill, you know. Seemed like the calmest guy I know but he told me once he was on some kind of meds for high blood pressure. Stress of all that must've pushed him over the edge"

Brad had heard enough but made the bold decision to test the depth of his resolve just a little further. The receiving line had dwindled to just a few. Not wanting to be last, he acted distracted and slipped between two obviously unrelated people in line.

He found himself looking into the eyes of young Tom Yates. His years in education trained him to recognize children who were hurting and he had seen more than his share. Tom Yates was not a child but Brad easily saw the depth of pain flickering in his deep-set blue eyes. Brad moved by quickly with a hasty "I'm sorry" without offering any introduction. Despite his determination, Brad could not make eye contact with Nancy Yates, mumbling a barely audible and ineffectual "sorry" to her as he squeezed her hand. When he reached his car after nearly bolting from the church, he felt his eyes begin to sting. He dug his handkerchief out of his back pocket and with a quivering hand pushed it hard against his face, as if applying a tourniquet to stem a hemorrhage.

*   *   *

Brad followed the investigation into the sinking of the *BiNaY II* through the weekly paper. The story generated considerable interest and the editor capitalized on it. Bill Yates had been a well-known and local figure but he was really only a part of the story. With most of the year-round population of the local communities surrounding Lake Winnipesaukee possessing boats of one sort or another, the tale of a midnight collision of a boat with a submerged rock held a certain fascination as well. The story stayed on the front page for three weeks in a row as the local police, the lake patrol, and eventually the New Hampshire State Police jostled with each other for press coverage of the incident.

The final report of the three agencies was presented at one of the few news conferences of its kind ever held, the type usually seen on television in some large city. Police officials flanked by local selectman, all elbowing each other and straining to be in camera range, took turns explaining the outcome of the investigation. Even WMUR-TV sent a crew from Manchester to cover the conference, and Brad watched the evening news to see the few short clips they allotted to this rare news story from the North Country. He smiled as he watched George Grover, assuming a "man of the hour" posture, deliver the dramatic opening line of the conference and wondered how the group had agreed to allow George the privilege. From the background, a familiar face jumped out at him. "I'll be damned; it's Gordon Tibideau," he said aloud.

"We have found no evidence of foul play in this incident and have concluded that the *BiNaY II* met with an unfortunate accident that resulted in the sad tragedy for the Yates family," Chief Grover announced, puffing his chest for the cameras.

When the local weekly appeared two days later, the story contained every detail of the "complete" inquiry. For Brad Wallace, there were no surprises. He skimmed the story to the section about the extensive efforts by the salvage company to bring the boat to the surface. The description of the damage to the boat offered in a long quote from George Grover reinforced Brad's belief that preconceived notions often affect perceptions of unrelated events. This happens even with "professional" law officers, as George referred to himself over and over. Brad knew it was more than likely that the boat was not out of the water five minutes before any investigators concluded that the damage was caused by a rock collision simply because that was what everyone expected to find.

Several paragraphs from the end of the story, Brad found the reference to Nancy Yates. As so often occurs in small local newspaper stories, the reporter's personal feelings mixed with the news, incorporating a combination of human interest and editorial comment. Brad read the account of Nancy's police boat trip to the scene of the accident, curious what effect a return to the exact place where she lost her husband might have been. The reporter, sprinkling adjectives throughout the description as though practicing her short story technique, described how she had wept when they approached the quiet cove where Brad had first watched them.

He put down the paper and supplanted the image of Nancy Yates with one of releasing his fully cocked gun into the hull of the *BiNayII*. After a few minutes of relishing his success, he began to plan the next one, another "open and shut" case.

* * *

The first loss of a human life because of events he set into motion unnerved him at first. As time passed and the case of the sunken Chaparral was entirely dismissed as an unfortunate accident, Brad reinstated his regular schedule. In a single session at the memorial, the term he now assigned to the grotto, he reasoned with Brad, Jr. that the military term "collateral damage" certainly was operable in the Yates' case. As much as the whole idea of situational ethics generally appalled him, in this situation the intent was not to physically harm anyone, therefore, no guilt applied. Besides, if the schedule for the conference he received in the mail stayed locked in place, he had a rendezvous with the *Belle* later in the summer and he needed as much practice as possible before late August arrived.

* * *

Educational conferences are planned years in advance. As an administrator of importance, Brad knew about the conference two years before he was retired by default. He actually entertained thoughts of attending when he first heard about it. Could it be possible that someone, somewhere, might actually have at least a small degree of vision? Soon after the complete descriptive brochure arrived, he decided that it was the type of conference that George Metcalf should attend, full of glitzy, high profile educational leadership and politicos intent on extracting every bit of juice they could from associating with "educational reform."

"Just another pile of horseshit," he said aloud as he read through the flyer, especially amused by the description of the evening cruise aboard the *Winnipesaukee Belle*, the finale of the conference.

"A last chance to share with your colleagues and newly-formed alliances what you've learned from this critical conference," the brochure read. Brad read it and immediately deposited it in his circular file.

"Doesn't mean shit," he said to his superintendent when asked why he likely would not be attending.

"It's like the drive off the tee in golf," he said to Metcalf, who had no idea what he was talking about. "It's what happens on the second shot that really counts. In this case, it's what happens next that counts. These men and women will supply all these wonderful pronouncements, rec-ommendations, and solutions. All the excited administrators will mouth the same words in their opening of school pep talks then the people in the trenches will do what they've always done to survive."

Visions of hundreds of classroom observations flitted through his mind in an instant. He continued his lecture. "They'll either be creative and innovative or so deadly boring that the kids will love to come to their classes to catch up on their sleep. In the meantime, the poor taxpayers will be footing the bill for this five day party disguised as an educational leadership conference." Brad remembered that his tirade was not well taken.

"Just your opinion, Brad. A lot of good stuff goes on at these things. Don't short-change it so quickly," Metcalf said, very much on the defensive.

*   *   *

Brad never allowed his subscription to *Administrators' Weekly* to lapse, although he was unsure why. The national journal kept him informed of what was happening in the field and, with only vague or non-existent interest in most of the items in the journal, he followed with increasing interest the burgeoning importance of this "search for solutions to the national crisis in education."

When it finally appeared on the foreseeable horizon, it received more print space in the small-town media than the local results of the "first in the nation" primary. As though they had been selected to host the Olympic Games, the Lakes Region towns in the immediate vicinity waited for the high powered political figures and educators to descend upon them, dragging with them all sorts of potential for glory and recognition.

Brad read the reports, paying special attention to the social event of the conference, a sunset cruise aboard the *Winnipesaukee Belle*.

"Perfect," he said aloud.

*   *   *

The tedious, time consuming and frustrating job of collecting physical evidence was fine for the police lab technicians but Parker loved interviewing witnesses. If his career in law enforcement had proven anything to him, it was that people were the best source of information. A friendly and skillful interrogation inevitably produced results for him. His keen perception of the quirks and foibles of human nature allowed him to separate the nervous sweat of a completely innocent man from the calm exterior of the most vicious criminal.

As he and Gordon discussed the boat sinkings, Parker decided that the only one involving a fatality was the best place to start. Without any jurisdiction, he remained skeptical of Gordon's insistence that it would be permissible to informally investigate the accidents.

"This is New Hampshire, not the big city," Gordon reasoned with him. "It's not like we're looking for a mass murderer or something. I'd just like an outsider's view to put my mind to rest that these things are just a string of incredibly bad luck and coincidence."

Gordon didn't prepare Parker for Nancy Yates. She was startlingly beautiful even with the shadows of sadness that drifted across her face at regular intervals. Parker was sure that the plush office remained just as it was on the day her husband left it to meet her. He looked at Gordon as she ushered them in, raising his eyebrows in the universal appreciative silent signal of men in the presence of a lovely woman. Nancy directed them to the soft chairs reserved for her real estate clients, seats that encouraged the comfort needed when writing checks for large amounts of money. She moved behind her husband's desk. As she sat softly in his large leather chair, another cloud of sadness scudded across her face, briefly darkening the room.

Parker looked around, absorbing details. This was a family man's office, the walls filled with pictures of his sons in various sports uniforms intermingled with the obligatory diplomas and certificates and community awards. An eight by ten photo of Nancy and Bill Yates standing next to the *BiNaY II* sat on the wide windowsill behind her. Nancy saw him looking at it.

"That's the one that went down but you probably already know that," she said. "I'm sure Gordon filled you in on the whole story. Anyway, what's this all about, Gordon? Not to be harsh but I thought that I was fairly safe in trying to move on here, at least as well as I could."

Gordon stammered out his answer. "I'm sorry if this is intrusive, Nancy, but we've had a string of these things and Parker's just helping me out a little. He thought it might be helpful to ask you just a few questions if you don't mind."

Another cloud passed through the room.

"It's OK, I. . ." She paused, staring over their heads at nothing. "I'll help any way I can, you know that. It's just hard, that's all." The two men shifted in their seats in an embarrassed choreographed unison.

"This'll be quick, Mrs. Yates. I know how awful this must be." He hated hearing himself say that because he didn't know; he actually had no idea how awful it must be. His first question surprised her.

"Do you remember anyone at the funeral who you didn't know, someone you hadn't seen before?"

"There were so many people there who were just acquaintances. Bill was a pretty well-known and active person in the area. I didn't know a lot of the people. Why do you ask?"

Parker didn't respond immediately and Gordon jumped in. "He's an old city detective, Nancy. Can't get rid of his suspicious nature, even up here." His interruption gave Parker an opportunity to rephrase his question in more palatable terms.

"Sorry, Mrs. Yates. It's just that situations like yours draw some strange characters sometimes. Morbid types, you know? That's more of what I was thinking about; people preying on the devastated widow, that sort of thing."

"As I think about it, there was a guy who for whatever reason got my attention. Came through the line right toward the end. I've even think I've seen him around town once or twice since."

Parker listened to Nancy's sketchy description passively then, to Gordon's surprise, stood up.

"We really appreciate your time, Mrs. Yates." He reached across the desk and shook her hand lightly. "I'm sorry about your husband. From all I've heard about him, he must have been a really special person." He turned to Gordon, who remained seated as yet another gloomy cloud settled over the office.

"Come on, Gordon, let's let Mrs. Yates get back to work. We'll show ourselves out."

"Thanks again, Nancy," Gordon said, trying unsuccessfully to slow their abrupt departure.

Parker didn't say anything until they got to the car. He looked up at the window of the office and saw Nancy Yates standing next to the photo on the sill, staring out toward the lake.

"Brad Wallace was at the funeral, Gordon. Now isn't that just the strangest coincidence yet?"

The Rehearsal

"The play's the thing . . ."
William Shakespeare

Brad drew some comfort from the well-known theory that a poor dress rehearsal of a play is usually followed by a flawless performance on opening night. The carefully planned practice session before his final liberation had not gone well at all. The sudden, violent thunderstorm that roared across the lake just after seven o'clock caught him by surprise, drenching him and all of the gear he had so carefully laid out. The *Belle* was in sight when he heard the first distant rumble, and he could only watch helplessly as she came about and headed back toward Wolfeboro amidst dozens of other boats scrambling for safety. The storm developed so quickly that many boaters headed for the closest shelter instead of returning to their own docks. Brad scrunched against the trunk of the shortest pine he could find for cover, cringing every time lightning hissed above his head. Several boats sped toward the cove and all he could do was hope that none would happen to stop close by.

The storm cell passed quickly and the late evening sun illuminated a spectacular double rainbow as the black cloud headed east toward Alton Bay. The occupants of the few boats that rode out the storm in what Brad referred to as "his cove" never were aware of his presence. He watched with relief as they slowly moved their crafts toward the broads, most of them looking back over their shoulders at the colorful display in the eastern sky. He turned to his equipment, pulling off the hastily thrown protective tarp and deciding what to do next. The *Belle* wouldn't be coming back out for the sunset.

His choices were simple. Either he could run through the whole exercise with an imaginary *Belle* turned toward the sunset or he could wait until the next week and carry out the finale without a dress rehearsal.

He sat down heavily against the same pine that had offered its protection from the storm and stared out toward the lake. Like the point and counterpoint in the song from his favorite musical, *The Fiddler on the Roof,* each reason for a rehearsal was met with an "on the other hand" argument. Internal disagreements with one's self can be terribly frustrating and Brad finally stood up and in an agitated voice made an announcement to the forest surrounding him.

"I came here to practice and by damn, I'm going to do it." Minutes later, after a careful check of the shoreline, he slipped beneath the surface of the lake on his way to an imaginary rendezvous with the *Winnipesaukee Belle.* As he expected, the extra weight of the explosive charge implanted into the arrowhead of his spear gun had no effect on his ability to swim and he arrived at the captain's favorite sunset viewing spot with minor exertion. Not wishing to disturb the surface in the event the chop in the lake had calmed since the passage of the storm, he slowly poked his head into the warm air until his eyes could scan the horizon. He looked back to the shore for the landmarks that told him that he was in the correct position. In his imagination, the *Belle* took shape fifty yards away, all of its passengers and crew focused on the sun setting over the western edge of the lake. Of all of his self-proclaimed missions, this one required the most care as it would be carried out in enough daylight for him to be detected should someone look in his direction at an inopportune moment. As he continued to stare at the imaginary image, an adrenaline rush coursed through his veins. The water lapped around his neck as he exposed his entire head and removed his mouthpiece.

"Destiny." The recitation was loud, as if he still needed to convince himself. "Destiny for the passengers, destiny for the crew and destiny for me. We'll just see what happens." He again slid beneath the surface and swam in the direction of the phantom vessel until he was twenty feet from the hull. Weeks before, a harmless conversation with the captain about fuel capacities in boats like the *Belle* led to a description of their location. As Brad raised his spear gun, he visualized the result of the penetration and the explosion caused by the impact. He cocked the gun and counted to three then sucked in a deep breath through his mouthpiece. The moment he imagined squeezing the trigger, he inverted his body and gave a fierce kick with both legs, sending him downward toward the bottom. In a week, during the real thing, he would be pulling on the line attached to his spear then staying underwater until well out of range of the chaos taking place on the *Belle*

Final Retribution

"Revenge is profitable; gratitude is expensive."
Edward Gibbon

Brad spent much of the afternoon sitting on the stone bench in a state of deep contemplation. He wandered through a mental maze, refreshing black periods alternating with complex emotional intervals of doubt and indecision. In the final fifteen minutes before he had to leave, he poured over the list of conference attendees, a list he had obtained from one of the proud local sponsors of the event. Many of the names he recognized as progressive leaders in the educational field, with a few of the more pugnacious critics of public school education mixed in. The symposium, a term used in public relations flyers and press releases to lend an inherent credibility and importance to the conference, provided an obvious attraction for political types of every persuasion. Brad wondered aloud how many of the influential people would be aboard the *Belle* for the evening extravaganza. The list in his hand was divided into categories, the final one being "Other Noteworthy Educators."

"This is where I would have been, son, right here under others," he said as he looked down at the marker by his feet. Quickly he read down the list, not expecting to see any familiar names. Halfway down the page, the word "Hartford" jumped out at him. He looked at the name associated with it and laughed, a low-pitched, maniacal giggle.

"Dr. George Metcalf, Superintendent of Schools, Hartford, Connecticut," the entry read. He stopped reading right there, barely able to keep from shouting an exuberant "YES!"

"I love it when a plan comes together," Brad said, folding the conference brochure and slipping it into his pocket as he prepared to leave the grotto to watch the boarding of the *Belle*. Several lines further down the list of other educators, in alphabetical order, the name of another old colleague was listed.

Dr. Harriet L. Stanton, a professor in the School of Education at the University of Chicago would be in attendance as well.

* * *

Josie followed the increasing coverage of the conference in the local papers with considerable interest. Like most experienced teachers, she looked upon any educational leadership conference that had no representation from those in the front lines of the classrooms of America as a probable waste of time and money. Her only hope that this one would be different and might actually make a difference was Harriet Stanton's attendance at it. With Harriet and Laura staying at the cottage with her for a full week before the conference and having Laura all to herself while Harriet attended the "symposium," she eagerly anticipated the last stay at the lake before the start of school. Her major regret had been that Parker would only be able to come to the lake on the weekends. When he surprised her with his announcement that he was able to arrange two weeks of his vacation to coincide with Harriet's visit, she was ecstatic.

* * *

After the conversation with Nancy Yates, Parker suggested another visit to Brad Wallace's cabin was in order.

"I'm not sure that's a good idea. We've got nothing to go on but your hunch. Maybe he was somehow acquainted with Bill Yates and Nancy just never saw him. We can't just go trespassing on people's property. Maybe we should get the police involved." Gordon Tibideau was nervous.

Parker laughed. "OK, let's go see Chief Grover and I'll let you explain all of this to him."

"Dumb idea," Gordon chuckled, "but I still can't see what another look around his property would accomplish."

"You're right, Gordon. I don't know what I was thinking about. We'll just pay real close attention to the next accident, OK?" Gordon was relieved on one hand but worried on the other.

"You think there'll be another accident, huh?"

"No doubt about it," Parker said, his voice a matter-of-fact monotone.

When Gordon stopped the car in front of Parker's cottage, he looked directly at him.

"I said I'd help you but you have to call the shots. Something's going on here but we'll just wait and see what happens next. I'm here for the next couple weeks so keep in touch, OK?"

The back door of the cabin opened and Josie poked her head out. Parker closed the car door and walked down the path. Gordon watched as Josie greeted him with more than a brief wifely hello kiss and led him inside.

Five minutes later, Gordon pulled off the Governor Wentworth Highway into a small town parking lot near one of the few public boat ramps on the north side of the lake. He maneuvered through and around the litter of boat trailers of every size and description and parked facing the lake.

"I don't know what the hell he expects to find but he's going to go back there. I just know it," he announced to himself.

*   *   *

Parker begged off on accompanying Josie on the trip to the airport to pick up Harriet and Laura.

"You'll have all kinds of girl things to talk about and I'll just be in the way," he said, and Josie let him wiggle out of it after a mild protest. The Monday morning flight from Chicago was scheduled to arrive at 8:30 and, as usual, the flight from O'Hare was running a full half-hour behind schedule when Josie called to check on it. At seven thirty, she kissed him goodbye.

"I'll be back ASAP. I love you," she said as she closed the door and headed for the airport.

Forty-five minutes later, Parker had pulled his car into a small side road a mile from Brad Wallace's mailbox and stopped well out of sight. He walked along the shoulder of the road toward the lane leading to Brad's cabin. Whenever he heard a car approaching in the distance, he would turn toward the woods, busying himself with the wildflowers growing between the forest and the road, confident that no passing motorist took the slightest notice of him.

As he had done when Gordon was with him, he picked his way through the woods, following the lane but deep enough in the woods that he couldn't be seen. Figuring that he had at least two hours before he would need to leave to be home before Josie and their guests, he found a flat rock embedded in an ancient stone wall and sat down. Through the thick woods, he could see the rising sun reflecting off Brad's car and the metal flashing around the chimney on the roof of the cottage. Only a small piece of the grotto and a corner of the stone bench were visible between the tall pines blocking him from view. He waited, passing the time by watching the squirrels and chipmunks chase each other around the floor of the forest. Five minutes into the second hour of his watch, he heard the cabin door open, followed shortly after by Brad's car starting. He peered through the trees as the car proceeded slowly down the lane. When he heard it speed away on the blacktop of the main road, he walked briskly into the yard, passing by the grotto with just a cursory look.

At the far corner of the property, a small storage shed, its natural cedar shingles weathered almost to the point of rotting, stood between the cabin and what appeared to be a pile of pieces of boat hulls. It looked like a section of the local town dump that was home to the carcasses of old boats, appliances, and various pieces of rusting machinery. Parker went first to the large sections of the hulls, some wood but mostly fiberglass. A few of them were intact but most had holes punctured in them, as though someone had deliberately stove them in. Puzzled, he started toward the shed. Two large hasps, both locked with heavy-duty combination pad-locks, sealed the door. He walked around to the single window, a six over six with several panes broken and the others clouded with dirt. He cupped his hands over his eyes and strained to see inside. A spear gun leaning in one corner caught his attention. On an old workbench on the far wall was a neat pile of scuba gear, topped off with red and black flippers. He was so intent on the task that he barely heard the car slowing down and turning in the lane. The crunching gravel sounded a final alarm, sending him running toward the woods. He found the safety of the same flat rock as he had during his earlier vigil, gasping in deep breaths as Brad's car rolled to a stop. When he felt that Brad was safely inside, he started off through the woods again, following what was becoming a familiar path.

"What in the hell is going on?" he said aloud as he started home to get ready to greet Josie, Harriet, and Laura.

*   *   *

The small airport, not a likely scene for any sort of criminal activity, still maintained all of the required federal security measures and Josie stood patiently at the baggage claim area, watching the balcony overhead for the arrival of Harriet and Laura. Her emotions bubbled to the surface when she saw them appear and start down the moving stairway. Laura was the first to the bottom, taking two steps at a time on the slow-moving conveyor. Josie greeted her, the annoying tears filling her eyes continuing as Harriet reached the ground floor. The fervent greeting, repeated by other travelers all around them with varying degrees of intensity, ended in a group hug as they moved together toward the circular conveyor belts.

"Sorry, I told myself that I wasn't going to cry but it's just so good to see you," Josie said.

"You look sensational, Mrs. Havenot!" Harriet said enthusiastically. "Life with Parker must agree with you."

Josie blushed slightly. "I guess it really does. I haven't been this happy for a long time."

A loud bell rang over their heads announcing the arrival of their luggage. The commotion around the baggage claim eliminated any chance at continuing the conversation. Letter writing and telephone calls invariably leave voids in the lives of friends separated by time and distance and the long ride back to the cabin passed quickly as they alternately filled in the missing details since they had last seen each other. Josie gently brushed aside Harriet's questions about Brad with the "It's such a long story" excuse, redirecting the conversation toward Laura and her impending adventures in graduate school at Michigan State.

"I'm looking forward to having you to myself for a while, Laura. I hope you won't be bored with your old Godmother. You surely must have a ton of young men hounding you all the time." Josie looked at her in the rear view mirror, struck as always by her beauty as she reddened and smiled widely.

"Just a few, actually, but nothing serious. I'm just enjoying life. We'll have fun; it'll be a good relaxing time for me but I've got to tell you that I can't wait for that boat trip at the end of the conference. Mom got me in as her companion. All those important people I'll get to meet . . .Wow!" Josie laughed out loud, charmed by her sincerity and wholesomeness.

"I hope Rich and Becky will be able to make it up here for that last weekend," Harriet said, interrupting just enough to prevent Josie from following up her discussion about Laura's young men. "It would be great to see them and I might be able to have a surprise for Rich as well if he's interested."

"They're coming on Friday morning. What's the big surprise, Harriet?"

"Let's wait to see if I can pull it off. I'll know after the first day of the conference."

*　*　*

"I knew it," Gordon said, "I just knew you'd go over there."

Parker ignored Tibideau's chastising interruption.

"Could we meet for coffee tomorrow morning? I'd like to tell you about this in person. I'm expecting Josie any minute and I'll need to hang out here with her friends this afternoon but by tomorrow morning they probably won't even miss me. I'll see you at Duncan Lake Coffee Shop about eight, OK?"

"Can't you give me a clue; I mean the suspense is killing me." Gordon couldn't cover his nervousness with the half-hearted attempt at humor. He waited for a response. Parker took a long time to answer.

"It's too difficult to explain by phone and it probably isn't anything anyway. I'd rather see you in person. You're so lovely to look at in the morning, you know?" Parker's laughter didn't cover the agitation in his voice.

Gordon was more nervous than ever.

"Sure. I'll see you tomorrow then." He hung up the phone and looked across the room to the map of the lake, large red pins marking the spots where each boat had foundered. "Random acts of a pernicious God, nothing more," he whispered to the empty office, failing miserably in his effort to convince himself that was indeed the case.

*   *   *

Brad was ready. His numerous trips aboard the *Winnipesaukee Belle* had provided all the information he needed. The captain, well trained and professional, was a model of friendliness and courtesy. He reacted to Brad's interest with an openness typical of small town residents far removed from the innate suspicious nature of so many of the touring city dwellers. He was happy to share the uniqueness of the paddlewheel, even giving him a tour of the engine and fuel compartments on his third trip. The boat certainly was one of the safest on the lake, a proud fact reiterated by the captain at every opportunity.

"I won't say that God Himself couldn't sink this ship," he joked. "We know where that got the Titanic but this is as safe a vessel as I've seen."

All but two of Brad's practice sessions on the smaller boats were successful, sending four expensive boats to the bottom of the lake. The gaping holes in the boats matched similar cavities in the wallets of some very wealthy people or, at the very least, in the coffers of some large insurance companies. His two failures were simple misses caused by unanticipated rapid acceleration by the drivers of the boats. The *Belle,* filled with all those special people facing the sunset, would not be a moving target.

The thunderstorm that disrupted his dress rehearsal was a passing memory and he felt that the odds were in his favor. As the cooler late August weather moved into New England, thunderstorms became rare occurrences. A more likely scenario would be a crystal clear evening with cool enough temperatures to keep most of the group off the open top deck.

With just a few days to go, he rarely practiced with the spear gun, more confident in his physical ability with that equipment than his emotional stability to execute his plan. He found the reassurance he needed at the grotto, his therapy sessions filled with images of the past. The residual catalog of faces whose fate had created such rage in him supplied his motivation. The image of Tyler Spence provided the final encouragement when it repeated his poignant plea.

"It's not fair, Brad. You've got to do something," he had said.

"I'm about to, Tyler; I really am this time," he said, a resolute conviction in his voice.

*   *   *

It was easy for Parker to ignore Josie's protest. The girls already were in the high spirits that accompany a close friend's visit and they considered his request to be excused from breakfast to have coffee with Gordon a minor intrusion on their conversation.

"Is everything all right with him?" Josie asked, a trifle perfunctorily.

"Oh yeah, we just haven't chatted for a while and I thought this would be a good time. I'll be back soon." He started to leave without kissing Josie goodbye and she brought him up short.

"Aren't you forgetting something, my dear?" she said, hugging him and surreptitiously slipping her tongue into his mouth. "I'll see you whenever. Tell Gordon I said hello." Parker, chagrined yet pleased by her audacity in front of her guests, left quickly, again promising to be home as soon as possible.

The small coffee shop near Duncan Lake served as an ideal meeting place. The small booths along the back wall each had exceptionally tall partitions that allowed for complete privacy. Gordon Tibideau greeted the regulars lining the counter and found Parker sitting in the last booth.

"So, what's up?" Gordon asked before he had even sat down.

"Aren't you even going to say hello?" Parker chided but with a detective's understanding of his friend's impatience.

Parker's moved directly into a description of the hulls of the boats at Brad Wallace's cabin. His vivid portrayal seemed to strike a nerve with Gordon Tibideau.

"Let's go look at a couple of the boats that went down," he said, losing interests in the cold English muffin in front of him. "They're still at the marina in town waiting for final decisions from the insurance companies."

They gulped down the remainder of their coffee and within minutes had driven across town to Watercrest Marina. The boat that had sunk most recently lay on its side at the used boat storage area. Gordon knew exactly where it was located, having been the one in charge of supervising the salvage operation to be certain that nothing valuable on board disappeared during the process.

"It looks the same to me but what do I know. You're the expert. What a damn shame, though. This boat is gorgeous."

"They're all the same," Gordon said. "It's like the damn rocks have grown in the lake like they do in New Hampshire gardens. They've all been similar but different. It all depends where the boat gets hit what the shape of the hole is."

Parker stopped walking and Gordon stopped two paces further along and turned to him.

"You want me to go look at the stuff at Wallace's, don't you?"

Silence.

"We're pretty stuck here, you know," Gordon continued. "You've got no jurisdiction and I look like a fool if I go to George Grover to try to explain things. I guess we need to confirm your suspicions but I sure don't like it. I mean, if the damage to the hulls looks the same as what you saw at Brad Wallace's place . . ." He didn't need to finish the sentence. "OK, you're the police detective. Tell me what we're going to do."

He waited for Parker's instructions.

*   *   *

Several days passed before Parker was able to show Gordon Brad Wallace's practice range. Gordon reminded Parker, harshly on occasion, that he still worked for the lake patrol and private investigating while on the clock would certainly be frowned upon by his superiors. This also happened to be the busy summer season, a season made more hectic by the large conference visiting the region. By Wednesday of the week after Laura and Harriet arrived, Gordon finally had a day off. Josie and Laura were bound for a day of shopping in North Conway, a small town to the north whose beautiful views of the White Mountains clashed with its reputation as the strip mall outlet capital of New England.

Their plan had a small but significant twist from the walk in the woods that Parker had nearly memorized. A single person stalking through the forest can elude detection easily but two men more than doubles the chances of being noticed. From previous experience, they decided to wait for Brad to leave, as he did every day for brief periods, then drive quickly down his lane, look at the pieces of the hulls strewn around the yard, and leave as quickly as they had come.

Parker backed his car into a narrow logging road across the main road from Brad's lane. It was close but not too close, well out of sight yet they could still watch for a car leaving the premises. The road narrowed dramatically as he backed in, each passing foot resulting in deeper and more damaging scratches from the low bushes and branches overgrowing the long untouched trail.

"How're you going to explain the scratches to Josie?" Gordon asked. "She'll probably think you've gone parking with some New Hampshire farm girl. Don't think I'll give you an alibi." He smiled, enjoying his role as sidekick, his original nervousness converted to excited positive energy.

"God, I haven't heard that phrase in a long time. Gone parking hasn't been an option for me in years. Now let's just hope our friend takes one of his little trips. If I'm going to be stuck in the woods for long, I'd rather it be with Josie than you." They settled in and waited.

Even though parked in the dense woods, the car began to warm as the sun rose higher in the sky. After an hour or so, they rolled the windows down, inviting the mosquitoes in for a morning snack.

"This must be what a stake-out is like in the city, right?" Gordon asked. "How exciting!" Parker started to respond but stopped suddenly and listened. Another minute passed and Brad's car left his lane, turned left and disappeared from sight.

Parker moved his car tentatively out of the lane. After making sure that nothing approached from either direction, they crossed the road and turned into Brad's long driveway, going faster than they should have and skidding to a stop at the end of the lane.

Gordon jumped from the car and led the way across the yard to Brad's practice range. He went from one hull to another in quick succession, running his hands gingerly over the wounds in each one.

"Holy shit! What in the hell is this all about?" He looked at Parker, a puzzled expression on his face. "This is just too weird," he said.

"OK, you've seen them; now I think we'd better get out of here. We'll talk about it in the car." Parker started toward his car and noticed that Gordon was not behind him. He turned and saw him leaning against the window in the shed. "Come on, Gordon. We've got to get going," he shouted across the yard.

Gordon glanced at him and waved. "I'll be right behind you," he shouted. Frustrated, Parker jogged back to the shed and took Gordon by the arm. "Just a second, Parker; look over on the floor under that workbench."

Uneasily following Gordon's request and feeling like a kid about to be caught, Parker peeked through the window.

"I'll be damned; what in the hell does that mean?" Then with adamant insistence, he pulled on Gordon's arm again. "We are going, right now!" he said.

* * *

"I've seen people with a lot stranger hobbies. I just don't know how I can help you boys." George Grover, ever the political police chief, was not convinced. They had proceeded directly to the police station after their discovery at Brad Wallace's cabin. "Seems like the only ones who did anything wrong was you two. A man has the right to do as he pleases in his own back yard. Maybe he's getting ready to buy a boat and wanted to test the different hull strengths. Unless you've got more to go on, I can't move on it. You got to admit it's a pretty bizarre claim you're making here. Not like you at all, Gordon, " he said, pointedly staring at Parker as though he had used witchcraft to influence one of Winnipesaukee's finest lake patrolmen.

"Live free or die, Mr. Havenot. That's the New Hampshire way." He continued. "Now we've already declared these incidents as accidents and we certainly wouldn't want folks thinking that somebody is sabotaging boats on this lake. Bad for business, as they say, especially with this conference in town. Now if this fella wants to keep chunks of boats in his back yard, that's his business. So, since this is entirely my jurisdiction, why don't we just say that I'll take your information under advisement for now? And thanks for stopping by." He stood, dismissing them without saying another word.

As they walked to the car, Parker was furious and Gordon was embarrassed but neither emotion was helping their cause.

"What a narrow-minded ass!" Parker exclaimed as he slammed the car into gear.

*　　*　　*

The finale for the conference had finally arrived. The Saturday event on the *Winnipesaukee Belle* presented the chance for the participants to revisit the conference in a social setting and Laura Stanton likely was the most excited attendee, even though she participated only vicariously through her mother.

Harriet waited until Saturday morning to announce her surprise for Rich Lane.

"You're going on a boat ride with us, Rich." She was determined not to allow him any time for protest until she finished. "You always were one of the finest teachers I've ever seen, and I thought it would be nice if we had someone on board who knows what it's like to be in the front lines. It's all arranged and you're stuck with Laura and me for the night. We'll get you on board first then Laura will stay with you while I get my stuff cleaned up from the conference. You can hold forth like you used to do at Pete's back in the good old days. I used my considerable influence to pull this off so you'd better not object. Becky can have an evening away from you for a change." She finished, her rapid speech leaving her slightly out of breath.

"She won't be able to stand an evening away from me but I guess it'll be a good trial for her." Everyone laughed at Rich's response until he faltered. "This is really nice, Harriet. I appreciate what it must have taken to do this and I am truly touched." Harriet went to him and hugged him.

"It's nothing, really. I just wanted a real person mixing in with this group of phonies."

Becky joined in with a final jab. "You can pick me up at the local pub after you're done, Rich, unless I've been picked up already."

"In your dreams," Rich countered.

*   *   *

Josie invited Gordon to join all of them for four o'clock cocktails on the deck before the event. The night was sure to be one of those bittersweet occasions; Josie thought she would try to extend it by having the small gathering to celebrate the wonderfully long visit with Laura and Harriet, as well as the end of Parker's extended vacation.

Parker, well aware of the political realities of police work, was sorry to see his vacation end for more than one reason. He had no choice but to accept Chief Grover's decisions on the Brad Wallace "situation," as he called it. From his perspective, there were too many unresolved questions. Philosophically, he had major problems with the whole "live free or die" thing. He'd much rather live free and resolve differences of opinion than live free or die. "Dying," he said to Gordon, "is so damn permanent."

Any one of the issues that bothered him would be enough in his detective job at home to motivate him to go further. Here, the combination of so many issues was driving him crazy: the boat sinkings; the matching holes in the boats and the pieces in Brad's yard; the unusual spear tipped with a large rock tucked under the workbench in the shed; and the grotto.

The night was perfect. As the group clinked their glasses and saluted each other with the classic "Cheers," Laura made her appearance on the deck. The final evening of a long visit with special people always brings the emotions to a level lurking just beneath the surface and when Josie saw her beautiful goddaughter step onto the deck in the shimmering black cocktail dress, she choked back her tears. She loved Laura as her own daughter but the emotional turmoil she felt came from a "what might have been" moment.

"You look spectacular, Laura. How about if I go with you and your mom stays home?" Gordon joked as he stood to greet her.

The next hour passed quickly, Josie ensuring that the lively conversation remained centered on the future rather than the past. After Harriet and Laura packed Rich into his van and left for the cruise, the conversation shifted toward a more uncomfortable subject. Parker needed to have his friend Gordon present and was happy that Becky was there for Josie's support.

"Josie, I think I need to tell you this just because it's only fair that you know," he began. She sat there, listening intently but acting distanced, as though she really didn't know the person they were talking about. "Anyway, George Grover thinks there is nothing to it so I guess that's the end of it," Parker concluded, glancing at Gordon with raised eyebrows, giving him the chance to add anything else. He was silent.

"So, if you think he's going to do this again, how do you prevent it?" Josie's interest was sincere but muted. The man they were talking about was, after all, a person she thought she knew rather well.

"It just seems likes he wants to get even, as illogical as that sounds. It's like he feels that these people have wronged him in some way. I don't know if it's because they're wealthy or what." Parker searched for his own explanations even as he tried to answer her.

"Then you'd think that logically he'd be going after people like George Metcalf. He surely got hurt more in education than anywhere else." Josie grabbed her chest with such severity that both men jumped from their chairs and went to her.

"Oh, my God," she whispered breathlessly. "Harriet told me that George Metcalf is at this conference. He was in one of her sessions. You don't suppose . . ." She couldn't bring herself to finish the thought, as if saying it would make it come true. "Harriet and Laura are on that boat," she said, clutching her blouse even tighter.

"Rich, too," Becky said. "He's so helpless . . ." She bit down hard on her lower lip, preventing any more words from escaping.

Parker looked at his watch. "The boat's already left. Now it's your turn, Mr. Lake Patrolman. What's our next move?"

*   *   *

Brad sat on the splintery wooden bench watching the dock closely as the passengers boarded the *Winnipesaukee Belle* for an evening cruise around the big lake. His beige Docker shorts and a gaudy "I Love New Hampshire" tee shirt allowed him to blend easily with the many blatantly obvious tourists filling the well-shaded town park adjacent to the public docks. Most of the people wandering the paths crisscrossing under the large oaks showed just a waffling interest in the boarding, glancing around as if searching for something more interesting.

Brad moved to the edge of his seat, leaning forward as though watching an exciting finish to a one hundred-meter dash. His posture emphasized the large red heart replacing the word "love" across the center of his chest. He had much more than a passing interest in those who would be touring the sprawling lake on the *Belle*. The night promised to be dark and clear; no moon would be reflecting off the water on this night, only faint beacons of light coming from the brilliant canopy of stars sure to appear after sunset.

In the summer, the large, double decked ferry-like boat with its simulated paddle wheels and ornate decorative wood paneling could be seen virtually every night, carrying a varied composite of passengers. With a capacity for one hundred and fifty passengers and a connection to the finest restaurant in the small resort town, the *Belle* provided a unique fashion of entertaining large groups. The popular cruises attracted capacity crowds and on the rare occasions when the entire boat was not reserved for a single party, the available spaces filled quickly. Humorously referred as "booze cruises" by the local populace, the three-hour cruises usually had no specific destination, simply motoring around the huge lake allowing the passengers to absorb the spectacular mountain scenery rising gloriously from every shoreline. On the nights when a few wispy clouds drifted across the horizon, the highlight of the tours came as the sun gradually dropped in the western sky. The captain would maneuver the boat into a north-south direction and drop anchor, allowing his patrons to marvel at the incredible beauty of the sunset. The boat stayed in place until the last bit of light disappeared, giving the passengers a last chance at snapping the photographs for the folks back home. The *Belle* would then resume its meanderings through the inlets, coves, and islands, arriving back at the docks at exactly eleven o'clock.

As Brad munched on the last bites of his sugar cone, small drops of vanilla ice cream slowly dripping toward his fingers, he reviewed his observations from the six different cruises that he had taken on the *Belle* during the summer. On more than one occasion, he engaged the captain in a seemingly innocuous conversation about how isolated and foreboding some of the areas of the lake became at night.

From his vantage point on the bench under the huge oak trees filling the park, he smiled to himself as the passengers continued boarding.

"Looks kinda like Noah's ark, don't it?" The loud voice from behind startled Brad, as much for its close proximity as for its volume. He turned and looked directly into a friendly, smiling face of a young man sporting a shoulder length blond ponytail.

"Sorry, sir, I didn't mean to scare you. I just meant the way they have to go on board by twos because of how wide the gangplank is." Brad continued to stare at him as though he was an intruder, violating his private space. The unspoken message had little subtlety and the unwelcome visitor started to walk away. Brad turned back to the boat, mumbling an answer intelligible only to him.

"Yeah, it does look a bit like the ark. Pretty damned ironic that God stepped in to help that story have a happy ending . . ." His voice faded to nothing as he realized that his companion had stopped moving away and was straining to hear what he was saying. The young man looked at Brad one last time then walked away, the friendliness replaced by a sneer and a final comment tossed over his shoulder in Brad's direction.

"Typical unfriendly flatlander," he muttered as he hurried away.

Brad's full attention had already returned to the boat. The image of the *Belle* and an ark overlapped but the brief reverie vanished in a puff of wispy haze when he caught the profile of one of the last women to board. He strained to get a closer look but two attractive young women, clad in short cutoff jeans and skin tight tee-shirts advertising the Wolfeboro Inn, the parent restaurant of the *Belle,* blocked his view. They handled the heavy ropes connecting the boat to the dock with surprising dexterity, deftly slipping them off the enormous spools and throwing them to the waiting hands of the sailors standing on the bow. The boat started its slow drift backward as the last vaguely familiar passenger disappeared into the enclosed lower deck. He stood and stretched, watching with natural male interest as the two vivacious young women continued their chores around the dock.

"Glad their destiny didn't include a ride on the *Belle* tonight," he said in a quiet whisper.

Quickly weaving his way through the parking lot adjoining the docks, Brad covered the two blocks to his car in just a few minutes, thinking the entire time about how well his plan was coming together. As he had hoped, the boat was filled to capacity with many rich and powerful people, formidable leaders in business, politics, and education, all gathered to solve what everyone called the educational crisis in this country. The thought of the arrogance and conceit of these pompous experts made his stomach churn—his furious rage frightening and exciting him at the same time.

He had spent his entire professional life preaching about the power of negative energy. Now, if he empowered his anger and bitterness, they would consume him. "Never give negative thoughts energy," he would say to anyone who would listen. "They will feed on it and take on a life of their own." He felt his personal demon assuming a life of its own.

"Most of them haven't seen the inside of a classroom for years but they have all the answers," he said loudly and bitterly, ignoring the quick glances thrown in his direction by those within hearing range. "The bastards are going to pay!"

He slid into the driver's seat and slipped the key in the ignition. The engine came to life as the face of the final passenger, the woman with the profile, formed again in his mind. "Harriet Long Stanton! Well, I'll be damned."

* * *

"No thunderstorms tonight," Brad said as he looked out to the western end of the lake. The evening sun, beginning its more rapid fall descent, was still well above the horizon but there was not a cloud to be seen.

After watching the boarding of the *Belle,* he drove to his cabin, allowing ample time to return to the secluded spot where he would launch his operation. The rehearsal of the week before had been helpful, despite its interruption. The timing was crucial and he had been able to practice at least that. He spread out his "tools" and pictured the boarding again.

"How in the hell did I miss Harriet Stanton's name on that list?" he asked aloud. "Wonder where that perfect daughter of hers is." As annoying as they were, he couldn't stop the memories from bubbling to the surface of his mind. As though saying them aloud would cast them aside, he started mouthing words. "Capaldi should've known, Harriet's damn adoption, Rich Lane, just was all too friggin' much . . ." He stopped suddenly. He was mumbling like a drunken wino on a packed city street. In the distance, the wail of the foghorn from the *Belle* floated across the lake.

"Let's get to work," he said, as if speaking with a colleague about preparing a school budget.

*   *   *

"If anything is going to happen, it's got to be when they're stopped. They always turn the boat toward the sunset and anchor to let people see the show," Gordon said as he gassed up the patrol boat. "We could get there just about in time but I'm going to radio the *Belle* and tell him not to stop for the sunset tonight."

Josie and Becky, both of them refusing to stay home when they realized what Parker and Gordon were planning to do, sat huddled in the back of the boat.

"I can't believe he would ever do anything like this. He's really not a violent person," Josie said. Parker moved away from the bridge and went to her. He squeezed her hands gently and tried to reassure her.

"It's a hell of a lot more likely that nothing's going to happen and we're overreacting but I think it's better to be safe than sorry, to coin a cliché." He smiled and she smiled back.

"Thanks," she said. "I'm sure you'll do the right thing." Parker returned to the front of the boat just as Gordon placed the radio handset back in its cradle.

"They're going to chance it," he said. "Can't say that I blame them. I mean we're not even sure if there is a threat and we know a lot more than they do. He's a great captain and he'll handle things until we get there; keep the boat in motion and all that. They surely don't want to disappoint that crowd tonight. I've got another boat that will be in the area around the right time just in case. So, let's go check it out and see if anything surfaces, so to speak." The feeble attempt at humor fell flat. He eased the boat away from the dock and within minutes they were up to full throttle, heading toward Rattlesnake Island and the *Winnipesaukee Belle*.

*   *   *

Brad conducted the final check of his equipment and satisfied that all was in order, he put on his wet suit. The *Belle* steamed into sight from around the large peninsula near Springfield Point and he knew that it was time. Allowing for at least a fifteen-minute stop to admire the glorious show in the west, he slipped into the lake as soon as the boat began its routine maneuvering into position. When he arrived at his first check point and surfaced, he assumed she should be stopped and all attention of passengers and crew directed toward the west as he approached from due east.

As he had done in his rehearsal, he slowly broke the surface for his first check.

"Shit, something's wrong," he said. The boat was still underway. He quickly went under and swam in a tight circle for a full five minutes. When he surfaced again, the boat had stopped and was aligned exactly as he had planned. He submerged once again and started toward his second and final checkpoint.

*   *   *

"If anyone is going to get out here, they'll have to come from the nearest land mass. I'm just going to position us between the *Belle* and the land and we can watch. We'll give you girls a good view of the sunset, too," Gordon said. The tension on the boat was obvious.

*   *   *

Brad made his way to the surface for a final position check, trying not to cause the slightest ripple. As the top of his head cleared the smooth surface, he heard the motor of a large powerboat roar to life behind him. By the time he turned to see what it was, Gordon had already slowed and was within twenty feet of him. He was between the *Belle* to the west and the Lake Patrol boat to the east. All of the attention aboard the *Belle* had now swung in his direction. Gordon was shouting at him but the water lapping at ear level garbled the words. He frantically looked back and forth between the two boats. Gordon expertly began to move his boat in ever decreasing circles and Brad finally understood what he was saying.

"Drop anything in your hands and come aboard; use the ladder on the port side," he commanded.

Brad cleared his mask and stared at the boat. Parker was leaning over the side, saying something that he couldn't understand. The familiar rage he had felt at so many injustices, so much that he saw wrong with the world, swept over him.

"Bastards!" He spat the word out viciously, as if ridding his mouth of some vile poison. He slipped his mask back on, took a deep breath and dropped below the surface.

The two women on the boat, following Gordon's earlier instructions to go below and put on life jackets, emerged from the cabin. They were in different stages of fastening the belts when they heard Gordon shout.

"Get off the boat, now! All of you, go over the starboard side." Reacting instinctively to the urgency in his friend's voice, Parker pulled Josie by the arm to the side of the boat, Becky following blindly. She kicked off her docksiders, put one foot on the railing and jumped.

"He's going to fire the damn gun. Jump! Jump right now. Get off!"

The seriousness of their situation was obvious. Becky followed Josie's lead and leaped into the water, paddling furiously away from the boat.

Parker, in an environment of law enforcement that was completely foreign to him, finally had something tangible to grasp.

"I'll take my chances here," he called to Gordon, who looked back over his shoulder, shaking his head.

"Hold on, then, you fool," Gordon called back as he prepared to open the throttle.

Fifteen feet beneath the surface, Brad cocked his gun. Less than twenty feet away from the patrol boat, he knew he couldn't miss. He pulled the trigger, sending the explosive ladened spear toward the stern then began his dive toward the bottom of the lake.

The attention of most of the passengers on the *Belle* was riveted on whatever was going on less than a quarter of a mile away. Becky's orange life vest contrasted with the black water as she closed in on the *Belle*.

When the explosion raised the stern of Gordon's boat several feet above the surface of the lake, their collective gasp was quickly followed by a louder groan as a second explosion shredded the boat into pieces.

Brad felt the shock of the second explosion. His mission hadn't been a total failure. He stopped descending and gradually surfaced. The scattered wreckage bobbed all around him. He removed his mask and the head covering of his suit, hearing nothing but a strange silence enveloping the scene, a silence soon replaced by the wailing of another patrol boat not that far distant. He looked west and saw that the *Belle* was already underway, apparently heading toward a swimmer bobbing along in the chop in a life vest. About fifty yards away, he heard a female voice calling for help. Stunned, he peered across the slight chop in the lake. Another swimmer, a woman, struggled to stay afloat as she seemed to be alternately wrestling with her life jacket and another person.

"Please, help me," she cried, sending her breathless pleas in his direction. He swam closer, well attuned to the loud wailing that was closing fast.

"Brad, help us, please!" Josie cried, fighting the debilitating effects of sheer panic.

The recognition of her voice caused him to stop and, for an instant, to recoil, kicking in the opposite direction.

"Josie! What the hell. . .?" Then he was swimming toward her, increasing his pace as all thought of his escape plan vanished in a deluge of memories. The life ring Gordon had thrown to him floated between Josie and her apparently unconscious partner. He grabbed the rope from it as he passed, dragging it behind him.

The sound of the patrol boat engine mingled with its siren and the *Belle* now was close enough that he could see the captain and first mate helping the swimmer aboard. Closer by, two men were assisting Gordon into the lake patrol boat. Brad looked back at the *Belle*. Squinting into the setting sun, he looked at the spectators gathered on the deck. With a flash of recognition, he screamed. A man in a wheelchair sat staring at him through the railing. The finality of defeat, the futility of failure crushed him. "Fucking Rich Lane was on board," he hissed.

"I had no idea you were there, Josie. I just saw Havenot and . . ." He stopped, as though just remembering something.

"I could've killed you," he said, deep despair seeping into his voice. "All I wanted was some justice . . . you know, a helping hand for destiny and justice . . ." The jumble of disjointed thoughts tumbled through his mind like clothes in a huge automat dryer.

"Oh, shit, Josie, what in God's name happened to me?" he asked softly. Then he let the straps of his air tanks fall from his shoulders. The tanks floated away. He tightened the weight belt at his waist then unzipped the front of his suit to just above the belt. He pulled the flaps aside, letting the water seep into the suit, slowly at first but then rapidly filling every crevasse and air pocket.

Josie watched helplessly as Brad lay on his back kicking away from her and Parker, as he quietly disappeared beneath the surface, leaving behind just a tiny ripple.